MW00963628

Other books by Mary Duncan

❧

Eyes of Garnet

SIGHTLESS

Sightless

An Eyes of Garnet Novel

To Dave –
Wellwish! Mary Duncan 4/18/09

Mary Duncan

Sense of Wonder Press
JAMES A. ROCK & COMPANY, PUBLISHERS
ROCKVILLE • MARYLAND

An Eyes of Garnet Novel: Sightless by Mary Duncan

SENSE OF WONDER PRESS
is an imprint of JAMES A. ROCK & CO., PUBLISHERS

An Eyes of Garnet Novel: Sightless copyright ©2008 by Mary Duncan

Special contents of this edition copyright ©2008
by James A. Rock & Co., Publishers

Address comments and inquiries to:

SENSE OF WONDER PRESS
James A. Rock & Company, Publishers
9710 Traville Gateway Drive, #305
Rockville, MD 20850

E-mail:
jrock@rockpublishing.com   lrock@rockpublishing.com
Internet URL: www.rockpublishing.com

Trade Paperback ISBN-13/EAN: 978-1-59663-715-3

Library of Congress Control Number: 2006926207

Printed in the United States of America

First Edition: 2008

*Cover Design and Interior Graphics
by Mary Duncan*

For Cathy Emmons
whose enthusiasm, support
and "why not" attitude
always amazes me.
Love you, sis.

മ ൽ

Part
One

Journey's End

Boston, Massachusetts, December 1746

The voyage was a tortuous, unending hell in which the only escape was to give in to the deep and drown. Those wretched souls were the lucky ones. Catrìona Robertson wasn't one of the lucky ones. She endured the two and a half months of rolling seas; gales so strong it felt as though the ship would crack open like an egg, spilling out all of its people into the sea; and dark, dank, pest-riddled, foul-smelling holds that she and the rest called home.

Cat was on the dock now, trying to remember how to walk on solid ground. For the first time in two and a half months she found herself laughing. It was just the release needed to let the rest of the emotions held in for so long spew forth, until she was on her knees sobbing on the wooden planks of Long Wharfe. Her dazed shipmates passed by without much sympathy; most were on the verge of doing the very same thing.

After she had spent herself, Cat wiped her eyes and, still kneeling, took in her surroundings. She was near the end of Long Wharfe. Ships were being emptied and restocked, destined for faraway places she cared not to think about right now. The place was loud with shouting men, scuffling feet carrying heavy cargo, and rhythmic singing on the ships in a cadence only the workers could follow. Further down the quay lay Boston. There were more houses than she could count; up and down the hillsides, right down to the sea. Massive chimneys emitted gray smoke that blended almost immediately with the featureless gray sky. Cat took a long, deep breath of the cold, seascented air. Then another. Then another. She could still smell the stink of the ship in her nose. She hoped it wouldn't be permanent.

Picking up her satchel of herbs and tinctures—all she had left in the world—Cat slowly started the walk towards the city. Her thumb absently rubbed her ring finger, wishing the ring her brothers had given her was still there. Something tangible to remember them by. She shook that off quickly. "Ye canna go back, lass," she muttered to herself.

Her task now was to find her father. He would have made port about the same time as she did, having left London just a day after her. She had no sense of him, still. Was he alive? He had to be, she reasoned. He would have come to her if he had died. They all did.

Once on the street, she looked for the harbour master's office. Passing a set of windows, she caught her reflection. She didn't recognize herself. No wonder she could still smell the ship on her, it had permeated every part of her. Her face was dirty and smeared, and though her kertch covered her hair, she could feel it was grimy and stringy from the salt air. Somehow, she had kept most of the lice at bay with her herbs, but she knew before she could start her search, a bath was in order. But where? This wasn't like Scotland where small wading pools were abundant, and so was privacy.

As she continued walking, many of the people she passed looked much the same as she did. They, unlike her, seemed to have a destination. She watched a young woman and her two daughters knock on a door, only to be turned out by an older woman, dressed, in Cat's eyes, like a queen. The old woman screamed that they could not enter her house until they had rid themselves of their filth, then pointed an elegant finger towards the back of the house. Cat watched as they disappeared behind a high fence. She walked over for a peek between the boards to see the young family undressing rapidly and climbing into a huge copper tub. Another woman, apparently a servant, handed them some soap. The young women washed themselves with abandon, relishing each cleansing stroke. They took turns washing each other's hair and backs, then the servant-woman dumped buckets of fresh water over their heads as they stood shivering in the icy breeze. When they had finished, they wrapped themselves in blankets and were ushered into the house.

The thought of being clean was too strong to resist. When the servant-woman went into the house, Cat dashed into the fenced-in yard, peeling off her filthy clothes as quickly as she could, oblivious of the cold. She climbed into the tub and immersed herself in the cool water. She found the soap and proceeded to scrub her hair and body until she could hold her breath no longer. When Cat came up for air, the servant-woman stood above the tub with a scowl on her face, but a twinkle in her eyes.

"What have we here?" she asked with her hands on her hips.

Cat, pushing her hair from her face, just looked up. Her eyes said everything.

"Just hurry," the servant-woman said. "I'll not lose my position here for you."

Cat smiled and ducked under the water to finish her cleanse. When she re-emerged, a linen was handed to her. Cat took it without a word and dried herself, wishing with all her heart she had something else to put on besides that dreadful dress. She wrapped the linen around her long, now-auburn-again hair, and shook the daylights out of her dress before crawling back into it. Handing the linen back to the servant-woman, Cat wrapped her kertch tightly around her still-damp hair, donned her woolen cloak, and promptly planted a peck on the servant-woman's cheek before exiting. Now she was ready to find her Da.

Catrìona Robertson knew she had not heard the man correctly. It had to be a mistake. There was no way her father wouldn't have made it through the months of torturous wounds and imprisonment only to succumb to the voyage. She thought of how difficult her own voyage had been *with* food and water, and shuddered to think of what he went through.

"Ye must be mistaken, sir. Please look again. His name is Angus Robertson," she said, bending closer to attempt to read the upside-down chicken scratchings of the ship's manifest.

The balding little man looked up at Catrìona for the first time and opened his mouth to repeat his first statement, but when he saw the young woman he was addressing, he remained quiet. He studied her tired eyes, realizing they were a most unusual deep violet. Her waist-length deep auburn hair was freshly washed and nearly glowed in the late afternoon light filtering in through the window. Though he was seated, he figured her to be taller than the average woman by at least six inches. She was taller than nearly every man in line.

When the man remained quiet, Cat looked up from the ledger, realizing she was being scrutinized. She stood to her full height and sent him a look that demanded an immediate answer. The man took the cue and turned the ledger around so Cat could read it for herself.

Under the column that read Deaths, the second name from the end was Angus Robertson. This still did not convince Cat that he was dead. She knew that he couldn't be the only man that bore that name, and besides, she would have felt him pass.

"Did this man hae any distinguishin' features that attest to him bein' my Da?" she asked, looking into the man's very soul.

He snatched the ledger from her and began searching the records for anything of the sort. Cat felt his frustration. He was genuinely trying to help her.

"Wait. Before ye do that, it may be easier to see if there's another Angus Robertson in the livin' column, aye?"

Seemingly cleared of the awful task of repeating the bad news, he carefully started at the top and went through each name, praying that he would find another man with that name in the Living column. Cat waited patiently, letting him do his job, never taking her eyes from him. After the eighth page, the man looked up with apologetic blue eyes and just shook his head.

Cat murmured her thanks and turned to leave the crowded room, when a strange feeling came over her. There was a tickling on her head, as though hands were touching her hair. She was being contacted, but by whom? Outside, she took a deep breath of the cold, sea-scented air, and actually smelled it, then walked behind a small shack for some privacy. Quieting her mind, she probed to inquire who might want to reach her.

"Da?" she whispered.

Aye, 'tis me, mo nighean, her father replied from someplace far away.

"Then it's true. Ye are dead," she said, feeling herself spinning into the depths of despair.

Three days past. I tried wi' all my heart to stay alive, but wi'out food nor water, my wounds began to fester and the sickness o'er came me. Forgive me, Catrìona. I kent ye followed me here to help me escape, but

I'm in a peaceful place now. There's no pain, and I'm wi' yer Mam and brothers. Go back to Scotland and get on wi' yer life.

Cat wanted more, but he was gone. It was like that when the dead contacted her, they said their piece with little embellishment. She sat against the shack until the tears abated. He wanted her to go back to Scotland, but there was nothing there for her now. All of her visions had come true with pinpoint accuracy; the death of her mother, the war, her brothers being killed. She had no money to return, and even if she did, what call was there for a Clan Seer when there were no clans left? Besides, she had seen a prophecy for herself. A new land of fir trees, rugged coastline, and dark-skinned people with long black hair living in log houses.

After a while, she got up and looked around. There were no trees here; no coastline that matched her vision. Boston must not be where she was to settle. Good. She didn't like it here. It was too crowded with English. But where was this new land and how would she get there? She had used the few pence Gregor had given to her, along with her garnet ring, to book passage here from London.

Pulling the woolen cloak tighter to her body, Cat began formulating a plan as she walked up the cobblestone path into town. First, she would need a place to stay, but she needed money for that. All right, first she needed a way to make some money. Taking stock of her skills, which weren't many, she decided work as a housekeeper would fit the bill.

Remembering a tearoom on the way from the docks, she walked past stately homes and small shops until she reached her destination. In front of the tearoom, a silver object on the ground caught her eye. A shilling. She bent to pick it up with a smile on her face. At least she would be able to buy herself a cup of tea and something to eat. Opening the door, she stepped into a warm foyer. It was mid-afternoon and the cozy room was filled with well-dressed women chatting. The smell of baked goods wafted to her nose and instantly made her stomach growl.

Scanning the room, Cat decided the best method would be to telepathically locate any prospects for a housekeeper position. She found an unoccupied table for two near the door to the kitchen and took a seat. A young woman dressed in a conservative brown dress took her order of a cup of tea and a scone.

Cat closed her eyes and began twirling a lock of damp hair she'd pulled from under her kertch. Her mind became busy with the thoughts of the women in the room. Day-to-day life was rather boring here, Cat thought. What was for supper tonight; that new settee was just the right size; wee Elizabeth was feeling better.

When the order arrived, Cat was just emerging from her task. Unfortunately, there was no one in need of a housekeeper. There was, however, someone in need of her help. Looking around, she noticed an exquisitely dressed woman sitting alone at the window. Cat studied her for a moment from behind her teacup, and noticed a deep sadness surrounding this light-haired woman. The woman kept her eyes on the street as though searching for someone. She also kept placing her hand over the left side of her ribs. Was she injured?

Cat probed the woman's thoughts and found out that she wasn't searching for someone, she was hiding from someone. A man. Her husband, whom she feared. She was smart, though, hiding in plain sight and in a room full of women. If these women were Scotswomen, the man wouldn't dare to raise a hand to her in their company without fear of being thrashed for it. Cat didn't know how Englishwomen would react.

Suddenly, a tenseness seemed to take over the woman and she hurriedly brought her teacup up to her lips, as though it would hide her. Cat took the initiative, walked over and took the seat across from the frightened woman. The woman seemed even more startled by this, but when she saw the look of compassion in Cat's eyes, she broke down in soft sobs.

"I'm verra sorry to hae scairt ye, Mistress," Cat whispered.

It took a couple of moments, but the woman regained her composure and dabbed her eyes discreetly with a lace handkerchief.

"It is I who should apologize. Please forgive me for acting like a fool," the woman said in a well-bred English accent.

Cat put her hand over the woman's, smiled and said, "I'm Catrìona Robertson, and ye're forgiven."

The woman gave Cat a slight smile, as though stalling, or trying to determine if she should give out her name. Cat watched this play over her face and decided not to press her.

"I'll be goin' now. Good to meet ye."

Cat returned to her table and finished her cup of tea and scone, then left the warm room. She had started down the street in search for another way to find a job, when she heard her named being called from behind. Stopping, she turned to find the woman hurriedly trying to catch up to her. Cat smiled and waited.

When the woman reached Cat she was out of breath. Cat thought it odd that such little exertion would tire someone out so much. She waited for the woman to catch her breath before asking if she was all right.

"Oh, yes, as well as can be expected. My name is Rose Carlyle," she said, extending her hand to Cat.

Cat shook it, noticing how frail it was. She also got a very distinct impression that Rose was very ill.

"What is the illness ye hae, Rose?" Cat asked quietly, as they continued walking.

Rose skipped a step and put her hand to her heart.

"How do you know I'm ill? Do I look so terrible that a stranger can guess it?" Rose asked, a little paler than she was in the tearoom.

Cat took her hand and said, "I'm a Seer. Do ye ken what that is, Rose?"

Rose looked up into Cat's eyes, then took in the rest of her appearance, trying to determine if she was genuine. Cat waited patiently under the inspection, getting a clearer picture of Rose's ill health.

A moment later, Rose made her decision.

"I am familiar with Seers," she said, "though I have never met one."

"Well then, ye hae now, hae ye no'?" Cat chimed.

This seemed to bring a slight pink to Rose's cheeks and a pretty smile.

"I'm pleased to meet you, Catrìona," Rose said, squeezing Cat's hand, "but I must get in from this cold. Do me the honor of staying to supper at my house, won't you? I believe we may have much to talk about."

"I would like that verra much, Rose."

ॐ

Arriving at 35 Newberry Street, the residence of Charles and Rose Carlyle, Cat thought they had to be wealthy beyond belief.

The large wooden house with its enormous center chimney was flanked on each side by equally large homes. Cat stopped for a moment to take in the grandeur of the place.

"How many people live here wi' ye?" Cat asked.

Rose heard the wistfulness in Cat's voice and said, "Just my husband and myself. And of course the servants."

Cat's hackles went up, reminded that her father would have been a servant working in someone's household or stable. Unconscious of the look that crossed her face, Cat turned to Rose and said, "Och, o' course." The sarcasm was barely veiled. Rose either didn't catch it or chose to ignore it, and opened the door for Cat.

When Cat stepped into the front foyer onto a hooked rug of every shade of blue, she knew Rose Carlyle was much wealthier than Alexander, her clan chief, or most of the other clan chiefs in Scotland. She never considered herself poor, but if this was how Americans lived, she had lived no better than a dog. The heavy door latched behind her and in an instant a much older woman appeared to take her cloak. Cat smiled at her and relinquished the heavy woolen garment.

"Emily, this is Catrìona Robertson. She will be dining with us this evening," Rose announced, passing her own cloak to Emily's outstretched hand.

"Aye, verra good, Miss," Emily said in a thick Glasgow accent.

Cat wanted to ask Emily a thousand questions as to how she got to America, but knew that would not be proper. Not yet, anyway.

"What does yer husband do, Rose?" Cat asked, slowly walking into the warm house with its wide pine floors, fireplaces glowing in each room, settees and beautiful silk brocade chairs everywhere.

"He's the captain of a merchant ship, the *Rose Ellen*," she answered, once again touching her ribs. "Much of this fine furniture comes from all over the world. In fact, he has just returned home from a rather lengthy voyage to Spain."

"Will he be joinin' us for supper?"

"I never know."

Rose directed Cat to a settee near the fire in the best room. Not a minute later, Emily came out from the kitchen with a tray of tea and scones. Cat once again smiled and took the teacup with a "thank ye." Emily just nodded and returned to her duty.

"So, Catrìona, how long have you been in Boston?" Rose asked, warming her hands on the teacup.

"A day," Cat said, reaching for a scone before her stomach started rumbling.

"Dear me, one day? Where are you staying?"

"At the moment, nowhere," Cat replied around the soft, sweet cake she had just bitten into.

Rose just stared at her incredulously. "Are you indentured to anyone? Oh, I'm sorry for being so blunt, but you just looked like you've been here for quite some time and ... and ..."

"Let me save ye a bit of embarrassment, Rose, and tell ye of my journey here."

Another Lifetime

Cat finished her scone with relish, resisting the temptation to lick her fingers. Rose took notice and offered her another, but Cat declined in order to tell her story.

"I will take ye up on another when I'm finished though," she said with a smile.

"Please, tell me everything," Rose said, nearly bursting with excitement, as though this was the only adventure she'd ever had.

"Och, where to begin," Cat said, grabbing a thick lock of her hair to twirl, as was her custom when deep in thought. This may take a while.

"First, may I ask ye how long ye've been in America, Rose?"

Rose thought for a moment, and said, "Nearly seven years, now. Why do you ask?"

"Are ye familiar wi' the Scottish Rebellion that began in 1745?"

"No, not really. We do not get much news from England. We're trying to distance ourselves from them in our own way here. Well, some of us are," she said quietly. "But that's a story I'll tell when you have finished yours."

"Ye are familiar wi' King James the Eighth wantin' to regain the throne for Scotland, are ye no'?"

"Oh, yes. Silly man, thinking he could fight the English and win." Rose made the statement so offhandedly, Cat had to laugh.

"Oh, dear. There I go again. I apologize once again. You just seem so cultured that I forget you are Scottish."

"Och, aye. And a Highlander to boot, even speakin' the savage language of the *Gàidhlig*," Cat said, good-naturedly daring any further slander. Flushed, Rose settled back into the settee, refusing to say another word.

Cat resumed her hair twirling and started her tale.

"Well, it must be three years past now that talk of a rebellion started. As usual, by spring, things quieted down and life returned to normal. I had been havin' visions since I was eleven—mostly about my family, if they were in trouble or if somethin' bad was goin' to happen to them—but at the Hogmanay divination, I got a vision of a terrible storm at sea wi' ships and lives lost. Later, we found out that it was the first of three attempts for Prince Charles to lead an army into Scotland and regain the throne for his father, King James."

"I never heard of any of this," Rose said.

"We didna hear of it again until April of 1744, when the rebellion failed yet again. Anyway, that's when I started havin' visions o' my brothers dyin' in a battle. When my Mam died, she said to my Da no' to let his sons fight in the rebellion because they would be killed. My brothers quickly chose to forget those words, but I made them promise no' to fight."

Rose was literally on the edge of her seat now, and asked, "Did they heed your warning?"

Cat looked at Rose with a brilliant smile, dropped the lock of hair she had twisted around her finger and said, "It took nine months of usin' the silent treatment on them, but I got promises from two out o' three no' to fight. I think it was easier for them to promise then because there didna seem like there would be a rebellion anyway."

"The following spring, on Beltaine, I was at my mentor's croft to help her wi' the divination, when I saw the final battle of the war yet to happen. I saw so many of my kinsmen slaughtered, I ken my family had to remain out of the fight or they would surely perish as well. But my Da was a laird and had to do as the chief wished of him. Alexander, against all o' my warnings, still chose to fight wi' the Jacobites, enlistin' my Da in that ill-fated war.

"My oldest brother, Seumas, who trained to be a soldier from the time he could lift a claymore, felt the need to fight wi' my Da. My two other brothers, Iain and Lachlan, kept their promises to remain out of it—at that time anyway.

"The Prince arrived in July, and when he and the Jacobites won each battle they fought wi' little or no resistance, it became a battle for my brothers to keep their promises. They wanted to be a part o' the victorious army o' the rightful King o' Scotland."

Rose opened her mouth to say something, but thought better of it and clamped it shut without a word. Cat picked up the lock of hair again and resumed.

"Then I had a vision of the aftermath o' the final battle on Culloden Moor. All o' my brothers lay dead, bodies of men still livin' were bein' burned in piles, and the war had ended. One hour was all it took. I went to the battlefield wi' three other women to tend to the wounded and dyin', but I ne'er found my brothers' bodies, nor my Da."

"How did you know they were dead then?" Rose asked, her blue-green eyes wide and her hand to her heart.

The look Rose received was filled with such sorrow, tears sprung to her eyes.

"They each came to me—their spirits—so I could send them home to the other side. When my Da ne'er came, I hoped beyond hope that he was somehow still alive. Little did I ken that it would've been better for him to die there, than endure what the Hanoverians did to him in prison."

Cat stopped there for a moment, transported back to Scotland; back to the filth and stench and abuse Angus Robertson went through in the cellar of the church in Inverness, never mind the prison ship and the long voyage here, only to die two days before arriving in Boston. A tear, released from its well, ran down Cat's cheek unnoticed. Rose's sniffle brought Cat back to reality.

"I do not think I could have survived what you have been through, Catrìona," she said, blowing her nose softly.

Cat felt the tear start to dry on her cheek and wiped it away. "Ye do what ye hae to do, Rose. And ye ne'er ken what ye are able to do until ye hae to." Suddenly, she felt much older than her twenty years.

Emily softly entered the room and announced that dinner was ready.

"We'll be right there, Emily. Oh, and would you have Claire fix up the green room upstairs. We'll be having a guest for a while."

Cat shot a questioning look at Rose.

"Where else will you stay, dear? I have this great big house and would very much appreciate your company for as long as you want."

"But what about yer husband? Wilna he mind a stranger in his house?"

"We may not ever see the man," Rose said.

Before Cat could question Rose on that cryptic statement, Rose was off the settee and heading towards the dining room. Cat got up and followed her new housemate into another room with a fireplace and a long table of dark wood with sixteen heavy, ornately carved high-backed chairs surrounding it. Cat thought the Carlyles must do a lot of entertaining—at least Rose anyway.

The table was set for two with fine china in a rich blue and white flower pattern. Crystal goblets were filled with a deep red wine, and the silver utensils were elaborate with flourishes. Cat had never seen such elegance and just stood beside her chair with her mouth open. Rose smiled at Cat's stare and asked her to be seated so they could begin.

The instant Cat was seated, Emily brought in a soup tureen filled with a creamy fish soup. The heady aroma made Cat's stomach cry out in anticipation. She put her hand over it, hoping to calm it down. A young woman Cat had not met yet brought out a loaf of bread and fresh butter. This must be Claire, she thought.

Not knowing where or how to begin, Cat waited for a cue from Rose. Rose sensed Cat's confusion and took the bread and broke off a small portion, then buttered it. Cat followed suit. Emily ladled out a bowlful of soup for each of them, then stood in the corner awaiting orders.

Cat couldn't wait any longer and lifted a spoonful of the delectable liquid to her lips. Cullen skink! She looked over at Emily and smiled. Emily just nodded slightly, but her eyes twinkled a bit in acknowledgement of the popular Scottish dish. When the soup was finished, Claire came in and took the bowls away and Emily disappeared into the kitchen.

"That was a fine meal, Rose, thank ye," Cat said, wiping her mouth with a linen napkin.

Rose just looked at Cat in dismay and said, "I hope you're still hungry, dear. That was just a starter."

It was Cat's turn to turn a rose flush. When she remained speechless, Rose giggled and said, "I'm glad you'll be staying with me for a while. Think of me as your social teacher." Remembering how she seemed to sound degrading, she quickly added, "If you don't mind, of course."

Cat giggled this time and patted Rose's hand. "I'm verra glad to hae ye, Rose."

After four more courses, Cat figured she wouldn't have to eat for at least three days. Unless there was a feast at Blair Castle, food was never this plentiful in Scotland.

"Shall we retire to the best room so you may continue your story, Catrìona?"

"Aye. But would ye mind terrible if I just stand for a moment. My corset seems to hae gotten much smaller."

From the kitchen she heard the giggles of Emily and Claire, then even Rose laughed.

"I take it you don't eat like this in Scotland."

"I hae ne'er eaten like this in my life!" Cat said, rubbing her stomach. "Would ye mind if I told the lasses what a fine meal they prepared?"

"I'm quite sure they would appreciate it. Go on."

Cat smiled and opened the door to the kitchen, where she startled Emily. Claire peeked in from the pantry to see who entered the kitchen.

"Can I be helpin' ye, Miss?" Emily asked.

"Och, no. I just wanted to thank ye both for a marvelous feast."

Claire and Emily exchanged glances, apparently unaccustomed to compliments. They both curtsied, then stood, as though awaiting a command. Cat was embarrassed to think they had to wait on her. She left the kitchen realizing that her father would never have been able to endure this kind of life. For a moment, she was glad he never had to.

"Come along, dear," Rose urged.

Cat followed her into the best room and sat at the edge of the settee. A little later, Claire brought in a tray with two glasses of sherry and placed it on the little table beside Rose.

"Well there be anythen' e'wos, Mum?" Claire asked in a squeaky little voice, thick with a London accent.

"No, that will be all." Then taking a cue that should have been automatic, Rose said, "And thank you for dinner, Claire."

Claire stood open-mouthed and pink, curtsied and quickly left the room. Cat smiled at Rose, thinking they would both learn about "society" from each other.

Picking up a glass of sherry and handing it to Cat, then taking the other one for herself, Rose settled back into the settee and said, "Now, please continue, my dear."

"Now, where was I. Oh, aye. After realizin' my Da was still alive, I had to find him. The Hanoverians took all the prisoners to Inverness and housed them any and everyplace there was room. It took my dear friend, Anne Leith, nearly a month to find him. He was in the basement of a church I walked by e'ery day, starvin', in need of treatment for his wounds, wallowin' wi' forty-three other men in their own filth. Anne and I went there e'ery day after that to give the men bread and blankets. I even managed to smuggle in an herbal poultice for my Da's wounds.

"Three weeks later, my friend Gregor Macgregor had a plan to break him out, but just before we could carry out the plan, all the prisoners were transferred to prison ships in the harbour. There they sat wi' no food or water for two days before sailin' to London for trial.

"We—Gregor and I—hired a privateer to sail us to London. A month later, the prison ships arrived at Tilbury Fort on the outskirts o' London. After a few days, even the Hanoverian soldiers started to complain about the cruelty towards the prisoners, and surgeons were allowed on board to tend to the wounded. There were many who didna survive that journey. Once the trials began, the government kent it could no' try each man, so the prisoners were made to draw straws to see who would be tried. It was just a formality though. The captured clan chiefs were all executed, but most o' the prisoners were sentenced to be sent to the colonies as indentured servants for seven years to life."

"So, had your father survived, even though he was a lord, he would have been a servant for the rest of his life?"

Cat looked at Rose, wondering if it really mattered to her. She had servants here. What difference would it have made to her that Angus Robertson, Laird of *Slios Mín aig Aulich,* would have been a servant?

"Might I be blunt wi' ye, Rose?"

"Well ... of course," she said tentatively.

"What of yer servants, Emily and Claire?"

"What of them?" she asked, truly not making the connection.

"Did they come here o' their own free will to be yer servants, or did ye capitalize on their misfortune?"

Rose didn't say a word. She finished the last swallow of sherry in her glass and left the room. Cat heard her climb the stairs to her chambers and close the door.

"Hmm. It must hae been the latter," she said, making no attempt move from the settee.

Irreconcilable Differences

Cat awoke the next morning with a stiff neck from lying on the arm of the settee all night. In the faint, early morning light, snow drifted lazily passed the windows. She sat up, noticing she had at least removed her shoes before napping. Listening for anyone else's stirrings, she heard noises from the kitchen. Rose had not come downstairs yet, and she really wanted to talk to Emily alone. Now would be her chance.

With the quietness of a cat, she walked into the kitchen barefoot, once again startling Emily.

"Och, I'm sorry, Emily. Should I hae knocked first?"

Emily smiled and shook her head, "No, Miss. It's just that noo one e'er coomes inta the kitchen an', weel, I dinna ken if I was gooin' tae be disciplined for soomethin' I didna doo."

Cat cocked her head and frowned, "Rose doesna beat ye, does she?"

"Och, dear me, noo," Emily said with her hand to her ample bosom. "I just always hated bein' hollered at, is all."

"I may no' hae kent Rose for verra long, but I hae a hard time imaginin' her hollerin' at anyone," Cat said.

"No, no. No' Mistress Rose. Mr. Charles," she whispered, as though the man would instantly appear if his name were spoken aloud.

Cat looked around warily, wondering if he was in the house. "Tell me about Charles. Why is everyone so scairt o' him?"

Emily thought for a moment, deciding if she should say anything or not. Cat caught her indecision and said, "If I'm goin' to stay here for a while, I want to ken who I'm livin' wi'."

Emily called Claire in from the back larder to keep watch before she would say another word. Claire came in with a snow-covered kertch and was posted at the kitchen door to listen for anyone attempting to intrude.

"Mr. Charles has a fondness for the drink. He doesna coome here often, oonly a coople o' times a year. He's in toown noow, but most likely stayin' on his ship 'til it's unloaded. Then he'll coome here an' the hoose will be all skittery and we'll all be walkin' on eggshells 'til he leaves again. Thankfully, he usually oonly stays for a week, but it's always a verra long week."

"Does he beat ye or Rose?" Cat asked, feeling she already knew the answer.

Emily looked down at her feet.

"Ah. Ye need no' say a word, Emily. Wi' that look, I ken the answer."

"When he arrived three days agoo, he came in and found Mistress Rose entertainin' a few o' her friends wi' tea, an' he called her into his study demandin' why she was entertainin' when she kent all along he was coomin' hoome."

"Did she ken he was comin' home?" Cat asked, feeling her blood start to heat up in her cheeks.

"We ne'er ken when he's coomin' hoome."

"Did he beat her wi' her friends still in the house?"

"Och, aye. Claire heard the commotion an' kent what was happenin'. She came ta fetch me an' I went oot an' apologized ta the ladies an' toold them they had ta leave. I dinna ken whoo was more fashed, me or them. They must hae heard the whole affair."

"Hae ye e'er tried to stop him from hittin' Rose?" Cat asked, trying to remain calm.

"I wouldna dare. He's a braw man, an' besides, I wouldna want to lose my position here," Emily said in a defeated tone, clearly afraid of the man and her precarious situation.

"Might I ask how ye came to be here?" Cat asked quietly. But before she could get an answer, Claire opened the kitchen door and said Rose was coming downstairs. "Can we continue this conversation later?"

Emily nodded and Cat quickly walked back into the best room where she had spent the night. Rose came in just as Cat was taking her seat on the settee. Not knowing Cat had spent the night there, Rose didn't notice her at first. When she caught Cat's movement out of the corner of her eye, she nearly jumped out of her skin and let out a little squeak. Her hands instantly flew to cover her mouth to quiet her alarm. Cat rose to calm her.

"Oh, dear me, Catrìona. You nearly scared me to death," Rose said, shaking like a frightened animal. "I didn't hear you come down."

"That's because I didna. I fell asleep on the settee. My neck is payin' for that mistake," she said, rubbing the sore spot and showing her dimples in an attempt to lighten the situation.

Rose stole a look at the kitchen door, then back to Cat. Cat got the distinct impression Rose was worried that she may have spoken to the staff behind her back. Refusing to apologize for her comment last night, Cat stood her ground, waiting to be thrown out into the snow. It was a stand off. Cat could read every thought going through Rose's head, but waited for Rose to make up her mind.

After a few moments, Rose made a decision. "I'm sorry I walked out on you last night, Catrìona. It was terribly rude of me. I should have been more sympathetic to you, with your father being thrust into that situation. Can you forgive me?"

"There is naught to forgive, Rose. I ken what ye've been goin' through wi' yer husband. I dinna believe that a man has the right to treat his wife like a beast, even though society says it's appropriate."

Rose turned the color she was named after, clearly embarrassed. Without looking at Cat, she said, "He only comes home a couple times a year. I can bear it for that long."

Cat knew she would not be able to make Rose understand that she had a choice. Not yet, anyway. She let it go and changed the subject.

"Well, would ye believe I'm hungry?" she lied, rubbing her stomach.

Rose smiled, appreciating Cat's delicate way of diverting the subject.

ﻉ❧

Later in the morning, the snow stopped and the sky took on yellow and pink hues. Cat needed a walk after eating too much for breakfast, and asked Rose if she would like to walk to the shore. Rose declined the offer, but told her that Emily was going to the fish market on Hill's Wharf if she would like to accompany her.

"Are ye sure it's all right wi' ye? I mean, ye dinna mind me askin' Emily questions, do ye?" Cat queried, fully intent on asking questions even if Rose forbade it.

Rose looked at Cat and assumed that sooner or later, Cat would get all that answers she was seeking, and said, "You'll find Emily to be very helpful, and I have a feeling that you would ask even if I didn't want you to."

Cat looked at Rose and burst out laughing, having been seen right through. "Ye're right, Rose."

Emily emerged from the kitchen with a heavy woolen cloak around her and a basket in the crook of her arm.

"Might I join ye to the fish market, Emily?" Cat asked.

Emily glanced at Rose, asking permission with her eyes, and received a nod from her Mistress. "Aye, lass, I'd like that."

The two walked out into the brightening afternoon that was becoming windier by the minute. This cold was so different than Scotland's. It cut right into one's bones and seemed to settle there permanently. Emily set a very quick pace and Cat, at least twenty years her junior, had to quicken hers by quite a bit just to keep up. She followed Emily down the cobbled lane then left onto Essex Street. The wind seemed to slap her in the face at this juncture and they both tightened their hoods against the biting cold. Cat attempted to ask some questions, but in the gale, the wind sucked the words from her mouth and blew them across town.

When they reached the fish market, Cat was relieved to see it was indoors. The shack was fairly large and was instantly warmer than outdoors, although the wind whistled through it, threatening to carry it off in the same direction as her words.

"Och, dear me, Mr. Phillips, it's right fierce oot there!" Emily said, rubbing her hands together and stomping her feet to bring the circulation back.

"I'll tend to be agreein' with ye, Mrs. Keith," he said, never looking up from the task of filleting a large fish. "Who have ye got with ye there?"

"This is Miss Catrìona Robertson. She's stayin' wi' Mistress Rose for a while."

"Is she new in town?" he asked.

"Oh, aye. She's just been here a couple o' days noow."

Cat wondered how long it would take for them to realize she was standing right beside them and could answer for herself.

"I thought as much."

"Her Da was on …"

"Pardon me, Emily," Cat interrupted quietly, "but I dinna care to hae my business all around town, thank ye," stopping the conversation before Emily ranted on about things she did not know.

"Don't worry yerself about who ye tell yer stories to, Miss, they always manage to get around town anyway," Mr. Phillips said, wrapping up the fish and handing it to Emily, who promptly placed it in her basket and dropped a coin onto the plank used as a counter.

"See ye in a coople o' days, Mr. Phillips," Emily said, then turned and walked back out into the gale without another word.

"Nice to meet ye, Mr. Phillips," Cat said, hurriedly pulling her hood back up around her head.

Cat left on Emily's heels, but closing the door behind her made her lose ground and she had to run to catch up. Still unable to speak, Cat wondered why Emily was so quick to speak of her dilemma to a stranger. At this rate, she was never going to find out.

Reaching Newberry Street, the pair turned right and, still nearly running, aimed for the fifth house on the right. Once inside, Emily headed straight for the kitchen, effectively terminating any chance of Cat questioning her. Was this behavior instructed by Rose? Cat never liked secrets. While she was glad for a warm roof over her head and plenty of food to eat, she would not remain here for long under these circumstances.

The house was quiet as Cat took off her cloak and hung it on the hook near the door. She decided to check out her room upstairs and do a little meditation. She needed some answers since no one was offering her any verbally.

When she got to the head of the stairs, she was thankful to see most of the doors open. She easily found the green room that was assigned to her and walked in, stopping at the threshold to take in the splendor of the place. It faced the harbour; the pale sunlight filtering in through fine lace curtains. The featherbed was covered in a sage green quilt, and rosy-pink pillows rested against a rich, tiger

maple headboard that arched high over the bed itself. At the top was
a scallop carved in gold. There were two chairs near the window
upholstered in silk in the same shade of green as the quilt, with thin
pink stripes. A wool rug in a darker shade of green with burgundy
flecks rested near the bed. An enormous armoire and a chest of drawers
made of the same wood as the headboard finished the room. In the
looking glass that topped the drawers, Cat saw in its reflection her
look of awe. She could live in this room and never come out, it was
so beautiful.

Cat walked the rest of the way in and closed the door behind
her. The overwhelming newness kept her eyes running around the
room, not allowing concentration enough to meditate just yet. At the
window she saw the ships' masts in the harbour dancing in the gale.
Taking a seat in one of the silk chairs, she just sat, burning the memory
into her mind for the future. She felt certain she would never see
such wealth and beauty again and wanted to savor it for a while.

After a few moments of bliss, Cat got a distinct feeling something wasn't right. The hair on her arms started to rise. At that very
instant, the front door downstairs slammed shut with such ferocity,
the windows shook. In her mind, she saw the man everyone in the
household feared. He was a little taller than her five-foot-eleven, but
not by much. His dark curly hair was pulled back in a queue. What
startled Cat the most were his eyes. They were a compassionless pale
blue that didn't miss anything. In her mind, she could see him listen
to the house. Cat knew he could feel her. She remained perfectly
still, not wanting to give away her position.

Suddenly, she heard Claire's voice greet him—a little louder than
was necessary. Was she trying to warn Rose? Cat tiptoed to the door
and opened it a crack. She could hear his voice, raspy and deep, with
a slight slur. He was drunk. No telling what he would do in that
state. She had to get to Rose. Listening for any clue to his whereabouts, Cat stealthily walked out into the hallway. Claire was doing
a good job in keeping him occupied by offering him a drink. Something he obviously didn't need, but didn't refuse.

At the end of the hallway was a closed door. Hopefully, that's
where Rose was. Cat crept to the door and opened it a crack. Relief
washed over her when she saw Rose asleep. Cat went in and touched
her on the shoulder, ready with her other hand in case Rose screamed.

Rose groggily opened her eyes and, at first, wasn't sure where she was or why Cat would be waking her. It didn't take long for Rose to understand Cat's intrusion into her bedchambers, when she heard the breaking of glass and a few incomprehensible shouts and grunts from downstairs.

"You must not be afraid. I'm quite sure he will not harm you," Rose said, getting out of bed and fixing herself up in front of the looking glass.

"I'm verra sure he wilna harm me, for I wilna let him," Cat said, lifting the pleats of her skirt to reveal the dirk she had strapped to her leg.

"Keep that handy, just in case," Rose said, walking out the door to greet her husband.

Cat followed closely, refusing to let Rose come to any harm by the brute awaiting her downstairs. When they reached the bottom of the stairs, all was quiet. Claire met them and whispered to Rose that, "Mr. Charles passed out."

The threesome walked into the best room and found Charles on the settee Cat had slept on last night. One leg was hanging off as though, once he awoke, he would be ready to bolt. His dark hair was coming out of its queue in an unruly mass of curls. Even in his sleep, he looked angry and menacing—three deep furrows between his brows remained, telling of fierce concentration. His mouth was open, and even from ten feet away, Cat could smell his rank, liquored breath.

"Come on. He'll be out for quite some time." Rose glanced at the mahogany grandfather clock, making a mental note of just how much time she had left. It read three-thirty.

Unwilling to risk waking Charles, Cat and Rose took their supper in Rose's bedroom upstairs. The enormous room took up the entire north side of the house and was divided into a suite consisting of a dressing room, bedchamber and a sitting room. It was done in glorious shades of rose and blue, with ivory accents. The rug was an intricate floral pattern of rose, burgundy and shades of blue. Two ivory silk chairs with small ottomans flanked a long tea table where there was plenty of room for a small supper to be set up. They weren't having a five course meal tonight, just bread, soup and a platter of sliced venison.

The clock downstairs chimed eight o'clock as Cat and Rose were finishing their dinner. It was very quiet in the house. Emily and Claire must have retired early to their own rooms off the kitchen.

"Tell me why ye let him hurt ye, Rose," Cat asked quietly. "Doesna he ken ye're no' well?"

Rose didn't look at Cat. She was staring off into the blackness of the night windows. Cat touched Rose's hand, indicating she was waiting for an answer.

Rose turned and searched Cat's eyes. "You have the most beautiful color eyes, Catrìona."

"Ye'll no' get out o' my question so easy, Rose, so I'll tell ye what I see. I ken ye hae somethin' eatin' at yer insides. It wilna go away and it's past time to heal it. I dinna see ye livin' much longer. Am I right?"

Rose's perfectly oval face was mirrored by the perfect oval of her mouth as it opened in shock.

"No one knows about my illness, only my physician. How can you know of it?" Rose got up from her seat to stand by the window. She turned to Cat when there was no reply. Rose studied her for a moment and noticed a far-away look in her eyes. It was as though Cat were somewhere else.

"Catrìona?" Rose moved back to Cat's side, but the look was gone when Cat looked up at her. "Are you all right?"

"Aye, but ye're no'. He's awake."

The shouting started in the kitchen area. Charles was looking for something and was not going to be happy until he destroyed everything that got in his way. Claire was the one who knocked on Rose's door requesting her presence downstairs.

As Cat and Rose descended the staircase, Charles' booming voice was heard demanding more rum from Emily. "But, Mr. Charles, sir, ye know there's oonly what ye brought in yerself this night," Emily tried to reason.

A smash of porcelain and a thump against the kitchen door prompted Cat to take matters into her own hands. She would not stand there doing nothing while this maniac frightened the staff and destroyed the house. Lifting her skirts, she deftly removed her dirk from its strap and opened the kitchen door.

Charles was in the middle of throwing a teacup that just missed Cat's head. She quirked an eyebrow, but stood her ground, as though dealing with a spoiled toddler. The dirk was held behind her back. She didn't want to antagonize the man further. Charles looked at her for a moment, trying to remember if he knew her or not. A sneer played along his wide mouth. Cat didn't like the look, and casually brought the dirk in front of her. Emily must have been the thump on the door, because she was still sitting against the wall, afraid to get up and give the man another chance at knocking her down.

Charles noticed the long blade, but still only stared at this tall, unfamiliar woman almost daring him to make a move against her. His eyes scanned the room for a weapon of his own, but it looked like Claire and Emily had had such run-ins before and there was nothing for him to use, save more china. His hands tightened into large fists, surely more than capable weapons. In a quick move, he started at Cat from the other side of the room. There was more than enough time to sidestep the drunkard and cold-cock him with the handle of her dirk as he went by. He landed in a heap against the door.

Rose and Claire started shouting Cat's name, assuming it was she who went down. They were banging on the door trying to get in, but Charles' body wouldn't be moved that easy.

"Help me move him out o' the way, Emily," Cat said, grabbing a leg.

Emily stood up and grabbed the other leg, dragging him to the middle of the room. The kitchen door flung open and Rose and Claire were amazed to see Emily and Cat standing, and Charles on the floor. Rose kept looking from him to Cat and back again, trying to imagine how this might have played out.

"I dinna ken what ye want to do wi' him now, but if I were ye, I wouldna let him stay here tonight," Cat said, sheathing her dirk under her skirts.

"He needs ta spend the night in gaol. Shall I fetch someone ta take him there, Mistress?"

All eyes rested on Rose now, but she still seemed to be reluctant to take any action to rid this man from her life. Cat stepped in once again.

"'Tis late to be walkin' the streets lookin' for someone to bring

him to gaol." Taking Rose by the shoulders to emphasize her request, she said, "Is there somewhere in the house where he can be
locked up until the drink wears from him?"

Rose looked up in defeat. She just shook her head, unable to
comply. Emily interjected with the suggestion of bringing him down
into the basement and tying him to a post until such time that he
can behave himself.

"Does that sound all right wi' ye, Rose? We can make sure he
stays warm down there, and this way he'll no' be harmin' any of us,
aye?"

Rose nodded her head and left the room, leaving the details to
the rest of them.

Nearly an hour later, Cat went upstairs to check on Rose. She
was sleeping on top of her featherbed, still fully dressed. Cat removed
Rose's shoes, but left the rest of her clothes on. She folded the quilt
over Rose and blew out the candle by the bedside.

Returning to her room, Cat undressed, crawled under the bedclothes and fell immediately into a sound sleep. She dreamt of being
captured and brought someplace against her will. When she awoke,
it was still dark out. She got up and went to the window. There was
a sliver of pink on the eastern horizon, signifying dawn wasn't far off.

Dressing, she went downstairs to see if Emily and Claire were
up. They were both in the kitchen when the clock struck half six.

"Hae ye checked on him yet?" Cat asked the two of them.

"No," they said in unison.

"Shall we then?"

The three went down the stairs to the damp basement. It was
cold down there and dark, the candle having gone out some time
ago. Emily lit the lantern she brought with her and held it high
enough for all of them to see. Still tied to the post where they left
him, Charles stirred when the light hit his face. He let out a little
groan, as though pained, and Cat walked behind him to make sure
he wasn't bleeding from the blow to the head she gave him. He seemed
to be fine, probably just a headache.

"Charles?" Cat touched his shoulder. She could see he was coming around. "How are ye feelin' this mornin'?"

In a deep, raspy voice, perfectly audible, he said, "Like someone hit me on the head."

"That's because I did," Cat said without remorse or apologies.

"Why? And who are you, anyway?" He sounded more curious than agitated, but Cat was not ready to release the man until she was sure he was sober.

"I'm Catrìona Robertson, a friend o' Rose's. Ye were drunk last night and tried to destroy this beautiful house and who kens what else."

"I was hardly drunk ... Catrìona, you said?"

"Aye, and I beg to differ wi' ye, sir. Because when a man comes at me armed wi' a teacup, I would hae to say that is drunk."

Charles chuckled a little at that, Cat seeing him try to imagine himself in that position. "Well then, I guess that is drunk. I do apologize for any mishaps that may have occurred in my inebriated state. You see, I was ..."

"I dinna care to hear any o' yer excuses, sir, for none will appease me," Cat interrupted. "There's no excuse for beatin' yer wife or destroyin' yer household because ye canna hold yer rum."

Once again Charles chuckled. Emily and Claire looked at each other, ready to run if the man was let loose. No one dared talk to him that way and get away with it.

"I see you will not spare my feelings in this matter, so I am in your command, my dear."

Cat turned and started for the stairs without saying another word, or setting Charles free. Emily and Claire followed close behind, neither having the courage to remove him from bondage. At the top of the stairs, they heard him chuckle again, a little more maliciously now.

"What will ye doo wi' him noow, Miss?" Emily asked, clearly frightened at the thought of his release.

"Leave him there for a few more hours. I dinna care for his attitude. He's no' sober yet."

Claire and Emily seemed to sigh in relief and continued on with the daily chores.

ॐ

It was nearly noon when Cat, Emily and Claire, and this time accompanied by Rose, ventured down to the cellar to set Charles free. He seemed to be complacent enough, and his only request was to relieve himself.

Luncheon was being set when Charles, having washed and changed, came down to the dining room and joined the living. He didn't say much, only courteous remarks when Rose asked him questions. Cat watched him with a wary eye. Every so often she would catch him looking at her with those dead ice blue eyes. While that was not a basis for alarm, his thoughts were malicious. He was planning something, and she decided right after luncheon, she would find out what is was.

"So, what brings you to our fair town, Catrìona?" he asked.

She had to choose her words carefully. He had no business knowing why she was here.

"I came to be wi' my family."

"Oh? And who is your family?" he asked casually.

Being evasive, she replied, "They've no' arrived yet."

He looked at her trying to read her mind, but Cat kept an unreadable face on. He seemed to give up after a few moments and just nodded.

Rose, in an attempt to break the tension in the room, chimed, "So what treasures have you brought from Spain, Charles?"

"Some spices and teas mostly. We have little room for anything else."

"I'm sure they're fine. Wouldn't you say, Catrìona?"

"Oh, aye," Cat said, with as much emotion as she could muster under the circumstances, refusing to meet Charles' eyes to elicit further conversation. She wanted very much to finish her meal and go for a walk. The sun was shining brightly and the frigid wind of yesterday had abated. But Charles persisted in his questioning, as though trying to catch something he could use later.

"So how many in your family?" he asked.

Cat glanced at Rose, not ready to trust that she wouldn't speak to her husband about the conversation they shared.

"Just one," she replied, not elaborating further.

"And who might that ..."

"Dear," Rose said, patting Charles' hand. "I'm sure Catrìona would rather not discuss this while she is trying to eat her meal. I'm sure we can all have a wonderful conversation later. Couldn't we, Catrìona?"

"Aye, that would be better; besides, I hae an appointment I must no' be late for." Cat quickly wiped her mouth on the napkin and excused herself before he invaded further. She left the dining room and walked down the hall to get her cloak, not even putting it on before she opened the front door, and left the smothering house.

"Ye're on yer own, Rose," she said to herself, walking briskly towards the waterfront, looking back every so often to be sure Charles wasn't following her. When she got to the end of Essex Street, Cat decided to do some exploring of this end of town. She took a left onto South Street then continued across Summer Street onto Cow Lane. Rows of houses flanked each road. The town bustled the closer she got to the waterfront. She took another left onto Long Lane to the very end where she took a right onto Milk Street and finished her journey to the end where she ended up at Greenleaf's Yard. Ships of every imaginable size were in the harbour, all seemingly going someplace, or busy being loaded or unloaded with goods beyond the imagination.

It was breezy down by the water and Cat shivered, pulling her cloak tighter around herself. She walked towards Long Wharfe taking note of the ships' names. It took her a while, but she finally found the *Rose Ellen*. Hordes of men were unloading huge crates and barrels from her hold and walking them down the gangways. She watched men the color of coffee and dun and blue-black labor effortlessly like ants, all with the same mission—empty the ships of their supplies to make Bostonians comfortable in this new world.

In the hour or so she had been away from the Carlyles, she had completely forgotten the tension of that house. It was nice to be able to breathe again, but she realized she had to do something different. She would not remain there with Charles under the same roof. She had a very bad feeling about him.

Finding a sheltered alcove, Cat sat on a barrel in the waning winter sun. She thought more about her vision of great fir trees, rugged coastline and the dark-skinned people. They weren't as dark as those she saw unloading the ships, again realizing that this was not where she was supposed to be. But where was this new place?

"May I help you, Miss?"

Cat was startled to see a man standing in front of her. He had cropped dark brown hair and the tawny-gold eyes cats have—ones that don't miss anything. He wore tan breeks and a red woolen cloak covering his creamy lace jabot. He reminded her of a Hanoverian on the battlefield of Culloden and she visibly flinched. He must have caught her action and took it for alarm, because he held up his hands as though calming a horse.

"I mean you no harm, Miss. Are you in need of help?" he asked again. His voice was soft and soothing.

"Och, I apologize for jumpin', sir. I was deep in thought and didna see ye there. No, I'm just takin' in the sights and sounds, but I thank ye for askin'." she said in her best cheery voice.

He smiled and touched the brim of his tricorn, ready to move on.

"But, perhaps ye can help me," she said out of the blue.

"And how may I be of service to you?" he asked.

"Are ye from a ship?"

"Yes, I'm a ship's surgeon. Are you ill?"

"No. Do ye sail around here, along this coast?"

"Yes."

"Do ye ken of a place where great fir trees grow along a rocky coast?"

He smiled again and said, "Yes I do. A more rugged coastline will only be found in Scotland itself."

Cat perked up at this and asked, "Where is it? Is it here in Boston?"

"No, no," he said shaking his head. "It's much further north in the Province of Maine. There are no real settlements that far up to my knowledge, only Indians."

"Indians? What are Indians?"

"Red Savages."

"What do they look like, these … Indians?" she asked, refusing to call them savages. It brought back too many memories of how Highlanders were regarded. Now she truly wanted to meet these people, speculating they would fit her ways better than these rigid and pious English who considered themselves superior to all others.

"They are dark-skinned with black hair. Depending on the tribe, they wear their hair long or shaved all around save for a tuft left on the top of their heads. They wear animal skins and live in crude huts.

They all speak different languages very foreign to ours, though I have heard tell of some speaking French."

"French? How did they learn that language?" Cat asked, excited more and more about meeting these people.

"From the French trappers who settled along Hudson's Bay and the St. Lawrence River. Why are you so curious about them?" he asked, watching Cat's expression. "You're not planning to locate them, are you? It would be folly on your part. I've heard many dreadful tales of how they capture white women and use them as slaves."

Cat gave the man a look of disgust. "Och, ye mean like the English use us Scots as servants? What's the difference, sir?"

The surgeon looked like he'd been slapped, had no comment and walked away without a word.

"I must hae said somethin' that hit a little too close to home," she said to herself, watching him disappear in the throng of people.

Cat decided to head back to the Carlyles' house. The sun was making its descent behind a cloudbank on the horizon and it would get cold again quickly without its warmth. Figuring Milk Street would connect her to Newberry Street at some point, she decided to walk its length rather than go home the same way she came. At the end of Milk Street, she turned left onto Marlborough Street and after walking its length, spotted Rose's house. She congratulated herself for finding her way around without aid.

Once in the house, Cat removed her cloak and hung it on the peg near the door. She listened for everyone's whereabouts, but the house seemed empty. She walked towards the kitchen to see if Emily or Claire could tell her where Rose was. Just before she got there though, a loud thump sounded over her head. She stopped to listen, her ear strained for anything to indicate what that was. Suddenly Emily blasted out of the kitchen, nearly running Cat over in the process.

"What is goin' on?" Cat asked, following Emily up the stairs.

"What we tried ta prevent, but ne'er seem ta be able ta," she said cryptically.

Cat lifted her skirts and drew her dirk. At the top of the stairs, the door near the end of the hall flung open and out lunged Charles. He banged into the wall on the other side of the hallway, knocking a picture from it, then turned to go downstairs. When he saw Emily and Cat standing there, he let out a low growl and stumbled his way towards them. He was so stupefied he could barely stay upright. Cat stepped in front of Emily and flashed her dirk. Again, he gave her that menacing grin. Cat felt Emily step back down the stairs, ready to run down if need be.

"So you think you can stop me with that little blade, huh?" he slurred, getting close enough for Cat to smell his foul breath.

"Oh, aye, I do," Cat said, stepping away from the stairs in case he lunged at her. "Ye better get downstairs, Emily. Charles will be needin' some attention when he goes down them."

"Ha! You Scottish bitch," he snarled. "When I get my hands on you, you'll regret the day you nosed your way into my business."

Cat took a defensive stance and waited for him to make the first move. He might be drunk, but he was a powerful man. She would need all her skills to gain the upper hand without getting caught. Ten feet from her, he made his move. As he started to run towards her, his foot caught on the rug that had apparently been rolled up in the scuffle with Rose. It seemed to hurl him at an unnatural speed directly at her, but he landed hard a little short of his mark. Cat quickly sidestepped him before he could grab at her legs and got behind him. He was very slow in getting up, but Cat was wary of the trick.

"Emily, bring up the rope we tied him wi' the other night, aye?"

Without a word, she heard Emily dash off towards the kitchen. "Oh, and bring Claire wi' ye when ye return. It may take the three of us to get him restrained," she hollered.

"Aye, Miss," was all Emily shouted.

Charles started to stir and Cat stepped back to watch what he would do next. He looked up as though getting his bearings. He must have either passed out or been knocked out for a moment when he hit the floor. Getting up onto all fours, he just rocked back and forth trying to get into a standing position. Cat waited to see if he remembered whether she was there or not. He fell over and landed in the fetal position, where he passed out for sure this time. Emily and Claire ascended the stairs slowly, fearing what they would find when they reached the top.

"Dinna fash, he's out," Cat said, sheathing her dirk.

Emily brought up the rope and Claire edged past Charles to

check on Rose. Cat and Emily had just finished tying Charles up when Claire emerged from the room with Rose's arm around her shoulder for support.

Cat rushed to Rose to see what the damage was. Her eye was already a blue-purple; there was blood dripping from her nose, though it didn't look broken. Her left arm seemed to dangle in an odd position, probably broken. What damage was under her clothes would have to wait.

"Get her into her room," Cat instructed. "Do ye hae any herbs in the house?"

"Oh, aye. I always make shoor we hae plenty. What doo ye need?" Emily said.

"Comfrey, arnica oil, mullein flowers, witch hazel and plantain if ye hae them."

Emily made a mental note of each herb and said, "I dinna hae mullein flowers, but I doo hae all the rest. I'll fetch them for ye."

"I'll be down to make my remedies in a moment."

It was nine o'clock when the three had tended and mended Rose sufficiently enough to let her get some sleep. They were exhausted. Emily asked if anyone was hungry and the three went into the kitchen to fix whatever was available to eat. They each settled on some sliced venison and bread.

"Should we feed Mr. Charles?" Claire asked, ready to get a plate together for him.

Cat looked at Emily and they said in unison, "No."

"What are we ta doo wi' him noow?" Emily asked.

"I found his ship earlier today. In the morning, I'll go down and hae his shipmates come get him. He'll no' remain here. Rose could hae been killed tonight. He will no' be allowed to do it again." Cat's amethyst stare dared Claire and Emily to challenge her. They just nodded their approval.

"I'm goin' to bed. Ye did tie him up good and tight, didna ye, Emily? I hate bein' woke up," Cat said, showing her dimples to lighten the mood of the house for a moment.

Emily smiled and nodded. "Good night, Miss."

Eviction

Morning dawned cloudy. If Charles had awakened during the night, Cat didn't hear him. She tossed off the bedclothes and got dressed. When she opened the door to the hallway, all was silent. Looking towards the stairs, Charles was still on the floor in the fetal position, hands and feet bound together. Cat walked to the end of the hall and opened Rose's door quietly. Peeking in, she saw that Rose was sleeping. She closed the door behind her and went downstairs to ready some more herbal remedies for when Rose did wake up.

Walking into the kitchen, Cat said good morning to Claire and Emily who were already busy. Cat put the water on to boil for her remedies without asking. After last night's commotion, she felt she had become a member of the household.

"How is Mistress Rose this mornin'?" Claire asked Cat.

"She was still sleepin' when I came down. I'll bring her some remedies and perhaps get somethin' in her belly. Any suggestions?"

"I hae a fine broth she shoould be able ta get doown," Emily said.

"Aye, that would be good. I'll bring it up to her when I finish my poultice," Cat said, stirring herbs and water in a small bowl to make a thick paste. "Then I'll be off to the quay to get Charles out o' this house."

Emily and Claire looked at each other with expressions of concern on their faces. Cat caught the looks, but chose to ignore them. She didn't come here to play nursemaid to a woman who would not stand up for herself. But she also couldn't let a man throw his rage around because he preferred to be drunk. If he wanted to act like an arse, he could do it in the company of his men.

When her poultice and the broth were ready, Cat put everything on a tray and brought it upstairs. As she walked past Charles, she noticed his eyes were open and they followed her down the hall. She neither spoke, nor acknowledged his existence. When she reached Rose's door, she heard him spit the words, "You'll be sorry you ever set foot in my house."

Inside Rose's room, Cat placed the tray on the table in the sitting room. She went into the bedchambers and put her hand on Rose's forehead. Good. No fever. Rose stirred and slowly opened her good eye. The other was still very puffy and bruised.

"Good mornin', Rose. How do ye feel?"

A single tear ran down her cheek. She did nothing to wipe it away.

"Oh now, dinna do that. It wilna make ye feel any better."

"This is the worst he's done. He doesn't like you here and he blames me for it. But before you tell me you're leaving, I told him that you were staying with me for as long as I wished, and that he had nothing to say about it. That's where this came from," she said, pointing to her eye.

Cat opened her mouth to give her opinion of the man, but clamped it shut. There was no need to voice her thoughts in front of Rose. She wanted to instill a positive atmosphere in the house; there was already enough negative. The first order of business was to rid the cause of the negative, and that meant the *prig* at the end of the hall had to go.

After tending to Rose, Cat closed the door to let her rest, not mentioning anything about kicking her husband out of his own house. What would be the purpose? It would only cause Rose to worry more. Walking towards Charles, she noticed he had been struggling to free himself of his ropes, and from the looks of them, he nearly succeeded.

"Dinna think for one minute ye'll get away that easy, sir," Cat said, putting down the tray and calling for Emily and Claire.

The two rushed up the stairs with the frightened eyes of wild animals, unsure of what they were summoned for.

"He almost got himself out of his ropes. Help me hold him down while I tighten them," Cat instructed.

With a look of pure joy, Emily sat directly in the center of his back, effectively squashing him into the floor. Claire let out a little giggle, and Cat was glad to see they could find some humor in the situation. Even as Charles let loose a string of profanities towards the threesome, their smiles grew larger, offering suggestions when he ran out of things to call them.

"I certainly dinna want to keep ye from yer tasks, ladies, but can one o' ye check on him e'ery so often while I'm gone? Dinna want him to get loose, do we?" Cat said, her dimples deepening just for Charles' benefit.

"Bitch!" he growled.

Emily gave him a kick in the ribs as she got off of him for that remark. He let out a grunt, but said no more.

Around mid-morning, Cat set out to see a few sailors about a wayward captain. The sky had turned a milk-white, indicating more snow was on its way—she could smell it. Patting the dirk that she strapped to her waist for easier access, she headed east down Marlborough Street, then took Milk Street down to the dock. She wasn't sure of the hierarchy of command; who to ask to fetch Charles. Refusing to ever get on another ship, she went to the harbour master's office at the head of Long Wharfe.

Letting in a *whoosh* of cold air when she opened the door to the small office, she saw an older man smoking a pipe. His brown weathered face told of a seafaring life. Small, observant blue eyes immediately questioned Cat's appearance in his office.

Without waiting for an invitation, Cat asked him who she should speak to about fetching Charles Carlyle from his house.

"Has there been an accident?" he asked in a loud, booming voice.

Suspecting the man was nearly deaf, Cat assumed he read lips to understand her question correctly.

"No."

"Then why can't he get to his ship on his own?" he asked, cocking his head and shifting his pipe to the other side of his mouth.

Cat didn't think this through enough. Should she tell him the truth? Or would that only serve to anger Charles further (as though that were possible)? She had no intention of ruining his reputation, she just wanted the man out of Rose's life.

"Och, I was just curious so if he was too drunk to make it back to his ship on his own, who could come to help him get there," she said, putting on her best smile to make light of the situation.

The old man chuckled and nodded his head, "He does love his rum. Been more than one occasion they sailed late 'cause of it. You'll be wantin' to speak with his first mate, Thomas Finch."

"Where might I find him?"

"Got a wife over on Water Street," he said, pointing his pipe in the general direction. "More 'an likely be there."

Cat didn't relish the idea of traipsing all over town for the man. "Who else could I see about it?"

"Him," he said, pointing his pipe once again, this time at the man walking past his window. "That's John Richards, the *Rose Ellen's* surgeon."

"Thank ye, sir," she said over her shoulder, just before closing the door to the office.

It took her a moment to locate the doctor in the throng of people, but when she saw the red cloak and tan breeks, she wasn't sure how to approach the man. She had, after all, not parted on good terms when he was just looking out for her welfare the other day.

Without much choice in the matter, she would make her apologies, then ask for his aid.

"Sir," she called from behind the man, tapping him on the shoulder. "Sir, might I hae a word wi' ye?"

The man turned with a questioning look on his face. When he saw who was requesting his company, he almost turned away without acknowledging her, but propriety won out.

"Have you stopped me to insult me further, Miss?" he said, not waiting for Cat to answer before continuing to walk towards his ship.

"I do apologize to ye, sir. My comment was uncalled for. Please forgive me," she said, keeping up with his pace easily in the crowd.

He seemed to think about it for a moment, then angled off out of the throng and stopped in front of a small building. He looked at her, as though for the first time, noting her height was the same as his. The hood of her cloak covered her auburn hair, but the cold had turned her cheeks a deep red, accenting her amethyst eyes. Cat let him make up his mind while looking her over. Finally he said, "How may I be of service?"

Cat smiled. "My name is Catrìona Robertson. Ye're the surgeon for the *Rose Ellen,* are ye no'?"

"Yes, how did you find out?" he asked, tilting his head in curiosity.

"The harbour master told me when I was in his office just a moment ago. He pointed ye out to me because I hae a question about yer captain."

He seemed to relax his guard at this, but was still curious. "What of him?"

Cat decided to trust the man with the truth. He was, after all a physician, a healer, and she was sure he would not approve of what his captain did to Rose.

"I need ye to fetch him from his house immediately."

"He hasn't hit his wife again, has he?" he asked, ready to assist in her aid, if need be.

"Ye ken of what he does to Rose?"

"Yes. When he drinks he becomes a different man."

"He nearly killed her last night," she said, feeling her temper rise. "Ye ken what he does, yet ye do naught to stop him?"

"What am I to do about it? I certainly do not condone what he does, but it's not against the law to strike your wife."

Cat stood there with her fists rolled tight, really wanting to punch him. She thought better of hurling another insult because she really needed to evict Charles before he caused further damage. So, biting her tongue until it was nearly bloody, she said, "Will ye fetch him and bring him back to his ship or no'?"

"How bad is Rose?" he asked, evading any promises.

"He broke her arm, her right eye is closed shut, she has lots o' bruises on her ribs and he nearly broke her nose. Now will ye fetch him?" she said through gritted teeth.

This seemed to rattle the man finally. His face grew red, obviously feeling some anger over the situation. He glanced at his watch fob and looked in the direction of his ship, planning who he would get to help him.

"Is he drunk now?" he asked.

"No. He's tied up and in a rare mean mood, though."

At that, he looked at Cat in a new light and burst out laughing. "Who tied him up?"

"Me, Emily and Claire. He had murder in his eyes after he finished wi' Rose, and the three of us wouldn't stand for any further mayhem. He fell o'er in a drunken stupor so we tied him up where he landed. Will ye fetch him or no'?" she said, her hands on her hips demanding an answer, or prepared to find someone else to aid her.

"Yes. I'll meet you there with a few of his men. Give me an hour." Cat turned to leave, but he stopped her.

"His men may or may not know of what he does. It would be better for all involved if he *were* drunk when we came to retrieve him. Fetching him when he's out cold is an easier way of explaining it to the men."

"Dinna fash about that. I'll make certain he's out cold," she said, then turned and disappeared into the crowd.

Cat returned to the Carlyles' and walked into a shouting match between Emily and Charles. She smiled as Emily clearly relinquished any fear of losing her position with the Carlyles. Cat hung her cloak and walked to the stairs where Emily was expounding Charles' shortcomings in graphic detail. Claire's giggling could be heard from the kitchen.

Cat climbed the stairs and stood at the top until Emily noticed she was there. Emily just glanced at her, smiled, winked, and continued on, barely skipping a beat.

Cat interrupted by holding up her hand, asking Emily to join her in the kitchen when she felt she had spoken her mind.

A few moments later, Emily walked in and Cat explained what needed to be done before Charles' men came to fetch him.

"But hoow are we gooin' ta get him drunk?" Emily asked.

"We're no'. I dinna plan on gettin' any closer to that man than I hae to. One smack to the heid should knock him out, then we get some rum and pour it on him," Cat said, watching closely for any mutiny of the plan. There was none. "How is Rose?"

"She seems to be restin'. Hasn't said a word about anythen' though. I've never seen 'er like that," Claire said, pulling a bottle of rum from the cupboard.

"I hope she isna givin' up, but I dare no' tell her of our plan. I canna chance her state o' mind in her condition," Cat said, grabbing a large wooden rolling pin from beside the bowl of rising bread. "Are we ready, ladies?"

"Ready," Emily and Claire said.

When Charles saw the threesome climbing the stairs, he was instantly on guard.

"What do you three bitches want?"

"He's no' verra polite, is he?" Emily said.

"He'll be a lot more polite in a few minutes," Cat replied, holding the bottle of rum in front of him.

Charles knew he was being set up, but had no idea what their plan was. "Do you actually think I'm going to drink that? You've probably poisoned it."

"Och, aye. Now why dinna we think o' that?" Cat said to Claire and Emily.

"It's no' too late," Emily chimed.

Cat chuckled, and traded the bottle for the rolling pin so quickly, Charles didn't know what hit him until the rolling pin struck him just behind the ear. Claire uncorked the bottle and poured it onto his shirt. For all intents and purposes, it appeared as though Charles had passed out from the drink.

"What do we do with 'im now?" Claire asked.

"Go fetch a blanket, Claire. We'll roll him onto it and drag him down the stairs," Cat instructed.

Emily giggled, enjoying herself thoroughly. "Why put him on a blanket when we can rooll him doown an' let him land where he may?"

"Ye're a right cruel woman, Emily," Cat smiled. "But we dinna want to kill the man, we just want him out o' this house."

An hour later, as promised, John and three burly seamen knocked on the door to fetch Charles, who was resting uncomfortably on the cold wood floor in front of the door. The three men hoisted their captain as though he weighed little more than a sack of flour and walked out the door with him. Cat put her hand on John's arm to hold him back.

"I would like ye to take a look at Rose, if ye wouldna mind, Mr. Richards."

"Oh, yes, of course. Where is she?"

Cat directed him upstairs and opened the door to Rose's room. She lay propped up on a few pillows looking like a battered queen.

"Dear Lord," he said quietly, walking over to check on Cat's method for splinting Rose's broken arm. "Did you do all this?"

"Aye. I use a poultice on her eye three times a day to bring down the swellin' and I keep rubbin' arnica oil on her bruises."

Three wooden spoons wrapped with linens served as a splint on Rose's arm. Cat touched her fingers to make sure there was adequate circulation. They were cool, but not cold.

"You did fine," he said. "I don't think I could've done better myself."

"Thank ye, sir."

Rose stirred and opened her eye. She took in her whereabouts, then saw John standing over her. Ever the lady, she asked if she could get him a cup of tea. The herbal concoction Cat fed her kept her rather sedated and pain-free. She probably had no idea that she was incapable of fixing him a cup of tea. Before he could answer, she was sleeping again.

"I can see she's in excellent hands, Catrìona. I'll make certain Charles remains on board for the duration of his stay. We are to set sail again at noon on Saturday. I'm quite certain I can keep him *sedated* for the next two days," he said, winking.

"We'll all sleep better for it."

Retaliation

The house was peaceful. Cat was in her room clearing away the negative energy from Charles' presence. Emily and Claire were in the kitchen preparing a wonderful celebration meal for supper. The smell of baking bread filled the house. As the light faded from her room, Cat decided to check on her patient before it got too dark. Opening the door to Rose's room, Cat was greeted with a warm smile.

"Hello, Catrìona."

"How are ye feelin' Rose?" She walked in and stood next to the bed.

Rose took in a deep breath, winced a little from the bruised ribs, but let it out again and said, "I feel … I don't know, at ease. I don't know why, but it feels like a weight has been lifted from me. Why do you suppose that is?"

"Charles is gone."

The joyful light on Rose's face seemed to dim a bit. "I'm truly sorry for what has transpired in this house these past few days."

Cat sat on the edge of the bed and placed her hand over Rose's. "There is no need for apologies, Rose. No' from ye, anyway."

A tear slipped down Rose's cheek again, but she wiped it away this time, trying her best to smile. "I'm fortunate to have you here with me, Catrìona. I truly do not know what we would have done without your bravery."

"Och, Rose. All I did was show Emily and Claire that he didna hae to be feared. They did the rest when they saw how easy it was to regain the upper hand. I think Emily was actually enjoyin' herself towards the end," she said, her deep dimples bringing a genuine smile to Rose's face.

"I woke once to hear her berating him so, that I knew he must be restrained to take her comments without retaliation."

Cat laughed softly and nodded, "Aye, we made sure he was tied tightly for fear of what would happen if released."

"Where is he now?"

There it was. The question Cat feared to answer, but she had to tell Rose the truth.

"I went to see the ship's surgeon, John Richards. Do ye remember him comin' in to visit wi' ye this mornin'?"

Rose's questioning look indicated she had no memory of the event.

"He said ye were doin' fine."

"You didn't hurt Charles, did you?" her blue-green eye wide with dismay.

"No, o' course no'. We did return him to his ship, though," Cat said, waiting for that piece of news to sink in before continuing.

Rose thought about it for a minute, then looked up at Cat and said, "I think, under the circumstances, that was a wise thing to do."

"Mr. Richards said he would keep him on the ship until they depart on Saturday noon. I dinna ken how long they'll be gone for, but ye wilna hae to worry about him for a while."

Cat saw the relief on Rose's face, but just as quick, sensed dismay. "What is it?"

"What happens the next time he comes home?"

"We'll no' worry about that now. There's plenty o' time to come up wi' a strategy ye can live wi'."

Supper was a marvelous feast. The highlights were venison stew, baked fish, and squash pie. Cat, Emily and Claire ate with Rose in her sitting room. This seemed to boost Rose's spirits, and the foursome relaxed in each other's company without the social bonds of servant and employer.

"Yer eye seems to be op'nin' more, Mistress," Claire observed.

Rose gingerly touched it, just realizing she could see out of its slit. "You're absolutely right, Claire. Catrìona's poultice must be helping."

Cat brought the lantern closer for an inspection. "Hmmm. I do see a bit of blue-green in there, but that shade o' purple around it doesna do ye justice."

They all laughed then began clearing away supper. It was getting late and all were tired from the day's events. By the time the dishes were washed and put away, it was nearly eleven o'clock. Cat said good night to Emily and Claire, then went up to her room. She filled the wash basin with water from the ewer and washed quickly in the coolness. Tomorrow she would see about getting her hair washed. She put on a clean shift and climbed under the bedclothes shivering, but fell asleep almost instantly.

She awoke before dawn from the same dream she had a couple of nights ago. This message was not to be taken lightly. It was a warning, a premonition, and she had to remain cautious. Although there was no indication that Charles was involved in her abduction, her feeling was that he masterminded the whole affair, but wasn't stupid enough to carry out the plan himself. He could easily get any of his men to do the deed and she would never be the wiser. Today was Friday. He would have plenty of time to carry out the plan before his ship sailed, but one thing stood in the way. Her forewarning of the deed.

"Och, aye, I ken about it, but what do I do to stay out o' it?" she asked herself out loud.

She heard the clock strike five downstairs. Too early to get up, but there was no going back to sleep either. She crawled out from under the warmth of her bedclothes, lit the lantern near the bed and quickly dressed. She held up her threadbare dress and decided she needed a new one, or perhaps even two.

Going downstairs, she took note that even Emily and Claire weren't in the kitchen yet. She started the fire and set the water on to boil for some tea. By this time, she heard stirrings from the servants' chambers in the back. A smile deepened her dimples when she decided to make them breakfast this morning. Finding all the ingredients for oatcakes, even marmalade to smother on the warm cake, Cat commenced with the baking.

Just before six, Emily came into the kitchen completely surprised to see breakfast in full swing.

"Oatcakes?"

"I hope ye dinna mind. I thought I would fix *ye* breakfast this mornin'."

"Mind? Ye're spoilin' us, Catrìona," she said, putting another log in the stove.

"It's the least I can do to repay yer help yesterday."

"It's ye we should be thankin'. Wi'oout ye here, he may hae killed her, aye?"

"I hae a favor to ask o' ye, Emily."

"Aye? What is it?"

"Someone's goin' to try and abduct me—take me somewhere I dinna want to go."

Emily frowned, assessing how she would know such a thing. Then a dawning showed in her eyes.

"I hae been away from Scotland for too long. Ye're a Seer, are ye no'?"

Cat placed the oatcakes in the oven, then poured herself and Emily a cup of tea.

"Aye. I was my clan's Seer before the rebellion."

"Charles?" Emily asked, already suspecting who was behind the deed.

"Aye."

"When?"

"Before he sails tomorrow noon is all I can say for sure. He'll want to see for himself that I'm out o' the way."

"Doo ye see hoow it will happen?"

"No. But I'm tryin' to decide if I should stay here, puttin' ye all at risk, or leave now."

Claire came in just then with the same astonished look on her face as Emily had. Cat smiled and poured another cup of tea. She brought Claire up to date on what they had been discussing and asked for her input.

"Yor a Seer?"

"Try to stay wi' us, Claire."

"Where well ye goo?" Emily asked.

"I dinna ken."

"I'm afraid of whot Charles' men would do to us if yor no' here," Claire said, effectively making up Cat's mind to remain where she was.

"When ye put it that way, will the two o' ye help me fight them off and protect Rose?"

Emily went outside for a moment and came back in with a healthy length of oak. She demonstrated how she could wield it as effectively as a club. Cat burst out laughing at the look on Emily's face, but sobered a bit when she realized it might come down to just that. A fight for her life.

ॐ

The day went by without incident. Cat sat in her room in the warmth of the sun. People walked by the house, their breath vaporizing in the cold air. From her vantage point she could see all the way to the harbour. Anyone trying to sneak up to the house would have to wait until dark to not be seen. It was mid-afternoon, plenty of time to relax.

She got up and walked down the hall to Rose's room to ask her about getting a couple of dresses made to replace her old one. Rose was looking better by the hour and was feeling bedridden.

"Catrìona, help me walk downstairs, won't you? I cannot remain in this bed any longer."

Cat helped her up and brought a blanket down so Rose could sit in the best room and stay warm.

"I would like to get a couple o' dresses made for myself, Rose. Who should I see about gettin' fabric?" Cat asked, tucking the blanket around Rose's legs.

"Me."

Cat just stared at her for a moment before realizing Rose must have done something to make a living when Charles was gone.

"Did ye make all o' yer dresses?"

"Yes, I did. I have bolts and bolts in every color and fabric, from silk to lace. Oh, do let me show you," she said, kicking off the blanket and getting off the settee.

"Are ye sure ye're up to this?"

"It would be my pleasure to make a couple of dresses for you for all you have done for me. I have more fabric than I could use in a lifetime. Follow me," she said, walking to a door off the dining room.

When she opened it, Cat's mouth opened in awe of the array in front of her. She reached into the large closet and ran her fingers over the fabrics. Some were smooth as glass, while others were warm and thick. Rose wasn't joking about the color variations. Every color in the spectrum was present.

"What's your favourite color, Catrìona?"

"I hae always liked green, the color of heather in the spring, or cinnamon brown, the color of deer in summer," she said, still feeling each bolt.

"Choose what you would like and pull it out."

Cat turned and looked at Rose with a questioning wistfulness in her eyes that made Rose laugh. "Yes, really. Go on, choose."

Cat had a hard time deciding, but after a few moments pulled out a bolt of forest green linen, then turned her eyes to a deep red silk with a navy, gold and green paisley print. She kept her hand on it and turned to Rose for her advice. It was more beautiful than she could imagine, but thought it might be too much for herself.

"Pull it out and unroll some," Rose instructed. "Hold the length up in front of you."

Cat did as she was told. It was a sumptuous fabric that at first seemed cool to the touch, but once near the skin, warmed to her body temperature. Rose looked her over with a critical eye, taking in Cat's coloring and figure.

"It suits you much more than it would me. It brings out your eyes even more. You have the coloring for garnet."

"That's what my mentor used to call me. Garnet. I've no' heard that word since I left Scotland," Cat said, fairly beaming that the fabric suited her.

"You'll need some lace for the green linen, choose what you like … Garnet," Rose said with a smile in her voice. "That name fits you better than Catrìona. Not that Catrìona is a bad name," she said quickly. "It's just that you are more than that."

"No need to explain yerself, Rose, I hae been told that many times."

"Good. Now, if you would help me, I can teach you how to make your own dresses, since I will be of no use for a while with only one hand," she said, lightly patting the three wooden spoons holding her arm together.

"Oh no, Rose. We'll no' start anythin' this day. Ye're goin' right back on that settee. We'll do this next week, when ye're stronger. Now, back to the best room wi' ye," Cat said, scooting Rose along through the dining room.

Just then, Claire came out with a tray of tea and scones, surprised to see Rose downstairs.

"We'll take that in the best room, Claire, thank ye," Cat said.

"Is she givin' ya trouble?" Claire asked.

"No, nothin' I canna handle," daring Rose to defy the two of them.

"I'm going, I'm going," Rose giggled, knowing full well they were bluffing.

At noon on Saturday, the household seemed to sigh in relief. No one came to steal Cat away; Charles remained on his ship. The day was warm, by Boston standards, and Cat was feeling housebound. After two o'clock, she asked Emily and Claire if either wanted to take a walk with her. They both declined, but she had to get out for a while. Donning her cloak, she decided not to go down to the shore, just in case. She knew Charles had sailed, seeing it in the meditation she did earlier that morning, but did not want to push her luck.

This time she walked to the common, a large, open area dotted with trees. In the distance she could see the watch house and powder house. The six inches of snow prevented her from taking a closer look. She stopped and studied the school, marveling at its size, then continued towards the burying ground. The charcoal slate stones marking the passing of earlier Bostonians were stark in contrast to the pure white snow. She kept walking up Treamount Street, amazed at how many buildings there were. There were booksellers at nearly every corner. Cat popped into a couple to see what they had of interest. She had no money to buy, so she didn't linger long, but found a wide array of titles she would have loved to peruse.

White mare's tails began to appear in the sky, filtering the sunlight now and then. Another change in weather was coming. It was getting late so she started for home, heading down Queen Street then taking a right onto Cornhill. She walked into Rose's just as the clock struck four and the sun went down behind the western hills.

Making sure the door was locked for the night, she went into the kitchen to see if she could help with supper. Emily kicked her out.

She went upstairs to check on Rose and found her asleep. Remembering that there were some books in Rose's sitting room, she went in and pulled a couple of interest from the shelves; Margaret Cavendish and Emilie de Breteuil. At least she could expand her mind while she was here. Taking them into her room, she lit the lantern and read until Claire came up a couple of hours later to fetch her for supper.

When supper was finished and Rose was back upstairs after her most active day since Charles left, Cat retired for the evening to continue with her reading. After hearing the clock strike eleven, she blew out the lantern and went to bed. After hearing the clock strike twelve and not having slept a wink, she decided to get up and pour herself a sherry. Perhaps that would relax her.

Just as she threw off the bedclothes she heard something downstairs. She quietly tiptoed to the door and opened it a crack, straining to hear it again. There it was; a click, like a latch being jiggled. Getting a mental image of what it was, she saw two men at the front door trying to get into the house. She had to risk running down the stairs to wake Emily and Claire. Hopefully she could get there before they got in.

Grabbing her dirk, she descended the stairs as quietly as she could, quickly looking around the dimly moonlit room for something to put in front of the door. Everything she found would make too much noise. She ran into the dining room, then through the kitchen to Emily and Claire's room in the back of the house. As she opened their door, she almost screamed because Emily was standing there with her oak weapon raised over her head.

"I take it ye heard it, too," Cat whispered, her hand over her heart.

"Aye, it doesna take much ta wake me. Claire, on the other hand ..."

"Wake her, there are two o' them out there," Cat instructed, getting her weapon of choice, the rolling pin. Between that and her dirk, she was covered.

Claire was roused and grabbed a heavy cast iron skillet. The three of them opened the kitchen door and walked through the dining room. Cat listened. The intruders were still outside fiddling with the door in an attempt to get in.

"How doo ye want ta doo this?" Emily whispered.

"I dinna ken. Do we unlock the door and beat them senseless when they come in, or do we just wait to see if they even get in before we start actin' courageous?"

"Let's wait," Claire said.

"Emily?"

"Waitin' soonds fine wi' me."

They crept into the front foyer and waited. After a few moments, the men seemed to give up. Cat went to the window to see if she recognized them, but it was too dark. After whispering something to each other, they skulked beside the house heading for the back entrance.

"They're goin' 'round back!" she whispered.

"They'll get in easy that way," Claire said.

"Good. This waitin' is killin' me," Emily said, walking quickly to catch up to Cat who was already in the dining room.

Not a moment after the threesome got into position beside the back door, it opened ever so slowly. Cat had instructed Emily and Claire to wait until both of the men were in before commencing with the beating. It was darker at this end of the house, and as the shadows of men walked into the larder, the trio were perfectly concealed in the deep, black corners.

Before the two men knew what hit them, they were being pummeled to within an inch of their miserable lives. They weren't quiet about it either. Cat hit the first man in the ribs with the rolling pin, feeling the bones give way more than they should. That man fell to the ground and she belted him on the back of the head for good measure. One down.

The second man was a bit larger, and even with the skillet and the mighty oak branch, he was still on his feet, screaming and striking out at his unseen assailants with thick, burly arms. One of these blows knocked Claire into the wall, where she landed with a thud.

All of a sudden the room was filled with light. Having heard the commotion from upstairs, Rose came down to investigate. The man couldn't believe his eyes. He was being thrashed by women. This fact seemed to spur him on. If his mates heard of such a thing, he would be shamed for the rest of his days. He came at Cat with a long blade which he managed to pull from his waistband. He was eyeing her dirk blade, not the rolling pin. Making his lunge, Cat swung the rolling pin and it found its mark on the thug's wrist, knocking the blade to the floor. From behind him, Emily swung the oak branch with all her might and caught him between the shoulder blades. He fell to the floor. One more swing and he was out.

Claire was just coming to and slowly rose from her spot against the wall. Without a word, she went to get the rope that was used on Charles and brought it into the larder. There, they tied the two up and closed the door. Hopefully by morning, the assassins would have frozen enough and would gladly be remanded into custody.

Cat knew she had to tell Rose what was going on. The foursome went into the best room and Cat explained the sequence of events.

"I'm afraid that this wilna stop them. They hae their orders and will keep sendin' men 'til I'm caught. I will hae to find another place to stay. This is too dangerous for ye all, and I will no' put ye in jeopardy any longer."

"Well, we certainly will not be able to stave off many more of those attacks," Rose said, "I'm very impressed at the three of you for holding your ground. You don't think they'll send more men to-night, do you?"

Cat thought about it for a moment and said that she didn't think so.

"Good. Then let's all return to bed."

By mid-morning, the two men were carted off to the gaol. Rose sent a courier to some friends who lived in Charles Town to see if Cat could stay there until more suitable arrangements could be found. In the meantime, to stay busy and keep their minds occupied with something other than last night, Rose started instructing Cat on dress-making. She found it complicated, but interesting and they worked until a knock on the door just before dark interrupted them. Emily went to see who it was and delivered a letter from Charles Town to Rose.

Rose read it quickly and smiled. "Henrietta said she would be delighted to put you up for as long as you need."

"I'll leave in the mornin'."

Having vowed never to board a ship again, Cat waited on the dock for the Charles Town ferry to take her to Henrietta Morrisey's. Emily walked with her to the dock, which was on the other side of town from where the *Rose Ellen* was launched. After Cat and Emily were satisfied that only respectable citizens were waiting to go to Charles Town, Emily headed back home.

The morning air was cold and dry, making the inside of Cat's nose stick together when she breathed in. She adjusted the shawl up higher to cover more of her face so only her eyes were showing.

There was a gathering of nearly fifty people to take the ferry. Cat marveled at how mobile Bostonians were. Judging from the conversations around her, it seemed that most people were acquainted with the surrounding towns. The wait was festive as people talked and laughed.

When the ferry was sighted in the distance she heard someone say it would be right on time, which meant it should arrive at ten. It looked like it would take another half hour to dock, so in an effort to stay warm, Cat decided to take a short stroll towards the point. The low sun hit the water in a blinding reflection. It was warm and she stood in its light for a time.

The wind was starting to pick up, making the cold seem even colder, and she decided she would probably be warmer if huddled with the crowd. Cat was off in her timing a bit because when she turned, she saw the ferry was already docked and people were filing aboard. She picked up her pace to a jog so she wouldn't miss it.

She was the last one in line, but ticket in hand, she was assured of getting on. Cat reached the gangway as two men took tickets on either side of the entrance. When she got to them she was stopped.

"One minute, miss. We may already have a full boat," one of them said.

This didn't feel right. Cat started to back down, saying she would catch the next one. As she turned to make her break, the two men flanked her, grabbing her arms in grips that meant business, and dragged her behind the ticket house. In an attempt to struggle from their grasps, she kicked at their legs. One of the men covered her mouth with his hand, and finding a bit of flesh, Cat latched on tight. He let out a yell and that was all she remembered.

From Bad to Worse

The space was dark and moist, smelling of sweat and ale. Cat knew she was in the hold of a ship. Whose ship it was, and where it was going, were two questions that first came to her mind. When she tried to sit up, she realized her hands were bound and she was attached to a pole. Wriggling herself to get into a sitting position, Cat drew her legs together to see if her dirk was still there. It was, but she had no idea of how to remove it from its sheath with her hands tied in back of her. Her head ached terribly as she tried to remember the last thing that happened. It wasn't the blow to her head, but that's what it must have been.

Closing her eyes to stave off a wave of nausea, she rested her head against the pole for support. Cat needed to locate her captors and the only way to do that was through her mind. It would have to wait until her head stopped pounding first.

After a while her head cleared. She was ready. Releasing herself from her body, she was now free to roam. She went up on deck in search of the name of the ship and was almost positive it was going to be the *Rose Ellen,* but it wasn't. Charles must be very well connected to hire someone else to do his dirty work and take her … where?

The ship cut through the waves as effortlessly as air. The wind was icy and the shadows of the sails danced along the deck. She searched the faces for someone she recognized. It was becoming clear that they knew her, but she didn't know them. She walked back below decks to locate the captain's quarters, hoping for an indication of her captor and destination.

The door to his small cabin was open. He sat facing the window, watching the foamy sea play along the back of the hull. His hair was the color of honey and fell freely around his shoulders. His frame was small and wiry, thin through the hips and lean legged. He must have sensed her there, because he turned around. She knew he couldn't see her, but she now knew who he was. He was in line at the office where she received the news about her father. There was no evidence that he was looking for her then, but he must have worked for Charles, since she was now a captive aboard this ship. The quest for *who* was complete, but where she would be relocated was still a mystery.

As he walked past her and closed the door, Cat stepped further into his quarters to read his ledger. At the top of the page, it read, *Marianne,* 23 December, 1746. After a few insignificant recordings of what went on during the first watch, Cat found her answer. They were bound for Virginia. She had no idea where Virginia was, but knew it wasn't where she wanted to go. This posed another question. How could she get off this ship?

Suddenly, she was back in her body down in the dark hold. Cat rested for a few minutes, then decided it was now or never to release her bindings. In her mind, she saw the rope that tied her hands together. She had done this a few times before—moving objects with her mind—but never on herself. It was a strange procedure, feeling the ropes move on her hands from behind her, but she soon had them loose enough to slip out of. Now that she was free, what was she going to do? Were there places to hide? Not for long, she imagined.

Cat got up and stretched, letting circulation return into her limbs. She rubbed her arms vigorously to eliminate the prickly feeling of being asleep. Her cloak wasn't offering much in the way of warmth; she had been cold for too long. She wished for some light to get her bearings inside the small confines, but the only glimmer came from under the door. She felt her way around the place, stubbing her toe on a crate. Ah, a place to sit. Anything was better than the dampness of the deck floor.

Edging her way to the door, she placed her ear to the wood and heard muffled voices in the cabin next to hers. They were whispering and she couldn't make out what they were saying, but the hair started to rise on her neck. Not a good sign. Pulling up her skirts, she unsheathed her dirk and stood behind the door. Slowly, the latch was lifted and with a slight creak, it opened. The light hadn't hit where she should have been sitting yet, but she saw two shadows in the flood of brightness that illuminated the floor.

A head poked in and she grabbed his hair and yanked him into the cabin. The second man hesitated for a moment, but in pure instinct entered the cabin to see what had happened to his mate. When they were both inside, Cat kicked the door shut. She had her dirk under the first man's neck. He was either very short or just a boy, because his head only came up to her chest.

"Please, don't hurt me," he cried. His voice cracked as teenagers' do.

His friend, though Cat could not see him, was already trying to get the door opened. He was nearly whimpering in fright fiddling with the latch.

"Stop," Cat hissed, "Or I'll slit his throat."

The boy stopped fighting with the door, but his whimpering increased. He was actually crying.

"Do ye hae a lantern wi' ye?" Cat asked.

"Aye," said the boy against her chest.

Cat released him and told him to light it, keeping the point of her dirk between his shoulder blades. When the lantern was lit, she saw clearly that they were indeed just boys, maybe in their early teens.

"And what might the two o' ye been plannin' to do wi' me when ye got a chance?" Cat mocked, staring at the wetness on the front of the boy's pants who was trying to escape.

"N-n-nothin', miss. Really!" he whined.

"And what about ye?" Cat asked the lad at the end of her dirk, giving him a little poke.

He exuded a little more bravery and cockily said, "We were goin' ta scare ya an' torment ya some."

Stifling a laugh, Cat said, "Oh really? And then what? What if I screamed and someone came in to see what ye were doin' to me?"

He just shrugged, not having thought his plan out all the way through.

"Well, I'll be glad for the comp'ny, lads. Go hae a seat at the pole. Ye'll hae to be tied up, but I'm hopin' ye wilna hae to be gagged as well," she said, indicating they had a choice in the matter.

The lads shook their heads vigorously to the gag. Cat tied their hands behind them and sat on the crate, placing the dirk beside her in plain sight.

"So tell me of Virginia."

ﻋﻼ

The lads were quite eager to talk and Cat learned all about indentured servitude, black slaves, white slaves, and where Virginia was. They said they would be going ashore again in Baltimore—wherever that was—before continuing the voyage to Norfolk. They were to pick up another shipment of servants for the growing population of wealthy landowners in the south. Not all were content to have black slaves working in their homes and tending to their children. Some preferred to keep whites for those tasks.

The pit in Cat's stomach deepened at the revelation, and while the lads were certainly helpful, none of this knowledge made her feel any better. There had to be a way to get off the ship between here and Baltimore. Land was always in sight, but while Cat was a fair swimmer, the icy water and the distance to shore would mean certain death. She wasn't quite ready to die just yet.

After picking the boys' brains for all they were worth, Cat turned the conversation to a more personal level. She found out that the two were orphans from outside London, and "pressed" into service in the King's fleet. Basically, they were kidnapped much the same as she was. This situation might work to her advantage. They talked openly for a long time. When the smell of food wafted to them, Cat asked if they would be missed for supper.

"Aye, they do a head count," Jim, the whiney one said.

"Perhaps we can help each other," Harry, the cocky one, teased.

"Och, aye, and how would ye propose to do that?" Cat asked, trying to keep the curiosity out of her voice.

Even in the dim light of the lantern, Cat could see the spark of conspiracy in Harry's eyes. He obviously had planned this for some time, but had waited patiently for the right person to spring it on.

"There's always confusion when we get inta Baltimore. We'll pick up over a hundred people there. We sometimes get ta get off the ship an' go inta town for supplies. If me an' Jim make sure we *have* ta get supplies, we can *all* get off."

"Ya mean an' stay off?" Jim asked his friend, just now privy to Harry's plan.

"Aye, what do ya think?" Harry looked at Jim for a moment, assessing Jim's misgivings for the plan. "Ya don't wanna stay on this ship for the rest of yur life, do ya now, Jimmy-boy?"

Cat could see that Jim didn't want to stay on this ship, but was too afraid to do anything about changing his lot.

"Where would I go?" Jim said softly.

Cat thought about what he had just said. Where was she going to go? She had to find the place in her vision. John Richards told her it was north of Boston in a place called Maine. She was heading in the wrong direction, getting further from her destination every minute.

"What if ye both came wi' me?" Throwing out the question to see where it would land.

The lads just looked at each other. A large smile blossomed on Harry's face. Jim raised his eyebrows, like *Yeah, what if . . .*

"I think we've come ta an agreement, miss," Harry said.

"Call me Catrìona," she said, getting up to untie her young friends. "We hae some plannin' to do, aye?"

୨ଈ

Jim brought Cat her supper, which wasn't much; a crust of bread and some sort of stew. She was glad for the dimly lit room. She didn't really want to know what she was eating.

"How many days 'til we reach Baltimore, Jim?" Cat asked.

"Five days, then another four ta Norfolk. Do ya think we can really do it? Leave, I mean." He was nervous and afraid. Not good. He could ruin the plan if he decided to back out or confide in someone else.

"Jim, I promise we'll leave and ye—we—can make a new life. Wouldna ye like that?" she asked, touching his hand.

"More than anythin', but what if somethin' goes wrong?"

"Jim, ye canna be thinkin' like that, or somethin' will go wrong. I wilna lie to ye and tell ye it isna dangerous, but if the three of us stick together and stay quiet, we can do this. Are ye wi' me?"

Cat could see on his face that he still wasn't one hundred percent convinced.

"Do ye hae any good memories, Jim? Places ye've been, or people ye ken?"

Jim pondered that for a moment, then a slight smile played along his lips.

"Go on, tell me." Cat urged, moving closer to him.

"It was when I was back in Dartford with me family. I wasn't orphaned 'til I was nine," he said, answering Cat's unasked question. "Me an' me brother, and me Mum an' Dad were all singin' songs. It was the happiest day of me life."

"Let that sit in yer mind, and believe ye can hae the same thing again, only this time wi' a different family—Harry and me."

Getting a little choked up he gave Cat a feeble smile, then nodded his head. He took the bowl from Cat and left her small cabin.

No one bothered her again until morning. This time, it was Harry bringing in a mug of ale.

"What did ye say ta Jimmy last night?" he asked, sitting down next to her on the crate.

"I told him to think good thoughts. He's verra scairt about this plan. I didna want him to ruin it. He thought o' his family, so I told him that it can be that way again when we get off this tub."

Harry laughed at the derogatory name Cat used to call one of the sleekest ships in the fleet. "There's nary a ship on the sea that can catch 'er."

"Ye sound proud of it."

"Aye, well, ya should see some of the 'tubs' that are out there."

Cat chuckled a bit, then asked, "How are ye keepin' the men out o' here?"

"Ah, that'll be Jimmy's doin'."

"Really? And what did he say to repel them?"

"He told 'em ya keep pukin' on yurself." When he saw Cat's confused look, he elaborated. "No sailor likes the smell of puke on a woman."

He said it so matter-of-factly, she burst out laughing, knowing full well he probably had no idea why that would repel a man, just heard it said amongst the men and took it as truth.

"Do thank Jimmy for me, aye?" Handing the empty mug back to Harry. His smile indicated he would.

ઢ

The morning of the fourth day, just outside the point that entered Chesapeake Bay leading to Baltimore Harbour, a loud crack and explosion was heard above decks. A thousand pounding feet ran above Cat's head in chaos. Shouting, then musket fire and blades clanging indicated to Cat that there was either a mutiny going on above her, or an enemy had boarded them.

No measure of time could determine how long it went on before the door to her cabin flew open. She was hoping it was going to be Harry or Jim, but this strangely familiar man from another lifetime kept Cat riveted to her crate. She knew his presence, but the backlight kept his features hidden as he filled the doorframe.

It took him a minute before his eyes adjusted to the dimness of the cabin, but when they settled on Catrìona, he took in a sharp breath. He picked up the lantern that rested on the floor near her feet, bringing it up closer to get a better look at her face. When he did that, Cat recognized those malachite eyes, those hardened features, somehow even harsher now.

"Catrìona?" he asked.

"Aye', 'tis me, Greame."

"What are ye ... ?"

"I could ask the same o' ye," Cat interrupted quietly.

"Are ye here of yer own free will?" Greame Hay asked, pulling Cat to her feet.

"Hardly."

He smiled a bit, reminding Cat of the first time he did that so long ago. It still had the same effect on her and she smiled back.

"Shall we then?" he asked, guiding her through the doorway.

"Aye, but I hae one request," she said, taking in his rugged profile.

"Name it."

"We take two young lads wi' us."

"What am I to do wi' them?" he asked, climbing up the ladder to the fore deck behind her.

"I'm takin' them wi' me back to Boston. From there, I dinna ken where I'm goin', except further north."

"There are no' many settlements north o' Boston," he said, taking in the sight of her in the light. "Lord, ye are a rare fine beauty."

Cat smiled at the compliment, knowing full well what she must have looked like after five days of no bathing or comb through her hair. When she looked him over, she noticed a deep red line from his right ear disappearing into the collar of his shirt. She reached out to touch it, but he grabbed her hand and stopped her.

"Stories for another time. We hae to find yer two lads and get away from here before we're spotted. Go fetch them and I'll meet ye back here in a few minutes. The captain and I hae somethin' to discuss."

Cat knew very well what "discussing" meant, and talk was not involved. She didn't give it another thought after she spotted Harry and Jim being rounded up on deck by Greame's men. She walked up to the lads, grabbed their hands and escorted them to the fore deck to wait for Greame.

"Do ya know that pirate?" Jim asked, shaking visibly.

"Aye," she said, then the word pirate sunk in. "He's a pirate?" she asked, amused.

"Don't ya see the colors he flies?" Harry said, pointing to the flag on Greame's ship.

Cat caught sight of the black cloth with skull and cross bones blowing out straight in the wind. How appropriate, she thought, then pondered on how he went from Tullibardine, the Jacobite Duke of Atholl's driver and personal servant, to becoming the captain of a pirate ship. Scanning the deck, she finally saw him climbing up from below decks with the captain's sword.

Her eyes took in each detail of him. Chocolate-brown hair going halfway down the center of his back, restrained by a leather thong. Wide shoulders straining the fabric of his coat, and thick, muscular legs in the form-fitting breeks. He was definitely battle-seasoned judging from his alert stance and commanding presence. He must have fought in the rebellion, being one of the lucky who survived and escaped. Cat thought of the last time she saw him. It was less than two years ago. Had she changed as much as he had?

Greame caught her stare and nodded in acknowledgement, barked some orders to his men, and started in her direction. When he reached her, he looked Jim and Harry over, then gave Cat a smirk. "Like lost pups, aye?"

"We're all lost here," Cat said in their defense.

Before further exchanges could be made, Harry pointed and said, "Time to go."

Emerging from the harbour, a man-of-war in full sail appeared. If they didn't leave now, they would be caught for sure. Apparently, Greame's men were no strangers at making a run for it. Taking only what booty they could easily carry, they piled off the *Marianne* and onto the *Revenge*. Greame grabbed Cat's hand and the foursome ran to the ropes that would get them over board. Cat went over first, then Harry and Jim. Greame made one last visual sweep, then swung over, landing on the deck at a dead run shouting, "Raise the sails and man the guns!"

His men were doing his bidding even before the orders were out. They had seen the man-of-war before Harry did and begun the escape process. The *Revenge's* sails unfurled and caught the west wind, taking it quickly out of the Chesapeake. Men were working in orderly chaos pulling ropes, unloading cannon balls, breaking open gunpowder flasks and hauling cannons into place.

Cat took Harry and Jim below decks to the center of the ship where they would be safest. She could feel the excitement running through the ship itself. Why men loved a fight was still beyond her. Glancing at the lads, she saw that even they were spiked with energy; wide-eyed and smiles on their faces.

Taking in her surroundings, Cat realized she was in a surgeon's cabin. She got up and looked through the jars of remedies, pushed around the assorted gruesome tools and saws, opened cabinet doors containing linens and bandages, and flipped through the surgeon's log book. Judging from the thickness of the filled pages, the man had been very busy. Anything from tending to cuts and burns, to removing limbs and setting broken bones; even writing letters to the families of the dead.

Overhead, an enormous *boom!* sounded. The man-of-war was close enough to shoot at. Cat silently wondered if this ship was fast enough to outrun a war ship of the Royal Navy.

As if reading her mind, Harry said, "Don't worry, Catrìona, this ship can outrun even the *Marianne*."

"How do ye ken?"

"Pirates always have the fastest ships. They might be smaller, but they're quick and able to get inta places those big rigs cannot," he said, sounding very knowledgeable.

"Hae ye had dealins wi' pirates before?"

"No, but we've heard the other men tell stories about 'em. Pirates don't like authority," Jim replied.

"Do they take captives?"

"Sometimes, but mostly it's the bounty they want. Taking a ship would be a prize, but that doesn't happ'n very often. Most ships are not as good as the ones they already have," Harry said.

Another *boom!* exploded above their heads, making all three of them jump.

"I canna sit here wi'out seein' what's happenin'." Cat said, pacing around the small cabin looking up at the ceiling attempting to see through it.

"Me an' Jimmy can help with the loadin' of cannons. That's what we did on the *Marianne,*" Harry stated with eagerness in his voice, ready to go if permission was granted.

"I think we should all go up and lend a hand where we're needed."

The threesome climbed up to the quarterdeck and found Greame at the wheel. He was concentrating intensely on something on the horizon. Cat squinted to see what it was, but found nothing of interest. She braced against the sharp wind and walked up to him. He never looked at her, but Cat felt he knew she was there.

"The lads are familiar wi' loadin' cannons. Might they be of help to ye?"

"Aye, and hae them load the muskets as well. It may come down to it." The lads heard their orders and ran below decks to be of service.

Cat turned to get a view of the war ship and took a sharp breath. It was very close and seemed to be gaining at a rapid pace.

"Harry told me your ship could outrun that one easily. Why are they so close?" Cat shouted into the wind.

A smile cracked his hard façade, making the creases beside his eyes deepen. Cat was again amazed at the complete transformation he took on when he smiled.

"I like Harry already," he said, chuckling. "And to answer yer question, I'll make a good getaway as soon as I can catch the wind beyond the point. Then ye'll see what Harry was so sure about."

"Och, aye, but will we make it to this imaginary place before they blow us out o' the water?"

Greame faced her squarely with a lifted eyebrow. "Ye o' little faith, lass."

Looking to port, he judged that, any minute, he would be away from the influence of land and free to let the wind whisk the *Revenge* out of harm's way. Suddenly, a lurch and a tearing of canvas came from above them. The man-of-war fired a cannon ball that seared through the mainsail, just missing the jib, and somehow missing both masts.

"Christ, just two more minutes," Greame growled.

Cat looked aft in time to see the short burst of flames as another shot was fired. The boom was heard shortly afterward. This shot missed its mark, splashing in the water in front of the ship. A explosion beneath her feet indicated the *Revenge* was fighting back. Cat watched as a splash hit the hull at the man-of-war's bow. It didn't seem to have any effect on it whatsoever.

"Hang on!" Greame shouted.

Cat grabbed at the nearest railing just as the wind blasted into the sails and jerked the *Revenge* forward at an amazing speed. Cat didn't get a good enough hold and fell to the deck on her bottom, feet splayed out in front of her. The wind whipped at her long hair, and filled her cloak, making it into a sail of its own. The sheer exhilaration of the event made her giggle.

Greame was about to ask if she was all right, but the look on Cat's face told him all he needed to know. He marveled at her for laughing. He knew all too well they weren't out of danger yet, but there she was, enjoying herself! He shook his head and chuckled a bit before the reality of getting to safety took over.

Cat got to her feet and glanced at the man-of-war behind them. She could actually see it falling behind. Harry was right. But now what?

A Pirate's Tale

At midday, Greame finally relinquished the wheel to his helmsman and went below with Catrìona. When he allowed himself a glance in her direction, her teeth were chattering and her lips were nearly blue, but she had refused to go below until they were out of danger—from the man-of-war anyway. Only then was she finally persuaded to go down to the surgeon's cabin to warm up.

"Christ, how do ye e'er stay warm?" She was still shivering when Greame sat down next to her.

"No time to think o' gettin' cold when ye're in a situation such as we were," he said, rubbing her arms briskly to bring back the circulation.

"Sit closer, ye feel just like a warm day," she said, scooting over to him in an attempt to capture his heat.

Greame wrapped his arms around her and brought her to his chest. Neither said a word to ruin the moment, they just sat embraced, enjoying the feel of each other, like trying on a new pair of shoes to see where the fit is too tight or too loose. Or just right.

Like all good things, this didn't last long. The door to the cabin flew open and Harry and Jim burst in with such exuberance, there was no time to move a respectable distance from each other. The lads either didn't notice or didn't care. They were much more interested in talking about their close encounter with the English war ship.

Greame stood and went to the other side of the cabin, attempting to look busy. From the way the lads told it, the *Revenge* was nearly captured and sunk! He chuckled as he watched them shake with excitement and their eyes get bigger as the tale went on. When he glanced at Catrìona, she looked enraptured by the story, persuading them to elaborate. She seemed to say exactly what they wanted to hear. Seers must just know what's going on in people's minds all the time. This made him stop short. What did she know of me? he wondered. Cat glanced in his direction and smiled. *Did she know I was thinking of her just then, or was it just coincidence that she looked at me?* He decided that there was probably something for him to do in his cabin and quietly snuck out.

The hourly watch bell was sounded. It was nearly dusk when Harry and Jim finished exploiting every detail of the hour-long ordeal. They each found a hammock after they ate, but Cat was restless. She wanted to know where they were heading, so she went in search of Greame. She found him in his cabin writing in his logbook. He hadn't seen her yet, so she remained in the doorway to study him for a moment.

He had released his hair from the confines of the leather thong and it flowed down his back in a rich brown cascade. His face was stern, uncompromising as stone. She noticed again the red scar running down into his shirt and wondered in which battle he received it. His shirtsleeves were rolled up, showing heavy forearms from his years of servitude. She could wait no more to find out about his life, so she cleared her throat. His head came up sharply at the intrusion, but when he saw it was her, he smiled.

"Ye hae a wonderful smile, Greame," she said, walking into his chambers and taking a seat across from him.

He looked at her for a long moment, then said, "Do ye ken what I'm thinkin?"

She cocked her head, giving him her full attention. "If I tried, I would ken. Does that bother ye?"

"Aye, but only because I canna do the same wi' ye. It must be a verra handy talent."

"No' wi what I hae seen. It's a terrible talent to bear, but it has saved my life on more than one occasion."

"Someone has tried to harm ye?" The frown making thick furrows between his green eyes. "Why?"

She explained her abbreviated stay in Boston and how she came to be in the hold of the *Marianne*. She also told him of her vision of the rocky fir-lined coast of Maine, and the Indians.

"I've been as far north as York, Maine, but there's only sand there, no granite shore."

"Hae ye seen the Indians?"

"No. I've no' been ashore for verra long in any place. I like the safety of my ship."

"Tell me yer story o' how ye came to be a pirate. What happened to Tullibardine?"

"Ye could probably look into me and ken all ye need to," he said, staring hard into her eyes, looking for a sign that she could do just that.

Cat smiled. "Aye, but I would much rather hear it from ye. Besides, I would only get the major events, no' the details."

"Och, so ye want the whole story," he said, sitting back in his chair to get comfortable.

"Aye, but before ye begin, would ye tell me where we're goin?"

"I'm takin' ye back to Boston, if that's where ye want to go," he said, frowning a bit.

"For now, that'll do, but I feel I'm no' safe there for long," Cat said, twirling her hair around her fingers.

"Ye said ye were bound for Charles Town when they took ye. Do ye want me to take ye there instead?"

"We hae a few days before I hae to make up my mind, dinna we?" Hoping with her eyes to not have to make a decision right then and there.

"Ye just tell me what ye decide. I'll take ye where e'er ye want to go," he said. "Just not further north than York 'til spring. Winter storms are just as fierce here as they were in Scotland."

Cat nodded her head in agreement, then settled in to listen to the series of events that led him to America.

Greame John Edmund Grant Hay had not always been a servant. His family lived in the shadow of the sea-bound ruins of Slains Castle near Port Erroll, on the northeastern coast of Scotland. They were fisherfolk and plied their living on the sea. Greame had been on the water nearly all his early life, but when he was seventeen, his father drowned in a storm. Greame was lucky to be in another boat at the time, or he too would have died.

Now, being the only male in his family of five sisters, and burdened with the responsibility to make a living for them, he left to find work elsewhere. That's when he met William, Tullibardine, Jacobite Duke of Atholl. Greame had been working in the Blair Castle stables and doing other odd jobs. When the Duke saw his determination to keep his family cared for, William offered him a higher paying job as his personal driver and servant.

"At first, I didna like the idea of bein' a servant to anyone—I hated it. But I had to think o' my family. Tullibardine always treated me well, and paid me well. I worked for him for nearly fourteen years."

"What o' yer family now?" Cat asked.

"My Mam died four years past and all o' my sisters are marrit. The croft sits empty, but no' for long, I hope," he said, sitting up and folding his hands in front of him on the desk.

"So ye want to go back to Scotland?"

"Aye. Dinna ye?"

Cat thought for a moment. She had only been in America for about two weeks. From the looks of things, prospects weren't much better here. But then she remembered her vision. She had to at least give herself time to find this place and see why it was so important to her.

"I hae to find the place in my vision before I can make any decisions."

Greame nodded his head, understanding the need to get all the facts before settling on something. "If ye're able to wait 'til spring, I'll take ye up to Maine to see if any of the coast matches yer vision."

Cat smiled, "Ye would do that for me?"

"Aye. I'm curious to see these Indians and why this place has such a hold on ye."

"Me, too. So, continue wi' yer story."

"All right," he said, settling back into his chair. "When Prince Charles was at Blair Castle—the day I drove ye back to Anna Macpherson's croft—Tullibardine asked me to volunteer. I couldna verra well refuse, now could I," he said with a wry smirk on his face.

Cat just lifted an eyebrow and shrugged.

"We made it through the battle at Prestonpans wi'out incident. A horrible thing to witness though."

Cat nodded her head in agreement, remembering all too well just how horrific that battle was.

"Then there were lots o' wee skirmishes that just kept the Hanoverians out of our hair. They werna fightin' wi' their hearts in it."

"That's exactly what my brother Seumas said. That's why he and my Da came home for the winter."

"Aye, many men went home that winter. I stayed wi' Tullibardine, and on the sixteenth o' January we took Stirling Castle at Falkirk. That's where I got this." He pulled open his shirt to reveal the entire length of the scar going from the back of his right ear all the way down across his right pectoral muscle.

Cat stood for a closer inspection. "Someone did fine stitchin' work on ye."

"Aye. I dinna think I'd hae lived if it were no' for Tullibardine's surgeon," he said, lacing his shirt back up. "Anyway, Tullibardine sent me home to mend, and I was out the rest o' the war."

A far away look came over him just then. He stared off to some distant place for a long moment. Cat waited silently, not wanting to interrupt his contemplation. When at last he looked at her, his face was full of regret.

"What is it, Greame?"

"If I had no' been home, Tullibardine might be alive today."

"Did he die at Culloden?"

"No, no' at Culloden, though he was captured there. The *Sassenaich* sent him to London for trial, and bein' as rheumatic as he was, he died in the Tower o' London, a prisoner."

"I'm verra sorry. I could tell ye were verra fond o' him."

"He was like a Da to me."

They were both quiet again, deep in their own thoughts, unwilling to share anything further. Without a word, Cat got up and left the cabin. Greame didn't stop her. When the door closed behind her, she stood against it and let out a long breath. She would wait for another time to hear the rest of his story. Too many fresh memories had haunted her during that conversation.

For the next couple of days, Cat and Greame stayed clear of each other. Cat did not regret knowing about Greame, but it consumed her, drowning her in the past. She knew he felt the same way because he didn't search her out either.

Harry and Jim fell into a routine on the ship and seldom came to visit. This gave her lots of time to think. It was really the first opportunity since she had landed in the colonies to have so much time of her own. She made full use of it by doing a long meditation the morning of the third day back to Boston.

The sun filtered into the surgeon's cabin through a couple of small windows. She sat in their small shafts wrapped in her cloak, trying to stay warm. A storm must be brewing because the waves were getting larger, giving the ship a rolling feeling. She didn't like it at all, but the vision she received made her forget all about her stomach's unsettledness.

She stood on ledges of granite overlooking many small islands just off the coast. The waves crashed onto the rocks splashing her with sea spray. It was warm, the sun hot on her face. Gulls drifted overhead as though tethered, gracefully and effortlessly floating on the breeze. They dropped mussels onto the rocks to break them open, then darted down to retrieve their booty before another of their brethren beat them to it.

There was an energy here, where the sea, sky and land all met. It was joyous, peaceful, exhilarating. It was a feeling of home. All things were as one here, working with nature in perfect harmony. Everything had a purpose, including her.

Cat came out of her vision with a smile. As far back as she could recall, that was the first time a vision didn't have a dire meaning or feeling when she emerged from it. She wished to have more information, but she knew it would come in due time. Now, more than ever, she had to find this place.

A knock on her cabin door brought her back to reality. "Come in."

Greame entered looking very serious, taking a seat next to Cat. She waited for him to speak, but he seemed to be collecting himself to break some kind of news to her.

"Tell me what's on yer mind, man. Dinna make me go into yer heid for what ye mean to be tellin' me."

"Ye said that Carlyle's ship was named the *Rose Ellen?*" he asked, looking deeply at her for any sign of fear.

"Aye, what of it?" she asked, getting a little testy.

"We're nearin' Boston Harbour and one o' my men just spotted it ahead o' us."

"The *Rose Ellen* is headin' back into port?"

"Aye. What do ye want to do? I can change course and head into Charles Town right away if ye want."

Cat thought about this for a moment. She really wanted to see Rose and explain what had happened during her unexpected detour from Charles Town, but didn't want to create more trouble with Charles. On the other hand, if Charles was heading back to his house, was Rose in danger again?

"Tell me what ye're thinkin'. Perhaps I can help ye decide," Greame said, putting his big hand over hers.

As she explained her dilemma to him, a smile cracked his face. Involuntarily, she smiled with him.

"What are ye plannin' in that evil mind o' yers?" She turned to face him, very curious at what was running through his head.

"Let's meet Charles together at Rose's," he said, with eyebrows as high as they could go, begging her to do it.

"So a battle at sea wasna good enough for ye, eh? Now ye want to take on a verra powerful man on land?" Cat was still smiling, despite herself.

"Ye dinna look all that worrit about it. I thought ye may be too frightened to appear in front o' the man and show him his men failed at kidnappin' ye."

"I'm hardly afraid o' the man," she boasted. His raised eyebrow indicated his doubt. "I can handle one man, especially when he gets as drunk as Charles. What I canna handle are men comin' out o' the woodwork in secret to abduct me. I wilna live my life always lookin' o'er my shoulder."

"With my men placed around town and me wi' ye at Rose's, I hae a feelin' he wilna bother anyone."

"To Boston it is then."

Greame got up and walked to the doorway. "We'll be there in about an hour," he said, then turned to leave.

"Before ye go, I hae a request."

"What is it?"

"I want to bring Harry and Jim wi' us to Rose's. I hae a feelin' they'll make a fine home there, and protect Rose in the process."

Docking in a cove around Wind Mill Point on the south side of town, Greame deployed his men to various locations to garner information about Charles Carlyle. Then he, Cat, Harry and Jim walked up to Rose's house. Cat had been gone over a week, but it seemed more like hours now. She knocked on the front door and within seconds, Claire answered it. The look on her face held many questions, none of which she dared ask.

"Charles is on his way here," Cat said, walking into the front foyer with her entourage behind her, then stopped and asked, "He isna here yet, is he?"

"No, 'e's no' 'ere. Why would 'e be 'ere? 'E just left a week past. I thought ya were in Charles Town wi' Mistress Morrisey?" Claire threw out questions faster than Cat could answer.

Just then, Rose emerged from the best room. "Catrìona? What are you doing here?"

"Charles is on his way here, the rest will hae to wait until we take some precautions."

Emily had entered the room halfway through Cat's explanation and knew what had to be done. She showed Harry and Jim to the kitchen larder—the easiest place to enter if unattended, and remained with them.

Greame watched them go into action with military precision, amazed at every detail covered. His services weren't needed here. He thought he would have to protect a houseful of vulnerable women, not an impregnable fortress—armed even, as Claire came into the room wielding her cast iron skillet.

He looked at Cat in yet another light now. She was strong, capable and fearless. Her deep red hair and her extraordinary height were arresting. His mother used to name people after objects in nature according to what they were most like. He wondered what she would have named Catrìona. Not something dainty like a flower, she was more than that. Something deep red, fiery, tough … like garnet. He looked at her again, watching her command easily, knowing what everyone needed for the task at hand. She had leadership qualities found mostly in men. Garnet. He liked the name, and it fit her much better than Catrìona.

"Rose, did ye want to wait upstairs? Cat asked.

"Absolutely not, my dear. He does not frighten me any longer. Now, do you have time to tell me what's going on?"

Cat and Greame took a seat on the settee across from Rose. Cat explained what happened when she tried to board the ferry, and Greame explained how he found her on the *Marianne* near Baltimore. They took turns explaining why they came back to Boston and who they saw entering port.

"Dear me, Catrìona, you have had quite a time in America. What can I do to help you?"

"Do ye think I could stay here wi' ye 'til spring?" Cat asked.

"Of course, but what happens in the spring?"

"Greame will take me up to Maine."

Rose's hand flew to her heart and her blue-green eyes grew wide. "There are Indians in Maine. Beyond York, there is no one. Why in the world would you want to go there?"

"I keep havin' a vision of a granite coast, and John Richards told me he has seen coastlines like that in Maine. I hae to find out why I'm to be there."

"I certainly cannot do anything to stop you, but I fear for your safety."

"I'll be fine, Rose, but I do hae another favor to ask o' ye."

"Yes?"

"Look after Harry and Jim for me?"

Cat explained their situation, saying that they were good lads and will be a great help around the house. "I ken ye wanted to hae children Rose, but can no', so perhaps ye can raise them up right. They need a Mam."

"Are you mad, Catrìona? How will I tend to them when Charles is here? He will certainly never approve of this at all."

Greame opened his mouth to say something, but Cat stopped him by placing her hand on his knee. A quick glance at her revealed nothing, but he knew not to say anything.

"Think about it is all I ask o' ye, Rose."

Just then a loud bang sounded from the foyer. Immediately, the energy changed in the house. Charles was home. It must be his signature entrance to slam the front door so hard it shook the entire house. The three of them remained seated in the best room when the door flew open. Charles stepped in, locking eyes with Catrìona's.

"Hallò, Charles," Cat said coyly.

He looked at Rose for an explanation, but she remained unflustered by his untimely appearance. "Where are your manners, dear? Say hello to Catrìona. Or don't you believe your eyes?"

Cat suppressed a giggle at Rose's defiance, but when she saw the look in Charles' eyes, she knew Rose crossed the line. Greame must have seen it too, for he stood up, placing himself in front of Rose.

Charles, as though just noticing Greame for the first time, snarled, "Who are you?"

"Greame Hay, at yer service," he said, with an exaggerated bow.

To Charles, it seemed the whole room was trying to piss him off, and he would stand for it no longer. He made a lunge at Greame's mid-section, sending the two of them to the floor. A moment later crashing was heard in the kitchen area. Charles must have brought some backup. Cat pulled her rolling pin out from under the cushion of the settee and waited for the opportunity to give Charles a smack with it. Greame seemed to be in good control of the brawl, so Cat stepped back. Charles got in a good punch, but this only fueled Greame's fury. They were about the same height, but Greame had at least a stone on Charles. Another crash in the kitchen, but Cat was confident that the foursome could handle a couple of men.

Greame somehow managed to get onto Charles' chest and began pummeling away, making short order of him, leaving Charles gasping for breath and bloody—without the use of Cat's rolling pin. In his sober state, Cat realized Charles was a formidable man and was glad for Greame's take-charge attitude and strength.

The door opened and Emily escorted two of Charles' men into the room, both a little worse for the wear. One had blood running down the side of his head, the other was walking strangely and holding his privates.

Rose stood up, put her hands to her hips and said, "Charles James Carlyle, I want a divorce. And the house is mine, so you are to leave now and never return. Am I understood?"

When Charles just glared at her, Rose went over to him and bent down so her face was very close to his. "Am I understood?"

"Answer the lady," Greame said, slapping Charles up side the head.

"YES! Now let me up so I may gather my belongings."

"Oh, no! I will collect what is yours and send it to your ship. You are leaving *now*!" Rose demanded.

"Do as the lady asks o' ye, and be warned; dinna return here," Greame said, his features hard and uncompromising. He removed himself from Charles' chest and stepped back to allow the two henchmen to follow their captain out the front door. Harry and Jim tagged along to make sure there was no funny business on the way out.

"I'll have the magistrate draw up the papers immediately." Rose was actually smiling as the three left her house. "I should have done this years ago."

When Charles and his men were out of sight, the door was locked and the entire household assembled in the best room where Emily and Claire were already tidying up. They all talked for a time, then Emily and Claire went back to the kitchen to start supper. Harry and Jim were given a room upstairs to share, and Rose showed Greame the room next to Cat's. It was a full house and Rose was in her glory, finally able to have people to fuss over.

When supper was finished, Greame wanted to return to his ship to discover what news had been garnered by his men. Cat asked to join him, since it was news that affected her.

"Aye, ye can join me. I have things to tell ye."

It was a dark night, with only a sliver of a moon to illuminate the street. There was no wind, not even a breeze, and it was so quiet Cat could hear her own thoughts for a change. They walked in silence until they boarded the *Revenge*. Cat could feel Greame's need to speak to her and wondered what about, but it would have to wait until he was filled in by his men.

They all met in the captain's quarters. Hot ales were passed around and the first man began telling what he learned. After hearing that most of the men shared the same information, Cat felt Rose might be in even more danger now.

Charles Carlyle controlled most of the waterfront merchant seamen. He got a cut from each of their hauls so they could keep doing business in Boston. This town was the hub of the new world and riches were to be made or lost here. Charles intended to make his, along with a healthy share from everyone else.

"And they call me a pirate," Greame snorted.

"Aye, well, it may take one to stop another," Cat said quietly.

"What are ye frettin' for, lass? Me and my men hae quite a few 'acquaintances' to help us out with this task."

Cat looked at him for a moment, wondering exactly what he meant to do with these "acquaintances."

"Would ye excuse me for a moment?" She went into the surgeon's cabin and closed the door. She needed to know what dangers there were to this whole affair and wanted no one else getting hurt.

She sat quietly, twirling her hair, listening to the tide playfully slap the side of the hull. Her mind cleared and then filled again with a vision of a storm at sea. She was seeing the *Rose Ellen* trying to ride out a winter gale. She looked around, but saw no other ships. Getting her bearings, she recognized the point where Greame let the wind take his ship to safety near Baltimore Harbour. Something was preventing Charles from making the safety of port. She surveyed the sails and noticed the mast for the mainsail was broken. The spar was snapped off, making the jibs flail uselessly in the wind. Had Charles run into an enemy or was this all storm damage? The vision ended without that answer.

Cat returned to the captain's quarters and asked to speak to Greame alone. She was unwilling to divulge her talents to the men just yet. Greame cleared the cabin and sat next to her.

"What is it?" He noticed a strange look on her face.

Cat explained what she saw and asked what her vision did not divulge.

He didn't say anything for a long moment, he just stared at her eyes. Cat sensed he was trying to see what she saw. She gave him the time he needed, but he was trying too hard and getting frustrated.

"Do ye want to see?" When he nodded, she put her hand over his and gave him the vision. He gasped when it came to him, then acclimated himself to it. Cat was impressed by his willingness to become part of it, and allowed him to see the entire premonition. When the vision ended, Greame's eyes could not get any larger.

"Well?"

"Is that what ye see when ye hae a vision? Wi' that clarity?" he asked, taking her hands in his.

"Aye, ye did fine, too. I would ne'er attempt that wi' most people. It's too frightenin' for them."

"How did ye ken ye could do it wi' me?"

"By the way ye were tryin' to get inside my heid to see for yerself," she said, smiling. "Now, what do ye think happened to the ship?"

He got up and paced the floor for a minute, running the entire prophecy back through his mind. "I saw no sails pitted by cannon, did ye?"

Cat thought for a moment, "No."

"Then it was a devil of a storm to weather. He'll probably no' make it into port like that. If he's lucky, he'll stay clear o' the shoals and sand-bars further south until the weather breaks. Otherwise he'll sink."

His ominous words rang through her head. She saw it. She knew it would come to be. There was no warning Charles about it; he would live or die.

Watching the thoughts play over Cat's face, Greame said, "Ye canna do anythin' about it, can ye?"

Cat looked up at him; in the soft light of the cabin, her eyes were the color of thistles. She just shook her head. For the first time, he saw vulnerability in those eyes that could make him do anything. He went behind her and put his hands on her shoulders, plying the tension out of them. She let him work his magic for a while, then asked softly, "How did ye come to be a pirate?"

His hands didn't skip a beat. He was not offended. She was ready for more of him, and he was glad.

"Should we no' get back to Rose's before we hae to wake some-one to get back in?" he asked, stepping aside to get his cloak.

Cat smiled and held up a key she pulled from inside her cloak pocket.

"Ye're a crafty one, lass," he chuckled. "All right. I'll tell ye all about Clan Hay and our wicked ways."

꒰ꕤ

For generations, the Hays worked the sea, but not always for fishing. The North Sea was a fickle woman; serene one moment, then changing her mind and turning herself into a frothy womb, where instead of giving birth to new life, she took it away. Some gave up the sea and moved inland, making a stronghold at Delgatie Castle, and later, Leith Hall, but the ones that remained tied to that watery witch learned her secrets well.

English ships, French ships, even Danish ships not respectful of the treacherous eastern-most coastline, would be washed up onto the rocks. It was the Hays' right to scavenge the shoreline for the wreckage and, in the rare cases when the ship could be salvaged and repaired, they helped themselves to that bounty as well.

"This ship," indicating the *Revenge,* "was a French ship. I dinna ken what happened to the crew, but she was foundering in a cove near Port Erroll when I was healin' my wounds after Prestonpans. Wi' the help o' my cousins, we brought her in and repaired her. Most o' my crew are family."

"What made ye decide to come here?" Cat asked.

"After Culloden, Highlanders were hunted like dogs, as ye well ken. Nearly all o' my crew fought in one battle or another and didna like the idea o' bein' caught and imprisoned. Wearin' our plaidies and carryin' weapons is illegal, and even the speakin' o' the *Gàidhlig* is forbidden. We did the only thing we could do, and that was to leave Scotland until the English forget about us again."

Cat thought about that for a few minutes and wondered if Scotland would ever really return to the way it was before the Rebellion. The English had so thoroughly destroyed their way of life, she didn't think it was possible.

"Why a pirate? Why no' a merchant seaman?"

"Most ports are English ruled. They wilna buy our wares, and neither I, nor my crew, want to go to the West Indies, Spain or France. There are still too many English laws there."

"And there isna here?"

"Well, there is in Boston, but there are so many unsettled areas it's easy to disappear for a while."

"Is that why ye want to take me to Maine?"

"One reason," he said, trying to gauge what she really wanted to know.

"A question I fear to ask, but must is, what's the other reason?" Almost wishing she hadn't said it out loud.

Greame looked at her for a long minute. Cat wouldn't meet his eyes for fear of what she would see in them.

"What are ye really wantin' to ask me, Garnet?"

Cat looked up sharply, wondering if she really heard him right. "What did ye call me?"

He stammered for a second, then repeated it. "I called ye Garnet."

"Where did ye get that name? Did Rose tell ye?" Cat stood and walked over to him, standing so close she could smell the scent of the sea on him.

His malachite eyes tried to figure out what she wanted to hear, but her face revealed nothing of use. Grabbing her by the shoulders he said, "The name suits ye better than Catrìona. Ye are a rare woman—strong and fearless. And this," he ran his hand through her hair. "This smoulderin' fire ye hae coursin' down yer back made me think o' my Mam and how she used to give people names that suited them from nature. When I saw ye takin' charge at Rose's, I kent it's what ye should be called."

Cat stood open-mouthed, staring into his green depths, knowing what she felt from the moment she first met him. A connection so strong, so real, so right she could not contain herself. She raised her hands and placed them on either side of his face. Her thumbs rubbed over his cheeks, rough from a couple days' growth of beard. She lifted her head and placed a soft kiss on his lips, holding her lips there for a moment to savor the taste of him before stepping back.

Greame was totally unprepared for this. He stood motionless, his body unable to react. His self-consciousness prevented him from ever thinking anything would ever come of this but friendship. He cringed inwardly every time she looked at him because of the depth she went into his soul. Now she was kissing him. He closed his eyes, taking note of the softness of her lips, the scent of her hair, the warmth of her hands on his face. All too quickly it was over. He opened his eyes to see she had stepped back; he assumed the experience was a disappointment to her.

"I'm sorry for that, Greame," she said quietly, not meeting his eyes.

"I'm sorry too. I wish ye would hae said ye wanted to kiss me. I would hae told ye I wouldna be any good at it and saved ye the trouble," he said through clenched teeth.

Cat was shocked into silence, and before she could explain why she was sorry, he stormed out of the cabin.

Elevation of Status

Cat woke with a start. She looked around at the shafts of pink sunlight filtering in through the windows of the captain's quarters. Her body was stiff from sleeping at the desk. Standing up, she stretched herself to the limit, popping the sleep from her tendons.

Voices filtered down to her from the deck above. Greame's voice. He was giving instructions to his men, but she couldn't hear exactly what he was saying. She thought about his furious attitude last night. She just didn't understand him. He took everything she said the wrong way. It was the same thing in Scotland when she asked the simple question of his name.

The more she thought, the angrier she became. Emotions ran through her like fire through dry grass. First, she vowed never to speak to the man again. Then she decided she should hear his side of the story. To hell with the man if he was so fickle! But, maybe there was something she didn't understand about him.

"Christ O'Jesus, woman!" What infuriated her the most was that now she was too pissed off to even do a meditation. "I may as well go back to Rose's for all the good I'm doin' here," she muttered to herself.

Just before she got to the door, it opened, startling her. Greame filled the doorframe. His manner had softened since last night, but Cat's was just getting started. She glared at him, only to be met with a smirk and a mischievous look. She refused to give into it and tried to push her way past him. He would not allow that to happen.

Cat stood face to face with him, seething. "Let me pass."

"No' 'til we talk."

"Ha! What for? So ye can go off on a tangent again, leavin' me to wonder what I did to provoke such loathin'?"

"Loathin'? Isna that what ye thought o' me last night?" he growled. "If ye remember, ye were the one who kissed me, then ye were repulsed by me and wished ye hadna done it, and ye think I loath *ye?*" He was shaking her by her shoulders, his eyes taking on the color of the fir trees she saw in her vision.

"Ye thought I was repulsed by ye?" All of a sudden it all became clear and she laughed.

"Now ye laugh at me?" he growled, squeezing her shoulders harder.

Realizing she would never be able to say anything to appease him, she wrapped her arms around his waist and kissed him hard on the lips. At first he went rigid, but Cat persisted, her tongue feeling the softness of his wide mouth. His big hands now pulled her shoulders into him and he returned the passion. Cat's hands explored his back under his waistcoat, feeling his solidness. They were both breathing very hard and paused for air to look into each other's eyes.

Cat's eyes smoldered a deep amethyst, her cheeks were flushed. "Do ye still think I'm repulsed by ye, Greame?" she asked softly.

"Then why did ye say ye were sorry for kissin' me last night?" Raw desire showed on his face.

"Because I didna ken how ye felt about me. I thought I may hae acted inappropriately."

His eyebrow raised. "Isna that how we parted in Scotland?"

Cat smiled as she recalled the first time she met him. "I remember standin' in Mrs. Macgregor's kitchen wi' Tullibardine, waitin' for Seumas to take me home. Tullibardine saw no use in waitin' when he had a driver who could take me. That's when he called for ye out the window. Ye came in to fetch me and when I saw ye, I couldna move. Yer eyes trapped me in their green garden. Then, in Tullibardine's rare fine carriage, we had started a nice chat, but ye got all huffy on me when I asked for yer name. We had only kent each other for a quarter hour, but I nearly destroyed my croft after ye left I was so angry wi' ye," she said, taking in every detail of his face. "Even my dog left the house for fear of his life."

His deep chuckle reverberated through her, filling her with a strange happiness.

"Garnet, ye are the most amazin' woman I hae e'er met. I canna think o' why someone like ye would want to hae anythin' to do wi' me ... but I'm verra glad ye do."

"Ye dinna hae a verra high regard for yerself, do ye, Greame?"

He looked at her for a long moment trying to decide if she was serious or jesting.

"Oh, I'm verra serious," answering his unasked question.

"No, I guess no'. Why would I? I ken what I look like," he said, releasing her and turning away, suddenly uncomfortable under her scrutiny.

Cat grabbed his arm and walked in front of him. She placed her hand on his big chest and said, "I see what's in here." Then she looked deeply into his eyes. "And yer eyes captured me from the first time I saw ye."

He bowed his head, embarrassed. This was much too new an emotion to take in. He truly had no idea how to feel. Cat sensed his confusion and stepped back, giving him space.

"I dinna want to make ye feel uncomfortable, Greame. Solitude is my guide, but I dinna want to make it my sole companion."

He looked at her, studying every feature, memorizing them. "Give me time."

଼ଈ

Cat walked into Rose's house just as the oak grandfather clock in the best room was striking ten. She was hungry, so she headed straight for the kitchen. When she walked in, Harry and Jim were eating oatcakes smothered in jam. They stopped just long enough to smile at her, before devouring the sweet treat.

"Are ye hungry, Catrìona?" Emily asked, holding out a plate with two oatcakes on it.

"Ravenous." She took the plate and ate as heartily as the lads.

"Is Greame wi' ye?" Emily asked.

"No, he stayed on his ship to get some work done. Is Rose up?" Cat asked, licking the jam off her finger.

"Aye, she's in her room."

"These two lads are no' givin' ye any trouble, are they?" Cat laid her hands on each of their shoulders.

"Angels is wot they are," Claire piped, rolling out dough for biscuits.

Cat showed her dimples and left the room in search of Rose. She found her laying out a pattern on the deep red fabric Cat had chosen for a dress. Rose was concentrating so hard on her task she didn't hear Cat enter the room, and jumped when she looked up to see her standing there.

"Oh, you gave me a start, Garnet," Rose squeaked, then laughed self-consciously. "I forgot that name until I saw this fabric again. I'm glad you're here; now we can work on these dresses together. I didn't dare start them without taking proper measurements."

"Let me get out o' this dress, then; I need to talk wi' ye," she said, unbuttoning it to just below her waist and stepping out of it. She stood in her rather worn shift and corset with her arms out to the sides ready for Rose's string.

"Oh, dear, is this what you wear under your dress?" Rose asked, the string dangling from her hand.

"I could probably use another shift or two as well, aye?" Turning pink from embarrassment.

"And petticoats. How do you stay warm without them?" Rose asked.

"I dinna."

"First things first, let's get you measured," Rose said, fitting the length of string around Cat's bust and moving down from there.

After transferring all the measurements onto a piece of parchment, Rose told Cat to get dressed and go down to get more fabric for her new shifts and petticoats. "Pick out some lace for your sleeves and collar while you're at it, Garnet."

Cat smiled at the ease at which everyone seemed to use her monicker, and went downstairs to pick out some more fabric. Opening the closet door she was once again overwhelmed by the colors and textures. Running her hand over the bolts she hit on a fabulous material for her shifts. It would feel so soft against her skin. She pulled out the bolt and set it against the door. Rose said petticoats would keep her warm, so she felt the fabrics again and chose a light-weight wool. Now for the lace. She wanted something very special to match the elegance of the deep red paisley silk. She pulled out a couple of samples, but they weren't right. After another five bolts had been burrowed through, there, tucked in back at the very bottom she found it. Creamy white and exquisitely detailed. It was perfect.

Cat picked up the bolts and ran up the stairs. She felt excited for the first time in more years than she could remember. Rose held the lace up to the garnet-colored silk, and with a practiced eye, nodded her approval. For the next four hours they worked, cutting and basting the bodice together. When it was complete it was fitted to Cat and adjustments were made. Catching her reflection in the looking glass, Cat saw why Rose thought the color was perfect. It was made for her, and she couldn't wait until it was finished.

When it was too dark to work anymore, Cat and Rose went downstairs. Cat heard wood being stacked against the back of the house and went over to the window to see who was working so hard. She smiled when she saw Harry and Jim earning their keep.

"Rose?" Cat asked from the window.

"Yes." Rose was lighting the lamps.

"Hae ye thought any further on Harry and Jim stayin' wi' ye?"

"No. But seeing how well they fit in around here, and are willing and apparently able to help around the house, I think they are quite welcome to stay. It will be nice to have a couple of men around for some of the chores. And now that Charles is out of my life, well, let's just say I like the house full and the quiet broken by laughter."

"I'm glad ye feel that way."

For the next few weeks Cat attended to her new wardrobe. The final fitting for the silk dress was today and she could barely contain herself. All of her petticoats and two new shifts were complete. Cat was sewing the lace onto the sleeves of the garnet silk now. Rose was working on the green linen dress, but Cat really wanted to have the red one done.

Outside, the snow was falling once again, but the house was warm. Earlier, Cat sent Harry and Jim down to the *Revenge* to invite Greame to supper. The lads had just returned, snow-covered and red-cheeked.

"Will Greame come to supper?" Cat asked, pausing her needle waiting for an answer.

"He said he'd be honored," Harry said, with a deep bow, making Cat and Rose giggle.

There had been no more kisses between Cat and Greame. If he wanted time, Cat would let him have as much as he needed. They saw each other a couple times a week, sometimes meeting for tea at a shop, or at Rose's, like tonight. The house smelled of turkey and bread and apple pie.

There were only a few more hours before he arrived, so she concentrated harder, hoping to speed up the miniscule stitches. Finally, she tied off the thread and cut it with the little scissors. She stood and announced to Rose that she was going upstairs to try it on.

"I'll be up in a minute to see how you did," Rose said, pinning the lace collar onto the green linen dress.

Cat ran upstairs and stripped down to her shift, put on her new petticoats, then slipped into the garnet silk and buttoned it up. The square neckline was much lower than anything she had ever worn before, but she was comfortable with it. When she looked in the looking glass, she beamed. It fit like a glove through the bodice, finishing tightly at her small waist. The petticoats added the extra volume to flare out the skirts, making them drape perfectly to the floor. She stepped into a new pair of shoes Rose had insisted on buying for her and adjusted the lace on her sleeves.

Just then the door opened and Rose stepped in. She stood and appraised her creation with approval. She walked around Cat, tugging here, frumping there, but nodding the entire time.

"What do you think?" she asked Cat.

"I canna believe somethin' so lovely could be created by our hands. Thank ye, Rose," she said, giving her a hug.

"You look beautiful. Are you going to wear it tonight?" Rose asked with a twinkle in her eye.

Cat smiled and nodded.

"Well, if he cannot make up his mind after seeing you in this, there's no hope for the man. Now, let's do something with your hair."

❧

At dusk, Greame knocked on Rose's door. He was met by Jim, who had been stoking the fires. After hanging his cloak on the hook, he followed Jim into the best room where Harry sat reading a book.

"Ye lads lead a verra fine life here," he said, rubbing the chill from his hands over the fire.

"We sure do, Capt'n," Harry said, looking up from his story.

"Where's Garnet?"

"She's still upstairs bein' fretted on by Miss Rose," Jim said.

"Oh? She's no' ill, is she?" Greame asked, a little concerned.

Harry smiled, "We have been sworn to secrecy, right Jimmy-boy?"

Jim uncharacteristically smiled and winked, making Greame very nervous indeed at what was transpiring upstairs. He took a seat nearest the fire, unwilling to pursue the questions for fear of what they would reveal. His tendency to blow things out of proportion always got the best of him. Cat pointed that out to him on more than one occasion.

About a half hour later, the best room door opened and Rose walked in. "Come on boys, let's go into the dining room. Hello, Greame."

"Hallò, Rose ..."

"She's on her way down," she said, answering his unasked question, making him even more nervous now.

As soon as he was alone, the door opened and Cat walked in. She stood in the glow of the lamps and firelight not saying a word. Greame was unable to speak. His eyes took her in from head to toe. Her hair had been masterfully pulled in a twist, leaving a few wavy tendrils around her face and down her back. Her long neck was accentuated by the deep neckline of her dress. The silk shimmered in the fire's glow. She looked every bit like the gemstone she was named after.

Greame walked up to her and without a word, kissed her. "I canna tell ye how beautiful ye look, Garnet—there are no words."

Cat beamed. She placed her hand on his proffered elbow and together they walked into the dining room. Awaiting their entrance, everyone was formally standing behind their chairs. Cat smiled and Greame glowed pink, but all attention was taken off him when Jim said, "Ye look like a queen, Garnet."

It was Cat's turn to blush now, as Emily and Claire fussed over how wonderfully the dress had turned out. They all took their seats and ate their fill, talking amiably about life in general. After supper, the members of the household became conspicuously absent, leaving Cat and Greame to themselves in the best room.

"What is goin' on around here tonight?" Greame asked, taking his seat on the settee next to Cat.

"I'm no' certain, but I think Rose has hatched a plan for us to be alone," Cat said, sipping her sherry.

"Well, we are at that." He turned to face her and took her hand, placing a kiss on top of it. "I could hardly believe my eyes when ye walked through the door tonight. I barely recognized ye. I still dinna ken why ye would …"

Before he could finish putting himself down, Cat silenced him with her finger to his lips. She smiled, then said, "Stand up, let me look at yer new suit. It is new, is it no'?"

"Aye." He smiled and did as he was told, standing and making graceful bows.

The camel brown coat was definitely his color. His breeks fit snugly, showing thick, long legs. His calves, well defined, were covered in white silk hose. The finely woven linen shirt was a creamy gold, and he wore a lace cravat around his neck. His waistcoat was the most impressive item he wore, though. It was a dark green with gold buttons and embroidered with gold thread.

"Ye look like a wealthy merchant, Greame."

"Good. That was the look I was hopin' for."

"Oh? What are ye plannin' on doin', openin' a shop?" she teased.

"I dinna think I could stand bein' off the water for that long, but I dinna want to be lookin' like a pirate, now do I?"

"So what are ye plannin'?" Cat asked, becoming very curious now.

"To break Charles Carlyle's hold on the waterfront."

Racketeers

Greame had kept a low profile since arriving in Boston Harbour. His ship was moored in an out of the way cove, and his men, though frequenting the local taverns, were on their best behavior. There was no room for drunkenness and disorder; besides, from the feeling in the air, a rebellion was about to be unleashed against the English. The docks were bristling with agitation over the continued policy of pressing men into duty, turning them into slaves for the Royal Navy. This turn of events could speed along Greame's plan to remove Carlyle from power on the waterfront.

A small storefront was rented by a couple of Greame's men on the pretense of being tea merchants. The first day the shop opened, Greame was out back tending to the orders of substantial quantities of the most expensive teas from around the world. Not more than an hour after his task was complete, the shop was visited by a pair of rather large men. Seamen to be sure, but with a certain look that spelled out what they were really there for.

"And what might I be doin' for ye gentlemen?" Greame asked smoothly, appearing oblivious to their malicious looks.

The larger of the two stepped up to the counter and asked, "Are you the owner o' this 'ere shop?"

"Aye, is there a problem?" Greame asked, noticing the man's rotting teeth.

"As a matter o' fact there is," the larger man said with an evil smile.

"And what might that be, sir?" Playing along for all it was worth, while slowly reaching under the counter for the oak club he had fashioned for just such a visit.

"If you want to stay in business 'ere, you're gonna need protection."

"Protection? From what?" Greame asked, looking as frightened as he knew how.

"From the Whigs, o' course. They want to run this 'ere waterfront an' will do anythin' to destroy yor business," the rotten-mouthed man said, smiling at how easy Greame was to persuade.

"How do I get this protection?" Greame asked quietly, as though this were secret information.

"By payin' us twenty-five percent o' yor earnin's every week," he said, leaning up close to Greame's face, nearly making him gag.

This figure brought Greame around from mild-mannered shop owner to furious ship's captain. Faster than the two thugs could react, Greame brought out his club and smashed it into the side of the man's head. The smaller thug, complacent until now, saw that he was outmatched and dashed out the door leaving his friend bleeding and unconscious on the floor.

"That ought to bring them around," Greame said smiling, then shouted, "Robbie, George, would ye come take this scum out o' my shop?"

His two cousins emerged from the back to find a large man on the floor. Laughing, they dragged him outside and deposited him against the building next door. Maybe someone would find him before he froze to death. No loss if not.

For the next two weeks the same pattern followed, always with the same results. Not very bright, these big ruffians. Greame kept men in the shop each night to be sure no tomfoolery happened when he wasn't there. There had been fires of suspicious nature along the waterfront and he didn't want his shop to be next.

By the middle of March, Carlyle had had enough of not getting the upper hand on this lowly tea merchant. Due to sail for South Carolina at the end of the week, he was determined to make the man pay before he left. He was curious to see what sort of army this tea merchant had working for him to keep maiming his men.

Accompanied by three of his best hands—those who had not been to see the teaman yet—Charles walked up Milk Street to the Worldwide Tea Emporium, where he would lay out his ultimatum in person.

When the mob found the storefront, they waited for two customers to leave before making their entrance. In those few minutes, Greame's men, having watched Charles' procession up the street, through an elaborate set of Highland signals, gathered around the teashop just out of sight. Robbie and George, who tended the shop when Greame wasn't there or just stayed out back in case of trouble, were alerted to the quartet waiting outside. They in turn alerted Greame who was just finishing up with two ladies.

As the women departed, Charles and his men made their move. One man was sent around back, leaving one outside to make sure the negotiation wouldn't be disturbed, and he and his mate went in.

Just for shock value, Greame decided he would man the counter when Charles came in. The effect was just as he had hoped. Charles looked at Greame, at first not fully recognizing him, but knowing he had at least seen him somewhere before. The dawning came when Greame said, "Hallò, Charles."

Greame had a hard time keeping a straight face as the range of emotions ran over Charles' face. A thud from the back room indicated to Charles that Greame was playing him for a fool. This of course, only fueled Charles' rage, and in a blind fury, he ran directly towards the counter, as though he could go right through it to get to Greame.

Greame quickly swung his oak club and it caught Charles squarely on the shoulder, sending him off to the side in agony. The man Charles had brought in with him was approaching with a cutlass and a more-than-ready look in his eyes. The lookout entered the shop to see what the commotion was about, and that's when the rest of Greame's men surrounded the place. The man with the cutlass was undaunted, and with one swing was able to encompass the entire front of the shop with his blade.

John Hay, a skilled swordsman, came in from the back with a cutlass of his own. Greame pulled Charles in back of the counter with him so he wouldn't get any ideas about interfering with his cousin, and stood guard over him with his club. But Charles, holding his shoulder and grimacing in pain, had no try left in him.

The two swordsmen commenced in combat. The *clang!* of steel reverberated throughout the wooden building, echoing off the tin tea canisters.

John had an odd way with the men he did battle with. He talked through the entire scuffle, distracting them completely.

"What's yer name, mate? My name's John Hay. Where are ye from? I'm from Port Erroll. 'Course, that's in Scotland, mate. I could tell ye were wonderin'." *Clang! Clang!* "Who might I send yer heid to when it hits the floor? Do ye hae a wife, mate? I suppose I'll hae to look after her when I'm done wi' ye."

The flustered man carelessly lunged at John for his remarks. John knocked the cutlass neatly out of his hand, nearly severing it at the wrist. Within a few minutes, Greame and his men were escorting Charles and his unfortunates back to the *Rose Ellen.*

"I suggest ye dinna try anythin' like that again, sir," Greame warned Charles. "The next time, I'll let none o' ye live."

"The *Rose Ellen* sailed for South Carolina a day earlier than it was supposed to," Greame said, sitting with Cat on the settee at Rose's, reliving the incident at the teashop. As he talked, Cat once again received the vision of Charles and the storm at sea. With this alteration in sailing dates, the *Rose Ellen* would now sink in the storm. She saw Charles and his men flailing in the water, then the deep taking them under.

"Now neither he nor his ship will make it home again," Cat said. "I hae to tell Rose."

"I thought ye only saw him in trouble, no' dead," Greame said, looking into Cat's eyes, noticing the far away look in them. "Oh, ye just had another vision, didna ye?"

"Aye."

"So they just come to ye out o' the blue like that?" Greame asked, genuinely curious.

"Sometimes. Other times, I hae to meditate on the event to get an answer."

"Can ye teach me how to hae visions?"

Cat looked at him closely, going deep into his psyche to see if there were abilities there to sharpen. He had true intent, which would be very beneficial, and a greater than normal intuition. She would do some tests with him to see just what she was working with.

"Ye remind me o' my brother, Lachlan. He wanted to learn the Sight. As we grew up, we were able to communicate wi' our minds verra well. I think ye hae the same desire to learn as he did, and I would be happy to teach ye."

"Do ye communicate wi' him now?"

Cat remained quiet for a moment, a ghost of pain floated across her face.

Greame, having no idea Lachlan was dead, put his hand over Cat's, sensing her apprehension. "Hae I said somethin' wrong?"

Cat looked at him with sad eyes. "No. Ye ne'er kent what happened to my family, so it was a fair question to be askin'."

She took a deep breath and told him the entire story of how she came to be in America. When she finished, he was shaking his head, further amazed at her bravery and strong will.

"I didna ken ye had been through such horrors, Garnet. Many *men* would no' hae been able to do what ye hae done. And ye hae done so much of it on yer own."

"Dinna feel sorry for me, Greame. My life is based on solitude, I ken that. I'm stronger for what I hae been through. Everything is a learnin' experience that I can use in different situations to move through faster wi'out the negative outcomes. If ye take yer life that way, it becomes easier to bear."

He stood and walked over to the fire, suddenly chilled. He wondered if he could be as strong as she was when it came to seeing things before they happened, and know what to do with the information when he did see it.

"Are ye havin' second thoughts?"

He looked at her and said, "Is it that obvious?"

Cat chuckled, then patted the seat next to her on the settee. "Come here and sit. Let's do somethin' together to help ye make up yer mind. It doesna hae to be all bad, ye ken."

He took the proffered seat with a little worry in his eyes, but his curiosity overcame his misgivings.

"This works best when ye hae naught in yer heid. Clear yer mind of everythin'. Now, I will think o' somethin' and put it in my heid. I want ye to tell me what it is, aye?"

"Do I hae to close my eyes?"

"Whate'er makes ye comfortable. I twirl my hair," she said, demonstrating her professional technique.

"I dinna think I'll do that, but I will close my eyes."

Cat called up her dirk, holding the image clearly in her mind. "Go on, tell me what ye see."

Greame concentrated hard with his eyes closed. The furrow between his brows turned into an excited lift when he saw the image come to him. He opened his eyes and said, "I see yer dirk. Is that what ye were showin' me?"

"Aye, ye did fine," she smiled. "Now somethin' more difficult."

He closed his eyes again with the same intensity. This one took a little longer, but he saw it. "Blair Castle."

"Great! Again."

"A great dog?"

"What color is he?"

He didn't close his eyes this time, just lifted them to the right. "A greyish-brown."

"What's his name?"

He looked at Cat and said, "J … J … Gent?"

"Och, ye got it all right! I'm verra impressed."

"What kind o' name is Gent?"

"Gent is short for Argentinus, what Alexander named him." She shook her head. "It just didna fit."

"That's an understatement." Greame began rubbing his forhead. "Am I supposed to be tired from this? Because I feel like I hae just finished a hill-walk."

Cat laughed. "Oh, I forget to tell ye that. It'll be easier each time ye do it, but for the first few times it takes all the strength from ye."

"Do I hae the Sight now?" He was truly excited making his face animated with joy. A look she would hold onto.

"Ye either hae it or ye dinna. Ye showed me ye hae it. Now we'll see how much o' it ye can use. But dinna get too excited about it yet. Ye've no' had a vision o' yer own. That will tell us whether or no' ye are pleased to hae the gift."

❧

Angry steel-grey clouds filled the sky the next morning. The crimson sliver of dawn indicated a storm was brewing. After breakfast, Cat took Harry and Jim to meet Greame at the teashop. Even though Charles was at sea, she didn't like going anywhere alone if she could prevent it.

Greame met her at the shop door and said, "I'll be wi' ye shortly. I hae to get my ship to a safer cove. The south wind will blow her onto shore where she is now."

"What can I do to help ye?" she asked.

"Just stay here. Once the wind starts, it'll be tough goin' in the long boat. I wilna be gone for more than an hour. George and Robbie would appreciate the comp'ny."

Harry and Jim went out back with George to play checkers. Robbie, dressed in a decent suit, manned the sales counter out front. Cat chatted with him, looking over the stock of teas on the shelves. She could hardly believe there were so many different varieties from nearly every corner of the world.

When she finished with the teas, she looked out the window, taking note that the wind had started blowing. Picking up a lock of her hair, she gazed out towards the sea, of which she could only see a fragment between the buildings. There was an excitement in the air, sending shivers through her. She wondered if Greame would pick up on an idea in her head and decided to give it a try. This would be a good test. If he could "hear" her in the midst of his considerable task, he would clearly have the Sight.

In her mind, she envisioned her croft that she shared with Anna back in Scotland. She knew Greame had never been inside, so she showed him around. She stood at her vision window in the west side of the house showing him the herb jars and remedies, the rocking chair next to the fireplace, the brightly colored quilt that covered Anna's bed, and her mother's writing desk.

Smiling, she released her hair and turned her attentions back to Robbie, who had asked her a question, but she only heard the last few words of it.

"Och, forgive me, Robbie, I was somewhere else. What did ye ask me?" She walked over to the counter, leaning up close to it, rubbing her fingers over the grain of the wood.

"Where did ye come from in Scotland?" Robbie repeated.

"The northern shores o' Loch Rannoch. My Da was laird o' *Slios Mín aig Aulich*," Cat said, picturing her family's house as though she had just left it.

"I dinna ken how ye stand to be so far from the sea," he said. "If I'm away too long, I take ill."

"I ne'er saw the sea until the week before Culloden when my family went to Inverness," she said, not elaborating any further.

He was quiet for a minute, reliving something Cat did not want to know about. The conversation ended when three well-dressed ladies entered the shop. Cat stood off to the side, letting Robbie act the salesman. He handled their questions knowledgeably, concluding with a rather nice sale. Cat shook her head in wonder at Greame's chosen front. Some people just had a knack for making money, and it looked like Greame was one of them. Before the three ladies left, a couple entered the store, and Cat decided to go out back and check on the lads.

"Who's winnin'?" she asked.

"Jimmy. He always wins," Harry said, getting jumped twice.

"'Tis only because ya don't look ta see what I'll do if ya make that move," Jim announced, attempting to give his partner a hint at what he was doing wrong. It didn't work, because the next move Harry made finished him.

Cat and George laughed. Robbie came in shortly afterward, wondering what was going on. Seeing for himself, he cuffed Harry alongside his head, saying, "Hae ye no' learned a thing from me, lad?"

The bell to the front door signaled another customer, and this time George got up to tend to them. Before he reached the door, Greame stepped in with a look of confusion on his face.

"What is it, Greame?" Cat asked.

He looked at all the faces staring at him for an explanation, then grabbed Cat by the arm and brought her out front without giving a reason.

"What is wrong wi' ye?" Cat asked again.

"I think I had a vision," he whispered with such intent on his face, Cat had to laugh.

"Och, I'm sorry," she said, trying her best not to giggle. "Tell me what ye saw."

For a minute, he just glared at her, but couldn't contain himself for long before launching into his vision.

"… And then I saw this old writin' desk, but what was most curious was when I saw ye, standin' by the window, twirlin' yer hair."

"Ye saw me?"

"Aye. What does it mean?"

"It means ye did better than I could hae hoped."

"What?"

"I wanted to see if ye could get thoughts under dire circumstances, so I sent ye a vision of the inside o' my croft at Blair Atholl."

She wasn't sure if he was pleased or upset, then the emotions charged across his face.

"What if …" he started.

"That'll be yer first mistake," Cat said, totally serious.

"What'll be my first mistake?" he asked, folding his big arms over his chest.

"Never ask yerself that question. Did anythin' happen? No. That question begs to hae fate toyed wi'. Ye canna change the past, so why cast doubt around a situation where naught has happened?"

"But …"

Cat held up her hand, "No buts, either. It's like this new thing called 'insurance'. Ye pay someone to protect yer wares 'in case' somethin' happens. What if ye put yer intent towards makin' sure nothin' happens to damage yer wares to begin wi'? Wouldna that make more sense? Especially since ye hae the power to see what will happen."

He thought about this for a moment, then said, "So I do hae the Sight?"

Cat laughed. With all she told him, that's what he gleaned out of the entire conversation. *C'est la vie.*

A Withering Rose

Word came, nearly a month after Charles set sail, that his ship had gone down in a storm off the Baltimore coast. All hands were lost, along with forty-seven black slaves he was transporting to the plantations in Charlestown, South Carolina.

Greame delivered the news to Cat and Rose on April third. There was no grief over Charles' death. Rose, however, turned white when she heard her estranged husband was in the slave trade.

"I feel terrible about those poor Negroes," Rose said. "I cannot believe he would do such a thing. He knew how I felt about slavery."

"I think the only thing that mattered to Charles was turnin' a profit. From where it came was o' no consequence to him," Greame said.

Rose had skeptically heeded Cat's suggestion to wait a while before filing for divorce, and also gave Cat the benefit of the doubt about her premonition of Charles going down in a storm. Everything happened just as Cat said it would, and she was now a free woman without the scandal of a divorce.

"Are ye sure ye're all right, Rose?" Cat asked, sensing something below the surface that Rose wasn't divulging.

Rose looked at Cat for a moment, nearly saying what was on her mind, but nervously coughed and said, "Please do not fret over me, Garnet, I'll be fine. As a matter of fact, I think we should have a small celebration tonight."

Cat's and Greame's eyebrows lifted.

"What for?" Cat asked.

"Why, for my freedom, of course." She got up from the settee and started for the kitchen.

"Ye're no' goin' to invite people here tonight, are ye?" Cat asked, following Rose.

"Catrìona, that would be rather inappropriate. No, this is just for us—Greame and the boys, you and I, Emily and Claire. All of us who had to live in fear of that man."

"What will ye do now, Rose?" Cat stopped just outside the kitchen door.

"What do you mean?" Rose had her hand on the knob, but she stopped too.

"How will ye live wi'out Charles' income?"

"My dear, I have more money right now than I know what to do with. Charles had life insurance, as well as insurance on his ship. I shall never have to worry over money again."

Cat stood open-mouthed and let Rose go into the kitchen by herself. She walked back into the best room where she left Greame and sat down next to him.

"What is it, Garnet?" Noticing her perplexed look.

"Rose is a wealthy woman now."

"Wasna she wealthy before?" he asked.

"No' wi'out Charles, she wasna. She just told me he had insurance on himself and his ship." Cat was twirling her hair. Something wasn't right about all this.

"Are ye thinkin' what I'm thinkin'?" Greame asked, looking into her eyes.

"Do ye think when I told Rose to hold off on the divorce because Charles may die, she took out insurance on him?"

Greame cracked a smile, "A smart thinkin' woman."

"Greame!"

"What? Ye're thinkin' she capitalized on what ye told her. Well, o' course she did. Why wouldna she? After what he put her through for so long, then actually havin' the strength to go through wi' a divorce—somethin' ye allowed her to proceed wi', I might add—and possibly losin' her home and livelihood if he contested it, why wouldna she take the opportunity to come out ahead? She's verra bright."

Cat couldn't refute his logic. It made perfect sense, but she still felt taken advantage of somehow.

"Perhaps it was all right to do, but I dinna care for it."

"Why, because ye wouldna hae thought to do it yerself?" He was still smiling.

She looked hard at him, then said, "It's just wrong," and stormed out of the room.

So much for telling her of the good news he meant to share with her. "It can wait," he said to himself. He had not known her to stay angry for long.

❧

At six o'clock, Jim knocked on Cat's door saying it was time for supper.

"I'll be down shortly," Cat said from behind the door. Her room filled with a warm orange light as she watched the sun go down. She was anxious tonight—Maine was calling her. Hopefully, Greame would tell her soon when they would leave to find the coastline of her vision.

She decided to dress in the new gown she finished a week ago. This one was a rich deep blue, the color of a Scottish loch after a storm. The white lace lay on top like cresting breakers. She tied her hair away from her face, letting it fall in deep waves down to her waist.

Just as she opened her door, Greame was standing there ready to knock on it, startling him, making Cat laugh at his expression.

"Verra funny. We're all waitin' on ye," he said, then took in her new attire. "It was worth it."

Cat smiled and took his arm. "I made this one all on my own. Do ye like it?"

"Aye, ye look beautiful, Garnet," his voice smooth and deep.

"Might I ask ye somethin'?"

He looked at her, knowing exactly what she was going to ask. "I would like to leave the first o' May, providin' the weather continues to remain fair."

Cat just stared at him for a moment, then smiled. "Ye're gettin' rather good at readin' my mind."

"Och, aye. A regular gypsy, I am," he said, walking her to the top of the stairs.

"No' all gypsies read minds, Greame, no more than all High-landers hae the Sight."

"Then why are people so frightened o' them?"

"Because most o' them are thieves and cutthroats."

He laughed and they walked into the dining room to find everyone seated and awaiting their arrival.

"Och, what a lovely dress ye hae on, Garnet," Emily said as she started passing around the first course.

The rest of the gathering chimed in their appreciation as well, and Cat smiled, feeling again like a queen.

When supper was finished, Cat, Greame and Rose went into the best room to have a sherry and conversation. Most of their talk centered around Cat and Greame's trip to Maine.

"Are you positive you won't reconsider, Garnet? I am scared to death to have you wandering around in that wild place with all those Indians around," Rose said, taking a deep sip of her sherry.

"Och, that reminds me. I didna tell ye of my most recent vision," Cat said, sitting on the edge of her seat. "I saw them."

"Saw who?" Greame asked, scooting to the edge of his seat so he could see her face.

"The Indians."

"Tell us," he said.

"They are a graceful people. Their skin is light brown and they hae rich, long black hair. Their eyes are dark brown, nearly black. They wear clothes of either heavy fabric or deer skin beautifully adorned wi' beads and embroidery."

"What do their houses look like?" Rose asked, fascinated.

"From what I could tell, they were sheets o' bark o'er a log base. Some were verra large wi' rounded roofs, while others were round triangles."

"Round triangles?" said Greame. "What do ye mean?"

"I canna explain it, but they looked like this." Cat held up her hands and put her index fingers together and touched the tips of her thumbs together to make a triangle. Then she twisted her creation around, indicating it was round.

"I'm not sure I understand," said Rose, her nose wrinkled up trying to picture such a thing.

Greame was searching the room for something. He found a piece of parchment on the desk and rolled it up to look like a funnel. He set it on the settee and looked at Cat for verification.

Cat cocked her head then took the model and folded one of the ends of the wide opening over to indicate a door. She looked back into her memory for any other distinguishing features, then started to explain as best she could.

"This was made from the bark o' birch trees attached to logs that started wide at the base and ended jutting out o' the top. I could see smoke, so they must keep their fires inside, like our crofts in Scotland," she said, looking at Greame for acknowledgement.

"Fascinating," Rose said.

"Anythin' else?" Greame asked.

Cat just shook her head, but seemed to be somewhere else. A moment later, she said, "I see a man whose shadow looks like a large beast."

"What kind o' beast?" Greame asked.

"Big. A long snout. Ears on the top of its head. Enormous paws, and it looks as though it can stand like a man." Even as Cat described the creature, she had a difficult time believing what she saw.

Suddenly Rose said, "Oh, that would be a bear."

All eyes were on Rose now for an explanation.

"They are black or dark brown, live in the forest eating mostly berries and insects, but every so often attack people in the outlying settlements. I have even heard of people using the fat from the beasts to keep the mosquitoes away. An Indian method, I'm told."

Greame was thoroughly intrigued now and barraged Rose for every description of the animal he could get out of her. As the two of them talked, Cat got the distinct feeling she would meet this man from her vision in Maine. He would be a teacher to her and she to him. He was like her; a healer, one who knew the plants for remedies, and one who could see into the future.

"… that describe what ye saw, Garnet?" Greame asked.

Giving him a look that indicated she just dropped in from somewhere else, Cat apologized. "I'm verra sorry, Greame. I didna hear yer question."

Greame laughed and said, "No, because ye were in Maine, right?"

Cat showed her dimples and turned a bit pink. "Ye're gettin' verra good at seein' into me."

"That one was just a guess."

Rose suddenly looked a bit pasty and started coughing. Deep, body racking coughs.

"Are ye all right, lass?" Greame asked, getting up to pat her on the back.

"Oh yes, just tired. I think I'll retire for the evening."

She got up, but sat right back down again. Alarmed, Cat sat next to her and held her hand. Instantly, she got a vision of Rose's illness. It was progressing very rapidly now. Greame caught the look on Cat's face and knew it wasn't good.

"Let me get ye to yer room, lass," he said, gently lifting her from her seat.

Cat followed them upstairs, opening the door to Rose's room for Greame. He sat her on the edge of her bed and excused himself, letting Cat tend to her.

"And here I thought I was getting better."

Cat didn't want to let on what she had seen, but knew there wasn't much time left for Rose.

Rose looked at Cat for verification, but Cat's face remained neutral.

"You are very good at keeping what you know from me, Garnet," she said before starting to cough again. "But even my physician tells me the disease has taken over my body, and doesn't give me much hope."

Cat looked at Rose's face, taking in each detail. Funny, she didn't look like a dying woman. But when it came to her eyes, that's where the telltale signs resided. The eyes—pathway to the life force—always gave it away. Cat helped her undress and tucked her in, then sat next to her on the plump featherbed. She smoothed the hair from Rose's forehead and placed a kiss on her unlined brow.

"Ye hae become a verra dear friend, Rose, and the answer ye seek from me, ye already hae. Why do ye want me to validate what ye already ken in yer heart?"

Tears streamed unchecked down Rose's cheeks. Her blue-green eyes shimmered in the light of the lantern, making them look like jewels.

"Can you tell me what you know of heaven?" Rose asked softly.

"I dinna believe in Heaven, Rose. I do believe that ye go to a place where there is no pain, no struggle, no hate or anger. When my Mam died, she said it was a beautiful place. My Da said the same. There is naught to fear about passin'. The hard part stays wi' those left behind."

Rose nodded and attempted a smile, then closed her eyes. Cat wiped away her own tears, got up and stoked the fire, then turned down the lamp and left the room.

When she entered the best room, Claire and Emily were sitting with Greame, all awaiting news of Rose. Somehow they all knew that the cough, which had been becoming more frequent, was not a good sign. Cat took a seat and proceeded to ask how much they knew of Rose's ailment. Emily and Claire had no idea she was ill at all. Cat thought it best to fill them in on the prognosis.

ε&

The next morning dawned bright and clear. Claire opened the windows to let in the sweet-smelling air of spring, while robins whinnied in the shrubbery out back. It was half nine when Rose finally made it downstairs for her breakfast. Cat was on the settee in the best room fashioning a more rugged outfit for her trip to Maine in a few weeks. When Rose walked in, Cat looked up and almost didn't recognize her. Overnight, Rose had aged ten years.

Cat had to work to not let her astonishment show on her face before greeting Rose. Rose, however, seemed to be in another world, not hearing Cat, or even noticing her. She just walked right through into the dining room without a word. Cat didn't follow, but a moment later, heard a loud crash in the kitchen when Emily and Claire witnessed Rose's rapid decline.

Cat went to the kitchen to see if she could be of help. When she opened the door, Emily was on her knees picking up pieces of a broken bowl. Claire just stared at Rose, who was sitting on the stool near the stove saying nothing. Claire grabbed Cat's arm and took her into the dining room.

"Wot 'appened to 'er?" Claire asked, truly frightened.

"The disease has taken o'er her body. She doesna hae much time left. An astonishin' thing to see, though," Cat said, staring at the kitchen door as though seeing Rose on the other side.

"Wot will 'appen to us when she dies?"

Cat looked at Claire for a moment, realizing again what a precarious life it was for a servant.

"I would say ye will be a free woman, Claire."

"But where well I go? I ain't got any money."

Cat wondered if Rose had made provisions for her staff in this case. "Let me talk to her to find out, aye?"

"All right, but I'm scared."

"Why? Ye must hae excellent credentials if ye want to stay here and work for someone else."

"I never thought about workin' for anyone else," Claire said, wringing her hands.

"Would ye prefer to go back to England?"

Claire thought for a moment, then said, "I 'ave some thinkin' ta do, don't I?"

"I think we all do."

Cat went back into the kitchen to see if Rose was up to talking. She was still sitting beside the stove, chewing on a biscuit. She looked up when she saw Cat and smiled as though nothing had happened. Cat asked if she could talk with her when she finished her breakfast and got a nod.

"I'll meet you in the best room," Rose said.

Cat caught Emily's eyes for a second and saw the same fear that was in Claire's. She tried to reassure her with a nod, but wasn't confident about how rational the conversation with Rose would be.

About twenty minutes later, Rose arrived with Claire in tow carrying a tray of tea. Now it all just seemed like a bad dream. Rose was acting like Rose again, only an older version. She settled herself on the settee while Claire poured two cups of the steaming liquid.

"So my dear, what's on your mind?" Rose asked, blowing on the fine china cup Claire handed to her.

Cat waited for Claire to leave the room before broaching the subject. She took a deep breath and began.

"Rose, hae ye made provisions for Emily and Claire in the event o' yer passin'?"

Rose stopped blowing, but kept her lips puckered. The look she gave Cat was a stunned one. She put her teacup down, got up and left the room. Cat didn't know what to do. Perhaps it wasn't her business. Perhaps Emily and Claire should be the ones having this conversation with their employer. She didn't know. She remained seated and waited for a few minutes, feeling like she was an inch tall. The door from the dining room opened and Emily poked her head in.

"Where did she goo?" she asked after her search came up empty.

"Up to her room," Cat said, shaking her head in anguish.

"We shoold hae been the ones ta ask her aboot our future," Emily said, looking exactly how Cat felt.

"I wish I could start this day all o'er again, because this wouldna hae happened," Cat said, getting up to apologize to Rose. But before she reached the door, it opened and Rose entered.

"Good, Emily, you're here also. Now we just need Claire and we may resume this conversation," she said, thoroughly unperturbed. Cat and Emily exchanged surprised glances and Emily left to fetch Claire.

When they were all present and seated, Rose unfolded a piece of parchment and began to read it aloud.

"I, Rose Elizabeth Buckley Carlyle, being of sound mind and body ..." Rose read the entire contents of her last will and testament to Emily and Claire, which gave them their freedom, the house and all its contents, as well as a healthy sum of money to live comfortably for the rest of their lives. They were in tears by the end of it, hugging Rose before returning to their duties.

Cat just stared at Rose with a large smile on her face. "Ye did real fine by them, Rose."

"I'm not finished yet."

"What do ye mean?"

"Last night, I added you and the two boys."

"Och, Rose, the lads, aye, but I hae no reason to be in yer will. I can take care o' myself."

"Of that, I have no doubt, Catrìona, but this is because I want to, not because I have to. Would you like to read it?" Rose handed the parchment to Cat, who took it, but didn't look at it.

"Oh please, Catrìona, read it." She pointed to the paragraph containing Cat's share.

Almost by their own volition, Cat's eyes scanned the text. Suddenly, a brilliant smile came over her face and she reached over and gave Rose a big hug.

"Thank ye, Rose, and Harry and Jim will thank ye as soon as they hear they now hae a home to call their own."

11

Setting Sail

Three weeks went by faster than Cat could have imagined. At first it seemed like an eternity before it would arrive, but as the first of May loomed closer, she began to feel like there wasn't enough time to complete her tasks before the departure date.

At Greame's suggestion, in spite of what Rose, Emily and Claire said, Cat fashioned a pair of breeks that fit her rather smartly. They were made of a lightweight canvas, and instead of stopping at the knee, like men's breeks did, hers went all the way to the ankle. She was admiring their fit in the looking glass, semi-scandalized by the way her entire figure was displayed, but smiling at the ease of movement she had. These would be much better suited to the rugged forests of Maine. She put pockets in them and created a built-in sheath for her dirk on the side of the leg.

"Ye can come in now," Cat said loudly.

The door to her room opened and Greame entered, his eyes locking onto her fitted form. Aside from the hint of pink rising on his neck and cheeks, he smiled in appreciation of the craftsmanship and practicality of the newfangled outerwear.

Cat took in everything he was thinking as he looked her over. She smiled, though a bit embarrassed at the hint of desire he allowed to surface. When he caught her eyes, they lingered for a moment, fully aware she knew what he was thinking. He walked over to her and put his hands on her small waist. She made no move to break the contact, instead reaching up to touch his smooth cheek with her fingers.

"Ye'll make it a verra long voyage dressed like that, Garnet," he said huskily.

She stared into his malachite eyes, letting her feelings be obvious on her face. He found her lips with his, at first softly, then more demanding. Cat let him explore, matching his desire without losing control. This was his move; she would let him proceed at his own pace.

The connection was broken all too soon. Greame stepped back, but didn't release her waist. He looked hard into her eyes, searching for something he wasn't sure she was ready to give. Finding it in her amethyst eyes, he kissed her hard again, but then quickly released her when a knock on the door ended the moment.

"Damn it!" he swore under his breath, while Cat giggled and walked over to open it.

"Oh, dear me, Catrìona! You absolutely cannot be seen in public wearing that!" Rose said from the doorway, pulling and tugging at the breeks, circling with an unerringly critical eye for fit. "Squat down, I want to see how they react to stress."

Cat did as she was told, glancing quickly at Greame with a smirk on her face. He was facing the window now with his arms folded over his chest, not finding the humor under the circumstances, which put an even bigger smile on Cat's face.

Cat stood and turned around slowly to let her check for fit.

"Well, Garnet, you did a marvelous job with them. Are they comfortable?"

"Aye. And I can lift my legs high wi'out restriction from those petticoats and yards of skirts. They're verra warm, too."

"Now, promise me you won't go outside this house wearing them," Rose said, hands on her hips as though reprimanding a small child.

Cat smiled and promised, then ushered Rose out the door. Greame followed, having cooled down, leaving Cat to get back into more proper attire.

A few minutes later, Cat walked into the best room to find Greame preparing to leave with Harry and Jim. Frowning, she asked, "Where are ye all goin'?"

"I need to check on supplies for the trip," was his brusque answer.

When she saw his agitated state, she said, "Harry and Jim, ye go on ahead. I need to hae a word wi' Greame."

When the room was theirs alone, Cat asked, "Tell me why ye're upset."

He stopped what he was doing to look hard at her for a moment before answering.

"I'm angry wi' myself, no' ye."

"Because if we were no' interrupted, we may hae made love?" She watched him struggle with the right words to express what he was feeling.

He started and stopped several times, trying to come up with an adequate excuse before blurting out, "It was a lustful thing and no' what ye would hae been expectin'. No' the, uh, *performance* ye deserve."

Cat looked at him, sensing something deeper, but unable to pinpoint the real reason, she ventured, "Did ye ever think how it might be for me? I dinna think I need to be coddled or treated like I'd break if handled too rough."

He looked at her with a kind of scandalized shock on his face at her bluntness, and was relieved that she didn't see further.

Cat smirked and lifted an eyebrow, finding his discomfort amusing. "What? Is it wrong to tell ye how I feel, Greame?"

"I just ne'er kent that women would speak as open as men about it." He was still unsure where the line was when talking to her.

Reading his mind, she said, "If we speak our minds, we wilna hae to try to guess what the other is feelin'. That's how I was raised. If ye hae somethin' to say, then say it. How else will we learn about each other?" She walked over to him and stood close enough to smell his seascented skin. "Or are ye afraid to ken what goes on in my heid?"

"Oh, aye, I'm afraid, all right. Ye scare me terrible! Ye scare me because ye're fearless, strong, brave … beautiful. And ye scare me because ye dinna need me at all."

She was quiet for a moment, fighting the tears that were threatening to surface. She blinked them back, then whispered, "Ye dinna think that I need ye?"

He bowed his head, unable to face the sorrow he placed in her eyes, and not brave enough to tell her the real reason.

Cat put her hands around his neck so he would look at her.

"When I first met ye, Greame, it was then my heart began to beat," she whispered. "In your arms is where I want to wake each morning and go to sleep in each night. Ye're my strength and my reason for being."

In her eyes he saw it was true. But would she still think of him that way if he wasn't a whole man?

The morning of the first of May was bright and mild. The breeze blew in from the southwest and there wasn't a cloud in the sky. The *Revenge* was ready to sail north in search of a place seen only in Cat's mind.

Rose had said her teary farewell the night before. She was sleeping more and more now, making Cat wonder if she would be alive to hear of her adventure when she returned.

Greame rowed the longboat out towards his ship and Harry and Jim waved from the quay, shouting, "Are ya sure we can't go with ya?" Unsure of what it would be like in Maine, Cat and Greame didn't want to have to worry over them in the unsettled province.

George and Robbie stayed on to run the teashop, much to their displeasure. Both were anxious to get back onto the water, but Greame wanted to make sure there was something to come back to if Maine didn't hold any promise for Cat's future.

The sails were unfurled and the wind caught them, once again amazing Cat at the surge the ship took when the wind filled the canvas. They were underway. Cat watched the land fade away as she had when she left Scotland. Her heart gave a little leap for her homeland, but she knew she had to see this through. There was no going backward, only forward.

Kelvin Hay, Greame's uncle, was the helmsman. He had gathered quite a bit of information about the coastal route to Maine from the seamen he met in Boston. He even managed to obtain a few sketchy maps of the waters past York.

"What else hae ye heard about Maine, Mr. Hay?" Cat asked the older man.

"Seems there used to be a town called Falmouth about forty miles north o' York. The Indians and French burnt it to the ground. Now Massachusetts wilna let anyone settle north o' Wells. Too dangerous, they say." Kelvin's clear ice-blue eyes held onto the horizon as he told Cat what he knew.

"Heard one man tell of a place called Pentagöet. There's been a settlement there for o'er a hundred years. A Christian Frenchman lived wi' the Indians that called themselves Penawahpskewi. Even marrit himself an Indian woman," he said, his voice as salty as the sea.

"Really? How far is it from here, this Pentagöet?" Cat asked, getting an interesting feeling about the name.

"Five, six days. An island called Acadia is further up, and also has settlements on it."

"Hmmm. From what I was told, no one dared live up there. Now, it seems there may be more people there than Massachusetts is willin' to admit to. I wonder why?"

"Wonder why, what?" Greame asked from behind her.

"Yer uncle was just tellin' me about a few o' the settlements in Maine. We may no' be as alone as we thought," she said. "Might I borrow yer wee map, Mr. Hay?"

Kelvin took it from his breast pocket and handed it to her.

"Might I come along wi' ye for that?" Greame asked, already falling in behind her.

Cat smiled, knowing he knew what she was going to do. "Aye. Let's see if we both get the same answers."

Inside the captain's quarters, Cat laid out the map on the desk. She instinctively reached for her garnet ring, only to be hit with the realization that she didn't own it anymore. Greame watched this action and saw the hurt on her face.

"What's wrong?" he asked.

Cat tried to scoff it off by saying, "Och, I was just bein' silly."

"'Bout what?" he pressed, seeing that she was truly bothered by its lack.

Cat turned away. "It was just a ring."

Greame took her by the shoulders and turned her to face him. "Where's the ring now?"

She looked up at him, the hurt not fully masked. "I had to sell it to book passage here."

"Did it belong to yer Mam or somethin'?"

"No. My brothers gave it to me in order to gain their forgiveness." She looked far away for a moment, remembering the event.

Greame closed his eyes and saw her sitting at a table with two young men. One of them—the younger one—presented her with a box. She opened it to find a pouch inside. Unlacing the pouch, she poured out the contents into the palm of her hand. It shone silvery with a deep red stone. The two men seemed very pleased with themselves, then the vision was gone. When he opened his eyes, Cat was watching him with tears threatening to overflow.

"Silver wi', let me guess, a garnet stone set in it?" he asked.

"Aye. It was the only thing I ever truly cared about ownin'. Oh well," she sniffed, "no sense cryin' o'er somethin' that's long gone. Anyway," changing the subject, "I need somethin' o' yers to use as a pendulum. Ye dinna wear a ring," checking his fingers, "or a chain," checking his neck. "Do ye hae somethin' personal we can use?"

Smiling, he walked around to the front of his desk, opened a drawer and pulled out a wooden box. He opened it and picked out a small round coin with a square hole in the center. "Will this do?"

"Perfectly. Where is this from?" Not recognizing the strange characters that encircled it.

"China," he smiled, as he watched her study each side.

Cat looked up at him to make sure he wasn't teasing her. "Really?"

"Aye. I told ye ships wrecked all the time along my coast. My cousins and I found a whole box o' them and split them up between us. I've had this since I was about twelve."

"Hae ye a length o' string?" she asked, still fingering the coin.

Greame pulled open another drawer and came up with a cord long enough to do the trick. He handed it to her and Cat threaded its length through the hole in the coin.

"Hae ye e'er seen a pendulum work?" she asked.

"No," he said curiously.

"First, ye instruct it how ye want it to work. I like to hae it go sunwise when the answer is correct, and no' move at all when the answer is no or wrong. I do that in my heid." Her eyes closed for a moment just then to state her intentions. "Then ye tell it what ye want to ken. We want to ken the location o' my vision."

Cat held the pendulum over the map and proceeded to trace the coast with her finger. Greame watched in fascination, but the pendulum remained still as she went into each cove and around each island on the map.

"Are ye sure this works?" he asked.

"It works. We just hae no' reached our destination yet," continuing with the tracing.

Nearly halfway up the coast where a large bay opened up, the pendulum started to sway. "We're gettin' close."

"Near Pentagöet on the map," Greame said, their heads nearly touching as they studied each location.

Cat continued further, going up the west side of Panawanskek Bay then down the east, but the pendulum was still just swaying. Her finger went past Pentagöet, then as she started going around a jut of land just south, the pendulum started a strong sunwise circular motion.

"That's it," Cat said, pointing to the very western-most point of land on the peninsula called Cape Rozier.

"That's where we're goin'?" he asked, scratching his chin.

Cat eyed him for a moment. "Ye look a bit worried."

"We'll hae to wait to see exactly what this jog o' land looks like, but it sure would hae been easier if ye'd picked a nice safe cove instead of some pinnacle juttin' out into the sea."

Cat laughed. "Ye act as though I had any say whatsoever in this vision."

He quirked an eyebrow and shrugged. "I'll go tell Kelvin where we're goin'. He wilna like it either."

She shook her head and smiled, then decided to take advantage of the quiet to see if she could get more details of this Cape Rozier. Still holding the Chinese coin, she closed her eyes and went inside herself. Once again, she saw the rocky shoreline covered in fir trees. Making a visual sweep, there were enormous oaks mixed in with the firs. Small deer and large black birds with red chins stirred on the forest floor. Osprey, like in Scotland, perched in the trees, along with another large black bird with a white head and tail. Turning to face the sea, she saw seals stick their heads out of the water like dogs, curiously wondering what she was doing there. She wondered absently if they were selkies like in Scotland.

There wasn't anything new here, so she concentrated on the voyage. Was there a safe place to moor nearby? The map wasn't very detailed. For all they knew there could have been a myriad of small coves to anchor in. Then she saw it. On the northern side of the

Cape was a deep wide cove, perfect for setting anchor out of the battering of the open sea. The vision ended and she went topside to tell Greame.

&.

The weather remained fair; the seas calm. They hugged the coast, amazed at all the coves, peninsulas and islands. As they sailed through Casko Bay past Falmouth, their heading was due east to get around the long fingers of land and islands that made for treacherous travel. Hector Hay, a lad in his early twenties, took to charting the coast in as great detail as he could from the ship. It was already a better map than the one they had purchased in Boston.

The first night, they anchored in one of the many protected coves. Cat wanted to see the entire coast in the daylight to get a better idea of her vision. Standing on the quarter deck, she watched the sun slip behind the hills in a blinding yellow, sending shards of gold over the entire harbour. The breeze had nearly died. The only sound was the sea lapping against the hull. Greame joined her just as the sun disappeared.

"I can see where one could take a likin' to the sea," she said softly, not looking at him. "It's so lovely."

"Aye, when she's calm like this, there's no' a better place to be in the world."

&.

The next morning was obscured by a thick fog that hung close to the ship. Since there was no rush to get to their destination, Greame informed his crew they would wait it out. If the thickness lifted later, then they would set sail.

Taking advantage of the lay over, Greame asked if Cat wanted to go ashore and see what the land looked like. Maybe even do some hunting. She was all too ready to explore. With a small party, they piled into the longboat and began rowing. It was a rising mid-tide. The fog was so thick that the lapping of the waves was their only indication they were approaching shore.

The pebbled strand they landed on was littered with bluish-purple mussel shells. Pulling the boat all the way up to the tree line, knowing the tides rose high here, they set out into the woods. They divided into two groups of three, armed with pistols and dirks. Cat had told them of the small deer she had seen in her vision. Fresh venison would feed the men for several days.

The spruce and fir were thick as thieves, sometimes so dense there was no way to get through the tightly bunched stands. Patches of snow lingered in the darkest areas and the fog clung to it like ghosts rising from the cold. There were large open areas of bogs covered in what looked like heather, and boulders strewn across the landscape much like the Highlands of Scotland. Amazing ledges of open granite covered with moss and lichen completed the terrain.

Strange peeping sounds were heard from deep within the woods. No one seemed to be able to identify if they were birds or some other kind of creature. The noise grew louder as they approached the bogs and ponds. Small splashes became apparent as they walked past these wet areas, and they realized they were tiny frogs. Hundreds of them making chirping, peeping, whistling noises; nearly deafening when the entire chorus came to a crescendo.

Cat liked the smell of the forest—fresh, pungent, earthy, fragrant with spruce and cedar. She was sitting on a granite outcropping when she started swatting at the bugs that swarmed around her. They were buzzing in her ears, getting in her eyes and hair, and if she tried to breathe through her mouth she would swallow them. She got up and started moving again, but now that they found her, they seemed to have invited their friends. It was an all-out assault.

"Greame, I canna take these midges anymore," swatting for all she was worth.

"Oh, aye, they are fierce," he replied, swatting and walking faster trying to escape them as well. "I wish we had some o' that bear fat Rose was tellin' us about."

"What's bear fat?" Hector asked, scratching his ears.

"The Indians use the fat from a great furry beast said to roam these woods to keep the ... what did Rose call them?" Greame asked Cat.

"Mosquitoes."

"Right, to keep mosquitoes away."

"I dinna ken if these are mosquitoes or no', but I'm goin back to the shore. They didna seem to bother me there. Ye can go on if ye want," Cat said, already making a brisk exit to the beach.

"We'll meet ye back there in a bit," Greame shouted.

Cat burst from the woods and ran down to the waterline. The bugs didn't follow—not all of them, anyway. It still seemed like they were all over her, but it was just a residual reaction to the vermin. Tiny red welts appeared on her hands and she was scratching at her neck and behind her ears. Whatever they were, they seemed to have had a lively feast at her expense.

After a few minutes she calmed down and started walking the pebbled beach. Many of the stones were worn into smooth ovals in shades of gray, with brown, white and burgundy showing up here and there. Some were flecked with pink and black. Some were milky white and shiny. Others looked like the spotted sides of a seal or had stripes on them. There were even green and ochre ones. The more she looked, the more variations she found. Jewels. That's what they were, unrefined jewels. Their beauty captivated her as she strolled further down the beach.

From behind her, very far away, she heard someone shouting. She turned to find that she had walked quite a distance, losing sight of the longboat in the fog. Lifting her skirts, she jogged back to Greame, who had one of the large black birds with the red chin in his hand and a large smile on his face.

"I ne'er even heard ye shoot," Cat said, breathing hard, looking over the dark feathers that also had deep shimmering green, cinnamon and gray.

"I dinna ken what it is, but there was at least thirty o' them in a clearin'. Big, isn't it?" Greame was turning the large bird around in admiration.

The second group flew from the forest like they were being chased by demons. Kenny Hay had two of the big birds and was trying his best to swat at the swarm of bugs around his head. Thomas and Edward were batting at the air in a frenzy. Cat and Greame couldn't help but laugh at the spectacle, but understood their discomfort.

"Let's get back to the ship, lads. I think we've had enough for today," Greame said, placing his bird in the longboat and grabbing an oar. The rest of the crew followed suit and they were rowing back within minutes.

ॐ

"Turkeys. That's what they called 'em in Boston," Kelvin told them when they boarded the *Revenge* with their booty.

"We had turkey at Rose's one night, remember, Greame?" Cat said.

"Aye. It was verra good. Roasted was how Emily and Claire prepared it. Stuffed wi' cranberries and apples and giblets, if I recall."

"Made an impression, aye?" she said, smiling.

He chose to ignore her comment and said, "Since it looks like we'll be here for the day, we may as well eat well." He handed the three turkeys to Kenny, the cook, then went below.

Cat remained topside, breathing in the fresh, moist air and marveling at the life the fog appeared to have. It would roll in, then all of a sudden seem to lift a bit, enough to see the trees on shore. When it went through the trees, it made them look ghostly—appearing, then disappearing, as though a veil was dropped in front of them then lifted. The effect was hypnotic.

It was three bells in the afternoon when the fog departed with such rapid speed, Cat understood how it could envelop a ship with very little warning, having seen it with her own eyes. With about five hours of good light left, she wondered if they would sail further up the coast or wait until morning. The breeze freshened, once again from the southwest, and before she could ask what the plans were, the anchor was weighed, men were pulling on the ropes, and sails were being unfurled.

They sailed until they reached the Popham Colony on the Kennebec River; a settlement deserted for over a hundred and fifty years. Cat asked if they could explore the old foundations in the morning. Greame told her it was her trip and that she could do as she pleased. She fell asleep full of excitement at the prospect of exploring. She dreamt of Lachlan. He would be with her in her quest to find artifacts left by those who tried to settle this wilderness.

Nearly all of the ship's crew milled around on the sandy shore near the forgotten settlement. All of the buildings had been burned, leaving one's imagination to fill in what each foundation was used for. Now and then, someone would shout out a small find, but usually it was just a shard of pottery or metal utensil, nothing that would lead anyone to believe this was once a thriving community.

It was interesting to note that no one had seen a single solitary human being—red or white. With the way Bostonians kept clear of the place, one was led to believe Indians were everywhere. Cat brought this up to Greame while sitting in the sand soaking up the warm sun.

"It does seem a bit odd, but then again we've no' ventured too far from shore. With the amount o' game in the forest, they probably dinna hae to resort to takin' to the sea for their food."

"Do ye think we should be sailin' instead of relaxin' on the beach?" Cat asked, her eyes closed and face arched to the strong spring sun that was turning her skin pink.

"No. I'd much prefer to sit here and watch ye enjoy yerself for the day." He touched her hair, shimmering like red jewels. "But then again, I dinna want ye to bake like a fish for too long. Perhaps we should be goin'."

Cat smiled and got up, and Greame whistled for the crew. They launched the longboats and were soon underway.

By late afternoon, they were sailing by an outcropping of granite ledges striated with long grooves that fell into the sea. They looked as though a very large cat had dug its claws deep into the rock as it was dragged out to sea. The light green waves crashed onto dark gray crags with such ferocity it sounded like thunder, leaving only white foam as the surge retreated back into the depths.

"There's a place ye want to steer clear of," Kelvin said, giving the rocks a wide berth before heading north to find a sheltered area to spend the night.

"What's next on yer wee map, Mr. Hay?" Cat asked.

"Due east in the mornin'. We'll hae to navigate through some wee islands before turnin' north once again." He pointed with a thick finger the route they would take.

Cat went below as the ship was anchoring for the night. She used the surgeon's cabin as her own, as the *Revenge* had no such crew member. Undressing for bed, she heard a soft knock on her door. Buttoning her dress again, she gave permission to enter. Surprise registered on her face at her guest.

"What might I be helpin' ye wi', Hector?" He was holding his hand. He walked over to the lantern before revealing two bloody fingers on his left hand.

"What happened?" she asked, getting a clean linen from the cabinet.

"Got 'em smashed lettin' out rope for the anchor," he said, watching Cat intently.

"Here, take a seat while I clean them and see if they're broken," directing him to sit on the stool while she got a pan of water. "Are ye all right?" she asked, feeling a malevolence from somewhere.

"Aye, I am now," he said, leaning close to her as she washed the blood from the wounds.

"Ye're in my light, Hector. Can ye no' get so close?" As soon as she said it, she felt the hair rise on the back of her neck. She stepped back just in time to fend off a lunge from the lad.

"What in bloody hell are ye doin', man?" Cat had already grabbed her dirk and was brandishing it to let him know she could defend herself.

"I've been watchin' ye and I can tell ye like me," he said, suddenly in no pain.

"I like ye fine, Hector, but no' in the way ye're thinkin'." She had backed up to the door and found the knob with her free hand.

"Och, now, Catrìona. Ye dinna hae to hide it from me. Let me hae just one kiss, then ye'll realize how ye feel about me." He inched his way closer.

Cat opened the door quickly and stepped out into the mess. There was no one in the dimly lit cabin.

"There's nowhere to go, Catrìona, except into my arms."

Cat sized him up quickly, realizing she would have a problem getting the upper hand on such a fully capable man. He wasn't drunk, therefore he probably wouldn't make any mistakes to capitalize on. She needed help. In her mind, she made her plea. *Hasten yerself to me right now, Greame!*

She had backed into a table and quickly scooted around it to get something between her and her assailant.

"Greame will be none too pleased wi' ye when he finds out about what ye're doin', Hector." She wanted to keep his mind working on something other than her, hopefully to put some sense back into it.

"He'll no' find out, because when I finish wi' ye, ye'll wonder what ye ever saw in him. What in the world do ye see in him, anyway? He has the face o' a dog and canna even get ..."

"What she sees in me is none o' yer concern, Hector-lad," Greame said in an even tone from behind Hector.

Cat watched Hector's eyes get wide for a moment before he whipped around, trying to come up with an excuse for his behavior. She had to suppress a smile when she heard his justification.

"She was all o'er me, Greame. I went to her so she could look at my fingers I smashed and she tried to kiss me and hug me. Couldna keep her hands off o' me. I had to chase her out o' that wee cabin wi' threats to keep her away. Told her I'd tell ye what she was doin' behind yer back."

Cat raised an eyebrow and saw Greame try not to smile. "Let's hae a look at those fingers," Greame said, placing a big hand on Hector's shoulder and turning him back into the surgeon's cabin. Before Cat could get back into the room, she heard a bloodcurdling scream. She rushed in only to find that she really did have fingers to fix now.

"And if ye ever hae the thought in yer heid to lay a hand—or anythin' else—on her, I'll kill ye," Greame growled in Hector's ear, releasing the two fingers he had bent backwards beyond their limits.

Cat opened the drawers looking for something to splint them with. Finding a couple of short sticks, she stepped to the light and took Hector's hand—Greame stood ever so close—then proceeded to probe for the breaks. His sharp intake of air through his teeth indicated their location.

"It's goin' to hurt," she said, looking him in the eyes.

"Just get it o'er wi'." he growled, gritting his teeth.

Cat grabbed one of the fingers and gave it a pull, ignoring Hector's whimpers. There, one set, now the other. Repeating the process, then feeling for the smooth transition of bone indicating alignment, she placed the sticks under each finger, and instructed Hector to hold them there while she wrapped the linen bandage around both fingers to keep them immobile.

"Ye're free to go now," she said. "But be warned. The next time I'll hae to charge ye for my services."

Greame let out a laugh at her boldness. She may have asked for his help, but she was certainly not afraid.

Hector left the cabin cradling his hand like a babe. Cat began to clean up, then looked up at Greame when she felt him watching her.

"Thank ye for comin' to my rescue."

"My pleasure. Now can ye tell me what that was all about?"

"He had the notion that I liked him and that I would welcome his advances. Greame, do I come across to ye as someone who would do that? Am I too friendly?"

He thought for a moment. "Ye are verra friendly, but I hae ne'er seen ye be flirtatious—no' even to me. I think wee Hector there was just thinkin' wishfully. No' likely he'll do it again."

She walked close to him and wrapped her arms around his waist, then placed a kiss on his cheek. "What did ye think when I called for ye?"

He smiled at her, his arms finding their way around her waist, pulling her closer to him. "At first my mind wanted to believe ye wanted me to come to ye for some lovin'." His face grew serious then. "But then I heard an urgency in the request that wasna fear, but … trouble. I flew off the quarterdeck leavin' old Kelvin to wonder what set me on fire, and I ran into yer cabin to find no one there. Then I saw the door to the mess was open and heard ye speakin'. When I saw Hector there, I still didna think anythin' was wrong, except wondered why he was nearly in the doorway and ye were behind a table in the mess. Then he started explainin' what he was goin' to do to ye. That's when my blood started to boil. It was nearly all I could do no' to kill him there on the spot. The only reason he's still alive is because he's my cousin."

He let her go and ran his hand through his hair, pulling it off his face, then looked hard at her. Cat sensed his thoughts.

"Ye wilna grow o'er protective o' me, will ye?"

"I was just thinkin' what would hae happened …"

"Remember what I told ye about tryin' to make somethin' out o' what didna happen."

"But …"

Cat walked up to him and kissed him hard on the lips. After a few moments all "buts" were forgotten.

ತಿ

Morning dawned cloudy and very windy. The waves had been building all night, rocking the ship like a cradle pushed by the south wind, and the smell of rain permeated the air. The harbour they sought shelter in last night was south-facing and Kelvin voiced his desire to locate a more suitable spot to wait out the storm. Greame agreed and they set sail on a heading of due east.

By afternoon, it started raining. Once they cleared the islands—none of which held promise of safe harbour—they headed north. They came upon a peninsula and sailed up the east side of it, finding a deep harbour entrance with an eastern exposure. The brunt of the winds died down considerably once in the sheltered cove, and they rode out the storm for the rest of the day.

"I dinna care for this wind," Cat said. They were in Greame's quarters watching the horizontal rain lash the windows. Cat was writing letters to Alexander and Gregor, keeping them up to date with her adventures, while Greame was entering figures in his logbook.

"Ye get used to it after a while," he said into his journal.

"I think it's the constant noise I dinna like so much. It's ne'er quiet." She got up and started pacing around the room. A moment later, she asked if he was hungry.

"I could use a bite to eat," he said, scratching his head, his concentration still on his entries.

"I'll be back."

Cat wandered into the galley and asked if she could fix a couple plates of food. Kenny gave her his blessing and she filled them with leftover turkey, a few pieces of bread and some dried venison. Walking back to the captain's quarters with a plate in each hand and the boat listing from side to side was a precarious journey. As she walked through the mess, she saw most of the crew playing cards or chess, some just talking with their mates, relaxing.

It was getting dark, but the wind didn't seem to be letting up. Cat wondered if it would blow like this all night. It brought back too many fresh memories of her voyage across the Atlantic. During those hellish two months, she rode out no less than a dozen days of these types of storms. There was no place to find shelter in the open sea. She remembered the stench of vomit and fear, vowing never to board another ship. Now look at her.

❧

She returned to Greame's cabin and plunked the plates of food down next to him. He looked up at her, sensing her restlessness. He put down his quill and watched her twirl her hair, wondering where she was. He closed his eyes and concentrated, becoming one with her memories. It was as though he were a shadow watching from another room—one she didn't know existed. They were aboard a ship in a storm. The seas were high and rough; the wind whipped through the sails with every intent of ripping them from their riggings, and the ropes made an eerie whining sound. Greame wrinkled his nose at the smell of the place; it was putrid.

Suddenly, he saw her sitting in a corner with several other women. She was holding a wee babe in her arms. It was screaming, but nothing she did could quell its shrieks. Tears were streaming down her cheeks. One of the women was scratching herself all over. She was covered with lice. A young lad, nearly green, sat in his own vomit, useless to help himself. A man stood in the corner with festering scratches on his face and a wild look in his eyes.

Christ, no wonder she didn't like ships. He opened his eyes having seen more than enough. He pushed his chair from the desk, walked over to where she stood and wrapped his arms around her, pulling her to his chest and stroking her hair. She seemed in need of comfort. Soon, he felt her shake with quiet sobs.

"Shh, shh, Garnet. That will ne'er happen again. We're safe here. By mornin' it'll be all over."

She never spoke, just clung to him, accepting his strength. He gave it all to her.

12

Retrieving the Past

The bay where the Panawanskek River emptied in the sea was littered with islands, large and small. Along the western coast were high hills and a myriad of sheltered harbours and coves. Kelvin marveled at the prevailing southwest winds that forced him to sail past a harbour, then sail "downeast" to catch the wind that would bring him in.

From the map Kelvin obtained in Boston, there was a route between two large island archipelagoes that would take them right to Cape Rozier. Seals were abundant and harbour porpoises led the way. Cat stood at the bow of the ship searching for the exact location of her vision. Some of the shorelines were granite now. The small islands that she saw from the shore in her vision were the very same ones she was passing by now. A smile brightened her face. She was almost home.

Greame came up behind her and stood quietly at the railing. A glance at her face made him smile. She had her breeks on, but this time they seemed appropriate on her. He felt no pangs of desire; they were just practical clothing. He deduced that since she was wearing them now, they must be close to her destination.

"Can ye feel it, Greame?" she asked excitedly.

He closed his eyes for a minute attempting to feel what she felt.

"I feel somethin', but I think it's ye—yer emotions—no' from this place."

She looked at him and noticed a slight holding back of his emotions.

"What's wrong?" she asked.

Cat watched the stone façade strengthen as he turned to face her square. He wasn't going to let her in.

"No' a thing. Why do ye ask?"

She lifted an eyebrow. "Yer no' goin' to tell me?"

"No," looking her straight in the eyes, "no' yet." He turned and walked up onto the quarterdeck and relieved Kelvin at the helm.

She didn't want to pry. He would tell her when he was ready, but she felt like he was distancing himself from her. She resisted the urge to look into his thoughts, although with the stony look he wore, he had probably blocked the access of his mind from her. He was learning very quickly and proving to have strong abilities.

Cat watched him at the wheel with the wind in his face. The sun creating strong angles on his already chiseled features. His eyes were squinted against the reflections off the water; a few strands of hair came loose from their confines. He was as strong as the sea itself; a mirror image of the granite coast they sailed past. The green of his eyes were the same color as the giant firs. He *was* this land, and Cat wondered if the feeling of kinship was bothering him or drawing him in.

The sea was getting narrower as they sailed north. Up ahead to the east was a jog of land cut with coves and inlets. Open pebble beaches lined with tall spruce.

"We're here," Cat whispered, watching her homeport come into view, perfectly matching what she had seen in her vision. She ran to the quarterdeck and stood beside Greame.

"We're here," he said to her, keeping his eyes on the land in search for a place to anchor.

"Keep north, then ye'll see a channel to the east that will lead to a protected cove," Cat instructed, twirling her hair.

Greame did as he was told and soon saw the channel Cat had seen between a small island and the mainland. They sailed through the channel right into the cove she predicted would be there. Orders were barked to lower the sails and let loose the anchor. Longboats were deployed and much of the crew went ashore.

From their vantage point they could see the dilapidated forts at Pentagöet across the bay. When they sailed in, Cat saw an area where the water from a stream roared into the bay, and wanted a closer look. When they got ashore they walked over to the area. After a short survey, Greame said it must go back the other way when the tide came in. It was a reversing falls.

They continued along the shore, sometimes walking on the beach, other times having to climb up onto the smooth granite to walk in the woods because the sea left no beach to walk on—the cliffs fell off sharply into the sea. The May sun was hot, but the breeze off the water kept the group cool. It also kept the bugs away as long as they stayed close to the shore.

A few hours later, after passing a beautiful horseshoe-shaped cove, Cat stood on a high point of land overlooking small islands, long stretches of land, and the hills they had sailed past in Panawanskek Bay. She breathed in her surroundings and let the earth speak to her. But now that she had found the place, what was she to do here? Was she supposed to stay?

Greame was not himself. Such an odd feeling washed over him when he saw Cat's land. He was still trying to make sense of it. So far, all he had managed to figure out was that he felt a strange connection to the place. He had no idea why—there was nothing here save rock and trees. The forts he saw across the bay held nothing for him. No, it was something else. He wanted to figure it out on his own, that's why he didn't tell Cat about it. He knew she didn't try to read his thoughts; they had made a pact not to do that with each other unless under dire circumstances.

Sitting on the ground at her feet, he felt her watching him now and then, smiling to himself at her desire to know him—know what he was thinking and feeling. The secrecy must be driving her mad. He knew it would make him daft if the roles were reversed.

Just then it hit him. The memories of when he was a young lad out at sea in a boat all by himself. The serenity, the peace, the feeling of oneness with his surroundings. He had not felt that for so long he had forgotten the comfort of it. Here, away from everything, the connection was reestablished.

He rose to his feet and kissed Cat on the cheek with a smile that radiated his innermost feelings. She turned to look at him and returned the grin.

"So, what hae ye figured out?" she asked, taking his hand in hers.

"It was so long ago that I felt at peace wi' a place I had forgotten it, but I feel it here."

"What do we do about it? Are we to **settle** this place? Wait 'til we find the Indians? I dinna ken why I'm **here**," she said, a crease between her brows forming.

"Does it matter? Right now all I **want to** do is enjoy the place. We can decide the what-fors later, aye?"

She looked at him, nodded and smiled. "I do enjoy seein' the joy on yer face. 'Tis a rare thing. I like the way yer eyes turn the color o' grass in the shadows and sparkle wi' the excitement of a bairn. Ye're right. Let's enjoy it for now."

Returning to the *Revenge,* they watched the sun set in a fiery sky of vermilion and gold. They ate their supper in the captain's quarters so they could talk alone.

"Might I ask ye a question about the ring yer brothers gave to ye, Garnet?" Greame asked as he chewed on his fish, picking a small bone out of his mouth and laying it on the edge of his plate.

Cat looked at him with a cocked head and squinted eyes.

"Ne'er mind trying to read me, just answer the question," he chuckled.

"Why?"

"Just answer the question."

Another minute and she still couldn't get beyond his barricade. He sat there staring at her with a curious look on his face.

She gave in. "It was fine silver; engraved all around wi' a heart-knot interlace pattern and topped with a garnet cabochon. Why?" she asked again, twirling her hair.

Greame reached in his pocket and pulled out a pouch. Strange how she was transported back to her kitchen table with Iain and Lachlan. He handed it to her. All she could do was stare at the thing, wanting to open it, but not wanting to open it.

"What are ye so frightened of?" he asked in all seriousness.

She looked up at him, her eyes the color of thistles. "I dinna ken."

"Well, open it then," he said quietly.

Cat untied the strings and pulled it open. Just as she had done so many years ago, she poured the contents out into her hand. She felt the same metallic weight hit her palm. When she saw it, she inhaled sharply, not believing it was the same ring, but knowing it was. Tears formed and threatened to overflow when she looked at him. "How?"

"I was talkin' wi' Kenny in the mess and overheard John tell Geoffrey he had bought this silver ring wi' a red stone when he was on the docks in London just before we sailed here. It got me right curious, so I went over to see it. It sure looked like the ring ye told me about, so I asked John if he would part wi' it. He said how dear it had become to him, but for the right offer, he may consider it—the pirate. I kent it belonged to ye, so I paid his price."

"Ye hae no idea what this means to me, Greame. 'Tis the only thing I've e'er truly had as my own." She stood and hugged him fiercely, leaving a wet spot on his shoulder from her tears. "I'll find a way to repay ye."

He faced her, holding her by the shoulders. "It's my gift to ye, Garnet. Ye'll no' be payin' me back for it."

Cat held it in her hand, staring at it. Greame took it from her palm, turned her hand over and slipped the silver circle onto her ring finger. He kissed her softly, then just held her for a long time.

"*Tapadh leat,* Greame," she whispered into his shoulder.

"My pleasure, Garnet."

13

First Contact

It turned out to be a beautiful three days. The weather on Cape Rozier was warm during the day with a constant breeze, and cool at night. On a peninsula jutting out of the northernmost part of the Cape, Cat and Greame found the first signs of the native inhabitants; a small village of wigwams and round-houses. But still no people.

"Do ye think they ken we're here?" Cat whispered, standing at the edge of the village.

"Aye, they ken," Greame returned. "I think they've kent we were here since we landed."

"Why dinna they show themselves? Do they think we mean to harm them?"

He looked at her for a moment with a smile on his face. "After the English hae called them savages and probably killed more than we can imagine, did ye expect them to send out a welcomin' party?"

Cat clicked her tongue at his condescending tone and sent him a angry look. "I want to meet them, and I think I ken how to do it. Will ye excuse me for a while?" Not waiting for him to answer before she ventured into the village.

Greame knew Cat didn't want him to follow, but he was curious as to what means she was going to use to meet the Indians. Choosing a good vantage point, he watched her enter the village, then stop when she came to the center of it. She removed the dirk from her breeks and did something he had never witnessed before. Facing east, she raised her arms to the sky, then bringing them down, she cut the palm of her hand with the sharp blade. Letting her blood fall to the ground, her mouth started working, like she was speaking. He was too far away to hear what she was saying, but she turned south, raised her arms, then let her blood drip to the ground again. She did this at each compass direction then sat down in the center.

Cat was still speaking; he could hear bits of words when the wind blew in his direction. A few minutes later she stood, reached in her satchel and removed the pink scallop shell she had found earlier, along with some of the light sage-green lichen she pulled from a spruce tree. Bending, she placed her finds on the ground where she had been sitting, then added something more personal to the offering; a plaited lock of her hair she cut with her dirk.

He watched her turn and start back towards him. There was something so primal, so instinctual, so ancient about her offering, he wasn't sure how to take her performance. It would surely be classified as witchcraft had anyone but himself seen her do it. Dangerous for her in Scotland, never mind here in America.

When she reached him, there was a kind of peace surrounding her, a glow emanating that he had not seen before.

"Are ye all right, lass?" he whispered.

Slowly her eyes focused on him, as though just realizing he was there. She smiled at him, but never said a word. She walked past him to the shore and dipped her hands into the water, cupping them to capture the saline liquid, then lifted them high over her head to let the water drip onto her face. Then she stood, unmoving, looking out over the water for a few more minutes.

Greame was mesmerized. He wondered if she would teach him this ritual. Watching her perform the ancient rite made something inside of him connect even closer to her. A surge of unexpected bliss bubbled to the surface, the likes of which he had never felt in his life. He was feeling what she was feeling.

"Dear God," he said to himself, holding his chest as tears sprung into his eyes. The emotion was nearly more than he could bear.

Cat returned, stopping when they nearly touched. Without a word, she placed her hand on his face and wiped the tear from his cheek with her thumb.

"I'm glad ye felt it. That means they will too."

ϩ♠

Back aboard ship, Cat spent the rest of the afternoon sleeping. After expelling so much of her energy on the offering to the Indians, she needed to recoup her loss. She knew Greame wanted all the details about what she had done, but he would have to wait.

Just before the sun went down, Cat awoke feeling like a new woman. She smiled when she heard a soft knock on her door, knowing it was Greame.

"Come in, Greame."

He peeked his head in with a look Cat couldn't help but laugh at. "I didna wake ye, did I?" he asked quietly.

"No. Come in. I ken ye hae questions …" Before she could say anything else, he rushed into the room and sat at the edge of her bed next to her, grabbing her hand in his. Her dimples deepened waiting for the barrage.

"Does yer hand hurt where ye cut it?" he asked, inspecting the bandage. She opened her mouth, but before she could answer, he asked, "Did Anna Macpherson teach ye that? How did ye ken what to do? What *were* ye doin'?"

She raised her eyebrow, waiting to get a word in edgewise.

"Och, I'm sorry, Garnet. It's just that I hae ne'er seen such a ritual performed, and then to feel such emotion … I was truly overwhelmed."

Cat thought for a moment whether to tell him of her past, wondering if he was ready for that yet. She started with a few probing questions.

"Do ye believe in the afterlife, Greame?"

He looked at her deeply, trying to see what she was getting at. After a moment, he gave up trying and just answered, "Aye."

"Do ye believe that we come back into another body havin' the knowledge of what we were before?"

He lifted his eyebrows and gave her a sideways look. "Ye mean bein' born again?"

"Aye. Do ye believe it happens?"

Looking back on all he knew, he tried to find an instance where he could say he even gave it a thought. Choosing his words carefully, he said, "I dinna ken if I believe it or no', but ever since I've met ye, there are a lot o' things that make me think there's more to this life than what I can see."

Cat smiled. "Verra diplomatic."

"All right. Just for the sake of argument, let's say I do believe in bein' born again. What does that hae to do wi' what ye did this mornin'?"

"That's where I learned to do such things. Ye see, I was my grandmam before. She was a great Seer, but was put to a tortuous death when she spoke the truth of her prophecy, and the Marquis did no' want to believe it. She lives inside o' me now and I remember what was done before. Many would call it witchcraft so I must be verra careful where I perform these rites. No' many hae ever seen me do them. Ye are the only livin' person now."

He stared at her for a long moment, still holding her hand, working out his beliefs in his head. Cat could feel his questions, doubts and fears, but he remained stone-faced. Finally, obviously coming to some agreement with himself, he nodded, then said, "I believe ye. Now will ye tell me what ye did this mornin'?"

Cat smiled, then explained that she called upon all living things—seen and unseen—and asked for permission to have a meeting with the people who call this land theirs. She made it clear that she was there without malice, and declared how she felt about their land—this Cape Rozier—that she was living in harmony with all.

"Why cut yerself?"

"It's a blood sacrifice to the Mother so she kens who I am, showing her that my intentions are honorable."

"Why the water afterward?"

"To cleanse any impurities I may hae brought wi' me."

"How will ye ken they will meet wi' ye?"

"Just like ye will ken. We'll both feel a pull to a special place when they're ready to meet wi' us."

"They want to meet wi' me, too?" he asked, shocked.

Cat wondered for a moment whether she took for granted his wanting to go with her when she met these people. "I just thought ye'd like to meet them wi' me, but if ye dinna want to, I'll understand."

He stood and walked around the cabin deep in thought, his hands behind his back.

"I'm sorry, Greame. I should hae asked ye first. I'll go on my own ..."

"It's no' that, Garnet. I want to go wi' ye, but I feel somethin' verra strange about this meetin'." he said, still pacing the room.

"It's *who* we'll meet that gives ye that feelin'. Remember at Rose's when I told ye of a person wi' the shadow of a bear?"

He stopped and faced her. "Aye, that's right. I forgot about that. What about this person has me frightened for ye?"

"I dinna think ye hae to be frightened for me. He's like ye and I—a Seer for his clan, only his powers are verra different than ours."

"Different in what way?" He returned to the edge of the bed.

"I'm no' quite sure I can explain it, only that he carries wi' him somethin' so ancient, it holds all the secrets o' his clan as far back as the first."

"The first what?"

"The first human."

꿈

"Well, it'll be a birthday celebration," said Greame.

"Today's yer birthday?" Cat asked, trying to find a calendar. "What's the date today?"

"May thirteenth. When's yer birthday?"

"October thirty-first—Samhain," Cat said, stuffing oatcakes, a small looking glass Rose had given her, and one of the Chinese coins into the satchel.

"Ah, makes sense. The day where the reality of the livin' and the dead is the thinnest," he said, plaiting his hair and tying it off with a length of cord.

"Verra good," she smiled. "How old are ye today?"

"Twenty and thirteen."

"I like a mature man," Cat said.

Greame grinned and said, "That's a verra diplomatic way o' tellin' me I'm old."

"Old is just a state o' mind. Now, let's finish packin' up this satchel and go ashore. We dinna want to be late for our meetin', do we."

꿈

The long boat with only Cat and Greame aboard rowed into the cove next to the reversing falls. The water was rushing upriver in a frothy, blue-green torrent. According to the dream both of them had, they were to meet with the Indians upstream at a fishing camp.

Pulling the boat onto shore, they walked along the river bank watching ducks and gulls ride along the waves, catching whatever they could from the deep. An osprey chirped at them in short, sharp repetitions from the top of a dead tree.

"*Iolair-uisge*." Cat stated, pointing to the white bird with the dark gray head and wings. "Just like in Scotland."

"Aye. Great fishin' birds."

Rounding the riverbank, it opened up into a long, narrow pond. Further upstream they could see smoke from the fires at the Indian camp. Walking a little further, they were met by three young Indian lads. Each was dressed in a deerskin breechclout. Amulets of some sort tied with rawhide rested on their naked chests. One had a blue downy feather attached to it. Their hair was a brownish-black, straight and long down their backs. Their eyes were dark brown, holding mischievous twinkles. It was the only giveaway to what lay beneath their serious exteriors. None said a word. One of them took Cat's hand and guided her and Greame to the village.

They arrived where the smoking fires were, and six women and two men greeted them. All had the same dark skin and wide faces. They smiled, but remained quiet.

The women had deerskin dresses that came just below the knees with deerskin leggings underneath. Intricate beading and embroidery covered the front bodices. The men wore only breechclouts, as they were in the water fishing with round nets.

When Cat glanced over at Greame, he looked positively scandalized at such a show of skin to strangers. She had to restrain a giggle, feigning a cough instead.

"It's their way, like Highlanders who remove their plaids in battle and fight nearly naked," she whispered.

"Oh, aye, but we mean it to scare our enemies. What do they mean it to do?"

She chuckled softly, unable to keep it in.

From a wigwam on the other side of the fires, the birch bark door opened and out stepped a tall man clad in breechclout and leggings. Cat couldn't see him clearly through all the smoke, but was drawn just the same, unable to remove her eyes from him. When he finally emerged from the smoke, Cat inhaled sharply. All around him was movement, as though he had other life forms growing on him. Nothing was distinct, just shadows. She realized he was the man with the shadow of the bear and involuntarily glanced at the ground to see the beast, but it was just his own figure.

He was lean and muscular, his chest and arms darkened by the sun. Tattoos of beasts were on his arms and over his heart. His wide face and pronounced cheekbones held a royal air. The front part of his nearly black hair was knotted on the top of his head, intricately woven with feathers and beads of white, yellow and red. The rest of his hair fell free down his back. His ears were pierced and small shells and carvings of bone dangled from them. In his hand was the scallop shell and the lock of hair she left in the village. When he stopped a few feet in front of Cat, he broke into a smile, his teeth white against his dark skin. Cat returned the greeting with her own dimpled grin.

Beside her, she felt Greame reach for her hand. She took it, then watched as the Indian turned his attentions to Greame. Still smiling, he held out his hand to shake. Greame released Cat and grasped the Indian's hand in a firm shake.

In very stilted English, the Indian introduced himself as Sees With Far Eyes, and his people were of the lobster clan. He told them he could be called Far Eyes.

"Greame Hay, sir, and this is Catrìona Robertson," he said in his rich, deep voice.

Far Eyes released Greame's hand and made a formal bow to Cat.

"Ye speak verra good English, Far Eyes. Where did ye learn?" Cat asked softly.

Far Eyes pointed to Pentagöet and said, "I speak better French."

Cat and Greame must have had the same expression on their faces, and Far Eyes laughed a hearty cackle.

"Come," Far Eyes said.

They settled by the fires watching the women clean the fish, then split them open on sticks and hang them to smoke. There weren't very many in the village, probably no more than twenty-five men, women and children, but some of the older people were gathering around to learn more about these newcomers and see what they were offering.

The children were like children in any culture. Some hid behind adults, while others stood brazenly alone forming their own opinions of these white people. A young girl of maybe three sat beside Cat, mesmerized by Cat's red hair. She lifted a lock and tickled the little one's face with it, eliciting a giggle from her before a wary mother scooped her up.

When the crowd settled down, Cat opened her satchel and laid out a piece of fabric, then one by one, pulled out the offerings and placed them on the cloth. Far Eyes watched intently, smiling at the oatcakes and looking glass. But when the Chinese coin was presented, he looked at Cat, silently asking for permission to pick it up. Cat smiled at his curiosity and nodded. Far Eyes looked the coin over with probably the same questioning look Cat had when Greame showed it to her.

"It's from China," Greame said. "A place on the other side of the world."

This fact seemed to satisfy Far Eyes, and he nodded as though knowing exactly where China was. Maybe he did.

Following some unspoken protocol, Far Eyes offered them nothing, but took the fabric, folded the contents into it and placed it behind him, identifying it as his property now. The small gathering around them dispersed, leaving Far Eyes to do his work. He looked at Cat for a long moment. She could tell he was looking into her, getting to know her. She let him. When he seemed satisfied with what he found, she returned the gesture. He was startled at first, but relinquished himself to her—partly anyway. Cat sensed a heavy guarding of questions she wanted answered. Those questions would have to be answered a different way.

ૐ

Greame watched this play of mind reading. It was much more advanced than he could follow, but he watched in fascination the multitude of expressions that wandered over each of their faces as they went into each other. He could tell Far Eyes wasn't prepared for Catrìona's probing strength. As she strolled around in Far Eyes' head, Greame watched Far Eyes' face intently, picking up on his thoughts and memories as they filtered through Cat. It was a strange and exhilarating feeling not to speak a word, yet know someone very intimately.

Cat seemed to be having a little trouble with something in Far Eyes' mind. Greame watched as Far Eyes smiled, and, obviously wanting Cat to comprehend whatever it was, put the tips of his fingers to her forehead, then lifted her hand for her to do the same to him. Within a minute, Cat was smiling, apparently solving the vexation.

During this melding of minds, Greame didn't feel left out. He was able, through Cat, to see some of what was transpiring between the two masters. Every so often he would get a different perspective and could only assume it was Far Eyes sending him direct thoughts. It was odd to think this was normal, but he was comfortable with his newfound abilities.

ン

The two *spoke* to each other of their customs, their homeland, their families, and each seemed to have war stories of the same magnitude. When Far Eyes showed Cat the decimation of entire villages by the whites, or even other Native nations, she wept openly. Far Eyes inhaled sharply at her views of Culloden; a deep frown between his eyes and a shaking of his head indicated their kinship in hardship.

When they had exhausted each other, Cat spoke out loud.

"And they call *us* savages," wiping away the wetness from her face.

"Why *you* called savages?" Far Eyes asked them.

Greame fended this question and recounted a brief history of the Highlanders under Roman, Norse, Norman, Saxon and English rule. When he finished, Far Eyes launched into the warring nations of the Iroquois, Algonquin, Mohawk, then the French, and now the English, as well. He called himself Penawahpskewi, a group from the Wabinaki nation. The French called them Penobscot.

"We have much in common together," he said.

Cat and Greame nodded their heads in agreement.

"Since Cape Rozier is not the name ye've put on this land, what do *ye* call it?" Cat asked.

"*Mose-ka-chick*. It mean moose rump."

"What's a moose?" asked Greame, curious to learn all the new beasts in America.

Far Eyes thought hard as to how to describe it, but found a better way. He got up and asked them to follow him to his wigwam. It was very dim inside; the light from the fire made the drawings on the wall of the birch bark come alive. Far Eyes pointed to what looked like a large deer, only with a much more pronounced nose and enormous antlers.

"Lives in woods and lakes. Eats plants. Very big," he said, indicating with his hand the height of the beast being taller than he was.

"Why moose's rump?" Cat asked.

"In early times, *Kolóskape*, our creator, chased moose with dogs over the land they call Pentagöet. When moose reach shore, it jump in and swim across water here," he said, pointing to Pentagöet Harbour. "The dogs could not follow, but *Kolóskape* jump across and kill moose. When he return, he scatter moose entrails on water. They on rocks today."

Cat and Greame shared the same puzzled look. Far Eyes smiled and motioned them to follow him once again. This time they walked towards the shore. When they reached an outcropping of granite, Far Eyes pointed to the creamy colored striations waving throughout the solid stone.

"It does resemble entrails, Garnet. Dinna ye think?" Greame asked, tracing the thin rock with his fingers.

"Aye, wi' a bit of an imagination," she said, nodding.

"What this *Garnet*?" Far Eyes asked, frowning.

"That's what I call Catrìona. It's her ... spirit name," Greame said, hoping he used the correct terminology.

Far Eyes eyed Cat for a moment. "You have *motewolon*?"

It was Cat's turn to frown now. "What is ... *m*' ... *DEH* ... *w*' ... *l'n*?" Trying to pronounce it correctly.

"What Greame said; spirit power."

"Perhaps ye should explain what that means to ye, then I'll tell ye if I hae it, aye?" Cat said, never really realizing that when Anna Macpherson gave her the name, it had a much deeper meaning than fiery, independent, determined and courageous.

Far Eyes fought with the words to convey his thoughts, frowning deeply and rubbing his smooth chin. Cat asked his permission to look inside him. His entire face changed with the dawning that he could show her what he wanted to say.

"Yes. Look inside."

Cat separated a lock of hair and started twisting it around her fingers. Far Eyes closed his eyes and wore a look of intense concentration on his face. Cat nodded as the conversation in their minds began to make sense to her. Far Eyes opened his eyes at the same time Cat dropped her hair.

"Dream, vision, see other side. Yes, you have *motewolon.*"

"We call it Second Sight, or in our native language, *dà shealladh,*" she said.

"You have other language? Like my language?"

"Aye, but it doesna sound like yers. We both speak French and English, but we also hae our own words."

Far Eyes nodded his head in understanding and the three of them continued sorting through each other's cultures until nearly dusk, when Cat and Greame returned to the ship.

Invading Neighbors

After spending nearly a week with Far Eyes and his people, Cat and Greame were asked if they would like to participate in an important ceremony to be performed at dawn the next day. Being very anxious to learn more about the Wabinaki culture, Cat was more than willing to partake in the festivities. Greame was more interested in learning the Penobscot hunting techniques, but also agreed to participate.

The Penobscot sagamore, or chief, Loron Saguarum, was arriving to negotiate fairer supply compensation from the English and French traders. These were difficult times, as the two sides were at war with each other, and the Penobscot were in the middle, being pulled both ways for allegiance.

It was the first night Cat had spent on land since sailing to Maine. Following Penobscot custom, she lodged with the other single women in a large communal wigwam. The floor where they slept was lined with balsam twigs and needles covered with deer and moose hides. It smelled musky and clean all at the same time.

Somewhere in the middle of the night, she was shaken awake by several of her lodge mates. Sweating and crying, she made her apologies and left the wigwam for some air. Needing to sort out what she just saw, she walked down to the shore and found a large rock to sit on. The moon was just a crescent hanging low in the sky. Stars more numerous than one could count in a lifetime winked at her, as though sharing her innermost secrets.

Had it been been just wishful thinking that she came to a new land in the hope of finding peace? After the vision she had just witnessed, life here was in the same warring chaos as Scotland. Why did men feel the need to conquer? Why couldn't everyone just live together, embracing their cultures and differences? Was there no place she could go to escape from battles and death?

She sat for a long time on the granite seat. Small nocturnal animals came to the shore in search of food, unoffended by her presence. Funny hump-backed creatures with what looked like masks over their eyes sauntered around her, picking at the seaweed and turning over stones. From behind her, a larger animal, this one walking on two feet, approached. She didn't need to turn around to know it was Greame.

"Would ye like to talk about it?" he asked softly, his rich voice soothing away the tension of the vision.

She looked at him, the light from the moon illuminating half of his face, making it appear smoother and gentler than in the sunlight.

"Would ye just hold me for a moment first?"

He sat beside her on the boulder and wrapped his arms around her, swaying back and forth, rocking her like a child. Tender kisses were planted in her hair and he began humming. It was an old tune from when she was a child. Her mother used to sing it to her when she had a bad dream. Cat smiled at the remembrance, wondering if Greame's mother had sung it to him as well.

When the faintest hint of dawn shone on the horizon, Cat started replaying her vision.

"They had most o' their heids shaven, leavin' just a thickness in the center from the nape o' the neck to the forehead. Shirtless, and in breechclouts and leggings, they had their faces painted red and black. Fierce lookin' men armed wi' short axes and pistols raided the village, killin' nearly everyone. Some o' the children and women were taken prisoner when they left, bein' beat savagely and disappearin' back into the forest."

"*Mekwe*," came the voice from the edge of the woods, startling both of them into defensive postures.

"Christ O'Jesus, Far Eyes! Ye near scairt the life out o' us," Cat reprimanded, watching Greame sheath his dirk.

"Now, who are these *Mekwe*?" Greame asked.

"They our enemy. They most feared by my people. The French call them Mohawk. You see them, Garnet?" He walked over to the boulder so he could speak softly.

"Aye, if that's who they sounded like to ye."

"Tell me when."

Cat thought for a moment if she had been able to get that far in her vision before being shaken out of it. "I canna tell. The trees didna look any different. Let me go back inside," she said, excusing herself to walk the shore, and twirl her hair around her fingers.

Far Eyes watched her, as did Greame, both still very curious at her process.

"Why she play with hair?" Far Eyes whispered.

"She says it helps her relax." Seeing Far Eyes' confused look, he clarified. "It helps her be still and peaceful."

"She have many dream?"

"This is her first since we sailed from Boston, three weeks ago."

"Do dream happen when she see it?"

Greame glanced at Far Eyes, catching a change in his voice. "Aye. Every time."

Far Eyes said no more, folded his arms over his chest and waited for Cat to finish her vision. A short time later, Cat returned to elaborate further on what she saw. By the time she finished with her premonition, the sun was just peeking through the trees. The drumming and singing for the sagamore had begun back at the village, and the threesome returned to partake in the festivities.

❧

"So now we hae to worry about the ... what did Far Eyes call the *Sassenaich* again?" He was sitting on the ground cross-legged, not paying much attention to the goings-ons around him.

"*Igrismannak*," Cat answered, never taking her eyes from the five men drumming and singing. The beat was heartfelt and she related to it on some ancient level.

"Right. Now it's the ... whatever ye called them ... the English, the French and the Mohawk?"

"Havin' second thoughts about America, Greame?" Cat smirked, stealing a glance at him.

Greame clucked his tongue. "Aye. 'Tis like a beehive o' conquerin' nations here. Everyone wants a piece. At least in Scotland, it was just the English to contend wi'."

Cat's hackles went up immediately.

"Oh, aye, *just* the English. *Just* men who would rather us all dead, stoopin' so low as to murderin' women and children. Aye, *just* the English," Cat spewed, breaking her contact with the drummers to glare at Greame. She could feel her cheeks burn and knew she was nearly ready to blow, but didn't want to cause a scene here. "I dinna care to talk about this right now."

Greame stared at her, wondering what she hadn't told him about her visions and real experiences from Scotland. He opened his mouth to apologize, but was stopped by her hand going up. She was done talking.

He left her to her demons.

She had a difficult time trying to get back in the festive mood after Greame brought up the same sour thoughts she had been having recently. Sorry for having bitten his head off and driving him away, she decided to go look for him. It took a couple times around the village before she found him by the shore.

The day was hot, and he and a couple of the young lads had shed their clothes and were having pushing contests in the freezing water. Cat watched quietly from the woods, her mood brightening at their laughter. Greame must have sensed her presence, because all of a sudden he whipped around to where she was standing, made eye-contact with her, then in a self-conscious fit, ran waist deep into the water, much to the hilarity of the lads.

Cat walked down to the water, her hands on her hips watching him turn blue and shake so much she thought he would break his teeth from their chattering. "Ye're no different from any other man I've e'er seen naked, ye ken."

"And just how many men *hae* ye seen naked?" he glared.

"Just my brothers, but I'm sure ye're designed no different, aye?"

"How I'm *designed* is none o' yer business, now turn around while I get my clothes, or I may freeze to death in here!"

Cat couldn't help but giggle, staring just a little longer before doing as he requested. "I ne'er ken a man to be self-conscious, Greame," she said over her shoulder, getting another reprimand from him as he gingerly walked on the stones to exit the frigid liquid.

"Well, cold water does strange things to a man that a woman should ne'er ken about."

"Och, aye, ye mean like turnin' yer ballocks blue and shrinkin' yer manhood down to a stub?" she said with a giggle in her voice. She couldn't help it, he was so easy to rankle.

"Christ, Catrìona!" he growled, coming around to the front of her as he finished lacing up his breeks. "Ye talk like ye've been aboard ship for too long. Hae ye no thought o' scandal?"

"I think the only one I'm scandalizin' is ye. The lads dinna seem to care that they're naked. Oh, perhaps if I were naked too, ye'd feel better?" She teased relentlessly, reaching for the buttons of her bodice.

He grabbed her by her shoulders and blazed his eyes into hers. "Dinna ye dare, Catrìona Robertson. I mean it. It's just no' proper."

Wrong thing to say. She wriggled out from his death grip and started running down the beach unbuttoning her dress. Since she had shoes on, he had no chance of catching her. The dress fell around her feet and she quickly stepped out of it, freer now. Her corset, one of the new-fashioned styles with the ties in the front, was the next to be shed. Now she was just in her shift, not bothering with petticoats on such a warm day. Ducking around a point of shrubbery, she looked back for a second to judge Greame's nearness. He was still pursuing her, but quite a distance away, shouting something inaudible to her ears. Over her head came the thin muslin, and in that instant of blindness before the fabric was removed from her face, what appeared in front of her stopped her in her tracks.

Naked as the day she was born, out of breath with the smile still frozen on her face, she came face to face with a beast standing on its back legs like a man. It was black and furry with a long snout and small ears on the top of its head. Its paws were huge; each claw nearly three inches long. The beast, as startled as she was at seeing something that didn't belong there, let out a guttural growl and made swipes at her with its paws. She had never been afraid of a beast, but this was much different from anything in Scotland. Slowly, she started to back up. It held its ground, still snarling and swatting at her. Back a little further, almost around the shrubs, then back to the beach. Suddenly, she heard Greame's voice behind her.

"Dinna move."

"Easy for ye to say," she whispered back harshly.

"I think that's a bear!" he said.

"Aye, but what do we do about it?"

"Och, no' a thing. I like the view from back here," referring to her naked backside.

"*Prig!*"

"Now, that's what got ye started in all this mess."

"No. What got me started in this whole mess is ye tellin' me I'm improper. Ye ken that I hate that," she hissed. "But, just for the sake of argument, if we were to run now, do ye think it would chase us?"

The shrubbery was now between them and the bear, and the beast wasn't making any attempt to change that fact.

"It may no' chase ye, ye're still wearin' yer shoes, but these wee stones are right hard on a man's feet. It would make an easy meal o' me."

"All right. We'll split up. I'll give ye a head start, perhaps it wilna see ye. Then I'll run back up the beach, collectin' my clothes on the way, and get back to the safety o' the village. Go!"

Cat turned to see why he was still there. He was preoccupied with her backside again. "If ye dinna go this instant, I'll let the bear hae ye, now GO!" she demanded.

Greame chuckled, but prudently started back as quickly as his tender feet would take him.

Cat kept stealing glances over her shoulder to judge where Greame was with the lead time she gave him. The bear still had not come around the bushes. Grunts and pawing noises indicated it was still there, but maybe it had forgotten about her. Backing up a little further as quietly as she could, she picked up her shift and dropped it over her head quickly. Slipping her arms through the sleeves to cover her nakedness, she turned and ran to catch up with Greame, which didn't take very long.

Greame turned when he heard her footfalls on the pebbles, and said, " Dinna worry, it's no' followin' ye. Perhaps those stories Rose heard werna all true about how bears attack people."

"Aye, well, that's as close to wantin' to find out as I care to get," she said, breathing heavily from the sprint. "Now," she said, sliding her arm through his elbow, "let's talk about what ye dinna want me to ken about cold water."

Nearly two months after reaching their destination, all of Greame's crew were familiar with the Penobscot people and were learning their ways and language. The rugged shore reminded them of their Scottish coast and a few were thinking of settling here amongst the natives. Both cultures were very similar, living off the land, hunting and fishing, always on guard for other clans, but what the Scots were finding out was that most of the labor was done by the women.

Native women hunted and transported the game from where it was felled, skinned the game and prepared the hides. They hewed wood, drew water, made and repaired all the household utensils, prepared the food, and sewed and decorated all the garments they wore. In addition, they made canoes, gathered shellfish, caught fish, and even set up camp when they moved, which was about every six to eight weeks.

"So, what do the men do?" Cat asked Far Eyes the day the village was moving to another area.

"We do all big hunting, deer, moose, bear, and we make war."

He said it so matter-of-factly, Cat doubted his sincerity. When she stole a glance at him though, she realized he was dead serious.

"Speakin' o' makin' war, I hope ye dinna think by movin' yer village, the Mohawk wilna come."

Far Eyes looked at her hard for a moment. Cat felt him try to come to a decision about that very thing. Without waiting for him to reply, she said, "So ye're decidin' on the best place to move the village to protect yerselves?"

He quirked an eyebrow, and said, "That what I was thinking. In dream two nights ago, I saw place on high hill. Difficult to attack, easy to defend. Will that change outcome of dream?"

"Let me see."

After a few moments, she returned to this reality and smiled at Far Eyes. The look on his face mirrored hers. By moving to the hill he had seen in his dream, it would indeed cause much less death and destruction, though still not all would survive. At least the Penobscot would now have a fighting chance. Cat verbalized what she saw to Far Eyes' ever-brightening face, and the village made preparations to move.

In a matter of a few hours, the women in the village took down the wigwams, disassembled cook fires and stretchers for skinning, packed everything onto litters and were ready to follow Far Eyes to the new, safer destination. Cat and Greame watched the military precision in which everyone knew their tasks and carried them out without question or debate. By mid-morning, the camp was on its way.

The destination for the new village was further inland on the Cape. It was a difficult climb with all the utensils, hides and household items they carried, but before the sun set, the wigwams were reconstructed and cooking fires had been lit.

"Amazin'." was all Greame could say.

From their pinnacle vantage point, just a few well-placed scouts were able to cover every angle coming up to their new village site. No one would be able to sneak up on them without the entire village being forewarned in plenty of time to defend themselves.

Sitting at the communal fire, Cat, Far Eyes and Greame made plans for their defense, as they knew the raid would be within the week. The Mohawk were a warring band who always had the latest European weaponry, but with the French and English at war with each other, firearms and ammunition amongst the Penobscot were scarce. That, however, did not mean they were without adequate skills to defend themselves. Over the generations, the French taught the Wabinaki many new techniques to defeat their enemies. Cat watched quietly as Greame pointed out possible shortcomings in Far Eyes' plan, then enthusiastically patted him on the back when his defensive schemes displayed pure genius.

After a few hours, Cat retired to her lodge with the other women. As tired as she was, sleep eluded her. She thought of her new surroundings and its people. Was she happy here? Yes, she thought. Happy enough to stay? It was possible, but still not a certainty. What was she looking for? Ah, that was the real question, wasn't it. She seemed to be wandering aimlessly. There was no purpose to her life. Her vision directed her here, but for what purpose? To warn a village of Indians against an onslaught of a murderous tribe? She didn't think so. Yet there was a strange connection to the Penobscot people and this geographical area. Back and forth, she pondered for what seemed like hours. In the end, her only solution was to give it more time, if Greame was willing to remain a while longer.

♒

Stepping out of the lodge at dawn, having no more than a couple of hours of sleep, Cat found Greame and Far Eyes still at the coals of the fire where she left them at last night.

"Did ye no' get any sleep, either of ye?" she asked, taking a seat on the log next to Greame.

Stretching his arms over his head in a gaping yawn, Greame shook his head. "We just now finished our plans."

"The Mohawk will wish they not leave village to attack us," Far Eyes said, looking tired and stifling a yawn of his own.

Before any of them could say another word, the scouts sounded the alarm. Far Eyes and Greame were off to inform the Penobscot warriors of the battle plans, leaving Cat alone on the log. She thought it strange that she hadn't sensed them coming. Closing her eyes, she saw that they were not Mohawk warriors, they were scouts. They had just come from the former site of the village, only to find it empty. The scouts had only climbed this hill to get a better vantage point to look for the smoke of cook fires that would lead them to the Penobscot's new location. What they had not planned on was the welcome they were going to get for their blunder.

Cat ran to find Greame or Far Eyes to tell them not to use the pistols. If the Penobscot could eliminate the enemy quietly, the Mohawk attack may be averted all together. Small twigs slapped at her face and tangled in her hair as she raced through the trees. Her pace slowed as she reached the edge of the hill, its steep slope allowing only for a cautious lope.

Stopping to get a bead on anyone's location, the hair on the back of her neck started to rise. She unsheathed her dirk from her breeks and stood perfectly still, becoming invisible in the thickness. Out of the corner of her eye she noticed a movement. There was a steep granite cliff off to the right, and a head was coming up from below it. The Mohawk pulled himself up over the rock face, a tomahawk in his hand. His head was shaved on both sides, leaving a thick tuft of hair running front to back. His chest was bare save some kind of claws hanging from a length of rawhide. A breech clout and leggings were all he wore.

He stood still, assessing the area, turning his head very slowly, straining to hear anything; his eyes taking in every detail. Cat wondered if he could hear her heart beating wildly. He was no ordinary scout, this one. There was something else to him—an air of superiority and confidence and menace. His eyes were searching the thicket she was in now. For a moment, they stopped and rested on her. She was invisible, she knew it, yet she also knew he could see her. No, that's not quite true. He couldn't see *her*—he could see her essence. Like a break in the flora, a shadow, not really visible, yet a disturbance. He never moved, never revealed whether he could see her or not, making her believe she was just imagining it.

Suddenly, his eyes darted off to Cat's right, a twig snapped indicating the presence of another person. He lifted his head ever so slowly, then Cat saw him register one of his own men. In a language she had never heard before, he began to give what appeared to be instructions to the other man. His hands were sometimes graceful in their actions, then sometimes abrupt. A moment later the other man dashed off into the thick woods, but the leader remained for a moment. He turned and once again looked straight at Cat, then he too dashed off. Cat took a breath of air, sheathed her dirk, and as quietly as she could, emerged from her hiding place.

The woods were silent. No shots were fired, no men yelling at the top of their lungs, no hoofbeats or footfalls. The silence was eerie, like she was the only person left in these woods. She shuddered and ran towards the lookout posts to confirm that she was not alone, only to find them empty. Something was wrong. She could feel it in her bones. Her eyes closed to get a better view, but before her vision became clear, a blood-curdling scream filled the air.

Whipping around, Cat bolted for the village. Out of breath and confused at what she saw when she arrived, she studied the smiling faces of the Penobscot. Why were they happy? What had she missed? Her eyes scanned the area and focused on Greame in the distance standing next to Far Eyes. Greame was not wearing a smile. In fact, he looked repulsed.

Cat slowly walked over to see what spectacle could have so many smiling, and one sickened. As she neared, the grizzly scene unfolded. Three Mohawk were on the ground with their tufts of black hair and scalps severed from their heads. The blood was absorbing into the needle-covered ground, leaving just a dark area.

Greame was too late to prevent her from seeing the barbaric aftermath. He walked over to her and placed his hand on the small of her back to let her know he was there. Cat looked into his deep green eyes with a pained, questioning expression.

In a voice barely a whisper, he said, "'Tis their way."

Cat looked back at the three men, their bodies brown and lean and muscular, full of life one minute, then dead the next. She looked up to find Far Eyes watching her; could feel him in her thoughts, so she closed herself off to him. This was her emotion and she didn't want to share it with him or Greame or anyone else. Without a word, she turned and walked away.

"She all right?" Far Eyes asked.

Greame was watching her disappear into the woods. He shook his head, but said, "In time."

"Did she not know what we do to our enemy when we capture them?"

Greame looked up into Far Eyes' nearly black eyes. "I honestly dinna believe she gave that a minute's thought."

"What did Scots do to their enemy when they capture them?"

"Huh," he scoffed, "many times, things much worse. But I think she is no' ready to see any more death." He shoved his hands in his pockets and walked off, realizing he wasn't ready to see any more death either.

There were no festivities in camp that night for two reasons: one, it may have led the rest of the Mohawk nation to the Penobscot's new village, and two, Far Eyes reasoned with the tribal leaders saying that, yes it was a victory to defeat their enemy, but to celebrate their deaths was causing harm to Red One That Sees, as they had begun calling Cat.

Greame understood Cat's need to be alone and he gave her that space. He sat next to the small fire in front of the lodge he and his men shared, throwing spruce needles into the flames. They would snap and sparkle, then disappear into the blaze. Kelvin sat beside him chewing on some moose jerky, content to just stare at the glow. It was well after midnight when Cat emerged from her hiding spot to sit next to Greame.

After a few minutes of watching the spruce needles burst into flames, she asked, "Why wasna there a celebration?"

Greame looked over at her, the orange glow danced over her face casting strange shadows that made her look enraged and giddy all at the same time. He told her what Far Eyes had said, then watched as a single tear rolled down her cheek, a miniature fire burning its way down her face, disappearing under her chin. He reached over and drew her to his chest; she let him. Kelvin quietly got up and walked into the lodge.

"Do ye want to tell me about it?" he asked into her hair. It smelled of balsam.

"I want to sleep on it." Then curled herself into him and fell asleep.

A Proposal

Mid-August and the bugs finally began leaving flesh and blood alone. The deciduous trees had an olive appearance now, readying themselves for their fall spectacular. Along the shore, the ochre-colored seaweed that covered all the rocks within the tide's reach began to dull. The birds were quieter, having reared their young and left the nest for places unknown. There was a change in the air and Cat was feeling it.

Torn in her decision to stay with the Penobscot or go back to Boston for the winter, she posed the question to Greame and his crew as they sat around the fire eating venison stew.

"This is no' a decision I make lightly and I would like yer opinions on it," she said, making eye contact with most of them, fiddling with her hair.

For a long minute the only sound was the snapping of the spruce in the fire. Greame cleared his throat and said he had just one question before stating his opinion. Cat watched him compose his thoughts, seeing Rose's face appear from behind a dark cloud.

"Does Rose hae anythin' to do wi' yer wantin' to go back to Boston?"

A troubled smile raced across her face. "Aye, though I fear it may already be too late."

"Do ye think the illness has taken her?" Greame asked, sadness hardening his fire-lit features.

Cat nodded and the rest of the men hung their heads. They had all been very fond of Rose.

"Then perhaps it would be for the best to see to her affairs for the winter, then return in the spring."

Greame spoke like the captain he was, not really asking if this was what she wanted or not. Cat could find no fault in his reasoning, and besides, Harry and Jim may need looking after for a while. And who knew what Emily and Claire were planning to do, if now they were free women.

Cat nodded, then simply said, "Aye."

After some teary eyes and long farewells, the *Revenge* set sail two days later. The sun rose as a vermilion orb in the blue-gray sky and thunderheads began forming on the western horizon. It was a sultry morning, the humidity created a sheen of perspiration with only the slightest exertion. There was a hot breeze, but the farther out they ventured in the slate blue water, the more comfortable the temperature became.

Cat had trouble getting her sea legs back and giggled often as she tried to navigate the deck. Greame seemed to have come home when he boarded his ship. Not that he was a fish out of water on land, but the sea was a more comfortable arena for him. She marveled how he could blend into any situation, taking command of his surroundings whatever they may be. She, on the other hand, was definitely a landlubber.

They decided to take pretty much the same route back as they had coming up, heading southwest into Panawanskek Bay, following the long island in the center of it. The sea remained strangely calm, even though the sky looked threatening. Distant thunder reverberated off the water in hollow echoes of itself. Shortly before noon the wind started gusting. Kelvin suggested they head for Meguanticook Harbour to wait out the storm and Greame agreed. By two bells, the gusts had became a gale and the rain was coming down so hard it threatened to pierce the skin. When they finally pulled into the protected harbour a few hours later, they felt beaten.

Cat's aversion to waiting out storms in the hold of a ship was made clear again. As soon as they anchored, Greame went below to check on her.

"I canna stand it, Greame," she sobbed, huddled in the corner rocking back and forth.

"Let's go ashore, aye?" he said, kneeling next to her and rubbing her back.

A look of relief washed over her and he helped her up. She blew her nose and dried her eyes in an effort to compose herself. She didn't want the crew to see her in this condition.

"Dinna fret, Garnet, it's still rainin' so hard no one will be able to see yer face, ne'er mind see ye've been cryin'." Greame chuckled, brushing strands of hair from her forehead.

Cat tried to crack a smile, but it was too labored to be more than a grimace. "I'm sorry for no' bein' strong enough for the sea life, Greame. I canna seem to get over the voyage from England."

He held her face in his big, rough hands, using his thumbs to wipe away the tears that were still spilling down her cheeks. "Lass, ye canna be sorry for that hellish trip. From the wee bit I've seen, ye hae every right to be squeamish in a storm. Besides," he kissed the tip of her red nose, "ye're so capable in every other thing, I kinda like bein' able to care for ye when ye're aboard ship."

"No' that I mind bein' cared for, but can ye do it on dry land? Now?"

His laugh was warm and deep and safe, then he took her hand and headed for the upper deck.

From an old sail, Greame rigged up a makeshift tent in the trees just off the shore. The rain continued for most of the night and the light show the thunderstorm created made the shrubbery and trees dance in eerie gyrations in the gale. Cat didn't seem to notice any of it though. As soon as she slid into the tent next to Greame's warm body, she was asleep, exhausted from the fear and stress of being aboard ship. He didn't mind, he held her body close to his, shushing her whimpers when a particularly loud clap of thunder cracked nearby. Stroking her hair, he wondered now what he would do without her. He had asked for time, but how long would she wait? In Scotland, the Clan Seer never married. It was said that a spouse's energy would interfere with the ability to see, so he knew their relationship would never be like normal people's—never getting married or raising children—but he didn't care. What they had right now was so much more than he could have ever asked for. He was content to be her bodyguard, and she never had to know of his handicap. But what about her? What did she want? They had never really talked about it. He spent the rest of the night thinking about what she might say to the different scenarios playing out in his head.

A tickle on her nose woke her around dawn. She slowly opened her eyes, but remained very still, pinned under Greame's thick arm, knowing he had kept her safe and warm all night. He wasn't asleep though, she could almost hear his thoughts. Keeping her promise not to spy, she whispered, "What are ye thinkin'?"

"I didna wake ye, did I?" he asked in a gravelly voice.

"No."

She lifted his arm so she could roll over and see his face. The early morning light didn't fully penetrate the canvas, but she could tell he hadn't slept much.

"I've kept ye up all night, haven't I," she said, sitting up and placing her hand on his bristly cheek.

"I was doin' some thinkin' is all. Ye didna keep me up," he said, propping himself up onto his elbow.

Cat waited for him to let her in, but he obviously wasn't ready to talk yet. She bent her head and kissed him on the forehead.

"What's that for?" he asked, smiling.

"For keepin' me safe last night." Then she crawled out of the tent, stood and stretched herself nearly backwards, rubbing the small of her back. "I must hae slept on a rock."

He looked around for the object in question, pushing aside some spruce needles to get to the rock the size of his hand she had slept on. Holding it up with a grin, he asked, "Might this be the culprit?"

"Oh, aye," she said frowning, continuing to rub the sore area.

Greame crawled out of the tent and started to massage Cat's lower back. After a few minutes of moans and groans as he loosened the tight muscles, his hands slowed to just touching her.

"Ye can ask me anythin', Greame," she whispered.

His hands stopped for a second, then resumed slowly. "What do ye want from this relationship, Catrìona?"

She remained quiet for a moment, wondering where that came from, but turned around to face him before she answered.

"I love ye, Greame Hay. I hae since the moment we met. When I was the Seer for the Clan there were a great many restrictions on my life. Now … well, now, I'm free to do as I please. I can marry, have bairns, be a normal woman."

She watched Greame's face while she spoke. He was very good at hiding his emotions, but Cat felt what he was feeling. His confusion baffled her, as though what she said was the only thing he had not thought of. He was scared. She put her hand on his arm and looked deep into his green eyes.

"Perhaps I should ask what *ye* want from this relationship?"

He looked her over from her deep auburn hair, to her violet-gray eyes, stopping on her full lips for a moment before answering.

"This was much easier last night," he said softly.

"Ye had no' expected me to be able to marry, did ye?"

He shook his head.

"We dinna hae to get marrit, but I do want to be wi' ye for the rest o' my life."

He took a step away from her and half-turned, hiding most of his face before he spoke.

"Ye've been honest wi' me, Cat, and now I hae to be honest wi' ye." He toed a pine cone with his shoe and stuffed his hands in his pockets. "Remember when ye saw me naked at the shore wi' the Penobscot lads?" He glanced over to see her acknowledgement. "Ye said I was made like any other man?" She nodded again. "It's no' true. I … I canna get a cockstand." He blurted out, turning away.

Cat wasn't sure what to say. Her mouth opened and closed several times, but nothing came out. She was embarrassed for him. It must have taken everything he had in himself to admit this to her. It took a moment to think of something to say. She knew how he reacted to silence, so she went with the obvious question. "How did it happen?"

Now that it was out in the open, he turned to face her again, armed with a bit of courage since she didn't laugh or run away. "I was fifteen at a Gatherin' at Leith Hall with my Uncle Andrew—now there was a tall man. He stood seven feet and two inches!"

Cat smiled, and feeling this to be a lengthy story, sat on the ground cross-legged. Greame joined her, his knee touching hers.

"Well, me and a few o' my younger cousins wanted to participate in the Games. We were too young to compete wi' the men, even though we thought we were more than capable, so we held our own Games with Uncle Andrew directin'. It was a queer accident really, we were workin' in pairs tossin' the caber—with much smaller poles than are normally used, o' course—when my cousin George lost control o' his caber and it came crashin' into mine. It took my caber right out o' my hands and when the high end came down, the end I had been holdin' came back up and hit me square in the ballocks. They were crushed. I dinna wake up for near a week. George stayed by my bed the entire time, feelin' it was somehow his fault. They tell me I nearly died, but I dinna recall anythin' after I was hit," he said, reliving the episode all over again.

"And ye've no' been right e'er since?" Cat asked.

He refocused to the present, looked into her eyes, and just shook his head.

They remained quiet for a time listening to the crickets chirping loudly in the clearing. Shafts of sunlight illuminated the grasses, and small insects floated through the light, destined for someplace only they knew. A seal's head broke the water just off shore, seeing if the coast was clear. The air smelled cleansed after yesterday's storm and it was much cooler than it had been for days.

"I think we should get back to the ship," Greame said moodily, getting to his feet.

"Dinna ye care to hear what I hae to say about what ye've told me?" Cat asked, looking up at him.

"I think yer silence says it all." His face was stone again, effectively closing her out.

He walked towards the tent and started folding the canvas. Cat watched him, not offering to help. She hated it when he acted this way, thinking he already had her all figured out. Fine, she thought, let him stew. When he's ready, he'll listen. She walked over to the boat and began hauling it to the water—not a far walk since it was high tide—sat in it and waited for him.

Once back aboard ship, Greame went straight to his quarters and closed the door, letting everyone know he was not to be disturbed. Cat stayed on deck next to Kelvin.

"So, what's happened to make the two o' ye want to be at opposite ends o' the ship?" Kelvin asked without looking at her.

"It's that obvious, aye?"

"He can be slightly pig-heided at times," he said, as though describing the traits of a pet.

"*Tcha!* That, my dear sir, is quite an understatement."

Kelvin chuckled and lit his pipe, never taking his eyes from the horizon. "I remember when his Da was still alive. Greame must hae been around eight years old—even then, he had a commandin' air about him. Anyway, we were all out in our wee boats fishin', and auld Alasdair made a remark that sent Greame's hackles up," he said, glancing at Cat for a second to see if she dared venture a guess.

"Too many options for me to take an accurate guess on, Kelvin," Cat shook her head smiling. "What did he say?"

"Ye'll ne'er amount to anythin' if ye dinna give all o' yerself in every deed."

"That's pretty sound advice," she said, cocking her head, waiting for Kelvin to reveal why it would have set Greame off.

Kelvin looked at Cat with a raised eyebrow and took a couple of long puffs on his pipe before answering. "Greame thought his character was bein' slandered."

Cat burst out laughing. "At eight years old he thought his *character* was bein' slandered? At eight years old ye dinna hae a character!"

"Greame thought he did. He didna speak to his Da for days. We all thought he was festerin' about it, like any bairn would do when their feelin's get hurt, but what he was really doin' was thinkin' about it. Thinkin' hard about it."

"What were his conclusions?" Cat asked, still smiling.

"He told his Da that he wanted to command his own ship someday so he could help support his family. Little did he ken that it would happen sooner than he thought," he said, making a slight adjustment to the wheel. "His feelin's run deeper than most. His thoughts are usually for someone other than himself, but he comes off as broodin' and self-centered. Dinna pay him any mind, Garnet. He's workin' it out in his own way."

"Och, I hae no doubt about that. But I do wish he wouldna take my silences as a trounce on his feelings. That's *my* way o' workin' things out. It would just be a lot simpler if he wouldna shut me out and come to the wrong conclusion wi'out hearin' my side o' the story first."

Kelvin's answer to that was a shrug of his shoulder. The conversation was over. Cat went to the bow of the ship and leaned against the railing. The wind had freshened and had a crispness to it; the season was changing. In a way, she was excited to get back to Boston, not that she missed civilization, but she missed the adoptive family she had found there with Rose. She thought of Rose again, trying to feel if she was really gone, but still just got her face behind a cloud. If Rose was still alive, it must be by the barest thread.

It's amazing how, if two people don't want to see each other—even on a ship—they can manage to avoid each other. True to form, Greame avoided Cat for three days. On the third day, Cat had had enough and walked into Greame's quarters without knocking. He was lying on his back in his bunk with his head resting on his arm; eyes closed and a smile on his face. He never opened his eyes to see who had come in.

"Where hae ye been, Garnet?"

Cat sputtered, shaken by the fact that he was in a good mood. It took her three days to get fired up enough to confront him, and now he doused her before she could launch into the tirade she planned. She stood by the door with her hands balled in fists; red blotches colored her cheeks and her eyes were murderous. She slammed the door, and in three quick steps, was at his bunk. Greame didn't have time to react to her violent outburst, but when he opened his eyes, it registered that she was not in the same mood as he was.

"Ye son of a bitch!" she hissed. "Ye make me fester for three days thinkin' I had hurt yer wee feelings, when all along ye were waitin' for me to apologize to ye?"

Greame managed to get himself into a sitting position before being pummeled by Cat's fists. His eyes were wide in amazement at her strength and quickness, being the recipient of a few good punches before he grabbed her arms and tossed her onto his bunk. She fought like a man, using her fists, not kicking and scratching like most women did. It took all of his strength to subdue her, and when he thought he had, she gave him a head-butt that made him see stars, effectively loosening his grip on her so she managed to slip off the bunk and get back on her feet.

She stood over him, breathing heavy, watching him rub his forehead. Nothing at all had been accomplished, but she sure felt better. Saying nothing, she turned on her heel and walked out the door.

≿❧

For more than an hour he looked everywhere for her, but she seemed to have disappeared, which was impossible to do for long aboard ship. He went back to his quarters only to find her sitting at his desk with her back towards him looking out the window. He stood in the doorway for a moment trying to get a feel for her mood. She wasn't letting him in.

Slowly, she turned around, peering at him over her shoulder. He could see she had calmed down, but he didn't want to say or do anything that would provoke her.

"I am a lucky man, Catrìona Robertson."

She turned her head back towards the window then he saw her shoulders shaking. Christ, he made her cry, he thought. He stood next to her and put his hand on her shoulder. When he did, he noticed she wasn't crying, she was laughing!

He was furious, confused, dumbfounded, and galled all at the same time.

"What … why … Christ!" he said, running his hand through his hair in bewilderment.

She whipped around and said, "That's just how I felt when I walked in here. Now ye ken how it feels!"

Greame just stood there with his mouth open. When he saw she was trying her best not to smirk, he let loose on her. He grabbed her by the shoulders, lifted her from the chair, and with his nose nearly touching hers, realized that she had not changed her mind about him. He pulled back a bit to see her eyes, then she let him in so he could see that she really did love him, despite his handicap.

"It truly doesna bother ye that we can ne'er be as proper husband and wife?" he whispered.

"There are lots o' ways to be husband and wife that dinna involve intercourse, Greame."

The way her eyes twinkled led him to believe she may know more about that than he did. It gave him a thrill to think of all the ways he could please her. As if reading his mind, she lifted her head and kissed him softly on the lips.

"We'll find out together, aye?" she said in a sultry voice.

He nodded and smiled, then asked, "Will ye marry me in Boston, Garnet?"

She smiled and nodded.

16

A Letter From Home

The voyage back to Boston was made in a little under a week, sailing only during the day and taking their time about it. Aside from the storm on the first day, the weather for the duration was warm, dry and sunny. Arriving in the harbour, the city looked very different than when they left on the first of May. The trees all had their leaves now and the grasses were a wonderful shade of gold. Late-blooming wildflowers, such as the deep purple New England Asters, and Queen Anne's Lace, along with Milk Weed and Golden-rod sprinkled the landscape with color. Even the color of the water was a lighter greenish-blue, not like the dark bluish-purple of winter.

Cat couldn't wait to get ashore. She stood in the wind on the stern as Kelvin maneuvered the *Revenge* into an opening on Long Wharfe. Greame came up behind her and asked if she wanted him to accompany her to Rose's.

"No. I'd like to go there by myself first, if that's all right wi' ye," she said.

"Fine, but as fetchin' as ye look, do ye think it wise to go dressed like that?"

Cat looked at him oddly, then glanced down at her attire. Still in her breeks and sark, with moccasins on her feet and her dirk hanging at her thigh, she giggled and ran below decks to change. Prim Bostonians would not take kindly to her being dressed like an In-dian.

When she emerged with her dress on, all of the crew looked at her in appreciation. They had become accustomed to her being dressed like one of them, having forgotten what a stunning woman she was.

"My dear, ye are a sight," Greame said, eyeing her up and down when she resumed her spot next to him.

"I feel rather odd in a dress now. It's so cumbersome, and this corset may well be the death o' me," she said, tugging at the pinching garment at her waist.

The ropes were thrown to the dockmen. They had arrived. The ship came alive with men in the rigging tying down the canvas sails, and men scurrying around the deck making sure the ship was tied down properly. The gangplank was lowered and Cat bounded down it to the dock, waving to Greame and shouting, "Meet me for supper." He waved and nodded, then she nearly ran the entire length of Long Wharfe, glad to be on *terra firma* once again.

When she arrived at 35 Newberry Street, the gardens were well tended and the house looked cared for. She took a deep breath and rapped the brass knocker on the front door a few times. Within seconds, Emily answered, looking no different than when Cat left over three months ago. An uncharacteristic smile brightened Emily's face, and Cat was given a warm hug.

"Och, lass, we hae missed ye terrible," Emily said into Cat's hair.

Cat pulled away and asked, "Rose?"

Emily shook her head somberly. "She passed oon two weeks agoo. Poor soul fought wi' all her heart, but she went peaceful in her sleep."

"What o' Jim and Harry, and Claire?"

"Coome in, we'll talk inside."

Not much had changed in the house. Cat followed Emily to the kitchen where she was met by a very excited Claire.

"Will ye be stayin' wi' us, Garnet?" she asked, after giving Cat a big squeeze.

"I was hopin' to for the winter, but then next spring we'll be goin' back to Maine to stay."

"What's it like up there? Did ye see any Indians? Or bears?" Claire asked.

Before Cat could answer, Harry and Jim walked into the kitchen. At first they didn't realize who it was, thinking this woman was just another caller for condolences for Rose. When Jim actually looked to see who it was, his eyes widened to enormous proportions. He elbowed Harry in the ribs, just to get his attention. Harry followed Jim's stare and Cat was greeted with that same cocky smirk. The two lads embraced Cat with all their might.

"I ken ye're glad to see me," she gasped, "but ye dinna hae to kill me to prove it!"

They released their death grips from her with their apologies.

"Christ, how hae ye both managed to get so strong in three months?"

"We've been workin' on the docks," they said in unison, before turning to each other and laughing.

"How's the teashop?"

"Prosperous," Jim said.

"I'm sure Greame will be glad to hear that."

Just then, Harry and Jim looked around for Greame, questioning his absence with their expressions.

"He's docked on Long Wharfe," shouting the end of her sentence, as they were already out the door running towards the dock.

Cat sat on one of the stools out of the way, and for the rest of the afternoon told tales of Maine and got caught up with the happenings of Boston. She helped with supper, making a celebration feast for their arrival. When Greame walked in with Harry and Jim around seven o'clock, he was greeted with the same lavish hugs as Cat had received.

"Well, I'd forgotten what it was like to be surrounded by women," he said, smiling at the array of savories on the table and the tidiness of everything.

"That's no' sayin' much for ye, Garnet," Jim said, before he realized how it sounded. When a blush crept up his neck and reddened his ears, that was all the reprimand he needed and the entire household laughed.

When nearly all the food was gone and each person sat back with their hands on their full bellies, Greame took his wine glass and stood. All eyes were trained on him in expectation.

"I would like to make an announcement," he said, his deep voice serious. When his eyes rested on Cat, everyone's eyes settled on her. "I want ye all to ken that I hae asked Catrìona to be my wife ..." Before he could say anymore, there was clapping and congratulations given around the table.

Harry, seemingly the only one there with forethought, asked, "What did she say?"

"Thank ye, Harry, as I was about to say, she said yes." He was once again drowned out with congratulations, so he sat down.

"Hae ye set a date?" Emily asked.

"Where will ye have the ceremony?" asked Claire.

"Are we invited?" asked Jim.

Cat stood this time and held up her hand to quiet the mob. "I'll … we'll answer all yer questions one at a time. First, we hae no' set a date, but we will be marrit here in Boston."

"I'd like to hae the ceremony aboard my ship," Greame said, looking up at her.

Cat took her seat and smiled, "That's a wonderful idea," she said, glancing all around the table, "and o' course ye're all invited."

It was nearly midnight when the party broke up. Jim and Harry looked like they were already sleeping when they crawled up the stairs to their room. Emily and Claire retired to their chambers, and Greame and Cat sat on the settee in the best room to say good night. Greame took Cat's hand in his and kissed it.

"Is it really all right wi' ye to be marrit aboard ship?"

To Cat, it really didn't matter much where they got married, but one thing was gnawing at her. She had never heard Greame talk of religion, but that didn't mean he wasn't part of some organized sect and wanted her to become part of it. It was the one thing she wouldn't do, not even for him. She would ask him, but not tonight. She was tired and wanted to sleep in a real bed for a change. Tomorrow would be soon enough.

"Aboard yer ship is a fine place to be marrit, Greame. All o' yer kin can be there, and this household is all the family I hae, so there would be plenty o' room for the festivities."

"When would ye like to do it? Ye'll need to make a dress. How long will that take ye?"

Cat thought for a moment. "What do ye say to the twentieth o' November?"

A broad smile lit up Greame's face, still amazing Cat how much it transformed his features. "The twentieth o' November it is then."

They walked to the door and kissed, then Greame left for his ship. Cat watched him disappear into the cool night, not closing the door until she couldn't see him anymore. Crickets creaked their song out to the night loud enough to be heard when the door was bolted shut. Cat took the lantern and walked up to her room, once again hit by the lavish beauty of it.

She shed her clothes, filled the ewer with water and washed the salt from her skin. A prickly sensation alerted her to the shadow in the corner. She smiled when she smelled the perfume. "Hallò, Rose."

I'm so glad you're back, Garnet. I'm also glad you were not here to see me die. There has been too much of that in your young life. You knew all along it would happen, didn't you?

"Aye, Rose, from our first meetin' at the teashop. Are ye happy where ye are now?"

Oh, my dear, yes. I am free of that sickly, weak body. Here there is no pain, only joy.

"Greame asked me to marry him."

Yes, I know. Put your fears to rest, Garnet, he will be all the man you need. I'll be watching you.

"Good-bye, Rose," she whispered, knowing she was gone. There never seemed to be enough time for all there was to say to those who pass, though she was grateful for the moment with Rose again, however fleeting.

Slipping a clean shift over her head, Cat slid under the bedclothes and fell asleep.

❧

It was after eight when Cat opened her eyes. Smells of sausage and eggs wafted into her room from the kitchen and her stomach growled. Stretching and rubbing the sleep from her eyes, she threw off the bedclothes and got dressed. Today she would pick out the fabric for her wedding dress. Remaining barefoot, she soundlessly padded down the stairs, effectively startling Claire from her dusting. She walked over to the closet that stored the myriad of fabrics that now belonged to her—the charity Rose left to her in the will—and started pulling out bolts of possibilities. Claire watched this curiously until realizing what Cat was up to.

"The dress?" was all she asked, excitement lighting up her face.

Cat glanced at her with a smile from ear to ear and just nodded, tugging at a gorgeous bolt of lace.

Claire set down her duster and helped Cat lift the bolts. Emily walked in to see them both in the closet and stood with her hands on her ample hips to supervise. When she saw the white laces and silks and brocades, she smiled and said, "Yer dress, Garnet?"

Cat and Claire nodded and smiled. Claire passed an armful of choices to Emily, who promptly laid them out on the dining room table, running her fingers over each one to savor the richness of the expensive fabrics.

When all the choices were laid out, Cat surveyed them with a critical eye.

"I sure wish Rose was here to help with this decision," Claire said.

Cat smiled, knowing full well Rose was there guiding her, but kept the fact to herself. She laid her hand on each bolt, silently asking Rose which one was appropriate. The white silk damask was out, as was the linen and cotton. When Cat placed her hand on the ivory-on-ivory striped silk brocade, it tingled. She smiled and lifted the bolt from the table. Now for the lace.

Point de France, Flandre, Mechlin, Valençiennes, Reticella, Point de Venise, Cluny, Bruge, and Argentella. Her fingers brushed each of the finely woven patterns painstakingly created with silk or bobbin threads. There were so many to choose from. She closed her eyes and let Rose guide her. After getting an approval from the other side, she lifted the bolt and laid out a length of the delicate lace over the brocade. The detailed Reticella was a perfect complement to the striped silk.

Suddenly, she got a picture of what the dress would look like in her mind. Rose knew precisely what fit Cat best: a low, sweetheart neckline, a fitted bodice with lace accented with what appeared to be pearls—where she would get those pricey items she did not know—lace sleeves with small strips of the silk brocade running down the arm, and finally, a full, pleated skirt. She studied the design Rose was sending her carefully, revisiting the lace bolts to select a complementing lace for the sleeves, settling on the Point de France.

During the entire time, Emily and Claire watched in amazement, as Cat seemingly knew exactly what to choose. When the final selection was made they looked at each other, and Claire said in an incredulous voice, "It's just wot Mum woulda chose." Emily nodded in agreement.

Cat unfurled the silk brocade and held it up to herself and walked over to the looking glass. "Will ye both help me wi' it? It may be a bit more challengin' than what I'm ready for."

"O' course we'll help ye wi' it," Emily said. "Do ye ken what it will look like?"

Cat nodded, approving of the choice of fabric she saw in the reflection. "I'll sketch it out for ye."

⁊♠

Greame entered his tea shop around dawn. He opened the door to the rich aroma and took a deep breath to capture every nuance. While tea was a rather expensive commodity, most Bostonians had the means to pay for it, no matter how much it cost. It was quite a wealthy town, but unrest whispered through the streets and pubs, according to George. Harry and Jim had brought George to the *Revenge* last night to bring Greame up on the local talk and doings.

"Oh, aye," George started, "local seamen are right fed up wi' it. Seems they're bein' pressed into service to replace deserters o' the King. Word is, there hae already been several riots in the past few years. One o' these days, and it'll be soon, mark me words, they're goin' to rebel again, and when they do, it'll no' be a pretty sight. I've seen the way many o' them handle a cutlass. I fear for the lads, here," nodding his head toward Jim and Harry. "We'd ne'er ken if they were took before they were too far out to sea to help 'em."

Greame listened intently. He knew George might exaggerate a bit, but never strayed too far from the truth. He would have to find the lads another place of work. Cat would not survive it if either of them were taken. He ran a big hand through his hair and let out a deep sigh. Was there no peace anywhere? He scanned the cabin full of his mates—family all of them—and knew they were waiting on his decision. Fight the English or fight the Indians and French. He tried in his head to figure which was the lesser of two evils. He stood and let out a pained snort, then went to his cabin to ponder on it.

⁊♠

"But we can hardly let them stay on the docks," Cat said, looking very concerned. She was twirling her hair, and Greame could see the thoughts darkening her eyes.

Jim and Harry were sitting with Cat and Greame at the kitchen table. They had firsthand knowledge of what being pressed into service meant. It was how they all met, after all, and Jim, uncharacteristically, was the one who spoke up.

"Garnet, we've been real careful. It's not as though the entire dock doesn't notice when the Crown sails in."

"We watch out for each other, Cat," Harry said in all seriousness.

Cat looked at him and realized how much he never wanted to relive that experience.

"Well, there has to be some kind o' safety measure we can take to be sure the two of ye are where ye're suppose to be at all times, but damned if I can figure what it would be. If the Crown is bold enough to take grown men, why wouldna two lads be more of a temptation?" Greame said.

"What if we check in at the teashop for luncheon every day?" Jim suggested.

"That's an excellent idea," Greame said.

"And just before ye come home, check in again," Cat said.

"Then we can work for the winter?" Harry asked.

Cat and Greame looked at each other and shrugged, finding no reason for them not to if they followed the precautions.

"One more thing," Greame said. "If the English do sail in, I want the two o' ye to stay together and get to the teashop. Safety in numbers, aye?"

Harry and Jim agreed in unison.

Emily dusted her way through the first floor, and admired Cat's handiwork that was nearly complete on the dress form. Just then, a knock on the front door summoned her and she walked over to answer it.

Mr. Phillips handed Emily a letter addressed to Catrìona Robertson, care of Rose Carlyle, Boston, Massachusetts. The handwriting was bold and flourished, as though written by a poet. It was made of a heavy parchment with a seemingly royal seal on the back. The return address was from Scotland. Emily wondered more than ever where Cat came from and who she knew in her homeland. With regret that Cat was down at the teashop with Greame, she left it on the kitchen table, propped up by the candlestick.

"So who is it from?" Emily asked as nonchalantly as possible when she handed Cat the letter. It was the longest two hours of her life, waiting for Cat to return.

Cat smiled when she saw the scrolling address, knowing immediately who it was from. "My Chief, Alexander Robertson," she replied, breaking the wax seal with the Clan Donnachaidh crest on the back.

Emily figured correctly, then. It was from royalty; well, as close to royalty as one could get in Scotland, since there was no ruler of the country, and she didn't think the King of England counted.

Cat went into the sunlit best room and sat on the settee, effectively letting Emily know that she wanted her privacy. Emily did her best to make busy projects within eyeshot so that she'd know just when Cat finished reading.

16 June 1747
My Dearest Catrìona,

I was deeply saddened by the news of your Father's death. I truly believed he would have survived the Journey, since he knew you would be following him. Gregor has been brooding over Angus' death even more. He feels responsible somehow. Please take a moment to write to him and Release him from this Burden.

I am not well, though I feared to tell this to you. The last thing you need is more loss in your Life. You've had far too much for one so young. But, alas, I felt you should know. The Country is still Tortured by the Bastard English. They think that by this harsh treatment we will Succumb to their new Laws, effectively banning us from being Scottish! They still do not know what we are made of, do they? They forget that we have been through this many times, and many times we have Risen again, like the Phoenix from the Flames. But, enough of that, for I could rant Forever on the subject.

And he did, for another six pages. Cat felt like he was sitting right beside her hearing his voice as he trounced the English for all he was worth. She was saddened when he told her that they burned down his Hermitage, knowing how much he loved that place. He even wrote a lengthy poem about watching the Hanoverians setting fire to it, as he watched in hiding atop Mount Alexander. The last of the poem brought back the horrors of what she had witnessed at Culloden.

And now the hellish Bands advance,
Bent to destroy whate'ver they meet;
Lo! While the furious Horsemen prance,
Poor peasants gasp beneath their feet;
Yet cruelty sits smiling on their Cheeks,
To hear the Orphans' Cries and Widows' Shrieks.

O Heav'ns! Let me resolve as far
If ever Ship so far could roll.
To freeze beneath the northern Star,
Or perish at the other Pole,
Ere I behold such an unnat'ral War,
Christians commit what Pagans would abhor.

What then remains, but that I go,
As Argentinus kindly bid,
Since there's a Fate that rules below
From whom there's nothing can be hid?
That Fate can bear me Witness of my heart,
How I have lov'd this Land, how loath I am to Part.

Retract not, O my Soul! I must
Perform what Destiny ordains;
In Providence I put my Trust,
Adieu to Woods, to Hills, to Plains.
Thou envy of the turbulently Great!
Farewell my sweet, my innocent Retreat!

She got to the last page and at the end, in typical Alexander style, he shocked her with a candid message.

> *I hope with all of my heart that you have started a new life in America, for there is truly nothing here to come back to. Meet a man, fall in love, find happiness, Catrìona, for you are deserving of it.*
> *Yours Forever,*
> *Alexander Robertson*
> *13th Donnachaidh Chief*

Cat folded the parchment and put it in her pocket. She wasn't sure what to make of the letter. What had Alexander really wanted to say? That he was ill and wanted her to go to him? That he was going to start another rebellion and would end his life trying to get back at the English?

Emily watched Cat thoughtfully reflect on what she had just read. The letter didn't seem like good news, and she discreetly went about her business in the kitchen.

Liberty and Justice For All

16 November 1747

A hint of yellow in the morning sky greeted Harry and Jim when they started unloading fish for the local market. By late morning, Mr. Phillips, seeing the lads heading to the teashop for their daily check-in before luncheon, stopped them.

"Here, lads," he shouted, and waited for them to reach his store. "Take this to Miss Emily with my affection." He handed them an oilcloth package containing a fine twelve-pound haddock.

Harry smirked and elbowed Jim in the ribs when he saw Jim's neck turning red.

"Aye, Mr. Phillips," Harry said, "we'll tell her just that," then sauntered off to the teashop with Jim following close behind.

"What did he mean by that, Harry?"

Harry sent a *don't-you-know-anything* look to Jim as they reached the door to the teashop.

"It means Mr. Phillips is smitten with our Emily, ya bonehead."

George heard this when the lads walked in and couldn't help but smile. He wasn't sure exactly how old the two were, but Harry did seem to think he understood women completely.

"So what's this I hear about Emily?" he teased, winking at Robbie who came out of the back room.

"Harry says Mr. Phillips is *smitten* with her." Making it sound like an infectious disease.

George could tell Jim had no idea what that meant, and remained stone-faced while he explained it.

Jim cuffed Harry on the side of his head. "That's not a bad thing; ta be smitten," he told Harry, over the laughter of George and Robbie.

"Ye'd better bring that wee fishy up to our dear Emily, then. She'll be a while filletin' that thing," Robbie said, secretly hoping Emily would have them all up for supper to help eat it.

Commodore Charles Knowles of the *HMS Lark,* commander of the royal squadron that fought the French at Louisbourg not a month ago, entered Boston Harbour that afternoon. He was a rugged looking man with a sharp, hooked nose and small, dark blue eyes that pierced whatever they looked at. His powdered wig sat back on his head to expose a large, broad forehead, and his wiry frame made him look always ready for a fight.

Charles needed supplies, then his orders were to return to England before winter set in. Morale was low amongst his men and the daily floggings weren't scaring them anymore. Disaster was imminent when sailors lost respect for their captain. He reasoned that his renowned temper (a view of any of his men's backs would attest), would make his men stick it out until they reached their homeland once again. Besides, it was unfathomable to think why any one of them would want to stay in such an uncivilized place.

He was wrong.

Overnight, he lost nearly fifty seamen to this new land, claiming they wanted a better life. At least that's what several of their mates uttered under the lash before blacking out. Just before dawn, he set out to capture these deserters by ordering a sweep of the waterfront. Failing to find the wretches, his men were to impress *other* warm bodies into service on the *Lark*.

17 November 1747

Jim saw them first. He had been wrestling with a sack of tea that weighed more than he did, and at the sight of the Royal Navy pounding their way down the wharf, he let the sack win. Jim looked around frantically for Harry. He was nowhere. Harry must have gone back aboard for another sack.

Closer now; he could see their faces. They were searching for something, or someone. Jim's only conclusion was to get aboard with Harry. They'd take their chances together.

He ran up the gangplank and headed for the hold. Harry was just emerging with another enormous sack and Jim nearly plowed him over.

"Bloody hell, Jimmy-boy, what's got ya so spooked?" he asked when he saw Jim's enormous eyes.

"Get back in the hold!" he hissed, pushing Harry in. "It's the Royal Navy and they're on the prowl. We've got ta get ta the teashop."

Harry took a peek to judge their distance. "Can't. They're too close."

"But, Greame said—"

"Greame will understand that things don't always go accordin' ta plans," Harry said, putting his hand on Jim's shoulder, pulling him further into the ship. "We're gonna have ta take our chances on this tub. Find someplace ta hide."

The heavy footfalls stomped up the gangplank.

≈

Robbie looked at his watch fob for the eighth time. "I dinna care for them bein' so late."

George was looking a bit worried as well. "John, grab yer pistol, aye? We're goin' for a stroll."

The teashop was just far enough from the docks to not know what was happening right away. As George and John got closer to the waterfront though, it became apparent they weren't the only ones who were looking for tardy family members. Boston rose to the occasion. By the hundreds, burly, hardened dockmen—black and white—amassed on the harbour protesting what they considered illegal impressment of sailors for service in the Royal Navy. Waterfront Bostonians had rioted against pressing several times since 1741, but this time it was going to end, once and for all.

≈

At half twelve, Greame was overseeing a shipment of tea at Charles' Wharfe on the northeast side of Boston Harbour when the commotion on Long Wharfe rose so loud as to silence the din around him.

"What do ye suppose that's all about?" he asked no one in particular. By the dozens, the men all around him were going to see for themselves. He finished his paperwork and gave directions for delivery to his shop, then he followed the masses.

Harry and Jim had no sooner secured the hatch over their heads when the crew began to shout and curse at the unwelcome visitors.

"Where are they?" demanded the lieutenant, scanning the dark confines.

"Who have ya come here for?" growled Captain Seth Bigelow, effectively blocking the lieutenant from boarding much further.

"The two young lads that just ran in here."

"The only lads aboard this ship are mine. What business have ya with 'em?" the captain said.

With the speed of a seasoned officer, a pistol appeared and was swung across the captain's face, sending him to the deck. "Search the ship. Find them!" shouted the lieutenant.

Scurrying footfalls were above them. The sacks were heavy and packed tightly. Harry managed to lift one enough for Jim to slide under, then he lifted another close to Jim's and edged his slender body under it.

"Are ya all right, Jimmy-boy?" Harry's voice was muffled under the heavy sack.

"I think so. I won't let them take ya, Harry."

Harry just chuckled. "You'll have little ta say 'bout it, Jimmy."

Suddenly, the cabin filled with light. The hatch had been opened. One of the English started down the ladder, followed by two more. They tossed the sacks of tea around as though they weighed nothing. Jim found Harry's arm and squeezed it tight. It was only a matter of time before they were found.

Jim felt the sack next to his leg lift away and he breathed in sharply.

Another set of footfalls started down the ladder.

At the same time, the sacks covering Harry and Jim were tossed away, exposing them to four seasoned royals bent on taking them. That didn't stop Harry and Jim from giving the sailors a handful of fury, though. As if sensing Jim would give them the least amount of trouble, two of the sailors grabbed Jim's arms and hoisted him up. Once in the standing position, the sailors thought the lad was too afraid to put up any resistance and loosened their hold on him while they went after Harry. It was just the moment Jim was waiting for. He broke free of the sailors' hold and lunged for the only weapon he could find, a broom. He swung the handle around and knocked one of the sailors square in the face, breaking his hawk-like nose. Harry was up on his own and laughing that devious laugh, making Jim smile in spite of the dire circumstances. Jim caught his second attacker hard across the thigh, sending him to the floor.

The lieutenant had had enough. Pulling his pistol that had already proved to render the captain incapacitated, he smacked it hard over Harry's head, dropping the lad where he stood. He then cocked it and aimed it directly at Jim's head, freezing him with the broom in mid-air.

Harry was knocked unconscious and bleeding from his ear. He was tossed over the shoulder of one of the royals and Jim was hauled out past a bloody Captain Seth. They were taken aboard the *Lark* and tossed into the hold. Prisoners once again.

Cat started for the teashop after one o'clock when Harry and Jim didn't show up for their luncheon. The closer she got to the waterfront, the more anxious she became. There seemed to be an extraordinary amount of people out this afternoon. There was also an energy so volatile in the air that a single match could have sparked an inferno.

Before she got to the shop, she saw Greame coming so she continued on to meet him.

"What's goin' on?" she asked.

"I dinna ken, but I dinna care for the feelin' in the air."

"Harry and Jim didna make it home for luncheon," she said.

Greame caught a glimpse of fear in her eyes. "Perhaps they're at the shop."

When they opened the door to the Worldwide Tea Emporium, Robbie looked up expectantly, hoping it was the lads. Greame saw the look on his face and knew immediately something was terribly wrong.

❧

By evening, thousands of enraged Bostonians converged on the waterfront. It seemed Governor William Shirley was doing nothing to stop it, so matters were taken into the hands of the angry mob. They forced their way onto the *Lark* and seized officers as hostages. Nothing could be done against so many if they wanted to live. Besides, many of the sailors were once victims of the very act the colonials were rebelling against, and therefore, would do little to aid the officers.

The next day brought no resolution and the people went even further in their efforts against the King. They seized a royal barge and dragged it through the streets with such ease, one would have thought the streets had flooded. First they brought it to the governor's mansion and then to the Commons, where it went up in a roaring fire, effectively sparking even more turmoil.

Governor Shirley, terrified by this point, called out the militia, but only the officers saw fit to come. The rest of the militiamen were part of the furious throng. When a mob surrounded Governor Shirley's mansion on suspicion that some of the royal officers had taken refuge there, he abandoned his mansion and retreated to safer quarters at Castle William in Boston Harbour.

❧

"God-damned English," Robbie kept spouting.

"How are we goin' to get the lads off that ship?" John asked Greame.

Cat had been pacing the small teashop for most of the day; hair twirling at alarming rates. Now, as darkness settled in once again without resolution, she grew moodier. Greame felt her turmoil and knew she'd boil over shortly if she couldn't do something. But there was nothing they could do through violence. That might only succeed in getting the lads killed. This would have to be done another way.

"Cat, would you come with me, please?" Greame asked.

Cat stood there for a minute, unsure if he had really spoken to her.

"Cat ... ?"

She turned at the sound of Greame's voice and saw his out-stretched hand beckoning to her. She took it and allowed herself to be brought outside.

"I think we need to convince some of the businessmen to speak to the General Court," he began. Still seeing that she was off somewhere else, he took her by the shoulders and squeezed them hard.

"Ouch! Greame, that hurts. What are ye tryin' to do?"

"I'm tryin' to talk to ye about gettin' the court involved. There has to be a compromise without violence. My only concern is for Harry and Jim, now will ye join me?" He said in a gravely voice tight with restraint.

She looked at him with eyes so full of despair and sadness, he felt his heart would break.

"I keep gettin' a terrible feelin' we're not goin' to be the same after this, Greame," she whispered.

His head cocked a little to one side, trying to get inside her mind. "Can ye tell me what ye see, because I canna seem to get anythin' to come to me."

"Jim. He's verra frightened, but no' for himself. For Harry," was all she could tell him.

"Is he hurt?"

Cat looked at him again and shrugged. "That's what I dinna see. I canna find Harry anywhere. 'Tis like he's no' with us anymore."

Greame frowned deeply. "Do ye mean he's … dead?"

Cat's head went slowly up and down, and tears welled in her thistle-colored eyes.

"Oh, Christ."

19 November 1747

Charles Knowles should have expected trouble. He knew full well how the laboring classes despised anything to do with authority, but he was going to serve the King to the extreme, if needed. On the morning of the third day of riots, the Commodore announced that he would bombard Boston from his warships. It did little to frighten the enraged seamen, considering the only damage that would occur would be to the property of the wealthy, not the rioters.

Finally, later that day, the General Court approved resolutions supporting the governor, acknowledging Governor Shirley's authority over military affairs in the province. With that, the militia assured the governor of its protection. The Court and Governor Shirley negotiated to trade the captured royal officers for the release of the impressed seamen.

"It was an accident," Jim told Greame in a steady voice when the crew of the *Revenge* went aboard the *HMS Lark* to fetch their young mates. Jim was sitting in a dark corner of the hold with Harry's head in his lap. Harry never regained consciousness. Jim never left Harry's side while Robbie and John lifted him from the hold. Jim's hand stayed on his friend's chest, unwilling to let him go.

Cat waited at the end of the gangplank, fearing the worst. When she saw that Harry was being carried off the ship, she ran up to meet them to see if there was anything she could do to aid him. A part of her refused to believe he was really gone. When she reached him and saw the pallor of his skin, she knew there was nothing she could do. Once again, the *Sassenaich* had taken a loved one from her. How many more would they take? Would Greame be next? Could she live through it?

She didn't think so.

Change of Plans

20 November, 1747

There was supposed to be a wedding today. No one would come, not even the bride and groom. Today was for death and it was a perfect day for it. The sky was the color of lead. Snow was imminent. The feeling of the entire city was not of joy, but revolution. Bostonians thought they had a foothold on independence. They thought that with the riots, and the subsequent ousting of the *HMS Lark* and her royal crew, they could repeat that whenever the Crown decided to wield its unwanted power from across the sea.

At 35 Newberry Street, the day was even worse. Cat had gone into a catatonic state, staring out her bedroom window, unaware of her surroundings. Her mind went into a defensive mode. It shut itself down. There would be no more pain, no more sorrow. It couldn't handle anything else that caused distress. Survival was overrated. Death would be welcome now.

Emily and Claire were beside themselves. Harry had been like the devil himself, but they loved him like a son. He had wound his way into their hearts with his cockeyed smiles and quick wit. What would Jim do without him?

Jim had made several attempts to console Catrìona, to no avail. He sat in the opposite chair waiting for her return. He wanted to tell her that it would be all right, that she still had him, and he would never leave her. He watched her until the sun left the room, then he got up and lit a candle and watched her until his eyes got too heavy to watch anymore. He fell asleep at Cat's feet, fearing that if he left her, she would never come back.

Greame sat in his chambers aboard his ship. He knew Cat needed time, and lots of it, if she was ever to return to normal. His only thoughts were for her, but when he broke his promise and entered her fragile mind without her consent, what he found was her return to the only time she'd been truly happy; she was back in Scotland, back to when she was just a bairn, too young to know about the world. Back to safety.

He'd cried hard; for her, for Harry, for Jim, for never being there to really change any outcome for the better. He knew he was feeling much of her pain, and it was a pain stronger than anything he had ever experienced. He wasn't sure how she could stand it. He wasn't sure if she could.

Greame checked on Cat every day for over two weeks. There wasn't even the most minute of changes. Jim was always with her, helping her drink and eat, which she did as though she were a babe. She could be guided around, but she never made the attempt to get up and around on her own. She needed something to bring her back. He feared that the longer she stayed inside herself, the less likely she would ever leave.

He wished for some kind of potion to bring her back, but he couldn't very well ask around town for a healer. Or could he? That's exactly what he needed … a healer, and he knew just where to find one.

"But the weather, Greame. It's too late to set off now," George stated, trying to talk some sense into his captain. But he already knew he was talking to deaf ears. Greame had made up his mind.

"Be sure we hae enough supplies to last a month or two, just in case the weather," he said, looking directly at George, "does turn bad and we hae to put in somewhere to wait it out."

Greame stood up and stretched in his cabin, patting Kelvin on the back before leaving to tell Catrìona of his plans. Whether or not she would hear him didn't make any difference. He already felt better just setting *something* into motion. He couldn't just sit idly by and do nothing.

"We'll leave on the morning tide," he announced to his crew, and left the ship.

By the time he reached the house, he felt ten times better. When he entered, he asked Claire if she would leave the door open for a few minutes. The air in the house felt like death. A little circulation would cure that.

Taking two steps at a time to reach the second floor, he walked into Cat's room to find Jim sleeping in the chair beside the window. The sunlight streamed over his dark curls. Cat was lying on the bed with her hair freshly washed. Thank God for Emily and Claire for taking such good care of her.

He sat down on the edge of the bed and absently brushed a few strands of Cat's deep auburn hair from her face, tucking it behind her ear. She smiled a little, but never woke. Greame decided to tell her of his plans anyway. He knew somehow she would hear him.

"We'll be leavin' in the mornin', my love. When we see Far Eyes, he'll ken what to do for ye. Ye canna stay in there fore'er," he whispered, tapping her on the head and kissing her cheek.

He stayed until Jim woke up when the sun went down.

"How are ye, man?" he asked Jim.

Jim just shook his head. Catrìona was bringing him further and further down with her.

"Pack ye're warmest clothes, Jim, and meet me at the *Revenge* before the tide in the morn. We're goin' to Maine."

Jim didn't argue, he just nodded and went downstairs.

The morning dawned bright, but frigid. The *Revenge* set sail, and despite all that had happened in the last month, all of it disappeared when they had the freedom of the sea under them. For the most part they would take much the same route as they did when they first went to Maine. The only difference would be when they got to the Panawanskek River; they would sail up it, past Cape Rozier. Far Eyes had told Greame that the Penobscot people went inland for the winter to a place they called Pasadunkec, which meant, above the gravel bar. Greame planned to take his ship up river as far as he could, then walk to the Penobscots' winter camp.

Cat rested quietly in the surgeon's cabin. Jim would be her companion for the trip, making sure she had whatever she needed. Greame's only thoughts were to get to Far Eyes as quickly as he could. He made his own blood sacrifice to the sea before they left, asking;

I see the moon and the moon sees me,
Lady, bless the sailors on the sea.

In a way, Greame was happy to be leaving Boston. He had made up his mind that taking his chances with the Penobscot was better than living with the English. He was sure Cat felt the same way. For the past few weeks, whenever he went into her mind, she was always with her brother, Lachlan. Perhaps there was some way of him helping his sister out of this state she was in.

As the day went by, the weather held perfectly. His heart seemed to get lighter the further from land he got. The air was cold, but the sun still had a bit of warmth to it. By nightfall, the westerly breezes were still favourable for sailing, so they kept going. Somewhere in the middle of the night, the wind direction changed and came out of the north at a good clip. He spent the next day tacking back and forth, not making very good time.

Kelvin relieved him every six hours so he could sleep. On the third day, a wall of clouds chased them from the south. The weather got warmer and moisture was fragrant on the wind. It would be snow, and he would take no chances with his precious cargo, no matter how close they were to their destination. Kelvin was at the helm and deftly made for Pentagöet and safe harbour.

By dusk, the entire crew of the *Revenge* was out of the weather in a small church in the ruins of an old fort. The wind whistled through the windows and doors, giving the impression that spirits were speaking.

Greame and Cat huddled themselves into a corner, but Cat didn't seem to notice her surroundings.

"Are ye well, lass?" he asked.

Cat turned to face him and a slight smile played on her lips, but then it was gone.

Greame held her close, as though to let her, or maybe it was letting himself know that they were safe. "Ye'll be well soon," he whispered into her hair.

Kelvin lit a few of the oil lamps, and the rest of the men made themselves comfortable on the floor and benches to get some sleep.

A few hours later, the sleet pelted the windows and the wind grew even fiercer, if that was possible. The wild sea, which was a few hundred feet from them, crashed with such ferocity onto the shore, it sounded like thunder.

"Christ, I'm glad we're no' on the ship tonight," Kelvin whispered, mostly to himself.

Greame heard him, though, and silently agreed. He knew it took a lot to rattle his seaworthy uncle, and this storm would prove to be one that stories are written about.

When daylight crept into the stained-glass windows of the church, it was nearly obliterated by the snow that stuck thickly to the lead. The storm raged on for three days. By the time it squeezed out its last snowflake, there was over three feet of heavy, wet snow covering what would have been easy ground to the Penobscots' winter camp. Greame wondered how they fared in storms of this magnitude. How could they possibly keep their wigwams up in snow this heavy? He would find out soon enough.

Return to the Past

Cat stared at the stained-glass window. She wondered where she was. She didn't remember leaving *Slios Mín*. Was she losing her mind? Where was Lachlan? She had just been speaking with him, now he was nowhere to be found. Turning her head to look at Greame, she wanted to ask him, but when she opened her mouth to speak nothing came out. Cat tried again, but still there was silence. This is ridiculous, she thought, what is wrong with me?

Wriggling out of Greame's arms, she stood up and brushed the dirt from her woolen cloak. It was very cold away from his side, but she just had to know where she was. She walked to the window and saw the snow sticking to the leaded glass. A frigid wind whistled through a small crack where the lead had pulled away from the glass, and blew in her face. She backed away slightly, then covered the opening with the edge of her cloak before going for another look. A clear glass piece enabled her to see outside. It couldn't be. Was that really Cape Rozier across that windswept channel? This made even less sense. She began twirling her hair then looked over her shoulder at Greame. He seemed quite intent on her for some reason.

She was quite hungry. It must be time to start luncheon. Lachlan should be back any time now. But how could Lachlan be here at Cape Rozier? He was dead.

☙

Greame watched her get up and go to the window. When she started twirling her hair, he thought for a moment she was back to herself again. She looked right at him, as though to ask him something, but remained mute. Her face was animate again for a few moments, but then the blank stare reclaimed it. She dropped her lock of hair and just stood there. Greame got up and walked her back to their corner.

"What happened to ye, lass? I ken ye were back wi' us for a moment. What sent ye back?" he asked, fingering the hair around her face.

Greame put his hand on her head and closed his eyes. He saw that she was back at *Slios Mín*. She was alone crying at the kitchen table. He felt her distress over a death, but not Harry's. She was reliving the trauma of her brothers' deaths. He watched as four men ran shoulder to shoulder in a blaze of musket fire, screaming their war cry, waving their swords and pistols. One of them was hit in the chest and fell to the ground dead, but the other three continued on. Then, two more were hit, one of them, Lachlan; a hole piercing his forehead. Then everything went black.

Greame opened his eyes and looked at Cat. She was sleeping, but tears were running down her cheeks. Once again, he wondered how she remained so strong after what she had been through. He held her close, rocking her like a babe, as much to comfort himself as her. She knew where it was safe, but now even that place was becoming too much to bear.

Janet was safe. Cat's best friend from childhood, who always wanted to live an adventurous life, but nothing ever happened to her. Cat had to go back further to remain safe from death. Back before the Rising; before talk of rebellion. Back to when the only thing she had to concern herself with was when could she play with the lambs. Janet would spend the night sometimes, and after the chores they would walk up to the summer shieling, picking wildflowers and heather, then sit amongst the broom until the lambs' curiosity got the better of them and they would skittishly approach. Cat and Janet would each grab one of the inquisitive critters and cuddle them for hours. This brought a smile to Cat's face. This was safe.

When Cat was very little, her Mam would rock her like she was being rocked now. Soft humming would lull her to sleep, only to wake up hours later wrapped in a blanket beside the hearth.

è&

By the fourth day, the wind had subsided enough for Greame and the crew to continue on their journey. He bundled Cat up and led her to the long boat, sitting her down with Jim holding her, then rowed to the *Revenge.* Once aboard, the crew swept off the snow and unfurled the sails, then headed northward up the Panawanskek River. The tide was flowing, so it would carry them right up it with or without much wind. From what Geoffrey Hay was saying, they should be able to reach Pasadunkec by dusk tomorrow. Geoffrey's natural ability to pick up on languages came in very handy when one of the Penobscot women, Willow Moon, whom he took a fancy to, explained the route.

"The river looks deep enough, why canna we sail further up?" asked Hector, as they were all taking their supper in the mess.

"Seems there are falls near an island … uh, Panawauske, is what they call it," replied Geoffrey. "Ye canna go further than that by ship unless ye got around the falls. It must be walked."

"We'll walk in the mornin' then," Greame said. "Jim, ye and Cat will walk behind so the snow will be packed down enough to no' hae to wade through. Geoffrey, ye'll lead us. Kelvin, pick a few men to stay on wi' ye. I dinna want to leave the *Revenge* unattended, since I dinna ken how long we'll be."

Greame looked over at Cat, eating happily from the spoon Jim was feeding her with. He wondered silently if she would really be able to come out of her trauma. As if reading his mind, Kelvin got up from his chair and laid a hand on Greame's shoulder, patting it a couple of times before heading off to his cabin. Greame accepted the show of support with a slight nod.

Later, Greame and Jim guided Cat to the surgeon's cabin. Jim usually slept in a hammock in the same cabin, just to keep an eye out for her. Greame wasn't far away if Jim hollered for anything, but tonight, Greame wanted to be with her and relinquished his quarters to Jim.

Cat lay bundled in her bedclothes so that only her nose to the top of her head showed. Greame sat on the edge of the bunk and stroked her hair, smoothing it away from her face. Cat looked up and smiled at him like a child would smile at a parent doing the same thing. She obviously knew who he was, but there was nothing else in her eyes. None of the passion he used to see. It bothered him greatly. What would he do if she never came back to him? Could he bring himself to take her back to Boston and let Emily and Claire tend to her for the rest of her days? Then what would he do? Go back to Scotland—without her? He hoped to get some answers to-morrow.

❧

The small group began their trek just after dawn. The weather was fine; no wind and sunny. The tide was flowing and even this far inland, its presence was felt.

Hector wondered out loud by asking, "I wonder how far the tide goes up this river?"

Geoffrey said, "Only as far as the falls."

By the time Cat and Jim walked on the snow trodden by the rest of the men, it was a smooth path. They walked for about eight hours before Geoffrey spotted smoke in the distant woods. Greame would have his answers soon enough.

❧

No one was more surprised to see them than Far Eyes when the village hunting dogs alerted him to the approaching group.

"I feel old friends get near," he said to Greame, meeting them on snowshoes fashioned from ash and strips of hide, "I thought it just in my heart," patting his fur-covered chest.

Greame smiled and shook Far Eyes' hand. Cat stood beside Greame and said nothing, seemingly more interested in the village than Far Eyes.

This captured Far Eyes' attention. He watched her for a minute, noting her child-like behavior. He looked at Greame for an explanation.

"I dinna ken if I should tell ye, or let ye see for yerself," Greame said, tapping his thick finger on his forehead.

"We do this in my wigwam," Far Eyes said. "More comfort there, and food."

"We all could do wi' some food, I reckon," Greame said. The small group needed no other invitation. They reunited with some of their friends and disappeared into the wigwams throughout the village. Only Jim stayed with Greame, having never seen an Indian before. He tried to maintain a respectful eye, but every so often was caught staring at Far Eyes. When Far Eyes winked at him, the ice was broken and the Indian became human.

"What your name?" Far Eyes asked.

"Jim."

"Your whole name?"

"James Thatcher, sir."

"James Thatcher, why you here?"

Jim looked at Greame for an answer. Greame smiled and said, "Well, answer the man."

Facing Far Eyes, Jim said, "I'm here for my dear friend, Catrìona. She saved my life, I expect."

"Good reason to be here then," Far Eyes said.

Jim just nodded. Then asked, "Can ya save her life?"

Far Eyes took a moment to stare at Jim this time. He saw deep sadness, but he also saw a great strength behind those blue eyes. Far Eyes then turned his attention to Catrìona. She was still silent, oblivious to any mental or physical interactions going on around her. A deep line formed between his eyes. He had seen this before, but only in people with severe life-altering events too dreadful to bear. He sent Greame a piercing look. Greame raised an eyebrow, his only show of explanation.

"You said she not bear more death. You right."

"Can she be brought back?"

Far Eyes closed his eyes and went in for a quick look. As soon as he entered Cat's mind, a man greeted him. He was her protector, even from the other side. Far Eyes knew this was an ally he could work with, but it would require a full ceremony.

"We eat, then sleep. Tomorrow, we prepare to chase away spirits." That was the end of the subject. They ate and talked amicably between themselves, with Cat never saying a word. When it was time to sleep, Far Eyes suggested they all spend the night in his wigwam. Greame knew how unusual this was, for, like Seers, Shamans also were meant to be alone. The energies of other people disturbed them. When Greame voiced this, Far Eyes told him that this protector might show him some secrets in his sleep. Greame gave him a little background on the man.

"His name was Lachlan. He was Garnet's brother and a few years older than she. He and Garnet shared a special closeness, even bein' able to read each other's minds, much like what we do. What we *used* to do," Greame corrected.

"How long he gone?"

"He died in the Risin', so that would be o'er a year now."

Far Eyes nodded, then crawled under the heavy fur and fell asleep. Greame saw that Cat was already tucked in, compliments of Jim, and he urged Jim to do the same. By the glow of the fire in the center of the large wigwam, Greame stayed awake for a while longer. It was an odd thing to watch people sleep. Facial expressions were softened and breathing became deep and rhythmic. It was so hypnotic that Greame's eyes grew heavy and he began to doze off. His head bobbed a few times, then he opened his eyes. What he saw in front of him brought him full awake, his heart racing as though he had just run a long distance.

There was a *ceilidh* at *Slios Mín.* Most of her father's tenants were there, as well as a rare visit by Alexander. The Duncansons had brought the pipes. Iain, Lachlan and Andrew Murray were on the *bòdhrain* and Mòrag was playing a tin whistle. Music filled the air, food was piled high on the tables, and everyone was smiling and laughing as couples did reels and jigs. Cat and Janet sat in the loft of the barn with their legs dangling over the edge, keeping time with the beat of the music. Well into the night they carried on, until, family by family, the crowd began to dwindle. Somewhere during the night, Andrew Murray climbed up into the loft and carried Janet down, fast asleep. Next up was Angus to get Cat, who was still awake, though groggy. She remembered it as if it had happened only yesterday. Her Da's warmth and strength held her tightly as they descended the ladder. She could feel him now; smell the wool of his plaid as he wrapped it around her. Cat clung to him, burying her face in his long, black hair as he carried her into the house and up the stairs to deposit her in her bed. He gently picked a few pieces of straw from her deep auburn waves, kissed her forehead, and closed the door behind him, just before she fell asleep.

Cat wanted to remain in that place forever. She could relive that day over and over again in a perpetual circle. Nothing could hurt her there. Nothing could break that blissful state. Nothing until Lachlan woke her the next morning with a shake and an order to get out of bed to help Mam with the chores. She could feel him now, uncaring of her slumber, just shaking and jarring her shoulder.

Cat opened her eyes to find him standing over her with a concerned look on his face. He was older than she remembered, and this was not her room.

"Ye canna stay in there forever, lass," he told her.

"Lachlan?" she whispered, sitting up under the furs. She tried very hard to get her bearings. As she looked around at the beasts on the birch bark walls, she realized that she was in Far Eyes' wigwam.

"Oh, aye, it's me. What are ye doin' to yerself? Why are ye hidin' in yer heid?" he asked, squatting down beside her.

Cat looked around the shadowed birch bark hut at the sleeping forms. Then her eyes rested on Greame who was watching her every move. He made no attempt to speak to her. His face revealed nothing of what he was thinking. She wondered for a moment what he would do if she got up and kissed him. The thought made her smile, but he remained stone-faced. Was he angry with her for something? She had no recollection of an argument with him. Then again, she had no recollection of having any interactions with him at all. That was strange, she thought.

"Lachlan, what's goin' on? Why canna I remember anythin'?"

"That's what I want to ken. Ye're a stronger lass than this, Catrìona. Why all of a sudden can ye no' be that lass who crossed the sea to save our Da; to brave all odds and send the fallen at Culloden to the other side; to be the fierce, independent, fiery and courageous woman ye've been named for?" He cocked his head to the side. "Hae ye lost yer powers?"

Cat sat there for a moment to think about what her brother was describing. She remembered those things. Remembered never being afraid because she had the Sight. The power to know what would happen to whom, and when it would occur.

She looked up at Lachlan and said, "I feel like I'm in a black room. There are no windows, no doors, no light. I dinna ken which way is up or down. I hae no direction, no will, no … nothin'."

"Hae ye given up then?" he asked quietly, stroking the fur that covered her.

A single tear fell from her lashes and she shrugged.

"What about him?"

"Who?" she asked.

"That man o'er there watchin' ye. Dinna ye love him?"

Cat once again looked at Greame. "He will understand."

Lachlan looked over his shoulder at Greame; looked hard at him, probing his mind. Then he looked back at Cat and said, "No, Cat, he doesna understand. If ye would look at him—inside—ye'd ken he misses ye terrible. He brought ye here to try and get ye to stop livin' in yer heid. Why else would he hae risked his ship, his life, and the lives o' his crew to get ye here? Remember when this happened before?"

Cat frowned. "When?"

"When ye saw yer fellow clansmen bein' tossed into the flames at Culloden."

Cat winced at the memory, as though it hurt her physically to remember it. "Oh Christ, Lachlan." She covered her face and wept. Wept for all the things she couldn't change. Wept for the abyss she had fallen into and wasn't sure she wanted to come out of.

Lachlan rubbed her back as she cried herself out. When he saw Greame make an attempt to come over and console Catrìona, he shook his head at him, telepathically telling him that she wasn't ready yet. He was amazed that Greame could see and understand so clearly. It must have been very hard to be halted by a ghost. Lachlan chuckled to himself. He wondered if he would have remained out of this *conversation* if roles were reversed.

Cat lay down after she'd finished crying. She fell into an exhausted sleep, retreating to the blissful dream of the safe time, fully realizing that Lachlan was still there, guarding to make sure she didn't go back too deep.

≥♣

Greame saw the whole thing. He knew he wasn't dreaming, but that would have been easier to explain. He wondered if Far Eyes had witnessed the conversation between Cat and her brother. He glanced over to see if Far Eyes was awake. The steady up and down of the furs indicated that he was sleeping like a babe. Greame wondered if the ceremony would make a difference or not in what Far Eyes saw. "I guess we'll find out in the mornin'." he said to himself, then slid under the furs and fell asleep.

It was called a sweat lodge. A dome-shaped lodge without windows, about ten feet in diameter and four feet tall. For the entire morning, rocks had been heating in the cherry-red bed of coals in the central fire pit. Many prayers were said in the Wabinaki language, and much like Cat had done with her own ceremonies asking the four *airts* for guidance, the Penobscot did the same. The rocks would be brought into the lodge four times during the ceremony, seven at a time, each time giving prayers to the four directions, always starting with the east. A fire keeper would attend to this. The area and lodge were cleansed with aromatic herbs and grasses, then the spirits were called upon from the four directions.

Greame watched with total fascination, wishing that Cat was able to see this. She would feel right at home with it all. Once the lodge was ready, the women took off most of Cat's clothes, leaving her in her shift. Far Eyes wore only a breech clout, and asked Greame to wear the same, if he was going to join them. His sense of modesty was overruled by the absolute curiosity to witness the ceremony, and he donned the cloth he was given.

When they were all settled—Greame, Cat, Far Eyes and Smiles at Everything, the fire keeper—a large pot of hot water was brought in and placed near the fire. Far Eyes opened a deerskin bag and started dropping pinches of herbs into the hot water and allowed them to steep. Then with a ladle, the medicine water was splashed onto the hot rocks, sending up billowing clouds of steam. The aroma was intoxicating. Far Eyes and Smiles at Everything sang songs each time this was done.

It was very hot. Greame was glad to only be in a breech clout. In the dim light, he could see Cat's shift was plastered to her body like a second skin. He tried not to think about that. She seemed oblivious to her surroundings. Her eyes were closed and her breathing was deep, as though she were sleeping.

Far Eyes began chanting and raising his arms, beckoning the spirits to come to him. He waved a smoldering bunch of herbs, making the air even thicker with fragrance. Out of the slowly moving fog, Greame began seeing faded shapes. At first, they seemed to be animals, then they turned into people. None were Lachlan. More medicine water was splashed onto the stones, filling the lodge so thickly with steam it was hard to see anything. Greame glanced over at Cat, and sitting between her and himself was Lachlan. Greame wondered if Far Eyes knew Lachlan was there.

Lachlan looked at Greame and smiled. Unsure of what else to do, Greame nodded and smiled back. Suddenly, Far Eyes stopped singing. The steam had retreated enough for him to notice Lachlan, then catch Greame's eye. Greame nodded in acknowledgement.

"Welcome," Far Eyes said.

As if he were flesh and blood, Lachlan said, "Thank ye."

In his native tongue, Far Eyes started asking Lachlan questions. Greame couldn't understand a word he was saying, but apparently, when you're dead, language isn't a barrier, because Lachlan answered him in English. Greame wiped the sweat from his forehead, and listened to the answers Lachlan was giving, therefore able to keep up with the conversation.

"I asked her that last night," Lachlan said. "She has lost her power to see. She is sightless and feels like she's in a black room wi' no way out."

Far Eyes nodded, as though understanding the situation better. He opened his bag of herbs and made a smudge stick out of many different plants. He tied it together with a thin braided grass strip then dipped the tip into the fire pit. Nearly immediately it caught on fire, but then reduced to a smolder. Far Eyes crawled over to Cat's side and started swirling the smoking smudge stick around her head, blowing on the herbs every once in a while to keep the smolder going. He whispered prayers in his language, then took a large feather and continued swirling the smoke around Cat.

Greame watched as Cat sat there perfectly still, allowing Far Eyes to perform the ceremony. Her eyes were closed, but every once in a while, a frown would crease her forehead. Her head shook back and forth a couple of times, as though something he was doing was making her angry.

"She's fightin' him," Lachlan whispered to Greame.

"I canna see what she's doin' in her heid. She has me blocked."

"Oh aye, she's still verra strong-willed, that one. Far Eyes is tryin' to pull her from the past. She doesna want to go; she's holdin' on tight to our Da." Lachlan turned to look at Greame, then said, "For her, there are more people she kens on my side than yers. She doesna want to return."

Greame held his response and tried to remain emotionless, but he forgot that the dead don't abide by mortal laws, and Lachlan saw right through the façade. Lachlan could tell that comment hit Greame like a rock to his chest. And Greame was right. If *he* couldn't keep Cat on this side, then who could?

Many hours later, the small group exited the sweat lodge. The cold air was invigorating and brought them back to life. Even Cat smiled and breathed in deep. The Penobscot women took Cat to the women's wigwam to wash and dress her. Greame followed Far Eyes to his wigwam, where they too washed and dressed.

Greame could see that Far Eyes was disappointed. He wasn't too happy himself.

"Dinna fash yerself, man," Lachlan said from the corner of the wigwam, startling both Greame and Far Eyes. "Ye just haven't found the right thing to tell her yet."

Far Eyes raised an eyebrow, and Greame snorted. "Do spirits usually behave like Lachlan wi' ye?"

The other eyebrow raised at this and Far Eyes just shook his head. "You see him last night?" he asked Greame.

"Aye. Everyone was sleepin' and all of a sudden, there was a *ceilidh* in the wigwam."

"What this *ceilidh*?"

"Oh. A gatherin' o' friends and family. Garnet was verra young at the gatherin'. She goes back into her past to when she was happy. Before all the death."

Far Eyes nodded and rubbed his chin, as though coming to some conclusion.

"Ye nod like ye hae an idea of how to help her. Do ye?"

"Yes. If Garnet goes backward to happiness, we find people from past to bring her back."

Greame shook his head and said, "We canna do that. They're all dead."

"All?"

"Aye. The only ones left are in Scotland and they would only remind her of what she's tryin' to escape from."

Far Eyes smiled conspiratorially. "Then we bring dead back."

ॐ

Life for the Penobscot was hard. The snow around the camp was finally packed down enough to walk on, rather than wade through by people who basically lived outside. Hunting was still carried out, though made even more difficult since the game tended to stay bedded down rather than be on the move. Smoke from the ever-burning fires floated lazily on the light air, making the valley seem like it was in a perpetual fog.

Greame and his crew settled in as though they had never left. He decided if Cat could not be brought out of her state within the week, he would send most of his men back to Boston for the rest of the winter. He couldn't leave the *Revenge* in the river for the winter, and the weather would not be getting warmer for quite some time.

For three days, Far Eyes remained alone in preparation for another sweat to reach more of Cat's family. Just after dawn on the third day, Greame and Cat entered the dim lodge with Far Eyes. As before, Smiles at Everything tended the stones and fire. The stones sizzled with the medicine water and the lodge filled with the aroma of herbs. Far Eyes sat next to Cat and once again began to sing and smudge all around her, making her nearly disappear in the thick smoke and fog. For a long time, nothing happened. There were no other visits from Lachlan that Greame was aware of since the last sweat, and he wondered if her brother had given up so easily. Another seven stones were brought in and set into the fire pit. More medicine water was poured onto the new stones, and Far Eyes continued to sing and chant, with Smiles at Everything joining in now and then.

As if from a dream, a shape began to manifest on the other side of the lodge, but the figure remained blurry. Greame could only assume it was Lachlan, but wasn't sure. Then, right beside the blurry figure appeared a man; a big man. Greame watched as the fog cleared for an instant, and he recognized Angus Robertson. Greame could tell Far Eyes had noticed the big man too, because he stopped singing.

From inside the heads of Greame and Far Eyes, Lachlan's voice stated plain as day that this was Cat's father. Angus nodded once, his eyes never leaving his daughter, his only acknowledgement of anyone.

"Catrìona?" Angus whispered.

Cat had not noticed him yet. She had her eyes closed in the steamy, herb-scented air. At the sound of her father's voice, her eyes flew open wide.

"Da?"

"Good to see ye lass, but what are ye doin' wi' yerself? Ye canna think to be stayin' in the past. What good will it be doin' ye?"

Cat seemed to get smaller. Her head bowed, unable to look at her father. "Ye dinna understand, Da. I dinna want to *see* anymore. I dinna want to ken what will happen before it happens. What good did it do me?" she said, lifting her eyes to her father's. "Everyone I loved is gone. I couldna stop any of it. I couldna change the outcome of anythin' I saw."

Angus shook his head, this time his head bowing just before he disappeared.

Cat closed her eyes again, rocking herself back and forth, dismissing all around her and retreating back into her abyss.

Far Eyes wasn't about to give up just yet. He splashed more of the medicine water onto the rocks and began singing again, only this time with more of an aggressive tone. A little while later, Smiles at Everything slipped out of the lodge and brought in seven more of the scalding rocks, placing them into the fire pit. Another ladle of the medicine water was poured onto the new rocks, creating an even danker atmosphere. Far Eyes reached into his herb bag and sprinkled a handful of flowery-scented herbs onto the steaming stones.

Like before, Greame and Far Eyes heard Lachlan's voice in their heads, this time introducing Cat's mother. Though Lachlan never appeared, his presence was felt in the lodge. In a swirl of smoke and fog, a woman materialized on the other side of Cat. Side by side, they looked very similar. Far Eyes glanced at Greame to see if he recognized her, but Greame only shrugged, never having met Isobel Robertson.

Cat opened her eyes and smiled at her mother sitting beside her. She reached out her hand to touch Isobel, but there was no tangible body there, only mist.

Undeterred, Cat said, "I've missed ye, Mam."

"Aye, me too, Catrìona. I've been watchin' ye grow into a fine woman, and ye've found a fine man to be wi'."

Cat caught Greame's eye and smiled at him, as though nothing was wrong.

"Hae ye heard from Janet?" Isobel asked.

Cat thought for a moment, she had just been visiting with her friend, but realized her mother meant in the real world. It took her a moment to work that out. Then she said, "Is she all right?"

Isobel smiled. "Ye'd ken if ye really wanted to."

"But I'm afraid to ken. What if she's dead too?"

"She's no'. She's no' in a good place, much the same as ye, but she's no' dead."

"What of her family, of Mòrag and Andrew?"

"Both livin', but the English hae no' made it easy."

"See," Cat said in frustration, "that's why I'd rather be daft than live so hard."

"Oh, Cat. Dinna ye think there are others worse off than ye? Had even more hardship than ye? What makes ye so different than those who lost everythin' and didn't even hae the love of a man and new friends like ye hae here?"

Cat looked around the lodge at Greame, Far Eyes and Smiles at Everything. She thought of Greame's family aboard the *Revenge* that had come to treat her like kin.

"Ye're still loved, Cat," Isobel said, touching Cat's cheek. "Only ye hae the love from both sides."

Greame could see that she was finally wavering, but she had yet to make the leap that would catapult her back to reality. He glanced at Far Eyes who nodded, seemingly convinced that she would choose to return, when musket fire shattered the moment and made all of them stop and look at each other to confirm its reality.

Screaming punctuated the air, immediately tearing all of them from the spirit world. This propelled Far Eyes and Greame to their feet. Greame grabbed Cat and they bolted from the sweat lodge just in time to see three Mohawk braves running through the camp firing their muskets indiscriminately into the wigwams.

Geoffrey and Hector flew out of their wigwam with their pistols blazing. One of the Mohawk braves was hit in the ribs, sending him sideways into the snow and landing at Cat's feet. Hector caught up to him and ended it with a shot to his head. The snow turned bright red. That's when Cat slipped out of Greame's grasp and fainted to the ground. Any thought of her return was now dashed like the skull of the Mohawk lying in the snow.

An arrow whizzed by Greame's head from one of the Penobscot behind him, finding its mark in the chest of the second Mohawk. Greame's only concern was for Cat, whom he lifted and ran to Far Eyes' wigwam, still barefoot and clad only in his breech clout.

The third Mohawk was heading for the trees and escape, but the Penobscot braves were heavy on this heels. He would not make it back to his people.

As quickly as it started it was over. Far Eyes opened the flap to his wigwam to find Greame wrapping Cat in furs. She was shivering, but he sensed it wasn't just from the cold. He stood silently and watched as Greame lovingly tended to her. He closed his eyes in an attempt to make contact with her other self, but he only saw Lachlan barring him from entry. Far Eyes doubted his ability to bring her back after this.

Part
Two

Clarity

The weather had made a great change. Small buds on the trees were turning to flowers, soon to be leaves. As the ground warmed, the air smelled of freshness, of a new start, and those strange miniature frogs were singing in every pond and lake where the ice had receded.

Greame, Cat and Jim had remained with the Penobscot throughout the winter. The rest of Greame's crew had returned to Boston by the middle of December, and most were expected back anytime to stay. Greame intended to settle on Cape Rozier, and his cousins would probably remain close by. The *Revenge* would return fully loaded with provisions for creating comfortable homes for all of them.

John Hay decided to stay in Boston to run the teashop. He told Greame that he had a feeling it would come in mighty handy someday soon. The rest of Greame's family wanted to be out of English domain—at least as far as they could be.

Sometime during the winter, Cat had emerged from her stupor, but she was not the same woman as before. This Cat was no longer called Red One That Sees, she was now called Lives Inside. Her entire demeanor had changed to a very quiet woman oblivious to nearly everything. Where animals and birds had always captured her attention, the only thing that she related to now was water. No matter the weather, Cat was at the river. She would sit on the bank staring at the current for hours. Greame or Jim would usually have to return her to the village where she could warm herself. Though she was able to get around on her own now, it seemed like she was just a young child in need of guidance.

"Do ya think she'll ever return ta us, Greame?" asked Jim one afternoon on their way to fetch Cat.

"I dinna ken, Jim. Sometimes I think we're goin' about this all wrong, but I hae no idea what else to do for her."

Jim placed his hand on Cat's shoulder and she looked up at him with a smile on her face. "C'mon Cat. It's time ta go back."

Cat nodded and stood up. Greame stepped beside her and brushed the dead leaves and grass from the back of her threadbare skirt. She waited patiently for him to complete his task, then she put her hand through the presented crook of his arm and the threesome walked back to the village.

Far Eyes met them at the fire. Greame had snared a couple of rabbits and they were cooking on the spit.

"I see your ship return," he said to Greame. "You leave soon?"

"Aye. When will ye return to Cape Rozier?"

"Next moon," he said, referring to the next full moon in May.

Far Eyes watched Cat for a few minutes. Greame wondered what he was seeing since he had not been able to get into her head since the Mohawk attack. Lachlan had not returned either, and still, there was the nagging feeling that there was something he was missing.

"Far Eyes, is there naught else we can do for her?"

Far Eyes shifted his eyes from Cat and peered into Greame's eyes. Before he answered, Greame noticed that the shaman's nearly black eyes weren't focused on him, he was looking inside for something. After a moment, he refocused on Greame's face and shook his head.

"You think another way?" Far Eyes asked as he poked the fire under the cooking rabbits.

"Aye, but I dinna ken what."

"How you meet Garnet?"

Greame sent a rare smile to Far Eyes.

"We met in a castle in Scotland. I was driving my master's coach."

"You have master?" Far Eyes asked, clearly confused.

"I was a servant to a verra powerful man. He helped me keep my family from starving, since my Da died when I was young. I couldna make enough money—wampum—to keep the family croft, so I worked for him. Anyway," he said, waving his hand to dismiss all of that, "I met Cat when she needed a ride home during the early days o' the Risin'. It was verra dangerous for a woman alone, so my master had me take her to her croft. We started off wi' a nice conversation, but she was verra forward."

"What this forward?"

Greame rubbed his chin in search of an explanation, then came up with, "She speaks what's on her mind."

Far Eyes nodded in understanding.

"We were verra angry wi' each other when I dropped her off at Anna Macpherson's old cott. Cat told me that she nearly destroyed the inside of her croft because o' me," he said, smiling at the memory.

"Who Anna Macpherson?"

A dawning look radiated on Greame's face. "Christ, that's it!" He grabbed Cat's shoulders and kissed her forehead. "We're bringin' Anna back to see ye."

Cat smiled and said, "That would be nice."

Greame spent the rest of the day familiarizing Far Eyes with the most powerful Seer he had ever known.

"Anna was verra old," he started. "Some say nearly one hundred years. She had been the Seer for Cat's clan for many years. She had great powers and the ability to heal wi' herbs. Cat was taught by Anna to use her Sight and how to use the herbs. When Anna died, Cat took over as Seer for the clan and lived in Anna's cott near the castle where her chief lived."

"You think we bring Anna Macpherson to Garnet, she get better?" Far Eyes asked.

Greame took a moment to think about it, then said, "Aye. They were verra close and from what Cat has told me, they were able to do great things when they were together."

"Does Garnet have something of Anna Macpherson?"

Greame looked wounded by this question. He looked at Cat; at her clothes, her ring, the solitary piece of adornment her brothers had given to her, and could think of nothing that was brought from Scotland that belonged to her, never mind that belonged to Anna. He shook his head.

"Where's Anna?" Cat asked, as though expecting her for luncheon.

Greame took her hands in his and asked, "Cat, do ye hae anythin' that belonged to Anna wi' ye?"

Cat looked at him; looked deep into his green eyes, and said. "Aye, the crystal and dirk."

A frown formed between Greame's eyes. He knew nothing of these items and knew she didn't bring them with her or he'd have seen them. They must still be in Scotland, probably in the care of Alexander. "Must she hae the objects wi' her, or can she just think about them?" he asked Far Eyes.

It was Far Eyes' turn to rub his chin and ponder on that for a moment. He turned to face Cat and asked her directly what the crystal and dirk looked like. In an instant, he saw the *clach na brataich,* the crystal that was unearthed when the Clan Donnachaidh standard pole was pulled from the ground at the battle of Bannockburn in 1314. It had been carried by all the Robertson Chiefs since then when leading the clan to battle. Then, in a dark red wooden box that was polished to a warm glow, resting in a velvet nest lay a silver dirk encrusted with garnets on the pommel and at the ends of the short, curved quillons.

Far Eyes' eyes went wide at the sight of such riches and he said, "You not see these things?"

Greame shrugged again and Far Eyes took his hand to send him what he saw. Greame's frown went even deeper. He had no idea Cat was the guardian of such things.

"We try another sweat lodge with these things in our minds. Maybe it work."

༐

The next morning dawned so foggy, it was impossible to see from one end of the village to the other. The air was cool and clammy. The sweat lodge was ready and the foursome entered as before. Far Eyes and Smiles at Everything chanted and sang for a long time. Seven new stones were brought in and doused with medicine water. The herbal concoction Far Eyes used this time was different from the previous fragrances. This somehow smelled of Scotland. Greame was taken back to his homeland in an instant. The smell of the moors and wood. He could even smell the heather, if that was possible. When he glanced over at Cat, she had a smile on her face and was deeply breathing in the fragrance of home. He chanced a look into her mind and saw that she was at Anna's cott. Her dog, Gent, was with her.

Far Eyes stopped singing and must have called up the crystal and dirk in his mind, because they appeared in Greame's head, and he again marveled at the beauty of the objects. Far Eyes then spoke Anna's name out loud, calling her to join them. Greame recalled Anna's face and put that in his mind, then looked at Cat. She was still smiling, but Anna was nowhere to be seen.

More medicine water was splashed onto the stones sending the Scottish aroma throughout the lodge.

"Hallò, Garnet," the voice said.

Greame saw no one, but heard Anna's voice clearly.

"Hallò, Mistress," Cat whispered.

"I see yer man here is verra smart to ask me to come to ye. Do ye think it'll help?"

Cat smiled, then started to giggle. Greame and Far Eyes just watched, having to smile themselves at the melodic sound of her laughter.

"I dinna ken why they're so frightened that I dinna hae the Sight anymore. I'm happy."

"*Phaa!* Ye canna lie to me, Garnet. Dinna ye remember how long ye worked to hone yerself into a rare fine Seer? Ye had more o' the Sight than anyone I'd e'er met, even yer Grandmam."

"But I am Grandmam … well, I was," Cat stammered.

"Ye canna remember how ye were put to death when ye were yer Grandmam, Garnet, because the last life is forgotten in the rebirth. But ye are to be told about it now."

Cat shook her head violently, not wanting to recall that horror.

"Ye were stripped naked, bound, then placed in a barrel wi' nails pounded into it from the outside so yer flesh was ripped from yer body as they rolled ye 'round in it. Then, just for good measure, since ye didna die quick enough, they boiled ye in tar for bein' a witch, even though ye had served yer chief loyally for many years. This was because he didna like what ye told him about a vision ye had concernin' his wife. The vision was true, o' course, which he found out a few weeks later when his dear wife tried to kill him in his bed," Anna spewed with disgust, recalling the incident with perfect clarity.

"Why are ye tellin' me this, Mistress?" Cat whimpered, holding herself around her shoulders as though warding off the wounds from the previous incarnation.

"Because right 'til the end, ye wouldna renounce yer vision. Hae ye forgotten the circle o' rebirth? Ye remained strong and sure of yer Sight, and ye kent ye would return to continue yer work." Anna paused, as if preparing for the final blow. "Do ye think for one minute, *Catherine Macinroy,* ye chose to come back in the wrong body—and at the wrong time?"

Harsh words meant to slap the senses. Cat was crying at this point, but she was also angry.

"How dare ye come here and reprimand me on how I live," Cat spat, no longer shaking and timid.

"I dare because ye need to hear it! Ye need to ken what ye're doin' to yerself, yer future, and to those ye love around ye. Do ye think they summoned me to hae a lovely *chat*? There's much more death comin', Garnet, whether ye like it or no'; whether ye're here or no'; it's goin' to happen. I would ne'er hae guessed that ye would take the easy way out," Anna admonished, as though speaking to a child.

"So what, ye'd hae me keep the Sight just so I could make someone else's life more comfortable? What about my life?" Cat screamed. "Dinna I hae the right to be comfortable?"

"As I see it, lassie," Anna chided, "ye hae the love of a good man, dear friends and a new clan. Ye've no right to complain. All ye hae to do is snap out of this hidin' within yerself, and LIVE!"

Cat was furious, her temper returning with a vengeance. She tried to stand, but in the low-ceilinged lodge she smacked her head on one of the curved branches. She curled up her fist and pounded on the branch, effectively shaking the lodge so violently, it nearly came undone. With her other hand, she rubbed her head, feeling the knot that was already forming. She glanced around the small space, just realizing she wasn't the only one there, and caught Greame and Far Eyes staring at her. This fueled the rage even further and she lashed out.

"What in bloody hell are the two o' ye lookin' at? Hae ye no' seen someone crack their heid before? And Greame, what are ye doin' in that breech clout? Christ, so much for ye bein' the bashful one, aye? And ye can wipe that bloody grin off yer face, too. It's too hot in here. I'm goin' to take a bath," she growled. She whipped open the deerskin door, nearly ripping it from the lodge, and stormed out in search of the river.

Greame watched in total fascination as Anna made Cat see what she *did* have, instead of what she didn't. When her renowned temper reared its head, he knew she had returned—at least for a moment, but when she raged on and on, he knew it was permanent. He was never so happy to be screamed at in all his life, and his smile couldn't be contained. He glanced over at Far Eyes, who had never endured the brunt of Cat's fiery outbursts. The look on his face, while mildly concerned, was also one of joy.

"She back," Far Eyes said, nodding.

A moment later, Lachlan appeared wearing a big smile on his face. "See, someone just needed to tell her the right thing."

Rebuilding A Life

The summer passed very quickly. Cat, Greame and Jim had traveled back to Cape Rozier from Pasadunkec with the Penobscot early in the spring, and picked out a piece of land on a high point overlooking the small islands to the south. They chose the parcel for its beauty and warm, sunny exposure. On the western side of the point was a small crescent beach with deep water to moor the *Revenge.* Settlement on the perfect parcel was determined by a couple of interesting factors.

"After that winter storm we survived last year, we'll want to build a distance from the water, aye?" Greame stated.

Cat looked at him with a blank look in her eyes. "I'm sorry I dinna remember it, Greame."

"Och, lass, dinna be sorry. Ye wouldna hae cared for it."

Jim laughed, "That's an understatement."

"But let's be close enough so the midges dinna bother us so much, aye?" Cat said.

"I think if we clear out enough of these woods, there wilna be anythin' for the midges to eat."

"Only us," Jim snorted.

So they started by cutting many of the tall, straight spruce down. Cat was in charge of limbing them so they would fit together as close as possible. Greame's cousins, the ones who wanted to remain permanently on Cape Rozier, chose plots nearby and began building a couple of cabins of their own. It was hard work, but they all saw progress at the end of each day.

Mornings were becoming crisp as the season changed to autumn. Hopefully, the snow would hold off until after the roofs were up. Cat was at the cook fire with Kenny, the ship's cook, making some biscuits to have with the deer jerky they were accustomed to for luncheon, when she saw Jim emerge from the western side of the property. He was whistling as he walked closer to the building site. She smiled when she noticed Greame look up at the strange sound.

"Ye're in a rare fine mood this day, Jimmy-boy. We obviously dinna hae ye workin' hard enough. Pick up the end of this log and help me set the header over the doorway," Greame instructed.

"What's it like ta be in love, Greame?" Jim asked quietly, hopefully only loud enough for Greame's ears.

Greame set his end of the log down and tried his damnedest not to smile as he took a seat on the hewn timber. Jim sat down beside him, intently anticipating clarification on the subject.

Cat had heard the question posed to Greame and moved a little closer to hear what advice would be handed down to the young lad.

"Well, Jimmy, love is …," clearing his throat, he tried again. "Love makes ye feel like …" he rubbed his chin pondering hard for a moment, then looked Jim square in the eyes and said, "It makes ye feel like ye're alive—like ye can do anythin'—and yer heart beats faster when ye see yer lover, and ye're foul and surly when ye dinna see yer lover. Ye dinna eat, ye dinna sleep, and ye certainly canna keep yer mind to anythin' whatsoever."

Jim looked a bit pasty for a minute, then said, "Huh. Well, I'm not so sure I want ta be in love then." He stood, then walked over to see what Geoffrey was doing on the lot next door.

Cat couldn't keep it in any longer and started giggling, which got Kenny chuckling, and as contagious as a yawn, started Greame laughing.

So much for love.

§♠

That night, as Cat handed Greame his plate of stew and took her seat next to him on the log, she asked, "Is that how ye really feel?"

After a moment of attempting to figure out what Cat was referring to, he looked at her with his spoon in midair and asked, "About love?"

"Aye, about love. I dinna think I e'er remember ye missin' a meal," she chuckled.

He slowly put the spoon in his mouth, giving her a look that could hurt if it weren't for the twinkle in his eye.

"Well, are ye goin' to answer me?"

He chewed with great pleasure and shook his head back and forth.

"No, really?"

Another spoonful effectively ended the conversation that never began.

"Well, I'll tell ye how I feel about love," watching him out of the corner of her eye. "It makes me angry."

Greame choked a little on his stew before swallowing the mouthful. "That, my dear, is exactly what I thought ye might say."

Cat sneered at him, but couldn't resist asking him why he thought that.

"Because love makes ye lose control. It means ye hae someone else to think about besides yerself, and that interferes wi' how ye live yer life."

She seemed to puff up in indignation at the jibe. Her brows furrowed. "So ye think me to be selfish?"

Greame put his plate down on the log beside him, realizing this was going to have to be handled gently. "No, that's no' what I meant." He looked directly at her and finished chewing before completing his statement. "I meant that ye take matters to heart verra easily. Ye're sensitive to other's feelin's and tend to put them before yer own. But ye tend to find it an inconvenience sometimes."

Cat's eyebrows went up, and she tried to hide the smile that threatened to deepen her dimples. "That was a verra well thought out way to get back into my good graces, my love."

A quirk of his lips told her that he was full of it, so she elbowed him in the ribs just to let him know he had it right, but never to bring it up again.

He picked up his plate and finished his stew.

੨੩

By the first of October, the shells of the cabins were finally complete. The last project to complete was to dig a privy hole a little distance from the "village." Jim and Geoffrey were tending to that, while Greame was helping Cat with the hearth inside their cabin.

"That's a fine piece o' stone ye found, Garnet." Greame had taken to calling her that again, explaining that it was her true name, one he hoped would remain forever on her. The stone he was referring to was a large, thin, rectangular piece of granite that was perfect for the hearthstone. It took six men to lift it into place, but it was worth it. The wood floors were next, but would take some time to put in. For now, the cozy space was looking more like a home.

"Where did ye get all the money to buy these fine cherry floor boards, Greame?"

"The Worldwide Tea Emporium is bringin' in a nice profit, enough for all o' this," he explained. "Oh, in Jimmy's room, there's a chest I'd like ye to open," he said, too matter-of-factly.

Cat eyed him suspiciously, but ran into Jim's room to see what treasure Greame's men had secretly stowed on the ship from Boston. She opened it and was rewarded with beautiful quilts for the beds, bolts of fabric for curtains, two cast iron cook pots, and behind the chest was a lush hooked rug, obviously a leftover from Rose. It was a vine pattern in shades of green and tan. Cat rubbed her hand over it and couldn't wait to see it on the new floor as soon as it was finished. She pulled out a couple of interesting bolts of fabric. One was a green linen matching the rug, and the other was a patterned burgundy and cream. She brought them both into the keeping room with a big smile, then put them down and planted kisses all over Greame's face.

"Enough. Enough, woman," he chuckled, trying to dodge the lip smacking that made his face wet.

"Was it Emily or Claire that put all these fineries together?" Cat asked, delighting in the feel of the fabric.

"Both, I expect. I take it they'll do."

"Oh, aye, they'll do just fine." She unraveled a few yards from each bolt and held each up to the window. "I think I like the green best, how about ye?"

Greame nodded his approval then returned his attentions to the fire, which was warming the room nicely.

Just after dark, Jim walked in, managing somehow to always know exactly when supper was being dished up. He had been helping out wherever help was needed, even in the Penobscots' summer camp.

"Just in time, Jimmy," Cat said, handing him a linen and pointing to the wash basin.

He took the linen from her and flung it over his shoulder, reminding her of her brother Lachlan.

Greame said, "I always ken when ye think o' yer brother. It brings a warm smile to yer sweet face."

Cat chuckled. "I'm glad ye got to meet him … well, kinda," she said, blushing.

It was Greame's turn to chuckle. "Oh, aye, it was right fine to meet him. I do hae a question, if ye dinna mind speakin' of it."

Cat shrugged, "Ask what ye want."

"Why didna ye other brothers come to ye when ye were … in yer state?"

A hurt look appeared on her face for just a moment. She opened her mouth to speak several times before replying.

"I suppose it was because Iain and Seumas werna so close to me at the end. Especially Seumas."

Her face now held a far away look. Greame didn't pursue the questioning any further. Some things were better left in the past.

A knock on the door broke the thickness of the air.

"Come in, Geoffrey," Cat said.

Greame and Jim turned to see who was coming in, as though expecting to catch Cat in error.

Geoffrey walked in. "It still spooks me when ye do that," he said with a smile, taking his seat at the table with Greame and Jim.

Cat brought the kettle of venison stew, ladled out a plate for each of them, then placed a pan of biscuits in the center of the table before taking her seat. The men talked amongst themselves, seemingly unaware of her inwardness.

It had been a very long time since she'd had a vision, and it took her a few minutes to get adjusted to the sights she was seeing in her mind's eye. More war? It couldn't be. The French and English were talking about a treaty to end King George's war. Was it going to come to blows before that and not really end? She refused to become included in any war of this new country. She was here for a purpose—she knew not what that was yet, but she was sure it wasn't to get into a war.

As she received more images in her mind, she realized it wasn't a war she was seeing, at least not here. They were Highlanders; thousands of them in full regalia walking behind something. She saw her surroundings and realized it was Carie, Scotland they were coming from. She marched along with them for a spell, then came upon the front of the line to where six men—men she knew—were carrying a wooden box on their shoulders. She realized now what had happened. Alexander had died. This was his funeral procession. But where were they taking him? She thought he would have enjoyed a peaceful rest at his Hermitage, but then remembered the English had destroyed it. After further consideration, she realized that he would want a proper burial in a kirkyard. But would they take him all the way to Struan Kirk? That was almost fourteen miles away. Cat smiled at the notion. It would be just what Alexander, the thirteenth Clan Donnachaidh Chief, would have wanted—and deserved.

Cat watched for a while, feeling like she was a part of something very important that would be remembered for generations. She also felt extra special witnessing such an event, as women were never allowed to participate in a chief's burial.

She looked around for the season so she could gauge when this would happen. The grasses were just starting to green up and small buds were on the trees. Early spring, she concluded. Maybe April. After a bit of calculating in her mind, she came up with the fact that Alexander would be around eighty years old when his life ended. A good long life, she thought.

Laughter brought her out of her trance, and she shyly looked around the table to see if anyone had noticed she wasn't there. Greame was staring at her with a curious look on his face. An eyebrow raised was his nonverbal question. Cat's head dipped slightly in acknowledgement. She smiled when she felt Greame's tension leave and he returned the gesture.

The meal concluded and Geoffrey took his leave. Jim retired to his room and his deep breathing was heard not long after. Cat and Greame sat near the hearth completing the day's tasks, waiting to have a bit of privacy.

Greame could wait no longer. "So, what was yer vision about?"

Cat smiled and faced him. "It was strange to hae one again after so long. It took me a while to fish out the details, but it seems Alexander is going to pass sometime in April."

As she told him what she saw, Greame was amazed.

"Thousands? He must hae been a verra important, dearly loved man to warrant such an extravagance. I truly canna think o' many men who would hae such devoted followers."

"I think perhaps I'll get a letter off ... well, perhaps no', since there's no way to get it to Boston from here."

"Aye, 'tis a bit isolated up here," Greame said, rubbing his chin. "The Penobscot hae runners between villages. We'll hae to come up wi' somethin' like that in the spring."

Cat absently nodded, realizing for the first time that now, no matter what, there was no going back to Scotland. Ever. In a way it was freeing, like closing a chapter on that part of her life. It was time to live this new chapter, wherever it led. Suddenly, she leaned over and kissed Greame's bristly cheek.

"What was that for?" He smiled and put down the paperwork he was working on.

She thought for a moment. "I'm not sure I can tell ye everything it's for, but mostly for stayin' by me when many a man would hae taken the chance to leave, and no' a soul would hae blamed ye for it. For bein' so strong. For takin' me to this wild place wi'out a question as to why. For helpin' me figure out what I'm here for. And because I truly love ye, Greame Hay."

He had no words, even though his mouth opened and closed several times. Cat reached her hand over to run through his chocolate mane, and he closed his eyes and smiled. He took her hand and pressed it to his lips, then sighed.

"I dinna think any man would e'er want to be rid o' ye, Garnet. Ye're a remarkable woman. What happened to ye only proves that ye're human and that ye can only take so much. It was yer mind tellin' ye that it needed a rest for a while."

Cat laughed, "Oh, aye, a half year gone from my life. That was quite a rest."

"Point is, ye've returned, and together we're goin' to make our lives here in peace and quiet. We'll forget about the past and all the bad things that happened. We'll start fresh and new, and whate'er ye're here for, I'll be here wi' ye."

Hell Hath No Fury ...

The snow had been so deep that winter not much could be done outside. A few times, when the weather had settled down, a hunting party consisting of Greame, Jim, Hector and Geoffrey went in search of meat. Deer bedded down during extreme weather and only browsed close to that area, but if one could find their yard, there was a good chance of a kill. The hunters were rewarded twice. They ate well during the long, cold season.

Winter was also a good time to spend finishing the inside of their cabin. The fine cherry flooring was laid, and there were now a settee and two armchairs in the keeping room close to the hearth. The hooked rug was on the floor, and the new curtains for the two windows that looked out onto the sea were hanging.

In Jim's room, there was an oak armoire and bed, complete with a straw-filled mattress. He told Cat after a long afternoon of splitting wood that he had never slept as well. Cat deduced that after that heavy work he could have slept on a bed of nails and would have been just as comfortable.

Greame and Cat had decided to share a bedroom early in the planning stages of this house they built. They didn't pursue marriage anymore. To them, they were as married as they needed to be. Their bed was an ornate tiger maple with a carved scallop shell on the head and foot boards. It was tall, taking up much of the wall. Small tables, each elaborately carved, flanked each side of the bed, and a matching armoire and chest of drawers completed the room.

The chests of linens brought from Rose's contained, among other things, two beautiful quilts. Cat chose the Mariner's Star finely made of silk in rich greens and burgundy with a cream border for a warm, cozy feel to chase away the winter cold. The patterned burgundy and cream fabric was a perfect complement for the window treatments. The "summer colors" quilt was a light peach and pink floral pattern on an almost bronze background of chintz; perfect for warmer nights. Greame had pulled out a few more hooked rugs from his seemingly inexhaustible booty and the floor became bearably warm to the feet.

"Ye can come in now," Cat said from the doorway of their newly completed bedroom. She had spent most of the day behind the closed door so she could surprise him.

He smiled and rose from his chair. "It's about time, lass. It's near time for bed anyway."

The cluck from her tongue made him chuckle, but when he stepped inside to the softly lit room so lovingly decorated, he was amazed. He reached around her waist and brought her to him. His mouth found hers in a soft kiss that lingered and probed, then became fiery. He closed the door with his foot and laid her down on the smooth silk. Passion would truly complete the chamber.

Sometime well before dawn, Cat was startled out of her slumber. She lay there listening for the source of the disturbance. Greame's even breathing and the wind was all she heard. A smile came to her when she remembered Greame's big hands exploring her body. She felt his touch lingering on her.

She looked out the window to see the moon floating in a veil of clouds that made a ring around it. It would be a cloudy day tomorrow, perhaps even snow. It was already waist deep. How much more would there be? It didn't snow this much in Boston …

A floorboard squeaked and brought her out of her wandering. She strained her ears to hear more. Silence. The wind whistled through the house sometimes making odd sounds. On more than one occasion, a tree nearby was heard crashing to the ground because of the wind's ferocity. Greame had cut several enormous dying spruce to eliminate the possibility of them coming down onto the cabin.

Another squeak, but this one *felt* different. She laid a soft hand on Greame's shoulder.

"Hmmm? Are ye wantin' me again, lass?" he said groggily, reaching over to touch her, more than ready to accommodate.

"Shhh. Listen." She fended off a greedy hand.

Her tone brought him to attention and he was quiet for a minute. A bump of a piece of furniture from the keeping room confirmed Cat's perception.

"Someone's in the house," he whispered, stealthily slipping out from the bedcovers, naked as the day he was born.

Cat got up and slipped into her shift, which had so hastily been tossed to the floor earlier. Before she could get around to Greame, the doorknob clicked. Someone on the other side was attempting to enter their bedroom.

Greame stepped back, allowing the intruder clear access. He was pretty sure the surprise would be on the trespasser. The door opened so slowly Cat was nearly ready to walk over and let them in, just to get it over with. Gradually, it opened further, and in the dim moonlight Cat saw Greame get into an offensive position. She stood perfectly still at the end of the bed.

Off to the side like she was, Cat had a better vantage point than Greame at whomever it was wanting to get in. Further it opened, until below the doorknob came a hand with a glint of metal protruding from it. He must have been on his knees holding the blade.

In an agonizingly slow act of stealth, a face appeared. Cat felt his energy more than saw it. As the door opened further still, Greame now got a glimpse of the knife. With all he could muster, he kicked the door closed on the hand wielding the deadly instrument. A scream permeated the house. Greame was leaning on the door now, effectively pinning the culprit. When the knife fell to the floor in a thud, Greame whipped open the door and began pummeling in a blind rage. Cat quickly lit a candle so Greame could see who he was beating. As soon as he saw, he ceased the bruising.

"What in bloody hell are ye doin' comin' into my house wi' a blade in the middle o' the night, ye sorry bastard?"

By this time, Jim, clad in his nightshirt, was standing outside the door with a club in his hand watching in disbelief.

"Answer me!" Greame growled.

Cat had wrapped herself in the quilt trying to chase the chill from her bones. A chill not from the cold, but from the hatred coming from him.

"It was her," Hector Hay hissed in a nasally voice, pointing a finger at Cat. Greame must have broken his nose in the fight.

"Talk sense, man! What's Cat got to do wi' this?" Greame said, pulling on his sark.

"She's no' stopped wantin' me, and told me to come to her bed tonight. I'm goin' to be her husband." He announced it so confidently it was almost believable.

Cat and Greame exchanged surprised looks, then Cat walked over to Hector, who was still lying on the floor, holding his wrist, blood seeping from his nose onto the floor. She squatted down next to him and just stared. Hector met her eyes with a grin of smugness.

"See, ye wanted me to come to ye, just tell him," Hector said.

"Ye've got somethin' wrong wi' yer heid, Hector. What signs hae I e'er given ye that I even like ye? And my *husband*, eh?" she said calmly, looking him up and down with eyes revealing his failure to meet any of her qualifications.

His reflexes were quick for an injured man. He grabbed his dirk from the floor at the very same instant Greame lunged for it. Hector slashed at the air wildly and Greame stumbled backwards out of the way, catching his foot on the rug that had balled up in the fray. He landed hard, striking his head on the bedpost as he fell.

Hector then grabbed Cat's wrist and tugged with such ferocity that she tumbled on top of his chest. His hands found her throat and squeezed hard.

Jim wielded the club he'd been holding onto Hector's knee. The sickening crack it made when the bone shattered was enough to make Hector relinquish his hold on the dirk, but he still held fast to Cat's throat. Hector's scream was that of a mortally injured beast. Cat, gasping for breath, saw the dirk. In one quick motion she grabbed the blade and plunged it into his chest. It went to the hilt with cruel accuracy. Hector's screams were silenced immediately.

Cat stood up and stepped away from the dead man, her arms at her sides with her hands balled into fists.

Greame was still on the floor trying to shake the stars from the hit to his head. When he made it to his knees, he saw the dirk protruding from the lifeless chest of his cousin. A dark moist spot was spreading onto Hector's cloak. Labored breathing from Cat behind him confirmed it wasn't a dream.

"Christ, woman, ye've killed him!"

Cat's eyes were flames. Her breasts heaved from her effort. She stood her ground, a battle woman to the core, making no apologies for her actions.

"I'll no' hae a man around us wi' such intentions as Hector had," she told him in a steely voice. "Jim, get him out o' my house."

Jim dropped his club and hoisted the lifeless Hector onto his shoulder. "What d'ya want me ta do with 'im?"

Cat started to say something, but Greame interrupted.

"Put him in the privy. We'll tend to him in the mornin'."

Greame waited for Jim to leave the cabin before turning his anger onto Cat.

Grabbing her shoulders hard he yelled, "What were ye thinkin', woman? That was my cousin ye just murdered!"

Cat's eyes reduced to slits and her jaw became rigid. She was still raging inside from the attack. Her throat had bruises on it already, and now Greame was blaming her for defending herself. In a dead calm voice she said, "Let. Me. Go."

"I dinna think so, no' until ye explain yerself."

"If I hae to explain myself for stayin' alive, then we may need to rethink our livin' arrangements," she said in a cutting tone.

She wrenched herself free from his grip and he made no further attempt to subdue her. She saw the fact in his eyes and sat heavily on the bed. Her white shift was soiled with Hector's blood and she pulled it off, tossing it on top of the small red pool where Hector's nose bled onto the floor. She made no attempt to get dressed, just grabbed the quilt and wrapped it around herself. All of a sudden she was exhausted. Without another word, she crawled onto her side of the bed and fell asleep.

Greame knew that kind of fatigue. The heart races so fast, it nearly explodes from the chest. All of the senses are heightened and it's as though the power of ten men is in you. But when the battle is over the body collapses. What Cat needed now was rest. He hadn't meant to yell at her. It was fear. Fear of coming so close to losing her. And at the hands of someone he knew and loved. It was more than his mind could comprehend and he had lashed out.

He spent the rest of the night on the settee, awake. Jim went back to bed, but Greame doubted he got any sleep either.

At first light, Greame walked through the snow to Geoffrey's cabin ready to explain where his roommate was. Hector's footprints were all that remained of the man.

"What do ye mean, he's dead. How? When? Where?" Geoffrey spewed in disbelief.

Greame explained the row to an open-mouthed Geoffrey.

"I really thought the time he tried that wi' her on the ship would be the end of it," Greame said. His eyes distant, remembering.

"Aye, well, ye remember back home when he had it in his heid that wee lass … och," tapping his head, "what was her name? Oh, aye, Ealasaid Cummin. He thought she'd fallen in love wi' him. If I remember correctly, she ne'er kent he lived, ne'er mind loved him. But he kept dreamin' o' her until one day he had to show her how he felt." He snorted mirthlessly, "He didna fair too well when her Da caught him, did he?"

Greame shook his head. "I had forgotten about that. Damn, why didna I remember that! I could hae prevented this entire thing. Damn it!"

"If ye ask me, Greame, he certainly had it comin' to him. He must hae planned on usin' that dirk on ye, then taken Garnet for himself. No' that she would hae let him …"

"Aye, but then after all she'd been through, I go and yell at her! What the hell is wrong wi' me?" Greame said, pounding his fist on his leg and dropping his head on the table.

Geoffrey got up and threw another log on the fire. "Go home, Greame. Tell her ye're sorry. She'll understand."

Greame raked his hand through his hair, nodded and left.

Cat woke when she heard Greame leave. She sat up, but stayed under the covers. It looked like snow any minute.

She relived last night, wondering if the outcome could have been different. Though Greame could have just sent him away—out of

Maine—he wouldn't have stopped his natural habits. And last night, it was him or her, and she wasn't ready to go anywhere yet. What she couldn't believe was Greame calling her a murderer. What was she supposed to do, let Hector strangle her without fighting back? Greame thought he was the only person who could stew for days? Well, he'll have a long time to think about it. The cabin was too small to avoid each other, but that didn't mean she couldn't make him more miserable than he ever thought possible.

She whipped off the bedcovers and got dressed. When she opened the door, Jim was sitting at the kitchen table rolling his hands around a mug of hot chicory. The fire blazed, meaning he must have been up for a while.

She placed her hand on his shoulder and patted it. "Are ye all right, Jim?"

Jim nodded. He started to say something, but kept it to himself. Cat didn't press him. He'd talk when he was ready.

She poured herself a cup of the steaming liquid and sat opposite Jim to watch the first of the snowflakes float to the ground.

"Does it hurt much?" Jim said.

Cat looked at him blankly for a second, then realized she had been rubbing the bruises on her throat. A slight blush crept up her face. "A bit."

"It's all my fault, Garnet."

Once again, Cat stared blankly at him before asking, "What are ye talkin' about?"

"Hector. It's because of me that he came to get ya."

"I dinna believe that for an instant, Jim. Why would ye think that?"

"It was a couple of days past when I was helpin' him an' Geoffrey in their cabin. I was tellin' 'em how nice it was ta have a woman in the house. Ta have all the nice things around ta make it look like a real home. Men don't seem ta know how ta do that."

Cat raised her eyebrow. "But, what would that possibly hae to do wi' Hector tryin' to kill me?"

He turned a shade of pink and lowered his head.

"Jim?" She touched his arm. "What was it?"

"I suppose I should've told ya about it, but I just thought he was full of himself, like usual." He looked up with eyes full of regret and continued, "He said that someday soon, he'd be takin' ya for his wife. Since he was the one ya truly loved, Greame would be easily forgotten. An' that Greame was keepin' ya hostage."

"*Phaa!* Well, Hector certainly was full of himself, wasna he? What did ye tell him?"

"I told him the only way for ya ta ever even think of becomin' 'is wife would be over Greame's dead body."

Cat nodded. That's exactly what he tried to do, but when Hector saw her contempt for him, he snapped and went for her instead.

"Jim, it wasna yer fault. He tried this once before."

His eyes opened wide. "What? When?"

"On my first journey to Maine. Greame had to intervene then, too. Let him off wi' a warnin', but it obviously wasna enough. The man was off somehow, Jim. Ye couldna hae kent about it."

He sat there and pondered for a few minutes, just nodding.

Cat got up to start breakfast when the door opened and Greame stepped in from the cold. His thick hair was peppered with snow-flakes and he shook it like a dog and stomped his feet to remove the snow from his boots. Cat kept her back to him and went about making oatcakes.

Greame sat at the table with Jim and waited for a cup of chicory. After a few minutes, he stood and poured himself his own cup, keeping his distance from Cat.

Jim watched in fascination, feeling their tension so heavily, it was as though the room was fogged in. He made no move to leave them alone. His curiosity of how men and women behaved was something that interested him greatly at the moment. He remembered how his parents behaved, but was too young to know why some things created tension. With these two very passionate people, it should be quite a learning experience.

He was startled out of his musings when Greame barked at him to help move Hector's body from the privy to a more permanent place … that they would have to build right now. So Cat's scowl must have meant, *get to work, 'cause there'll be no lovin' here 'til ya do!*

Nearly frozen to the bone, Greame and Jim walked into the cabin about three hours later. Cat had a venison stew and biscuits ready, but never came out of her bedroom to serve it to them.

"Well, Jimmy-boy, it looks like we're on our own for luncheon," Greame stated, dishing up a plate for the each of them.

"I told Garnet that it was my fault this happened," Jim said, reaching for a biscuit.

Greame's spoon stopped before it reached his waiting mouth. He trained his green eyes on Jim expecting an explanation, and quickly.

When Jim finished telling him what Hector had said, then what Cat's reply was, a dawning twinkled in those green eyes. "So that's what the trouble is."

Confused, Jim asked for clarification.

Greame clapped a big hand on Jim's shoulder and smiled. "She's a bit peeved that it wasn't me who ended up takin' action for what she perceived to be my duty."

"What?"

"It means, Jimmy-boy, that we're on our own for a while."

Part Three

Death of a Poet

28 April 1749, Carie, Scotland

Gregor Macgregor rose at dawn from his room in the barn. Not much to tend to these days. The English had made fewer and fewer raids in the years after the Rising. There was nothing left to pillage or plunder, so why make the effort. They had taken everything from the Scots, including their means of making a living, the land. Smoke from fields of barley and oats didn't permeate the air as much now. The Scots were effectively beaten and the Crown knew it.

He slid into his breeks and donned his sark and wool cloak. It was a cool morning and looked as though it would rain at any minute. He opened the doors and led the horses out to the greening pasture before going to check in on Alexander. As he was hobbling his horse, he had the strangest sensation that Catrìona was nearby. He actually stopped and looked around, so sure of her presence. He scratched his thick beard and chuckled. He wondered what brought that on. Perhaps *he* was getting some of the Sight and there would be a letter from her today.

The longtime guard of Clan Donnachaidh's 13th chief walked in to his master's humble croft like he did every morning. Alexander appeared to be asleep in his favourite chair; crystal goblet of whisky clutched in his hand. Gregor went to remove it but Alexander's fingers were impossible to uncurl. As Gregor looked closer, he noticed his chief was not breathing. Gregor placed a large hand on the eighty-year-old chest, but there was no heartbeat. The Poet Chief was dead.

Word spread on the wind through clan territory. Within the week, an army of Highlanders, some two thousand strong, was escorting their beloved chief to his last resting place at Straun Kirk, some fourteen miles away. Clanswomen fed the mob before they left and packed food for their journey, for women were not allowed to participate in the chief's burial procession.

Gregor had never married. He was alone now with no one to watch over or protect. Many times he had thought of what he would do when this time came. He had made up his mind that living under English rule was not what he wanted to do anymore. He had reveled in the letters Alexander had received from Catrìona about this new place called Maine. With just one last thing to do before he set off for the coast, he packed what few belongings he owned, collected Gent, Cat's Irish Wolfhound, and went to the dùn to fetch what rightfully belonged to Cat.

è▲

The *clach na brataich* belonged to the clan. Gregor retrieved it from its hiding place deep in the bowels of the faerie dùn, just where Cat had left it before leaving for America. Safe from the hands of the English. Alexander thought it safe there as well, since the English harried him regularly. The ensign stone would go to the new chief, Duncan Robertson of Drumachuine. What Duncan would do with it was now up to him, not Gregor anymore.

The old clan system had been unable to continue after the Rising. The English had foreclosed on Clan Donnachaidh's estates due to the clan's participation in the revolt. Broken men were everywhere without leaders. Many were leaving their homeland, scattering to the far corners of the world in search of a better life and rebuild their fortunes.

What belonged to Cat, though, was the dirk, left to her for safekeeping by Anna Macpherson. Gregor unwrapped the dark red wooden box and ran a thick finger over the smooth surface, tracing the brass oval engraved with Anna's name, a gift from Tullibardine, the Duke of Atholl. With great care he opened the box. Just as it had the first time he laid eyes on it—the dirk, encrusted with garnets on the silver pommel and at the ends of the short, curved quillons—made him gasp. He lifted it from its purple velvet nest and once again marveled at its balance.

"Perfection," he said out loud. The earthen walls muffled his voice. Gent whined, as though agreeing.

He replaced it in its box, wrapped it once again and placed it inside his satchel. Still cautious, he watched through the waterfall to see if anyone was nearby before going behind the flowing veil and out through the gorse and twin oaks. The hiding place would remain a secret under his watch.

꙱

After placing the ensign stone safely in the hands of Duncan Robertson, Gregor spent the next three days heading for the coast and settling on Dysart on the Firth of Forth to catch a ship to America. He thought of the last time he had seen the sea. It was with Catrìona when he said farewell to her just outside of London. Now he was to embark on the same voyage she had. He booked passage for himself—and with a bit of haggling, Gent—on the *Falcon*, bound for Boston in three days. Just enough time to get supplies for the two-month long journey. God willing, he thought to himself, they'd arrive sometime in late June.

꙱

The quay was overflowing with masses of people. Some were dockhands loading and unloading items from around the world. Most were awaiting their ship to wherever in hopes of a new life.

Gent stayed close to Gregor.

"Ye ken who we're goin' to see, dinna ye, ol' boy," he said, rubbing Gent's ears without having to bend over.

Gent's brown eyes, nearly hidden under his coarse hair, seemed to beam a bit brighter.

The call was made to board, and with many people wary of a dog so large, a wide berth was given, so Gregor was one of the first to walk up the gangway.

The smell from the hold permeated the entire ship. He wondered if Catrìona had to endure such a stench. The passage he booked was one where he worked with the crew. He figured it would make the time aboard go faster since he wasn't one to idle about. He was glad he did that now and couldn't wait to get underway. The freshening breeze would help clear his nostrils.

He found the captain, who, after eyeing Gent with little less than disdain, assigned him a job hoisting the ropes. With his build—a few inches over six feet, and nearly sixteen solid stone in weight—his strength would come in handy. Gent was left to guard Gregor's chest with its supplies and treasure.

The day had all the beginnings of perfection. Blue sky, light breeze from the northwest and comfortable temperatures. Once underway, the breeze picked up and the ship hurled along the waves with little effort. By the time he got a chance to bid farewell to Scotland, it was little more than hills on the horizon.

Night came before he knew it and his hammock felt like a featherbed. Gent snored under him with the same intensity as the rest of the crew. By first light, the bell was rung and the day started in the same ordered chaos of ropes, wind and barked orders. There was little time for much of anything else. The sea rolled on forever, never giving away where they might be at any given time. Only the true seamen knew that, having a sense about those things. They'd look at the stars and could project with great accuracy just where in that great expanse of blue they were.

Day after day was the same, save the weather. The first storm, Gregor thought surely they would perish. The few men he worked close with laughed at him when his complexion turned a bit green.

"Och, this is no' a storm, laddie. This is but a wee blow. Dinna fash yerself, though, we'll be hittin' a real one before we get to Boston, mark me words."

His name was Gordon Buchanan. He stood on legs so bowed it seemed he was molded for a horse, not a ship. His plait was black and tarred like a rat's tail, but his muttonchops were as white as the foam that crashed onto the hull. He may only have reached the middle of Gregor's chest, but his arms were thick with muscles. Gregor marveled at the quickness which Gordon climbed the ropes, using his arms more than his legs. He had adapted well with what he was given to work with.

"Why, I've sailed on this sea for twenty and ten years. Only been in one wreck. Hit the rocks close 'nough to shore that most of us swum to save ourselves. Lost the ship, though. Been in waves so tall they'd be higher than the maintops'l. Hae to stay on yer toes for those," he said with a mischievous twinkle in his ice blue eyes.

"I dinna care to hear any more from ye on the subject. And dinna be callin' me laddie, I'm the same age as ye," Gregor said through gritted teeth. The thought of this ship rocking more than it already was … well, he just didn't want to think about it.

Gordon left him to his work and shimmied up to the mizzen topsail as the captain hollered out orders. Gregor chanced a look for Gent, but he must have been below. Probably sleeping through this entire event.

Sunset, which had turned the sea the color of blood, marked the storm's end. When Gregor found his way to his hammock, Gent was stretching languidly under it. When he caught his keeper's eye, he stood to his full height and wagged his tail.

"Just as I suspected, ye slept through the whole thing, didna ye?" Gregor said, peeling off his wet clothes and tying them to the ropes to dry. The entire hold looked like a laundry. Below him, where the passengers were, he heard crying and moaning. It must have been hell down there with no air. He thought again of Catrìona and her voyage. Her first letter to Alexander telling him of her father's death never mentioned the horrors she must have faced aboard ship. She had never complained, so how could he.

The next morning was calm and they drifted on the currents, but made no headway towards America. The captain let the passengers up for air. After such storms, the dead were hauled on deck and thrown into the sea. Most children and the elderly never made it to their destinations. This morning, thirty bodies were tossed to the depths. Sickness wasn't tolerated either, as it could devastate the entire ship. Often, even the sickly who weren't dead were thrown overboard. Gregor didn't want to watch, but his eyes had a mind of their own when the screaming woman with the lifeless child in her arms was brought up. She refused to let it go. The captain sent her and the babe over the side. It was a cruel and unforgiving life.

Gregor could stand no more. He spotted Gent on the bow and walked over to him. The feel of something alive was what he needed to reassure himself that life could also be good. As Gent got his ears rubbed, a young lad walked up to the tall hound, unafraid, and petted him. The youngster stood eyeball to eyeball with the great dog. When Gent's tongue washed his face, it was the first time laughter had been heard on the ship. It was a foreign sound, one that made everyone in earshot turn to find the reason for it, as though needing to put a stop to it immediately. The mother of the lad ran over and snatched the boy away, paddling his bum for all she was worth. There, crying. Now that was more like it. Gregor just shook his head. He wondered how much longer before they reached their destination. They had to be at least halfway there by now, he hoped.

"Oh, aye," Gordon said, chewing the salty brisket with the few teeth he had left. "Two weeks, maybe, if the weather holds. Remind me tomorrow and we'll see if we can spot Newfoundland on the horizon."

By the next morning, a thick fog engulfed the ship, making the world around it seem nonexistent. Gregor thought it was much like being a ship in a bottle. As he stood near the rails, he heard a strange hissing noise looming in the murk.

"Whale!" someone shouted from above.

Suddenly, Gregor located the source of the commotion as the blowhole opened right beside the ship and sprayed it with a fine mist. Gregor's heart raced. He'd heard tales of such monsters that took ships down with them, but his fear was overwhelmed by curiosity, and he leaned on the railing for a better look.

The enormous dark flesh gave the impression it was rolling, as its slippery back arched in a slow dive ending with its tail, which stood erect for a moment, nearly fifteen feet across, before it slid into the gray calmness with barely a ripple. A few minutes went by and he heard it again in the distance, but he never got another look. Despite himself, Gregor smiled at the event. He would bet Cat never saw a whale.

The calm water and fog remained for the rest of the day into the night. Somewhere in the predawn hours, the wind changed direction and blew in from the west, allowing for a clear sunrise. Finally, they were moving again. The breeze was warm, and by the end of the day Gordon was able to point out the distant jog of land as Newfoundland. With that sighting, an excitement ran through the ship. They were almost there and everyone felt it. Gordon told Gregor that the rest of the voyage would seem endless. Gregor had no doubt.

ε&

Shouts were heard from below decks. Tempers were flaring. It happened on nearly every ship just before their destination; someone getting overanxious to be back on land. The captain took his burliest seamen down with him to stave off any rioting or damage to his ship. His roster included Gregor.

As they descended the ladders, the darkness was nearly absolute. When they reached the hold, only small shafts of light from above were visible. Gregor let his eyes adjust to the gloom. A rat scampered over his boot. He kicked it away. It squealed its indignation. He couldn't breathe; the stench of humankind packed too tightly was nearly overwhelming. He held his sleeve over his face.

As he searched in the darkness for the source of the trouble, his eyes lingered on a child whose hair was moving on its own. Lice so thick it became a living entity on the poor thing's head. Gregor looked away. Nothing he could do about it. In the far corner, two men were dancing around each other with their fists in the air. One of them had blood coming from his nose.

"I've put up wi' yer slow takin' o' me space since we left, and I'll no' take it anymore, ye hear? Now move it back into yer corner, or I'll blacken yer eyes!" The non-bloody one shouted.

"I told ye time and again that there's no room in my corner! I hae three children, ye dinna hae any. O' course I need more room, ye slovenly pig!" the bloody one retorted.

"Slovenly pig! Hae ye looked at yerself in a lookin' glass lately, mate? And yer brats, pissin' themselves day and night … well, it's disgustin'." Non-bloody said just before he let a punch fly, finding its mark yet again.

"All right, the two o' ye," the captain scolded, directing two able-bodied seamen to break it up.

Gregor watched for another minute, but the scuffle seemed over. He followed the other seamen back on deck, where he took a deep, cleansing breath. Christ, how had Cat done it? He felt that they had shared so much heartache when searching for her father in Scotland. Now they were sharing yet another tragedy of sorts, and his heart went out to her. She was stronger than anyone he had ever met—man or woman. He couldn't wait to see her again. Then he wondered if she had found a man in America. If not, perhaps she would consider him as her husband. Funny how that thought came so easily to him. He rolled it over in his mind for a while, for size, and found it not offensive in the least.

Discoveries

30 June 1749, Boston, Massachusetts

As the *Falcon* approached Boston Harbour that warm early summer afternoon, Gregor's spirits were high. Gent stood beside him near the railing, wanting just as much to get onto dry land as everyone else aboard ship. Gregor's crumpled note contained the address of Rose Carlyle, 35 Newberry Street. He would stop there first on the chance of catching Cat at home.

His first step onto the solid dock was as though he had stepped onto the moon, so foreign did it feel to his sea legs. Even Gent walked a bit awkwardly, which made Gregor smile.

"Perhaps we'd better walk this off for a bit before makin' our entrance, eh ol' boy?"

The pair staggered along the cobbled streets, noting the painted plaques on the corners of buildings with the street names. A squeak overhead made Gregor look up to see a sign for the Green Dragon Public House. It was like destiny. He smiled and walked in, taking a seat near the window. Gent sat obediently beside him while he ordered his ale. The barmaid lifted her brow at the sight of the enormous dog, but said nothing.

When she returned with his drink, Gregor asked where Newberry Street was.

"Just south of the Common, due west of 'ere."

"Do ye ken Catrìona Robertson?"

The buxom brunette scratched under her kertch, "No, mate, can't say as I do."

No less than four ales later was Gregor ready to find where Cat made her home. He tossed a few shillings on the table and left, with Gent in tow. He walked over to Hanover Street until he reached the Common. He took a left down Winter which brought him onto Marlborough Street. A little further, then Newberry Street.

The houses were fabulous. Everyone here must have riches beyond belief, he thought. He brought out the crumpled address paper from his pocket while standing in front of the house numbered 35 just to be sure he had it right. He strolled up the walkway and lifted the doorknocker. A heavyset woman about his age opened the door for him.

"What might I be helpin' wi'?" she said, eying him with curiosity.

Gregor cleared his throat and said, "My name is Gregor Macgregor, miss. I'll be lookin' for Catrìona Robertson. Is she here, by chance?"

"Gregor … Gregor … why is yer name familiar ta me? Hoow doo ye ken our Garnet?" Emily asked, rubbing her chin with one hand while her other arm rested on her great bosom.

Gregor smiled at Cat's monicker. "*Garnet* and I worked together to find her Da, Angus, when he was shipped here from London, a prisoner."

Dawning came quickly to her blue eyes. "Och, aye, now I remember! Coome in, coome in!"

Emily ushered Gregor and Gent to the best room and urged Gregor to have a seat.

"Claire, bring soome tea, dear, we hae a guest," she shouted.

"Och, no, miss, I dinna want to take up yer time, I just want to find Cat. Besides," he said, looking at the state of his clothes, "I'm no' fit to be in such a fine place. I just came off the ship."

"Hae ye a place ta stay then?" she asked, once again eyeing him up and down as though taking his measurements.

"Uh, no, no' yet. I figured to stay at the Green Dragon. They've rooms upstairs."

Claire had just walked into the room carrying a tray of tea and scones, piping hot with honey drizzled over them.

In unison, Emily and Claire said, "Ye'll do no such thing."

"We've moore rooms here than we ken what ta doo wi', an' no' one ta fill them. Ye'll stay here, in Garnet's room," Emily said, folding her arms over her chest, daring Gregor to say no.

Gent whined his approval of the invitation. Gregor eyed the fresh scones as their aroma by now had reached his nose. He breathed in deep and smiled. "Well, if it's no trouble …"

ঽ৶

The bath was better than anything he had ever experienced. Warm water, the fragrance of lavender … peaceful. Before he went into this *bath room,* he asked if there was a straight edge to shave with. Claire fixed him up with Charles', along with a looking glass and comb. Gregor brought his trunk upstairs and set out a clean pair of breeks and sark for when he finished bathing.

When he finally came downstairs, Emily and Claire barely recognized him. He had shaved off his beard and managed to tie his thick mop of dark hair into a queue. His wide shoulders strained at the fabric of his sark and his narrow hips were accentuated by the tight-fitting breeks.

"Oh aye, that's mooch better," Emily said, once again appraising him up and down.

Claire smiled and said, "Yor a fine lookin' ge'n'el'man, Gregor."

Gregor was never praised for his looks and his beet-red face showed it. He allowed himself a shy smile and was ushered into the dining room where a feast was laid out on the table. Gent was greedily eating scraps from a bowl on the floor.

"I thank ye, ladies, for treatin' me like royalty, but I dinna think I deserve it," he said standing behind his chair.

"Sit, sit. We'd be treatin' any o' Garnet's friends like this. We miss her soo," Emily said, taking her seat.

"An' Greame and Jimmy, too," Claire added.

Gregor's heart fell a little. So she did have a man, and from the sounds of a son as well.

Emily must have caught the look and asked, "Did she no' tell ye oov Greame and Jimmy?"

"No. It that her man and son?"

"Well, Greame was the man who saved her from that sonofabitch … pardon," Emily waved, "Charles."

"Who's Charles?"

For the next hour and a half, Claire and Emily flooded Gregor with what Cat had been up to for the past couple of years. The three of them ate their fill, retired to the best room and continued the saga over a nice whisky. By the time they finished, Gregor was spent.

"Christ. It's a good thing she ne'er wrote to Alexander about all that went on here. He would hae demanded her return." He stood and stretched his muscles. They weren't used to inactivity for this long. Then he laughed out loud, a rich, melodious chuckle, and said, "She really directed a military operation in yer kitchen? Ha!" He laughed again. "If only I could hae been here to witness it."

"It dooes seem laughable noow, but when she was kidnapped, well, it was frightenin' indeed."

"And that's when she met Greame and Jim. What's Greame's family name again?"

"Hay, Greame Hay. Garnet said he was a driver for, ooh, what was his name … began wi' a T … Tull … Tulla … soomething," Emily told him.

"No' verra tall, thick build, ugly as a stump?" Gregor recalled.

"Aye, that's 'im," Clarie said. "No' a very 'igh opinion of 'im, though."

"My apologies. Aye, I ken who he is now. Can't say as I ken much about him, though. Quiet sort."

"Only speaks when he has soomething ta say," Emily said. "His men think verra highly oov him. They're runnin' his teashop doown on Milk Street. Perhaps ye should goo talk wi' them in the mornin'. They'll be better able ta tell ye where Garnet is, since they've all been to Maine."

"I'll do that. Now ladies, I feel I must retire for the evenin'. I'm dead on me feet."

ҙ♣

The morning dawned foggy, warm and humid. Gregor dragged himself out of the softness of the finest bed he'd ever slept in and got dressed. He looked out his window only to see the murk as thick as it was aboard ship. The harbour was nowhere to be found.

Gent was sprawled out on the hooked rug, taking up most of it. He must have been pretty comfortable, for he never moved. Only his eyes followed Gregor's motions around the room.

"C'mon, ol' boy. Let's go see who Cat's new friends are."

The pair trotted down the stairs and almost made it to the door when Claire appeared holding a mug of warm ale.

"Emily said ya didn't seem like a tea sort o' man."

"Well, she'd be right."

Gregor followed Claire into the dining room when Emily walked through the kitchen door with a tray of sausage and eggs.

"Ye canna possibly expect me to eat again after last night's meal."

"Ooh, please," Emily said sarcastically.

He sat and ate with gusto. Gent even got another bowl. "That'll hold me for a week. Truly," he said, when Emily was about to say she didn't believe him.

"Leave 'im be, Em. That's 'ow 'e keeps 'is boyish figure," Claire giggled.

With that, Gregor took his leave. He walked over to Marlborough Street and took a right onto Milk Street. Emily said the Worldwide Tea Emporium was nearly to the harbour. He found it without trouble and walked in, closing the door after Gent.

A man behind the counter eyed Gent suspiciously, but asked courteously, "What might I be helpin' ye wi', sir?"

Gregor introduced himself and got much the same reaction as Emily and Claire had given him. A few more men filed out of the back room and shook hands as though they were all long lost friends.

"Cat, uh, Garnet, must hae really spoke highly o' me for ye all to extend yer hospitality so easily," Gregor said.

"There werna many she did speak of, so we guessed there werna many o' her family left," Kelvin said, taking a long drag on his pipe.

"Emily and Claire said ye all hae been to Maine. How can I get there? Does a ship leave regularly or do ye ride?"

Kelvin and George exchanged glances. A silent word was passed, then a smile came over their faces. Gregor wasn't sure he wanted to know what was going on in their heads.

"It's near time for a visit, anyway, right cousins?" Robbie said.

Kelvin nodded. "We'll leave in a week wi' provisions for the new settlement they hae built by now."

"Settlement? How many cousins did ye leave up there?" Gregor said.

"Seven. Some stayed wi' the Penobscot and others stayed with Greame and Garnet."

"Penobscot?"

For the rest of the morning, Gregor was filled in on the native population, the war, the climate of this new land, and what Cat had been through. Things they never shared with Emily and Claire for fear of making them sick with worry.

The fog had lifted and hazy sunshine was making it very hot when Gregor finally left the teashop. He found his way down to the waterfront for some cooler air, but his sark still clung to him. Gent was panting heavily even in the shade.

"Did ye hear that, Gent, our Catrìona's as close to marrit as she can be. I guess it was just a silly dream to think she might take me as her husband, me bein' near as old as her Da. I'll at least remain her friend. From the sounds of it, she can use all the friends she can get. Trouble just seems to find that lass."

The week went by quickly, and by the time the *Revenge* left Boston Harbour, Gregor's breeks were pretty tight. He had never eaten so much in his life.

Greame's cousins had loaded the ship with what looked like enough for a worldwide expedition. Furniture, fabrics, kitchen utensils, windows, tools, food and a myriad of other staples would be going to Cape Rozier for the new settlement. Gregor wondered how he'd fit in, but figured he could make himself useful somehow. Right now, he had to work off this weight he'd put on and made himself useful on the ropes.

The westerlies and fair weather remained for the entire voyage, bringing them to Cape Rozier in record time; three days. Kelvin steered the *Revenge* into the deepwater cove and dropped anchor. The long boat was lowered, and as Gregor got in, he chanced a look on the shore and the sight he saw brought tears to his eyes.

Cat was standing on the pebbled beach waving like a mad woman. His eyebrows raised when he saw her in a pair of breeks that showed off her figure scandalously. Gent got in beside Gregor and barked until their boat reached shore. Gent was out before they reached dry land, and was uncontainable. He rushed to her, unmindful of his size, and leapt onto her, dropping her to the ground. By the time Gregor got there, she was laughing so hard, tears were running down her face as she tried to fend off Gent's wet kisses.

Gregor pulled the beast off her and grabbed her wrists to haul her to her feet. She squealed with delight and wrapped her arms around his neck in a show of affection he hadn't felt since she left him in London.

"Dear Gregor," she said smiling, kissing his cheek. Her deep auburn hair was nearly on fire in the sunlight. Her amethyst eyes and deep dimples looked more mature, but not hardened by her ordeals.

"Och, it's good to see ye, lass," he said, giving her another squeeze.

"I couldna believe it when I saw ye in a dream. Comin' here to this new, wild place. I saw other things, too." A little sadness crept into her voice. "Alexander."

"There are no secrets wi' ye, now are there? Aye, he died on April twenty-eighth. He was still holdin' his glass o' whisky. No' a better way to go, I say."

"And what of ye, Gregor? How did ye find me?"

"Well, I found ye through two great ladies in Boston who nearly fattened me to the point o' no return. I still dinna fit into these breeks the way I should," he laughed, trying to put a finger into the waistband. It was easy to laugh with her.

Cat laughed that wonderful melodious sound that he remembered so well. "Emily and Claire. How are they?"

"More important, lass, how are ye? And speakin' o' breeks ..."

She put her arm around his waist and walked him up to the cabin filling him in on her life in this place called Maine.

A Dog, A Lobster, and An Indian Walk Into A Cabin ...

Greame and Gregor remembered each other from Blair Castle. Tullibardine had been a regular visitor there, and where he went, Greame went. They each told stories. reminiscing about their former lives, and Jim and Cat listened to the tall tales as the two men did their best to outdo each other. It brought Cat back home to when she would listen to her father's and brothers' stories. She and her mother would roll their eyes as the tales got bigger and bolder, with hardly a word of truth by the end of them.

As the weeks went by, Gregor's impressions of this wild, wooded land were those of incredible freedom and a bounty of natural resources. Game was plentiful, and he assumed the land was fertile, if one could find a spot where there weren't any rocks. He loved the look of the sea and its ever-changing moods, telling Cat and Greame over supper why he had never considered living near it when he was in Scotland. "I'm no' a fisherman," he said. They all laughed trying to picture him in a dory with a net.

By the middle of August, the stone foundation for Gregor's cabin was complete and logs sat upon it waist high. As well as building a cabin for Gregor, Cat and Greame had also decided to put an addition on their cabin to serve as a dining room. Cat wanted to keep the extended family fed well, and with all the men working, going home to cook supper for themselves didn't seem right. Greame's men stayed on for the summer to complete the village, so there was plenty of manpower.

One afternoon as Cat was folding bedsheets, a knock came on the door. She turned to see Far Eyes and Smiles at Everything standing at the threshold with an enormous lobster. She squealed with delight to see them, but steered clear of the giant crustacean.

"You know how to cook?" Far Eyes asked.

"Aye, but no' one that big, unless I cut it up first." Cat said.

"Cut off claws and tail. Use rest on ground to make better."

"Better for what? All we can grow is rocks."

Far Eyes laughed. "That why make ground better. Use seaweed, too. Next year, you have planting place."

Gregor and Greame had just set another log in place, hewn by Geoffrey and Kelvin, when Gregor spotted the half-naked men entering Cat's cabin.

"Who are those men?" he asked with a bit of alarm in his voice, putting his hand on his dirk ready to save Catrìona.

Greame followed Gregor's stare, and said, "No need to worry. That's Far Eyes and his man, Smiles at Everything. They're Penobscot."

Gregor pulled his eyes from the natives for a moment to see if Greame was fooling with him.

Greame smiled, raised his eyebrows and nodded.

"Ye allow them in yer house nearly naked like that? Is Cat all right wi' them in there?" He said, still not convinced.

"Oh, aye. We lived wi' them the first winter we came up here. They're as close to us as ye are. Let me introduce ye."

Gregor nodded and followed Greame to the house.

Ð

The lobster was on the floor of the kitchen, backed into a corner. It was a dark reddish-brown with blue areas on its claws, and over two feet long. Gent was eyeing the odd looking creature with restrained curiosity, sniffing at it just out of reach of those lethal-looking claws. When its antenna twitched, Gent growled and backed up a step in anticipation of an attack.

When the creature went still, Gent ventured a little closer. The lobster remained motionless, and Gent found courage enough to put his front paw on its head. In one quick movement, the lobster

lunged and got Gent to barking. This caught the household's attention and they watched as the giant claws snapped opened and shut.
Gent was wild with indignation as the lobster scampered around his
legs, snapping those enormous claws. Smiles at Everything, of course,
found this more than amusing and had to sit down, he was laughing
so hard. Far Eyes was yelling at Greame to get behind the lobster and
grab it by the body. Lobsters in Scotland didn't seem to get this large,
but he'd had experiences with their claws.

The lobster seemed to read Greame's mind when it noticed the
rear attack. Those eight little legs propelled it backwards so quickly,
it nearly ran over Greame's feet. He let out a yell, tripping over the
rug as he danced beside the crustacean trying to steer clear of those
claws. Gent was now in protective mode, barking and snapping his
own teeth at the claws. Far Eyes yelled at Cat to get Gent outside so
he didn't get his nose bit off. Smiles at Everything was now on the
floor in hysterics with tears streaming down his face.

Cat grabbed Gent by the scruff of his neck, but Gent was in no
mood to be ousted from the fray. He wrenched free of Cat's grip and
leapt onto the lobster, biting at the snapping claws. Greame, Far
Eyes and Cat were yelling to get Gent off when Gregor stepped in.
He somehow tiptoed around the angry lobster, pulled Gent off and
literally threw him outside and slammed the door.

When the lobster realized the furry beast was gone, it set its
sights for the next thing on the floor. In an angry lunge, the lobster's
claws attached themselves to Smiles at Everything's breech clout,
just missing his manhood. Smiles at Everything screamed and tried
to detach himself from the nasty death grip, looking a little like a
lobster himself as he crawled backwards on the floor. Gregor and
Greame were both roaring with laughter. Gent was still barking outside and clawing at the door, wanting a piece of the action. Cat and
Far Eyes each went for a claw. Cat managed to grab the claw that
wasn't attached to anything at the moment and held on. Far Eyes
couldn't make the death grip on Smiles at Everything's breech clout
release. He stood and surveyed the kitchen for a weapon, then grabbed
a cleaver from the table. He stepped a foot on the lobster's back and
brought the blade down onto its arm, severing the claw from its
body.

Smiles at Everything was still screaming because the claw didn't release its grip. He danced around the kitchen pulling and tugging at the claw between his legs. He finally tore off his breech clout altogether, which now made Far Eyes and Cat burst with laughter. Smiles at Everything opened the door to a seething Gent, backed up a step, then ran past the angry dog without looking back.

"So this it how ye entertain yerselves up here, eh?" Gregor said, mopping his face.

"I canna remember the last time I laughed so hard," Greame said, wiping his eyes.

"Poor Smiles at Everything," Cat said, still giggling. "He'll be back to yer village by now."

"What in bloody hell is goin' on up here?" Kelvin said from the doorway. "We just saw Smiles at Everything runnin' stark naked from here screamin' like a *bean-sidhe*."

Kelvin stepped in and saw the discarded breech clout on the floor with the lobster's claw still attached. He looked around at the smiling faces and nodded, not needing any other form of explanation. He left chuckling.

&

The lobster dinner, complete with mussels and clams, biscuits and a few berry pies, was the perfect ending to a great summer day. The sunset was painted in shades of peach, apricot and lavender, ending with a vermilion orb that fell into the sea. A warm breeze stirred the fire as Gregor and Far Eyes exchanged war stories. Cat and Greame sat contentedly on the rocks making plans for the next day, while Gent sprawled himself out on the cool boulder next to Cat, close enough to get his ears rubbed. Jim and a pretty young Penobscot girl called Jumping Turtle were strolling down the beach hand-in-hand.

No one was paying any attention to the ship on the horizon. No one on that side of the Cape, anyway.

Smiles at Everything had seen the humor in his undoing … after a few hours. Though not in time to return to eat the cause of his humiliation. He walked along the shore of his summer village then up into the woods overlooking the bay and the hills to the west. His keen eye spotted the ship, but couldn't make out the flag it was flying in the waning light. If it was a French ship, that meant trading supplies for his people. If it was an English ship, it meant trouble. He would have to wait until morning to find out for sure.

ॐ

Gregor was invited to Far Eyes' village the next day. Far Eyes told him there was someone he should meet.

In the morning, as the rising sun sent dappled shafts of light through the woods, Far Eyes set off with Gregor to his summer village on the other side of the Cape. If Gregor wasn't shown where it was, he would have never seen it, the wigwams were camouflaged so well.

In a clearing he noticed her. She was squatting down over a deer hide rubbing it soft with a stone. From behind, her figure was shapely as it fit snuggly in the deerskin dress. She was barefoot and her long, dark hair splayed over her back. Turning her head when footsteps came up behind her, she stood when she saw her brother and Gregor. Her widening eyes were her only expression when she saw him.

Gregor gave a sideways scowl to Far Eyes, indicating that he did not need to be set up with a woman.

Far Eyes ignored him and said, "Gregor Macgregor, this Sings Like Bird."

Sings Like Bird smiled and said, "Pleased."

Her voice was deep and soft, something a man could listen to for a long time. Gregor noticed a fresh pink scar about three inches long on the right side of her face near her hairline. He tried not to stare, but at the same time wondered what or who had done that to her. He regained himself and cleared his throat. "My pleasure, miss."

"Sings Like Bird my sister. She need man ..."

"Whoa, Far Eyes," Gregor protested. "I didna come here for a match makin' visit. I'm well past the age o' takin' a woman—too set in me ways to care for anyone but me, beg yer pardon, miss. No offense."

Far Eyes smiled but seemed to ignore Gregor's plight. "Come, I show you around village."

Once out of earshot of Sings Like Bird, Gregor laid a hand on Far Eyes' shoulder. "What was that all about?"

Far Eyes stopped and looked up at the big man. It took a moment, but when he spoke he said, "You not true to self."

Gregor just opened his mouth and watched Far Eyes walk on.

"Wait," he said, catching up in just a few strides. "What makes ye so sure I'm not bein' truthful?"

"I see."

"Ye see?" He paused for a moment remembering that he was a shaman. "Oh great. Ye see. Ye mean like Cat sees, dinna ye?"

Far Eyes smiled and nodded.

Gregor took in a deep breath and let it out, defeated. "A man can hae no peace around the likes o' ye."

Far Eyes laughed.

"But I'm still no' wantin' a woman."

"In time you will."

Smiles at Everything found Far Eyes and Gregor at the reversing falls and he told them about the ship he'd seen just before dark last night. In their native tongue, the two put a plan into motion to find this mystery ship, since it had not anchored in Pentagöet, as was customary with the French ships.

Smiles at Everything ran in the direction of the village and Far Eyes told Gregor the plan.

"The English still have bounty on Indian scalps," Far Eyes told Gregor.

"What? How long hae they been doin' that to yer people?"

"Many years. They do not care that some scalps come from women and children, they want all Indians gone. Two summers ago, white man's sickness killed almost all Mi'kmaq people. Not many left. English not want us here. Want land for self. Take, but not give back."

"Aye, I ken what the English are like. That's why I've come to this country. All that I had in Scotland is gone, taken by the English," Gregor said. "I want to help ye to fight them. Tell me what I can do."

At low tide later that afternoon, three canoes set out for Pentagöet each carrying four Penobscot braves. Gregor went with Far Eyes and Smiles at Everything. It didn't take long to reach the old settlement.

The canoes were hauled up high on the shore, and the braves scattered in search of the vessel, disappearing quickly into the woods.

Gregor followed Far Eyes through the village, noting the French, Dutch and English influences in the architecture. The dilapidated fort was armed with cannons aimed at the harbour, but no one was around.

Up on a knoll overlooking the harbour and the bay, the two men waited. It wasn't long before they heard several shots fired behind them. Gregor felt naked with only his dirk at his side.

"Are ye able to *see* what's happenin'?" Gregor asked, crouched low to the ground.

"I not see like Garnet. I make ceremony or dream, then see," Far Eyes explained, he too on his belly.

This fact made Gregor realize now what an asset Alexander had with Cat giving him such detailed information about the battles in the Rising. He wished she were here right now to tell him who was shooting at them.

Cat was in the middle of mixing a bowl of bread dough, smiling again at the lobster attack in her kitchen yesterday. The creature had to weigh nearly two stones, but its meat was tender and sweet. She dumped the dough onto the floured table and started folding and pressing the bubbles out of it. The chirping of birds just outside the window made her look, and she caught sight of vivid yellow and black bodies swooping and diving through the woods with such speed, she wondered how they didn't dash themselves against the trees.

Her hands ceased the kneading process when the birds suddenly changed to men. They were Penobscot braves and Smiles at Everything was with them. They were being chased by white men in red coats. English! What were they doing up here? She watched to see one of the soldiers stop and take aim, then disappear in a cloud of blue smoke as the musket fired. The shot missed the braves, but then she noticed Gregor and Far Eyes. The braves were leading the soldiers right for them. Where were they? Desperately, she tried to see if this was happening now or would happen in the future, but couldn't tell.

She ran to the door and screamed, "Greame!"

Greame and his men were taking a break beside Gregor's cabin chewing on some deer jerky. Cat's scream sent him bolting to the house, followed by the rest of the crew.

"What is it? Are ye hurt?" He asked breathlessly, looking her over for a wound.

"Where's Gregor and Far Eyes?"

"What? I dinna ken. Why?"

The men picked up on the fear in Cat's voice, but couldn't figure out what had caused it.

"English soldiers are shootin' at Smiles at Everything and some other braves and they're leadin' them right towards Gregor and Far Eyes."

"Kelvin, did Gregor tell ye where he and Far Eyes were off to this mornin'?"

Kelvin shook his head, "He only said Far Eyes told him there was someone he wanted him to meet. I figured they were just goin' to the summer village."

Turning back to Cat, he asked, "Do we go?"

"Aye, since I canna tell when this is happenin'." she said, wiping her dough-covered hands on her apron before whipping it off. "I just hope it's no' too late."

❧

When they arrived at the summer village, all seemed peaceful enough. Cat asked Sings Like Bird, who was tending the smoking fire, where Far Eyes was. Sings Like Bird announced that Smiles at Everything had seen a ship, so Far Eyes took many braves and Angry Giant to Pentagöet to see it.

"Angry Giant? Who is that?" Cat asked.

"Big man, black hair, not smile."

"Gregor?"

Sings Like Bird nodded. "They leave not long past."

Cat turned to Greame, "Perhaps it hasn't happened yet."

"Is there a canoe we can use?" Greame asked Sings Like Bird.

She pointed to the shore. "If any left."

The five of them ran towards the shore. Two canoes were tied in the brush above the tide line. The boats were released and rushed to the water. Cat was about to get in when Greame stopped her.

"Ye're no' comin, it could be dangerous."

"Oh, for the love of *Brighid*, Greame, ye ken by now I can take care o' myself, now let's go before we're too late!"

To emphasize the point, a shot was fired from Pentagöet. No time for arguments now. They paddled for all they were worth, and within minutes were dragging their canoes alongside the three others.

Another shot, then bursting from the woods came a few Penobscot braves, then Far Eyes and Gregor, with Smiles at Everything ending the group.

"Ye're just in time for the fun!" Gregor shouted to Greame.

"How many?"

"We counted seven, and us wi' no pistols or swords! Such a pity," Gregor said with a broad smile on his face. "Now go!"

The group dashed back to the canoes and quickly got underway, paddling for their lives. Cat chanced a look on shore to see the redcoated soldiers emerging from the woods, but not setting up to fire upon them.

"They've stopped the chase," Cat said to her boat mates.

"How did ye find us?" Gregor asked, breathing heavy from paddling.

Cat just raised her eyebrow.

"Oh, aye, well ye cut it a bit close, didna ye? Ye usually get yer visions well ahead o' time. What happened?" Gregor chided.

Cat sent him a kick, which he was unable to avoid in the close quarters.

Greame filled Gregor and Far Eyes in on their detective work and irresistibly added, "So, *Angry Giant,* what made ye leave wi'out yer pistol?"

"What did ye call me?"

"Och, it's no' me that called ye that name that's fits ye so well. Sings Like Bird called ye that when she told us where ye went," Greame said, his face lighting up with mischief.

Far Eyes laughed, agreeing on the name.

Gregor scowled at them and tried to change the subject by saying, "I didna ken I needed to be armed in these woods. It wilna happen again, but what were the *Sassenaich* doin' up here?"

ॐ

The English, having nearly decimated the white pine stands in Massachusetts, set their eyes on the thickly wooded coast of Maine for their ships' masts. The Crown's insatiable appetite to rule as much of the world as possible meant building more ships. More taking, and giving nothing in return but hardship, taxes and exploitation. Someday they would be made to pay.

Back To Nature

As the summer turned to autumn, Gregor had somehow managed to procure enough guns and ammunition from the French to arm the settlement and the Lobster Clan. Cat no longer asked where he went for days on end, taking only Smiles at Everything with him. She still had not regained her full capabilities of the Sight after losing it for all those months. 'Course, she really didn't practice strengthening it either, choosing not to see too much, unless her family—immediate or native—were in trouble.

Far Eyes knew only that they went nearly to New France and traded with the Maliseet, as well. He feared disease to his people after having so much contact with the whites.

Greame's men made several trips to Boston and back, bringing with them items of great use in the trade system. If the English had thoughts of harassing their settlement, or the Penobscot, they were in for a fight.

Everyone watched the seas with more caution now. Living so close to the well-established Pentagöet and its ever-changing inhabitants, the French could easily lose control if the English wanted it for themselves. Cat voiced her concerns one night.

"Greame, I still dinna ken why I'm here. And now there seems to be more unrest wi' too many countries wantin' a piece of America. I canna be someone who would hae a hand in how this all sorts itself out, can I?"

"Perhaps," Greame said, stroking her hair, "but perhaps, ye're just supposed to live. Ye and I both found our way here, perhaps we were meant to be together and that's the only reason. Dinna ye think ye've been through enough? Why are ye askin' for more?"

"Oh, aye, I've definitely been through enough, but I dinna think that's why I returned to this life. There has to be another reason. I just wish I ken what it was."

"Ye dinna think tryin' to change the outcome o' the Risin' was enough? Ye came here to find yer Da, but also to stay alive. If ye had stayed in Scotland wi' what's gone on after the rebellion, do ye think ye'd have been better off than ye are here, lass?"

Cat thought about that. Could that have been the entire reason for her existence? And then to have failed at it? Well, Catherine Macinroy must not be very pleased with her selection of the mortal to come back as. Cat fell asleep with more questions than answers.

The dream began in a field. She was lying in the tall grass with the warm sun on her face, watching as the clouds curled and dissipated in the upper air currents. Crickets chirped and creaked all around her. A tree began to take shape next to her, spreading its enormous branches to shade her. The tree was an oak and the sunlight dappled through the leaves. A bird landed in the thick branch above her head. An owl. Its round, flat face with its large yellow eyes looked right at her. It seemed to be saying something to her, but the language was garbled. From a hole in the oak came a tiny faerie with translucent blue-green wings. The faerie landed on Cat's forehead and tweaked her ear. After that, she could understand the owl perfectly. It was telling her that she was asking the wrong question. Then it started saying "Whoo. Whoo."

Cat awoke and slipped out of bed. Greame's even breathing indicated that he had not been disturbed by her departure. She wrapped a shawl around her and walked outside into the crisp night air. The dream was certainly a message. The oak, a symbol of ancient wisdom. The owl, a messenger, for sure, but not usually a good omen. She felt the owl had more to do with the call it made, than the bird itself. But, "Who?" Who what?

She looked up at the stars, thick enough to walk on and close enough to grasp. A fox barked in the distance. The fragrance on the breeze was sweet from the sea, and the waves lapped gently onto the pebbled beach. A voice filled her head; soft, yet demanding to be heard.

Who are you?

Well that was a question she didn't know the answer to. She smiled at the reason for the owl in her dream.

"Who am I?" she said out loud. "Indeed."

When she started to think about who she was, the answers were shallow. She had a feeling the question should be, *who am I in this world?* A deeper look. In relation to the stars, who was she? In the grand scheme of life, who was she? Did any of it matter? If she were to die this very instant, would some catastrophic event happen to change the world? Would she even be missed?

Lass, must ye always be so dramatic?

Cat smiled, recognizing Anna's voice. "Hallò, Mistress. Ye ken verra well I dinna hae a gift for drama. But I do need some help wi' who I am."

Ye ken who ye are, but yer no' usin' yer powers anymore.

"I'm frightened of what I see. Besides, it really helps no one. The same events still occur. Nothing really changes."

What about yer new friends?

"Far Eyes? He has his own powers. Why would he need me to tell him what's to happen?"

Tcha! His powers are nothin' like yers, Garnet. He needs yer help. His people are in peril.

"Why, what do ye see that I canna?"

There were no more answers from Anna Macpherson. Cat would have to regain her powers if she was going to help the Penobscot.

When Cat walked into the house, Greame was sitting in the light of a single candle at the kitchen table. Cat stood behind him and wrapped her arms around his neck.

"So, what did ye find out?" He said, stifling a yawn, rubbing her chilled arms.

"That I hae a lot o' work to do. Let's go back to bed."

Cat was up at dawn getting breakfast for the men. After cleaning up the dishes, she told Greame she was going to talk to Far Eyes.

"I'll take Jim wi' me. I'm sure he wilna mind waitin' for me at the village," she said, indicating he would get to spend some time with Jumping Turtle.

"When should I expect ye back?" Greame asked.

"We'll be back before supper."

Clouds filled the sky with grays and whites. The forest-dwelling songbirds had moved on to warmer climates. From overhead, a flock of geese headed south, honking periodically, as though asking questions like, *are we there yet?* The poplar and birch had already begun to turn yellow.

Gent tore through the woods catching the ever-present animal scents, only reappearing twice on the hour-long walk to Far Eyes' village. Jim was his usual quiet self which gave Cat a chance to look at the flora in a medicinal light. Something she only did for wound care. There were many different plants she didn't recognize, therefore didn't know how they could be used. That was one of the items to discuss with Far Eyes. There were very few plants here that also grew in Scotland, so it would be learning everything anew.

The other item to talk to him about was what he needed help with. Cat didn't think that was going to be as easy as learning the medicinal uses of all the new plants.

When they arrived in the village, Cat was struck by the efficiency of everything, noticing with new eyes how simple life was for them. They could move on a whim, following game with the seasons. They could also disappear from their enemies. Far Eyes told her that carrying no burdens meant survival. The Penobscot could scatter for months when enemies like the English invaded, meeting up again at a designated place when it was safe. Cat wondered why they would need her help when they could already do that.

"Good to see you, Far Eyes."

"I dream last night. You in it," he said, walking towards the shore, his hands behind his back, making him look fatherly.

"What was it about?" Cat said, matching his slow stride.

Far Eyes took a seat on a large boulder at the water's edge. Cat sat beside him, picking golden grasses and braiding them together.

"You come learn about medicine."

"Aye …" she said, indicating there was much more to the visit.

"More?"

"I, too, had a dream last night."

Far Eyes looked at her quizzically.

"In my dream, the owl flew to the oak tree and asked me who I was."

"You know answer." It wasn't a question. He spoke it as though she should already know what it meant. It rankled her a bit. She had to ask.

"Do ye ken who I am?"

Far Eyes smiled. It was a sad smile. He nodded.

Cat looked at him square on and touched his arm. "Will ye tell me?"

"I can not."

"Why must everything be so difficult? I'm supposed to help yer people. Help them do what? They hae ye. And ye already ken, so why would ye need me?" Cat said, becoming frustrated and throwing the braided grass away.

"I see what *will* happen. You see what *could* happen."

Cat thought about that for a minute. It still made no sense to her. How would that small difference be of any consequence?

"It in your heart." When he saw she didn't understand, he said, "The answer in your heart."

"But …"

"Come. We learn medicine today."

Cat had no choice but to follow. There was no arguing with Far Eyes.

By the end of the day, Cat had learned about yarrow, lily root, acorns, goldenrod, juniper berries, and so much more. The Penobscot were masters in herbology and made strong decoctions and teas to aid in everything from wounds and pain to deworming, to childbirth. Cat was glad to relearn some old things and gather new skills to add to her abilities. It felt like the right time to get back into healing.

Later, she found Jim and began their walk back home. He was still very quiet.

"Is there somethin' on yer mind, lad?"

Jim stopped for a moment and stuffed his hands in his pockets, looking everywhere but at her.

"Ye may as well tell me."

"I want ta go with Jumpin' Turtle ta her winter camp." He didn't dare meet her eyes for fear of what was in them.

"Really?"

Jim nodded and chanced a look because her tone wasn't what he was expecting.

"Ye're a man now, Jim. Ye dinna hae to ask my permission for anythin'."

"I want ta marry her … if her father will let me," he said, toeing a pinecone.

"Who is her Da?"

Anxious to finally talk to someone, it all flowed out of him. "His name is Blue Feather. Her Mum is Raven. Jumpin' Turtle is their only child. That may pose a problem with her marryin' me, but I know I'll be a good husband ta her, and I'll make her parents proud ta call me their son."

Cat did her best to hide a smile. Jim would no doubt make any woman a good husband. He was a caring and sensitive young man.

"Would speakin' wi' them help ye?"

"Really? Ya'd do that for me?"

"O' course! I'll speak wi' Far Eyes tomorrow and ask if it would be permitted."

He gave her a hug and they both headed for home a little lighter.

Cat walked in to see Gregor home for the first time in over a week. He and Greame were at the table drinking mugs of chicory and looking rather serious.

"Hallò, stranger," she said, giving Gregor a peck on the cheek. "What are the two o' ye conspirin'?"

"I've just returned from the St. Lawrence. That's Mi'kmaq territory. The English have raised the price for their scalps to ten pounds each," Gregor said, staring into the dark brew in his mug.

"Christ," Cat said. "What does that mean for the rest of the tribes?"

"It means the English want this land and will go to war again to take it from the French or the Indians. There's talk of the French and Indians fightin' the English together. The only tribe who are on the English side are the Mohawk."

"That figures," Cat said. "We've already had a run-in wi' them."

Gregor looked up from his mug with a surprised expression on his face.

Cat explained the incident with the three Mohawk braves in the Penobscot camp last year, with comments from Greame rounding out the story. She also told him of the mysterious brave who seemed to have mystical powers like Far Eyes and herself. Greame now had a surprised look on his face, that being the first he'd heard of it.

"Was that brave killed in the camp wi' the others?" Greame asked.

Cat thought back, realizing that he had managed to escape, but to where? She shook her head, meeting Greame's eyes. The Mohawk shaman would be back and they would meet again. She had to be ready for him, since he held a power that was stronger than hers. It was time to go back inside herself for answers and strength, the two things she had lost over the past year. She needed Far Eyes' help.

"I'd best be startin' supper," she said, excusing herself from the table, mostly to have some time to think.

Greame knew her well enough to leave her alone, but Gregor said, "That's it? Ye're no' goin' to say anythin' else?"

Cat looked back at him and said nothing. Subject closed. Gregor knew that expression and didn't pursue it.

ℰ❧

In Greame's arms that night, Cat recounted what she had learned from Far Eyes, and Jim's plans to marry. Greame's deep chuckle made her smile.

"I kent he was smitten, but no' to that extent."

"I promised to speak to Far Eyes tomorrow about it," she said.

She felt him get serious. He knew it wasn't the only thing she was going to speak to Far Eyes about.

"Ye will be careful, wilna ye? I ken ye're strong, but ..."

"That's why I hopin' Far Eyes can shed some light on the powers o' this man. And he is just a man. Unfortunately, I've lost much o' my powers, but I'll get them back. After what happened last year, I didna want to hae anythin' to do wi' the Sight, but now I'm ready to get it back."

ℰ❧

Cat and Jim left at dawn for the Penobscot village. The woods smelled of balsam. Some rain was needed though, because the ground crunched under their feet. A red squirrel sat in a low branch and scolded them for intruding. Out on the water, a loon called its mournful cry. A moment later, its mate answered. Jim pointed out a porcupine in a copse of alder. It watched as the pair passed by, knowing it was too slow to make its escape, taking its chances that it would be left alone.

When they reached the village, Far Eyes greeted them, and Cat explained Jim's plight. Far Eyes smiled and patted Jim on the back.

"Blue Feather good man. He know Jumping Turtle want Jim for husband. I set parley for next full moon. You bring big gift to make Jumping Turtle wife. Give to Blue Feather. He tell you good or bad."

Jim's face lit up, agreeing to the stipulations. He took his leave to find his love.

Far Eyes turned to Cat with knowing eyes and said, "What on mind?"

Cat recounted the incident with the Mohawk shaman to a very concerned Far Eyes.

"Why you not say before?"

"If ye remember, that's when I went a bit daft," she said, pointing to her head.

Despite the seriousness of the situation, Far Eyes laughed, repeating the word daft and pointing to his head.

Cat rolled her eyes, but smiled just the same.

"His name Black Devil," he told Cat when he decided to get back to business.

"Aye, seems a fittin' name. I ken he could see me through the bushes—could *feel* him see me. Tell me what he can do wi' his powers, then I will find a way to meet him on his own ground."

"You not want to meet him again. He take your power last time. I not know this until now," Far Eyes said, convinced it was the truth.

Cat thought about that for a minute. If he was powerful enough to remove the Sight from her, maybe he was more than a man.

"Are ye strong enough to do that to someone, Far Eyes?"

"That not what I do. I heal, not destroy. Black Devil strong with other power. You not want to know about this thing. Very bad medicine."

"How do ye expect to keep him from destroyin' ye if ye dinna ken about his power?"

Far Eyes thought about that for a moment, putting his finger to his lips. "On this we have ceremony."

"Right. Ye hae yer ceremony, I'll hae mine. Sweat lodge again?" She said, not looking forward to that intense heat.

Far Eyes cocked his head and smiled, "You no like sweat?"

Cat shook her head.

"We use herb then," he said with a devious smile that made Cat laugh.

"What herb are ye speakin' of?"

"Hemp. We smoke in pipe. Make dream easy. See much. Make happy."

"No sweat lodge?" Cat asked, following him into his wigwam.

Far Eyes shook his head and told Cat to sit while he readied a pipe, stuffing a pinch of the herb into the carved bone bowl. He sat next to her and took a twig from the fire and lit the pipe, taking several long drags before handing it to Cat. She inhaled as Far Eyes did, but it made her cough and sputter. She tried it again, at Far Eyes' insistence. After a couple more times, she got the hang of it.

At first, she had a sense of total relaxation. Her vision got a little blurry in the low light of the wigwam. Then the animals on the walls started to move. She pointed to them and laughed. Far Eyes chuckled along with her, but seemed more in control of himself than she was. She took another drag, then jumped as she saw something moving in the smoke coming from her lips.

"What's that?" She asked, as though Far Eyes could see it too.

"What you see?"

Cat tried to focus on it, but it had disappeared in the haze. She shook her head and blinked. Far Eyes told her to take another puff, and be ready for the image. She did as she was told, but it was hard to concentrate, and she giggled.

Far Eyes took the pipe from her and took a deep drag from it, slowly releasing the smoke in front of Cat.

"There! Do ye see it?"

"No."

Cat squinted then jumped back with a squeal when the image lurched out at her.

"Tell me!" Far Eyes demanded.

"A beast. Red eyes. Great fangs." She was scooting backwards trying to get away from the thing. When she reached the wall, she cowered there and put her hands over her eyes.

"Fight, Garnet! It not real. Fight!" Far Eyes shouted, realizing Cat was seeing more than just smoke.

Cat chanced a peek from between her fingers. It was still there. She grabbed her dirk and lunged at it. In her head she heard laughter. Malicious laughter, taunting her. She swung at the beast again, having no effect. Now it was starting to make her angry. If it wasn't real, than how could it harm her, she thought. She stood up to face it, then took a step towards the moving fog. If it was a confrontation it wanted, a confrontation it would get. The beast stood its ground. Cat took another step, then another. She was right inside the smoky beast now. It wasn't attacking; it wasn't doing anything. Cat continued out the door. When the beast encountered the fresh air and light, it disappeared.

By this time, the drugged state had subsided and she felt light-headed and ravenous. She turned to see Far Eyes emerging from the smoke-filled wigwam.

"What in bloody hell was that?" she growled.

"It in head. Not real," Far Eyes said.

"I dinna care for yer kind o' ceremonies, Far Eyes. I'll stay wi' my own from now on. I trust what I see in them. They're real."

Far Eyes couldn't help it, he started chuckling, then cackling. At first that infuriated Cat further, but she couldn't restrain it from bubbling to the surface. She smiled, then she too was giggling.

"You hungry?" Far Eyes asked, wiping the tears from his face.

"Starvin'."

They walked over to the cooking area and grabbed a few pieces of jerky. As Cat chewed, she thought about what she'd seen. It was more than smoke, she would swear to it, but when she stood inside the hazy beast, it was unable to physically touch her. If the mind was that powerful, and one could harness that power … well, that's what she needed to do to fight Black Devil on his own terms. Then out loud, she said, "But no' wi' hemp."

Secrets

The Penobscot were leaving for their winter camp in a few days and Jim was going with them. Blue Feather was pleased with Jumping Turtle's selection of husband. He was also very pleased to be presented with the useful array of pots, blankets, and pair of flint-lock pistols for his only daughter. Under the guidance of Smiles at Everything, Jim prepared a wigwam to be used for Jumping Turtle and himself on their wedding night.

Greame told Cat that Jim looked as though he were going to his death. He said Jim had asked him how to proceed with the wedding night, and that during the entire conversation kept giggling and breaking out in waves of shakes and sweats.

"Much like ye probably did when yer Da told ye of yer weddin' night, eh?" Cat teased.

"No. My Da ne'er spoke o' such matters to me. Probably figured if I couldna use it, who would hae me."

Cat looked into those beautiful green eyes, stroked his smooth cheek and said, "Yer Da sold ye short."

The ceremony was a simple affair, but lasted the entire day. The drums and chanting and dancing were accompanied by plenty of food prepared by all the women in the village. Cat brought along several items; a venison stew made with vegetables she had received in trade with the Penobscot, several loaves of bread, and a berry pie.

Gent had several four-legged companions of his own and stayed close to the food, just in case there was a bone to be rid of. Two of the village dogs looked curiously like wolves. Cat had asked Far Eyes about it when they arrived, only to have it confirmed.

"We find when we hunt. Make good hunters. Breed with others, become good protectors."

"But, they're wild beasts. How do ye train them no' to attack yer weans? Wolves are greatly feared in Scotland."

"Have plenty food. No need to attack."

"Well, if ye say so." She wasn't totally convinced, but as time went by, she saw that they were indeed amiable beasts.

The day ended happily. Cat squeezed Jim hard before she left and tried not to cry. He would be missed greatly.

"Och, dinna fash yerself, lass," he said in a perfect Scottish imitation. "I'll be back in the spring."

Cat laughed and gave him another hug. Greame and the rest of his men bid him a happy winter, along with some rather bawdy remarks that made Jim's face glow in embarrassment. Gregor took him aside and spoke too quietly for anyone to overhear. Jim nodded somberly and they shook hands. Cat and Greame exchanged quick looks, wondering what that was all about. When Cat asked Gregor about it later that evening, he said he told Jim if he needed anything, to let him know. Somehow Cat didn't think that was quite all of it, but didn't press the issue.

&

The blaze of color on the maples, ash and beech was now coated with white. It was October twelfth and it had snowed overnight. Too early, Cat decided, not that there was much she could do about it. She'd just finished gathering the medicinal herbs and roots two days ago and they were drying in the newly completed addition.

Gregor was settled in his modest cabin, telling Cat one day that he'd never had a cott of his own, but was enjoying the freedom of it.

Cat laughed. "Freedom? Ye're ne'er there! But I guess that's freedom. How is Sings Like Bird, by the way?" She teased, knowing that Gregor still got flustered over the woman.

He gave her a half-hearted angry glare then smirked. "She's a rare fine lass."

"Will she be making an honest man out o' ye soon?"

This time the angry glare was real. "I am an honest man already," he said, then stormed from the house, nearly running Greame over in the process.

"What's got his ballocks in a knot?" Greame asked before giving Cat a peck on the cheek.

"I only asked him if Sings Like Bird was going to make an honest man out 'o him soon and he got right frothy."

Greame shrugged, then asked if she'd seen Kelvin lately. She told him that he'd been working on something quite secret-like. Wouldn't let anyone see it until it was ready. This piqued Greame's interest.

"Really? And no one kens what it is?"

"No one's sayin', if they do."

"Where are my gloves? I thought they were in the wardrobe, but I canna find them," Greame said, already dismissing Kelvin and his secret.

Cat opened the top drawer of the chest of drawers and pulled them out. "Right where ye left 'em. What are ye off doin' today?"

"Puttin' the finishin' touches on the root cellar. Gregor's made a hidey-hole for the guns. Says it reminds him of yer secret place. What's he talkin' 'bout? I dinna care for all these secrets," he said, pulling the gloves tightly over his big hands.

Cat smiled and told him of the faerie dùn. When she was done she donned her cloak and followed Greame to the cellar to see this secret place for herself.

"Oh, and Gregor told me to remind him to return yer gift from Anna. He said he'd forgotten all about it until he saw how much the cellar reminded him of the dùn. Another secret?"

"He brought it with him? I ne'er thought I'd e'er see it again," she said, quickening her pace to find Gregor.

"What was the gift? Hae I e'er seen it?"

Cat stopped and put her hand on Greame's arm. "Ye may hae seen it. It was a gift to Anna from Tullibardine as payment for a profitable outcome Anna predicted for him. It's a rare fine piece o' workmanship, and worth a fortune, I'm sure. Anna left it to me when she died. C'mon!" she said, trotting the rest of the way to the cellar with Greame left to scratch his head.

Cat was thrilled to see the secret hiding spot Gregor built. In a strange sort of way, it did remind her of the faerie dùn. He took Cat and Greame to his cabin and rummaged through a few chests before he came up with a satchel. He laid it on the table and unfolded it from the protective cloth. The reddish wood box glowed on the table and Cat ran her fingers over it, once again tracing around the brass oval with Anna's name engraved in it. Slowly, carefully, she lifted the lid.

The silver dirk encrusted with garnets lay just as it had when she saw it last, in its nest of purple velvet. As one did when in its presence, Cat felt like she was all alone. She lifted the masterpiece and was thrilled at feel of its weight.

Greame's movement caught her eye and she presented the dirk to him. His eyes were wide with awe, as were everyone's who first saw it. He held out his hands and Cat laid it in them. He gripped the handle and slowly turned the blade in his hand, testing its balance for himself. A smile transformed his face and he looked at Cat and Gregor, nodding his approval.

"This is what I saw in the sweat lodge with Far Eyes when we called for Anna to help ye. 'Tis a fine dirk. And Tullibardine gave this to Anna? What was it used for, do ye ken?"

"My Da said it belonged to our 4th Chief of the Clan, Grizzled Robert Duncanson. It was his ceremonial dirk given to him by King James II for capturin' Sir Robert Graham, who assassinated his father, King James I, o'er three hundred years ago. Where Tullibardine got it, we'll ne'er ken," Cat said wistfully. She turned to Gregor, and asked, "Where's the *clach na brataich?*"

"I delivered it to the new chief, Duncan Robertson, before I set sail. He's the rightful owner, but I felt this belonged to ye. Did I assume correctly?"

"I used to think so, but now I'm no' so sure."

"Why no'? Anna did give it to ye for safe keepin' for a reason. If the chief should have had it, wouldna *she* hae returned it to Alexander?" Gregor said.

"Ye told Alexander about it, didna ye?" she asked.

"No. I told him that the *clach na brataich* was in the faerie dùn. I thought ye told him about the dirk."

"Well, it's of no consequence now, is it?" Greame said, laying the dirk back into its velvet resting place and closing the lid. "There must hae been a reason Tullibardine didna return it to Alexander, so we hae to assume he gave it to Anna for safe keepin' and it was to be kept away from the chief."

Cat and Gregor looked at each other and both said, "Why?"

"That seems to be yet another secret," Greame said.

৵

Two days later the sun and warmer temperatures had melted all the snow. Cat took the opportunity to fetch buckets of seaweed for the garden area. Squashes and corn, carrots and onions, as well as many other root crops could certainly grow here and she wanted them in her own garden. She also wanted to have some apple trees of her own nearby now that there was sufficient cleared land around the village to plant a small orchard. Relying on the fine orchard of apples and pears left by the French at Pentagöet was fine for now, but wouldn't do forever.

Greame had taken the men on a hunt. A couple of deer would be a good start on the winter's cache. The root cellar had quite a bit of food in it, but wouldn't go through the entire season. Next year would be better, she vowed with each bucket of seaweed she hauled from the shore.

As she stuffed the greenish-brown nodules into the wooden pail, she glanced out to sea. The islands looked as though they were floating on the surface of the water. She wondered why. They never did that in the summer. She'd have to remember to ask Greame.

As she returned to her duty, she had a strange feeling someone was watching her. Discreetly, she glanced around, but could see no one. She trained her ears, but heard nothing except the water lapping the stones. There wasn't a breeze to speak of, so even the leaves weren't rustling. She resumed her seaweed gathering and started up the embankment when she heard a twig snap above her. She looked up and was startled to see Gent standing beside one of the wolf-dogs. Both were wagging their tails, thank goodness.

"Laddie, ye had me spooked. Who's yer wee friend, eh? She'll no' be takin' me hand when I go to touch her, will she?"

Gent sat, as though giving Cat permission to give it a try. Cat put her bucket of plunder down beside her and squatted down to eye level with Gent's friend. The tail was still wagging. Cat slowly put out her hand and the wolf stretched as far as she could, inching ever closer until her wet nose touched Cat's fingers. When that seemed well and good, she moved even closer, allowing Cat to stroke her ears, then her neck and body, until she was licking and whining and jumping around, ready to play.

"Well, I must hae passed her test, aye?"

Gent stood and barked his approval, then the two ran off towards the woods.

"Have fun, ye two. Be home for supper."

Cat picked up her buckets and dumped them into the garden. She had enough in there now and hoed it all in to the sparse soil. She added leaves and grasses so they too would break down and add to the rich mix. As she finished up, a tingle ran up her spine and the hair on her arms rose, despite her warmth. Glancing around in search of the onlooker, which she was convinced was out there somewhere, she saw an owl land in a dead spruce. What was with these owls lately, she wondered? It sat watching her intently and she got the distinct feeling it was spying on her for someone. But who?

She headed for the house, away from its prying eyes. Two could play this game. After washing her hands, Cat sat beside the window and pulled a lock of hair from under her kertch and started twirling it. As she gazed out at the brilliant trees, her mind went to the owl. Without a moment's hesitation, she was looking out through the owl's eyes. Her head bounced back at the clarity with which it saw things. It was surveying the ground, then its eyes rested on her house. If the windows didn't have a reflection to them, she would have been able to see herself. But she needed to see who was behind the owl's mind. She thought about that for a minute, then turned herself around in the owl.

She nearly screamed. Those red eyes again! Far Eyes told her the hemp-induced vision was all in her mind, that it wasn't real. If that were true, then who or what was looking at her? And she knew damned well it was real. She took a moment to regain some composure. After all, it couldn't hurt her, it was only looking at her.

"Let's try looking back," she said out loud.

It wasn't as easy as she thought it would be and after trying everything she knew, she let her hair fall to her breast. She had never attempted anything like that before. Did she need a surrogate, like an owl of her own? She had no one to ask. This was beyond Far Eyes' area of knowledge, and besides, he was on his way to his winter village. She got up and rummaged through her herb stash. None of that would help her. She needed help from someone who had become another being. Even in Scotland she didn't know of anyone who had actually accomplished that, but she had heard stories how, throughout the ages, select people were able to shape-shift into faeries and others into wolves.

She bolted to the door and hollered for Gent, effectively scaring the owl from its perch. A minute later, Gent and his new friend bounded from the woods, stopping at her feet. Cat sat on the cold ground and positioned Gent beside her. He laid his big body down as instructed.

"Now, lass, first ye need a name for me to be callin' ye," Cat said to the wolf.

Cat thought about it for a bit stroking the thick fur on the wolf's neck. The beast sat, as though patiently waiting for her name to be announced. Cat looked her into those round, golden eyes and smiled. "Bogle. Aye, that'll do. What do ye think?"

Bogle continued to stare at Cat, seemingly thinking over the name. But when her eyes wouldn't let Cat's go, Cat felt she was trying to tell her something. Cat closed her eyes and dug her hands into Bogle's thick nape, rubbing and scratching.

In her mind, Cat saw Bogle's pack running. They were chasing down a deer. Bogle was just a pup so she wasn't participating, but was watching from a rocky outcropping from above. When the deer went down, the adults ate their fill, then by some unseen signal, the pups were allowed to join the adults and eat. Bogle and her siblings ran down the steep escarpment and proceeded to tear into the deer's flesh. When they got a piece, they took it aside to devour it by themselves.

A footfall from behind didn't give her enough of a warning before she was hoisted up by the scruff of her neck and stuffed into a blanket. Try as she may to scratch and chew her way through it, she was trapped. Strange whispers were all around. Her muzzle was held so tight she couldn't cry out for help. Her whining went unheard as these strangers carried her far from her family.

Finally, after a long time of being carried she was plunked onto the ground and unwrapped from the blanket. The bright light stung her eyes and before she could get her bearings, hands were all over her. So many hands. She didn't know what to do. They weren't hurting her, but every time she tried to get away, the hands pulled her back.

This went on for many days. At night she was tied around her neck with a very short strip of hide. She was fed well and was allowed to play with others of her kind, though they did not have the same instincts as she did. They were different. Not wild. As time went on she forgot about her family and became one with these people who fed her and later allowed her to roam freely. But she remained different from the others and didn't know why, until now.

Cat opened her eyes to see Bogle still staring at her, but her mind was clear. A kindred spirit snatched from all she knew and loved for a higher purpose.

"Well, Bogle, if ye're willin' to let me become ye for a while for an important task, it will help us both."

Bogle's only reply was to put her front paw on Cat's knee. Cat took that as a pact.

Greame returned home just before dark. When he opened the door, he was greeted with angry growls from Bogle's snarling lips.

"What in bloody hell!"

"Bogle, he's mine," Cat shouted, and the wolf scampered under the kitchen table and laid down next to Gent, who hadn't raised an eyebrow at the commotion.

"What is that wolf doin' in this house?" Greame demanded, not ready to set down his rifle just yet.

"I need her to find out who's been watchin' me and for what purpose, though I doubt it's anythin' good."

Greame shook his head, hoping that might clarify what she just told him. It didn't. He unloaded his gear and reluctantly set his rifle down, keeping it within reach.

"Might I hae a seat at the table or will she chew my leg off?"

"She's fine. Really," she added when she saw Greame's hesitation.

Greame pulled a chair out away from the table and sat down, ready to hear Cat's explanation. Cat wiped her hands on a linen and took a seat next to him then told him what had happened with the owls.

"Owls? Plural? Where was the other one?" Greame said, loosening the cord that held his hair.

"The other one was in a dream I had. I didna tell ye?" Greame shook his head. "It was askin' me who I was. Far Eyes already kent. Said I was the one who could see what *could* happen."

Greame held up his hand to stop her. "Woman, yer makin' no sense that I can understand. Can we talk about this later? I'm hungry and tired, and the rest o' the lads will be here shortly."

Cat got up and resumed supper without another word.

૨

Greame was beat. His hunting party had killed two fine bucks. Without horses, they had to pack them out on their backs. He would change that fact in the spring and have a few horses brought up to the village. By then, he could have a barn built.

The family sat down to supper and Greame hoped Cat had forgotten about his curtness towards her. He had a lot on his mind and her confusing story was too much to take in. And what was that wolf doing in his house? Was Cat reverting again? He ran his hands through his hair, not listening to the conversation around him. He hoped there was a logical explanation to it all, but he couldn't hear it tonight.

What he had to figure out tonight was what Gregor was up to. Greame looked over at the big man talking with Cat as though nothing was going on, but he knew Gregor was meeting someone in the woods. At first he thought it was Sings Like Bird, but then he saw her leave with Far Eyes. Was he conspiring with the French? Greame understood the hatred for the English, but thought Gregor would have more sense than to drag Cat back into that hell. His mind was whirling when he heard his name being repeated. He looked up to see Cat and his family staring at him.

"Are ye well, man?" Kelvin asked.

Greame nodded, then shook his head. "If ye'll pardon me I'm goin' to bed."

When Cat started to rise, he said, "I'm fine, Garnet. Ye tend to the men, aye?"

Cat nodded and returned to her seat, watching him disappear into the bedroom.

After Cat had cleaned up from supper, she threw some more logs on the fire and took the lamp to her bedroom. When she opened the door she could hear Greame's deep, even breathing. She stood in the doorway for a minute, taking in his form under the bedclothes. His long hair tumbled around his wide shoulders and her hands ached to run through it. He said he was just tired, but she felt it was much more than that. At supper he hadn't participated in any of the conversations—something he always did. She wondered what was bothering him, but assumed he would tell her in the morning.

Cat set the lamp down and took off her clothes, folding them over the chair in the corner. She slipped into bed and lay still, letting the night enfold her. Even though her eyes were closed she could still see the events of the day. Bogle was the one highlight and the meeting brought a smile to her face. She absently wondered how to find out who was watching her. She knew she could connect with Bogle's mind, but could she actually become Bogle and weed out the spy? What would she do when she found out who it was, tell them to stop? What did they want, and why didn't they just come out and meet her? She fell asleep with no answers.

Cat woke before dawn and snuggled close to Greame. He was already awake.

"What's on yer mind, *a ghaoil?*"

Cat smiled. "That's what Lachlan used to call me."

"I'm sorry about last night."

"Perhaps I should be askin' ye what's on yer mind," she said, slipping her leg over his and running her hand through his chest hair.

He was quiet for a moment and Cat wondered if he was going to tell her or not.

"It's Gregor."

"What about him?"

"He's up to somethin', but I dinna ken what. He skulks off and I ken he's meetin' wi' someone, but I dinna ken who or why. Do ye think he's workin' wi' the French?" His voice was soft but held an agitated tone.

It was Cat's turn to be quiet. She ran several different scenarios over in her mind, but none made sense.

"Do ye think I should look into him? I feel it would be a betrayal though. Hae ye spoken to him about it?"

"No. I dinna ken what to ask. 'Gregor, what are ye doin' behind our backs?' just isna a good idea," he said, slipping out from under her to sit on the edge of the bed.

Cat got up on an elbow and rubbed his back. "I'll speak wi' him. We've been through a lot together. He'll tell me."

"And if he doesna? I dinna ken why it has me frightened, but I think we need to ken."

"He'll tell me, Greame." She lifted the bedclothes invitingly. "Now come back under the covers."

Greame glanced over his shoulder at Cat's nakedness and surrendered to her.

è.

The rain plopping on the window woke Cat. Greame was on his back snoring, but when she got out of bed he woke.

"I'm goin' to start breakfast," she said while slipping into her shift.

"Thank ye, Garnet."

Cat stopped buttoning her dress. "For what?"

Greame chuckled. "For takin' my mind off Gregor."

Cat bent over him and planted a deep kiss on his lips. "Ye're welcome."

è.

It was a cold rain that would probably turn to snow before the day was over. Cat ventured over to Gregor's cabin holding her cloak tightly around her. She had a basket of oatcakes left over from breakfast. She knocked on the door and Gregor answered it quickly.

"To what do I owe this pleasure, lass?" he said, smiling.

"Can I hae a word wi' ye?"

His smile faded from the tone in her voice, but he guided her through the doorway and took her cloak. Cat set the basket on the table and took a seat.

"Tea?" He asked.

Cat smiled and nodded.

"So what did ye need to speak wi' me about?" He set the teapot on the table with two cups and took the seat across from her.

Cat opened her mouth, but didn't quite know how to start. She wished she had rehearsed how to ask the question.

Gregor raised an eyebrow. "Lass, ye're ne'er at a loss for words. Just say it."

She looked him straight in the eye and said, "Who hae ye been seein' in the woods?"

Gregor's other eyebrow raised. He poured each of them a cup of tea and slid hers over to her. He got up and brought two plates over with some honey for the oatcakes.

Cat waited patiently.

Gregor sat and placed both arms on the table. He faced her as though bracing himself for her temper. Cat was getting more concerned as the minutes ticked by, but then he spoke.

"The French have great tracts o' land to the west of us in New France. The English are encroaching little by little. The Indians, no' the Penobscot, but a large nation called the Iroquois, hae lived on that land forever. The French hae lived peaceably wi' the Iroquois for many years and now want to band together to stop the English from settling their territory."

"Band together for what?"

Gregor took a swallow of tea as though to wash down the idea, then said, "To fight."

Cat just stared at him and felt herself getting hot with emotion. She stood up and went to fetch her cloak.

From the table, Gregor said, "What, ye're no' goin' to say anythin'?"

If he had just kept his mouth shut.

Cat turned to him with her hands on her hips. Her face got red with fury. "Tell me, Gregor, is it because ye didna get a chance to fight them on Scottish soil? Do ye feel cheated out o' the killin' and canna pass up the opportunity to hae another chance?"

Before he got to answer she was out the door, slamming it behind her with such force, it shook the teacups in the cupboard.

28

Conjuring Spirits

What better day than Samhain to probe the mysteries of the other side. Cat had practiced melding minds with Bogle for a couple of weeks, and now felt she was ready to flush out the spy. She figured out that to be successful, you had to project yourself and the "vessel"—in this case, Bogle—back to the watcher. It would involve either another round with hemp—which she would only do if nothing else worked because she had no control while in the state, and she needed her wits about her for this—or, if she figured correctly, an extremely deep meditation. For this she asked Greame to be present for two reasons; first, not to be disturbed and second, to help her if needed. This was uncharted territory, one only her spy was familiar with. She didn't know where it would lead her.

Bogle seemed to know it was coming. The "ceremony" wouldn't begin until nearly midnight, so the day was excruciatingly long. Cat had the house all tidied up, the chores finished and even had time to do some much-needed mending, but there were still four more hours before she could begin.

She thought about Anna and how she had prepared for such momentous events. There were candles, a silk square, herbs and talismans. Cat went to the chest of linens and dug around until she found the perfect silk fabric. It was a wash of emerald green, deep indigo and raspberry all swirled around each other. She took three new tapers out and placed them into candleholders. Scouring her new herb stash, she chose some balsam needles, tansy leaves and bayberry leaves to steep a fragrant tea. If only there was cinnamon, but alas, it was too expensive.

The kitchen table served as the altar for her ceremony and after laying out the scarf and candles she decided to add a talisman. She thought about her ring, but felt it had to be stronger for some reason. She walked around the house a few times in search of whatever it was she was looking for. When she entered her bedroom she knew she had found it. On the dresser was the wooden box that held the ceremonial dirk. Perfect. She took the silver blade out of the velvet nest, brought it to the table and placed it on the silk square.

Greame was seated at the table, watching quietly. He had never witnessed one of Cat's rituals and was fascinated. When she brought the dirk out from the bedroom and set it down, he wondered what she thought she would encounter to need such protection. It made him a bit nervous, but he didn't interrupt her preparations, as he was certain they would go over what to expect from this rite.

Cat called Bogle over to the table. She took off her ring and strung a length of cord through it then tied it around Bogle's neck.

"This is a part o' me, now I need a part o' ye."

With her dirk, she grabbed a small thickness of fur from Bogle's chest and cut it off. She placed the fur in a small leather pouch and tied it around her neck. She went over to the chest of drawers and opened the bottom drawer. After a little bit of rummaging, she came out with a raven's feather, black and shiny. With a short piece of cord, she tied it onto the leather pouch so it hung down between her breasts.

Glancing at the clock she was pleased to see that it was ten o'clock. One more thing to do then she'd be ready to go over the process with Greame. In a cupboard in the dining room she kept a few smudges. Far Eyes told her to clear the space before performing any kind of ceremony so there were no "bad spirits," as he put it. Cat grabbed one of the rolled bundles of herbs, along with a wooden bowl and carried them out to the table. She lit one end, and as it smoldered, walked around the room letting the smoke circulate, making sure the corners were saturated, as they were the places that became stagnate.

Cat surveyed her altar and mentally did a checklist, making sure nothing was missed. She was ready. Taking a seat next to Greame, she handed him her dirk then requested something personal of his.

"Like what?" He asked, setting the blade on the table.

"Do ye hae anythin' ye've carried around for a long time?"

Greame thought for a moment. "I hae no jewellery, but what about the Chinese coins?"

"Aye, they'll do."

Greame got up and went into the bedroom. A minute later he laid three bronze coins with square holes cut out of the centers in the palm of Cat's waiting hand.

"All right. I'm goin' to begin by askin' for protection. I just state my intentions and ask that those who are wi' me on the other side keep me safe. I want ye to do the same even though ye're no' goin' in. Like I said, this is a first for me, so I want to make sure we are all protected."

"How will I ken if ye're in trouble?"

Cat thought for a moment. "I remember once when I saw terrible things about the war, I lost myself and couldna come out of it. Lachlan put the ensign stone on my forehead and had me breath in the fragrance o' lavender. We hae neither here, but the fragrant herbs I brought to steep will do. Then, if more is needed, use the dirk," she pointed to the garnet-encrusted one, "on my forehead for the power o' the stones. I'm hopin' we'll no' need either."

"Are ye sure about this? There's no other way?" Greame said with a worried expression on his face.

Cat smiled and touched his cheek. "We'll be fine."

She looked at the clock. It was time. The candles were lit, the herbs were placed in a pot and boiling water was poured over them to steep. Their sweet, earthy fragrance wafted through the kitchen.

Bogle sat beside Cat and put her paw on Cat's knee. Cat grabbed Bogle's nape and closed her eyes. Out loud, she began her protective prayers. Greame whispered his, watching Cat intently. Not long after she stopped speaking, she relaxed herself so much she seemed to melt into her chair.

Cat was now one with Bogle. It was an interesting feeling of freedom. She was running through the woods following a strong scent. She ran for many miles seemingly without tiring, to a place she did not recognize. Rock cliffs surrounded deep valleys with raging rivers running through them. She was surrounded by thick woodlands filled with more leafy trees than the spruce and pine of Maine. For many more miles she ran until she reached great stretches of farmland. Indians were tending the fields. Mohawk Indians.

She stopped before a clearing, taking shelter in the brush so she wouldn't be seen. Around each person there was a colored cloud. It undulated around them, getting larger then smaller, and the colors changed sometimes. Cat watched in fascination wondering what it meant. She looked deeper into the village, but was too far away to see much. The open field was surrounded by brush and scrub so she followed it around, remaining inside, unseen. Round houses came into view and people milled about, tending to their work. One of the round houses was set away from the others. She knew this belonged to a shaman, but so far there was nothing here out of the ordinary.

A river came into view so she decided to follow it for a while. There weren't any Indians here. Up ahead were only steep rock crags. She was about to turn around when a reddish glow emanating from a large, protruding outcropping caught her eye. Atop it stood the Mohawk shaman, the same one she had seen in the woods at the Penobscot camp. Cat ducked into some tall grass and watched. With her enhanced abilities to hear, smell and see better, she picked up his chanting on the breeze. Despite the cold he was naked. His hands were raised to the sky and there was blood seeping over his stomach from a long, horizontal gash across his chest. The red glow he emanated was tinged with purple and silver. Then, yellow and white flashes like sunrays danced around his head. She wondered what it all meant, yet had a feeling it was his power she was seeing.

Even disguised as a wolf she knew she would have to become invisible, but wondered if that were possible with this man. She wished she could see his face, but didn't dare move closer. Suddenly he appeared in her mind, as though summoned. She thought like a wolf; she looked like a wolf; she buried her humanness behind a protected wall, but somehow she knew that he felt her.

Cat remained still, watching. He roamed around Bogle's mind for a moment, never lingering on anything in particular. Perhaps he saw no threat. She projected herself further into his mind while he was preoccupied. What she found was as amazing as it was disturbing.

His ancestral line were all powerful shamans, teaching and pushing the next generation further and further, until they could become whatever they wanted. Their sacrifice for these abilities was complete isolation. They were closer to the natural world than they were to other humans. As Cat went deeper, creatures scurried about, but were unafraid, never being on the receiving end of a probe. There was nothing good in them; their only purposes were aggression and maliciousness. She was just about to back out when she saw them. Those red eyes! They'd found her. She stood her ground as they circled and examined who had invaded their territory. The creatures recognized the threat too late.

In her own mind, she kept repeating that she was a wolf. Over and over again, she replayed her first encounter with Bogle's mind as a pup, then taken and raised by man. There were no other thoughts in her mind. She became the wolf and had to remain that way while she was in his mind.

Cat heard him say, *If you are really just a wolf, then how did you enter my mind and for what purpose?*

Cat was tempted to say, how do *you* like it?

He become frustrated and agitated when he received no answers. She knew she had to leave before he found her out. With all the power she possessed she sent out a blinding white light and escaped from his mind, but not before she heard him say, *Now I know who you are.*

Back in Bogle's mind she felt herself tiring. Cat had to get back now or risk becoming too weak to defend herself and Bogle if this madman wanted to exact his revenge.

In a flash, Cat was at the kitchen table. Greame was on the edge of his seat with eyes wide with wonder and fear. He got up from his chair so quickly it toppled to the floor. He grabbed her and held her close, as though she were hurt or frightened.

"Are ye all right?" His voice filled with anxiety.

Cat nodded and held onto him. Not from fear, but for the feel of reality.

"Are ye sure?" He asked.

"Aye. I'm fine."

"What was it like? Did ye see who it was? Did they see ye?"

Cat started to explain, but noticed Bogle hadn't come out of it yet. Cat pushed herself from Greame's arms and bent down to Bogle, feeling her chest. Bogle's heart was beating rapidly and her paws were twitching as though she was dreaming of running. Was Black Devil chasing her?

"Give me the silver dirk!" She shouted to Greame.

Startled by her tone, he grabbed it from the silk and handed it to her.

Cat began whispering something in *Gàidhlig,* then placed the dirk on Bogle's head. Cat took her ring that was still around Bogle's neck and held it, continuing to chant. Bogle's legs began flailing; Black Devil was definitely after her and she didn't know how to get back. Cat had to go back in or Bogle would die.

Cat raised her voice to the heavens and said, "With all the power in the universe and all who hae come before me, I ask for yer protection to face this demon on the other side and bring us back to safety."

Greame was truly frightened. This was something he could not see or do battle with. Cat was chanting in a language older than he knew, only catching a few recognized words here and there. He watched her place the silver dirk on Bogle's head and continued with the chant. When Cat spoke her prayer out loud, he saw her become bathed in white light. He backed away from her, unsure of what to do. On the table the candles flickered wildly as though there was a stiff breeze, but the room was still.

He looked back at Cat to find her on top of Bogle. She had blacked out. He threw the chair out of the way and knelt down beside the pair. He picked up the silver dirk from the floor where it slid off Bolge and placed it on Cat's head. He was more scared than at any other time in his life. He didn't know what to do.

"Damn it, Garnet!"

He raised his head and closed his eyes. He was going in. But first he shouted, "Anna Macpherson, if ye're there, we need yer help!"

In his mind he could see Cat and Bogle fighting an Indian. Bogle just got kicked hard in the side, yelped and went down, but got back up quickly. Cat was in a defensive posture lunging at the Indian with the silver dirk. He absently wondered how it got there, but he was quickly brought to focus when he heard Cat shout, "What took ye so long?"

Greame found that he could move, so he picked up the dirk that Cat gave him at the kitchen table and ran towards the fray. The Indian noticed him and laughed.

You bring such weaklings to save you.

"Dinna be fooled, Black Devil, he's stronger than he appears."

Out of the haze came a cackling laugh. Cat looked at Greame and smiled. Somehow, under the circumstances, he couldn't return the pleasantries, but was glad to know they were being joined by a friendly face.

Anna Macpherson held up her oak staff with the ancient interlace carvings and purple amethyst. The stone glowed eerily of purple and white. She chanted something under her breath, much like Cat had earlier, then pointed the wand at Black Devil.

At first, nothing happened. Cat was still doing battle with the shaman and Bogle was trying to stave off another powerful kick, while attempting to chew on Black Devil's leg. Greame now entered the fray from the rear, but found that this man, if that's what he really was, was impervious to harm. It was like he was shielded somehow. Every time Greame lunged, the blade would veer away, never finding its mark. He noticed that Cat was having the same problem. Black Devil seemed to be enjoying himself until Anna appeared above him, held up by some unseen forces, then swung the powerful staff and hit Black Devil right between the eyes.

He went down with what sounded like thunder in the distance. A long rolling event that lasted long after he landed. Bogle was immediately on top of him and Cat and Greame each plunged their dirks into the demon's chest.

With all the force of a hurricane, the event vanished before their eyes. Cat, Greame and Bogle were back on the kitchen floor. Anna was nowhere to be seen, but Greame heard her cackle again before the sudden silence.

"Christ!" They both said together.

"I ken there was a reason I loved ye so. Ye saved us all wi' yer quick thinkin', Greame! I should hae called upon Anna from the beginnin', but I guess I thought I could do it on my own. Almost did, but I didna count on him keepin' Bogle on the other side," she said breathlessly, stroking Bogle's ears.

"Do ye think we killed him?" Greame asked sitting close to Cat on the floor.

"No."

"Do ye think he'll watch ye anymore?"

"No' for a while. He kens my—our—strength now. I felt he was curious about me, but now he'll try to be stronger than I am."

"So what we did served no purpose but to anger him further?" Greame said, running his hand through his hair.

Cat looked at him and shrugged. "I only wanted to find out who was watching me and for what purpose. I had no idea it would be him, and I still dinna ken what he wants wi' me."

Greame got to his feet and held out his hand for Cat. She took it and stood, feeling the full results of the metaphysical battle.

"I just want some sleep. We'll look at it wi' a fresh mind in the mornin'."

Greame glanced at the clock and said, "It is morning."

The clock read three-fifteen. "No wonder I'm tired." She wrapped her arm around Greame's waist and guided him towards the bedroom. Greame stopped and blew out the candle snubs. A howl from far away raced a shiver up his spine, making him wonder if it was really a wolf, or Black Devil letting him know it wasn't over.

An Sgeulaiche

Gregor burst into the house just after dawn. Gent and Bogle were startled to the point of chasing him back out again with bared teeth and fierce barking. Gregor made it out just in time. A few minutes later, Cat and Greame stepped out onto the porch to see what was going on. When they saw it was Gregor and that he was a bit paler than usual, they feared the worse.

"Christ in heaven!" Gregor swore. "There's a wolf in yer house!"

Cat laughed so hard there were tears running down her face as she sat on the porch holding her stomach. Greame, remembering his first encounter with Bogle in much the same fashion was a bit more sympathetic, but wasn't about to keep the smile from his face.

Since Cat was in no condition to explain, Greame said, "Aye, her name's Bogle. Gent brought her home a few weeks ago. Cat needed her for … somethin'," not willing to divulge too much. "Is there somethin' we can be helpin' ye wi', man?" The smile was still lingering around his mouth.

Gregor regained his composure in spite of the fact that Cat was still giggling periodically.

"English ship."

"Where?" Greame asked, sobering as though a bucket of ice water had just been poured on him.

"Lurking around the islands on the west side."

"When did ye see them?" Cat asked, wondering how he could have made it back here in the short amount of time it's been light enough to see.

"I didna. Smiles at Everything sent a runner. I just received the news myself."

Cat and Greame just looked at each other trying to see if they both heard him right.

"Smiles at Everything is here?" Greame asked.

"Perhaps ye'd better come inside. There are questions needin' answers," Cat said, getting up from the porch.

Gregor spent the next hour explaining that he was only trying to protect the settlement and the Penobscot's summer grounds from harm. A few Penobscot braves were set up around strategic areas on the Cape to keep watch. They would spend the winter here, bunking with Gregor when the weather became too fierce. Even the English wouldn't attempt to navigate these waters in the dead of winter.

Without considering what Cat's feelings were on the subject, Greame told him that he thought it was a good thing to do and thanked Gregor for his forethought. Cat walked into her bedroom and slammed the door.

"I'm sorry for puttin' ye in the middle o' this, Greame."

"In the middle o' what? Did the two o' ye already hae a chat about this?"

Gregor snorted mirthlessly. "She dinna tell ye she nearly chewed my head off a few weeks past about me missin' my chance to fight in Scotland, so I could fight here to make up for it?"

"Ha!" he barked. "She told ye that? Well, one thing's for sure, she speaks her mind plain, doesna she?"

"Oh, aye, bitingly plain. And dinna get me wrong, I love the lass, but when she gets somethin' in her heid it's hell gettin' it out."

"Well, in all fairness to Garnet, she's been through her own hell since she's been here."

"Aye, I ken about some of it. Yer men told me in Boston. But what she doesna seem to understand is that there's a war brewin' and there's naught she can do to stop it, so it's best to be prepared," Gregor said in a hushed voice.

"Tell me what it is I can do. I ken well enough about Garnet's feelin's towards war, but I want to protect her and I canna do that if

I dinna ken what's happenin' around us," Greame said, matching Gregor's quiet tone. He'd have to find a way to make Cat understand that this was the best way.

≥●

As winter approached, life grew quiet, making it easy to forget about what the outside world was doing. Snow fell nearly every day in November, adding an inch or two or six during each storm, piling up to over two feet by December first. The days were dark and short, making everyone want to sleep them away. During breakfast, Cat suggested that after supper instead of going back to their cabins, everyone would remain for a while and revive the old Scottish way of story telling. This made several of the men very pleased. Kelvin, whom Cat would have never suspected as wanting to talk about anything for any length of time, was most excited. He practically begged to be the first *sgeulaiche*. That night after supper, they all gathered in the keeping room and took whatever seats they could find for themselves. Greame brought out a bottle of whisky he'd been saving and poured everyone a dram. Cat sat closest to the fire, smiling that everyone seemed to be enthralled by the simple pleasure of talking.

Kelvin had brought in a satchel earlier, storing it in Jim's room, and now went to fetch it. He placed the mysterious sack in the corner, only adding to the drama, then as though making his entrance, stood in the center of the room.

He raised his glass for a toast and everyone followed suit.

"*Slàinte mhath!*"

When all the glasses were drained of the precious amber liquid, he began.

"This is a story from the district o' Sandness, which is near Papa Stour. It's called the Fiddler O' Gord.

"The croft was occupied by a man that got away one night, away to the craigs to fish for fish. So he was comin' home one night wi' his booty o' sillocks and wand and as he passed a certain knoll, he was aware that there were a light shinin' out. He got up to examine this and he said that the trolls was dancin' inside. So he got in, bein' a fiddler, and the knoll closed up behind him until there were nothin' left to show of any doorway.

"His folk that night waited for him to come home wi' the fish, and he ne'er came. All night they waited, and in the mornin' they sent a search party out. They looked and hunted the coast and they found no sign of him. Time got by and it was put down that he was gone o'er the craig, and the sea and tide had taken his body.

"So time got by, and eventually his family grew up and moved away, and his name were forgotten. The time came when there were a whole century passed since that thing happened, and there were a new family livin' in that croft. So one night in the heart o' the winter, the old granfather was settin' at the fire, the son and his wife was settin' in the chairs, and their bairns was playin' around the floor, when the door opened. There appeared an old man in the door, clad in rags wi' a long white beard, carryin' in his hand a fiddle. O' course the bairns they laughed at this, they thought this man was silly. He came in and he says, 'What are you doin' here? This is my house!' They thought it a great joke and they laughed at him and they made a fool of him—everybody but the old granfather settin' at the fire, smokin' his pipe. He listened.

"He says again, 'What are you doin here? This is my house, ye've got to get out of it. Where's yer folks?'

"Every time he would say his piece, the young'uns laughed at him, 'til at last the old grandfather speakin' by the fireside says, 'Well, what's yer name?' He told him his name. 'Well, there were a man o' that name that used to bide here long, long afore my day, but, he … he disappeared one night, and ne'er came home.'

"Now the laughin' fell silent, and everybody was aware that there were something queer goin' on here. So this figure in the door says, 'Well, where is my folk then?'

"The old grandfather by the fireside says, 'Yer folk is all dead.'

"'Well then', he says, 'if that's the case I'll go and join them'. And he turned and left.

"Now there were one grown lad among the family that didna laugh at him. He stood and went after this old man; followed after him and crept up through the yard along the keel to watch him. An' this old fellow wi' the fiddle goes up around to the back o' the yard deck where there were a wall, and he lifts the fiddle to his neck. He looks up o'er the knoll to where the Merry Dancers was shinin' in the northern sky and he plays a tune once or twice o'er. The boy inside the yard deck watchin' all of a sudden sees him collapse.

"The boy out o'er the yard deck ran, and he came to the spot where the man had fallen at the side o' the wall. There he found the remains of a man that had been dead for a hundred years and a tiny fiddle. He always minded that tune, and when that boy grew up he could play that tune. That tune's been handed down to this day."

Cat surveyed the room to see smiles on everyone's faces. She clapped her hands a few times and everyone joined in. Then Kelvin went into the corner where his satchel was and opened it. At first, Cat thought for sure it was a fiddle, given the story and all, but what emerged was a set of great pipes.

Cat looked at Greame for confirmation that he did indeed play. Greame nodded and said, "So this is what's had yer attention so for the last few months."

Kelvin's eyes twinkled with a smile. He put the blowpipe in his mouth and started blowing up the bag, then positioned it under his right arm, giving it a smack then squeezing it firmly in place. The chanter was positioned in his fingers and he played a note to tune the drones. The sound was deafening, making both Gent and Bogle bark with fright. Greame got up and put them outside, then took a seat next to Cat.

"Ye haven't lived 'til ye've heard Kelvin play the *pìob mhor,*" he told her.

"I canna remember the last time I heard the pipes," she said in his ear.

When the drones were adjusted correctly, Kelvin quickly folded the blowpipe under the bag to prevent any air from escaping, then asked if there were any requests.

"Do ye ken *Fair Maid o' Perthshire?*" asked Gregor.

Kelvin nodded and put the blowpipe into his mouth and blew a couple of times. His fingers splayed out over the chanter and moved quickly with practiced precision. It was a lively tune that put everyone's feet to tapping. After several more reels and jigs, he toned it down with a slow air, signaling the end of the show. Its haunting tune lingered long after it was over. The room burst with the sound of clapping hands, and Kelvin took a deep bow and beamed with pride.

The men took their leave and suddenly the house seemed abnormally quiet.

"I enjoyed that, didna ye, Greame?"

Greame was stretching his body out and stifling a yawn. He smiled and agreed. "It was always like that at home. Someone would be tellin' tales and someone else would be playin' tunes. In my family, all my sisters played either the fiddle or the whistle. I had the *bòdhran*, but wasna home very often to keep the beat for them."

"In my house, it was just the *bòdhran*. Iain danced the swords and Lachlan kept the beat for him. Seumas was only interested in fightin'." she said with a bit of irony in her voice. "My Mam liked to sing, though. She had a fine voice."

"I'm verra pleased that ye thought of this for entertaining ourselves, Garnet. It meant a lot to them."

Cat wrapped her arms around his waist and pressed a kiss on his lips. "It means a lot to me. I feel responsible for gettin' everyone up here, so I want them all to be happy."

"How about I go make ye happy?" He purred in her hair.

Hogmanay called for a celebration. The Penobscot braves Gregor enlisted had little to do but wait out the winter, so they were also invited to the festivities. Geoffrey and Gregor had set up a spit outside and were roasting a couple of turkeys. The weather held nicely with a sky so blue it seemed unreal. Even though the temperature was cold, it wasn't so bitter it made one's teeth hurt to breathe.

Before leaving for their winter camp, the Penobscot showed a few of the men how to make snowshoes. These wide ash-and-gut frames were proving to be very handy for outdoor chores. Most of the dooryards had been stomped flat, making it easy to tread over the deep snow without sinking past the knees, and paths connected each of the cabins with smaller trails to the privies.

Kelvin was out on the rocks overlooking the cove playing the bagpipes. The drone echoed off the granite shoreline with an eerie melancholy that pierced the quiet in such a way that everyone in the village came out of their cabins to hear it. Somehow, the sound seemed to fit this place. The small group gathered behind him in the cold and listened. Some, like Geoffrey and Robbie, had their eyes closed as though remembering another time and place. Gregor stood stone-faced, but swayed slowly with the music. Smiles at Everything and the two other braves, Gray Eagle and Little Hawk, sat at Kelvin's feet enthralled by the instrument and how it was played.

Kelvin must have felt his audience's appreciation because he played for long time. When he finally did stop and turn around, he took a bow and smiled a rare smile.

"For a while, I was back in Scotland," Geoffrey said in a wistful voice, still staring out at the ocean.

"I think we all were," Greame whispered to himself.

Cat walked up to Kelvin and placed a kiss on his scruffy cheek. "Thank ye, Kelvin."

"Dinna be doin' that to the man, Garnet, or we'll no' get any work out o' him for a week," Kenny teased.

Kelvin walked back to his cabin as though Cat's kiss was merely a show of respect, but Greame saw him put his hand to his cheek with a hint of a smile. Cat could make any man feel good about himself; he was a testament to that.

Greame watched her walk back to their cabin with the three Penobscot. One of them would say something and she would laugh. Then, as though to make sure she was entertained enough, one of the others would say something else to make her laugh. He knew how they felt. Her laugh was the best medicine for any ill and thank Christ she laughed a lot.

Cat rotated the turkeys a couple of times. They were almost ready and the heady aroma made her mouth water. She went inside to finish with the rest of the meal. Gent and Bogle greeted her with furiously wagging tails as though she was going to let them out.

"Oh aye, I'll just bet ye'd love to go out and sit beside the roastin' turkeys, wouldna ye?" She waved her finger at them. "No' a chance." The pair knew they weren't going to get sympathy from her, but they'd try it again on the next person to walk through that door.

By the time anyone walked in, the turkeys were off the spit and onto two large pewter platters brought in by Greame and Geoffrey. All at once the house filled with men and they all headed directly into the dining room. Cat began dishing up the squash and beets when Greame came in and asked if there was anything he could help her with.

Cat smiled, her dimples getting deep. "Pull the bread from the stove and put each loaf into a basket, if ye'd like."

"Where are they?"

"Oh, I moved them the other day. They're in the first cupboard by Jim's door."

Greame opened the cupboard and pulled out the stack of baskets. He lined the top one with a linen towel and placed a hot loaf in it. He took the next basket from the stack and jumped back with a holler.

"What is it?" Cat said, holding her hand to her chest.

"Hae a look for yerself."

A few of the men came in to see what all the noise was about. Cat peered cautiously into the basket, along with Kenny and Gregor. The nest of naked, newborn mice put such looks of disgust on their faces, Cat couldn't help but laugh.

"For the love o' Pete, just toss them outside," she said.

"Aye, but what about the rest o' the family. They're still in here," Greame said, searching the other cupboards for the vermin after handing the basket over to Gregor to dispose of.

"We'll look for them after supper, now get another basket, the food's gettin' cold," Cat said in a mock reprimand, the smile never leaving her voice.

Cat handed the side dishes to Kenny and Gregor while she took in two dried apple pies. Greame was left with the bread.

The table was filled with food and the men dug in with gusto. Little Hawk said he was happy to take his meal with his new white friends. Gray Eagle and Smiles at Everything agreed as they filled their plates.

Greame, seated at the head of the table, stood and raised his glass. The men did the same and waited for him to speak.

"May we all hae a safe and prosperous new year. *Slàinte mhath!*" Then downed his dram.

Cat stood next, getting frowns from some of the men. "I ken this probably isna a proper thing for a woman to do, but this is my house too, and I hae somethin' to say." She glanced around the table ready to smack anyone who challenged her.

Greame tried his best to hide a laugh behind a cough as he passed around the whisky bottle. Cat sent him an evil eye.

"What I want to say is this, it has been my pleasure to ken all o' ye. I ken none o' ye would be up here in this wild place if it werna for me and I want to thank ye for …" she tapped her chin, looking for the right word, "well, for puttin' up wi' me. Then to actually want to stay here is more than I could hae asked any o' ye to do. For whate'er reason ye remained, I just want to tell ye that I couldna hae found a better family to share in this fate."

She downed her dram to *huzzahs!* from the men and took her seat. Catching Greame's eye at the other end of the table, the expression he wore could only be described as proud. He lifted his glass to her and winked.

ༀ

After all the men went home, Cat called Gent and Bogle over for a chat.

"Between the two o' ye, there shouldna be a mouse, squirrel, rabbit, or any other kind of beast in this house. Do ye understand me?"

They looked at her with expressionless faces, trying to act like she couldn't read their minds and hear their thoughts.

"And dinna give me those looks or ye can spend the winter out in the cold."

Suddenly, the severity of the situation registered on their faces. Cat could hear them agreeing with her terms and they bolted from her to sniff out the vermin who nearly caused them to be expelled from their own home.

Greame was listening from the kitchen, and said, "Really think that'll work?"

"O' course," she said with total conviction.

ༀ

Two days later, Smiles at Everything, Gray Eagle and Little Hawk announced that they were leaving for their winter camp in Pasadunkec. With winter firmly entrenched there would be no English venturing this far north. Cat asked why they decided so abruptly.

"Want to be away from coast before storm," Smiles at Everything said.

Cat, standing on her porch, looked out at the cobalt blue sky with a few mare's tails floating in it and said, "Really? There's nary a cloud in the sky."

Greame came up behind her and said, "Weather breeder."

Smiles at Everything smiled and nodded before he turned and left.

"Give our love to Jim, aye?" Cat said, waving them goodbye. Turning to go back into the house, she asked, "What's a weather breeder?"

"It's when the sky is clear like it has been for the past couple o' days. Then the wind freshens, bringin' wi' it a storm. Usually bad ones start out this way."

"It ne'er occurred to me, but I think ye may be right," she conceded.

"Well o' course I'm right," he said. "I've been on the sea long enough to ken the signs."

"When will it be here?"

"A day or two most likely. Ask Kelvin to confirm it."

"How will Kelvin confirm it?"

"His left knee always pains him fiercely when a big one's a'brewin'."

Not a minute later Kelvin was knocking on their door. Greame opened it.

"Storm's comin'. What do ye want to do wi' the ship?" Kelvin asked, rubbing his knee.

Greame looked over at Cat with a smile.

"All right, I believe ye, I believe ye!" she said, holding up her hands in defeat.

"The safest place would be in Pentagöet Harbour. Get the men. We'll meet on the *Revenge* in an hour and unload whate'er's left on her, then sail her around to the harbour," Greame instructed.

Greame headed out to the cove where the *Revenge* was moored. By the time he had dragged the long boats onto the beach from beyond the high tide mark, the rest of the men were arriving. There was an excitement in the air from getting back to the sea and the impending storm.

"I wonder if it'll be as bad as that one we weathered the first time we arrived here," Robbie said to whoever was listening.

"Aye, that one hopefully doesna bear repeatin'." Kelvin said, stepping into the boat.

Both long boats pushed off and were rowed to the *Revenge*. Once aboard, the men went below to gather what had been left there, mostly a few chests of personal items. Greame only had one more chest to come off and he instructed Geoffrey and Kenny to take good care with it.

"Is this another surprise for Garnet?" Kenny asked.

"No. It's whisky and tea."

"Dinna worry, Capt'n. We'll handle it like it was a babe," Geoffrey said with a grin.

When everything that was coming off was loaded into the long boats, they were rowed back to shore and unloaded. Kelvin, Greame and Gregor remained aboard to take the two-masted schooner to Pentagöet Harbour.

The sails filled with wind and the *Revenge* cut through the chop with ease and speed, making the short trip feel even shorter. When they arrived, the harbour was theirs. The current was very strong at low tides so he anchored the *Revenge* close to the island, out of the wind as much as possible, then lowered the sails and hoped for the best.

The last long boat was lowered and the trio got in and rowed to shore. The boat was pulled high onto the embankment and tied securely to a tree. Snowshoes were donned and they made their way back to the village. When they arrived, everyone began bringing in extra wood and food for themselves; enough for three days.

Greame found Cat in the root cellar with baskets of vegetables loaded and ready to be brought into the house. He noticed Bogle had a mouse in her mouth and was waiting beside the door when he got there. He patted her head and told her what a good wolf she was. Bogle just wagged her tail, but wouldn't move. She must have been waiting to show Cat—obviously the only one that mattered—that she was doing her job.

By sunset, the mare's tails filled the sky, making for a beautiful sunset of pink, apricot and violet. All they could do now was wait.

A Wicked Blow

Two days later, Cat was awakened before dawn by thunder. At first she wasn't sure that's what it was, but after a few lightning flashes filled the bedroom with light, she was positive. It was like a dream. She knew she went to bed and it was winter, but now there was a thunderstorm outside. Compared to Scotland, where one could count on the fact that it would be drizzling and cool for much of the year, Maine definitely had some strange weather anomalies.

Another loud clap of thunder and Greame stirred.

"What the hell is it doin' outside?" he asked in a sleep-raspy voice. "Is that thunder?"

"Aye, it's thunder." The room lit up with a flash of light again.

Greame sat up and looked out the window. Cat could see his masculine form silhouetted in the strange light making her want to touch him to assure herself he was real. Outside the wind had picked up in earnest. Greame got up and opened the window.

"It's too warm to snow," he marveled.

Cat got up to see for herself. She put her hand out the window and felt the breeze. It was indeed too warm. "How can this be?"

"I dinna ken, but I dinna care for it at all."

A flash of lightning hit the beach somewhere close. The thunderclap was so loud that Gent and Bogle came running into the bedroom, whining with fear.

"Dinna worry, ye two. Ye're safe in here," she said, almost to reassure herself as much as them.

Greame closed the window and got dressed.

"Ye're no' comin' back to bed?" Cat asked, crawling under the bedclothes.

"No. I want to watch what happens wi' this storm."

Cat debated whether she wanted to get up and watch it or go back to sleep. The sharp clap of thunder made the decision for her. She put on her wool dress and went out to the kitchen to make some tea. Greame was stoking the fire. There were already two cups on the table.

"Change yer mind?" He asked.

"Oh aye, like anyone can sleep in this commotion. I may as well be doin' somethin' useful."

"I fear for Smiles at Everything and his friends," Greame said, standing by the window.

Cat immediately had a vision of them hunkered down under moose hides in their winter village. They must have run much of the way to go so far so quickly. "They're safe."

Greame smiled, pressed a kiss on Cat's cheek and opened the front door. Lightning flashes were fewer now, even the thunder was a distant rumble. The air smelled fresh and clean. After a few minutes a heavy, wet snow started to fall. Gent and Bogle bounded through the doorway out into the snow. Greame closed the door and took a seat at the table.

"It's snowing."

Cat poured the tea and said, "I'm no' sure if that's good or bad."

"I remember a storm as a lad on the sea wi' my Da like this. We were on our way in for the day when as sudden as a blink, the wind came up and we heard the low rumble of thunder. Before we kent it, we were bein' tossed about like the sea was a cat and we were mice. We could see land, but it seemed the harder we rowed, the further out we were goin'."

Cat listened intently, reliving it with him.

"Then a lightning bolt hit the water no' fifty feet from us. My Da started rantin' and ravin' to God, sayin' how angry this was makin' him and that he wouldna want to be goin' to heaven in that angry state, so He—God—had better stop toyin' wi' him."

"Did it stop?" Cat asked.

"No. We were battered for near an hour before just as quick as it started, it stopped. We rowed back to shore in the dark, drenched to the skin and half froze. My Mam and sisters had put a fire on the shore to guide us in." His face softened and a rue smile played with his lips.

"They must hae been verra frightened for ye both."

Greame thought about it for a minute before answering.

"My Mam was a verra strong woman. I dinna remember e'er seein' her weep or show much emotion. It was her duty to do what she did and she did it without complaint. But early the next mornin' I was up before the rest and I saw her at the kitchen table sobbin' silently into her hands."

"Did she say why she was cryin'?"

Greame looked at Cat and said, "I didna console her. I went back to my pallet and stayed there until I heard my Da get up. By then my Mam was bustlin' in the kitchen."

Cat nodded and touched Greame's hand. "Ye did the right thing."

A quizzical look appeared on Greame's face. "I did?"

"Aye. If ye had acknowledged her sorrow, ye would hae taken away her strength."

Greame thought about that for a moment. "Aye, she would hae been weaker in my mind, unable to hold up in dire circumstances. Then I would hae worried for her."

Cat nodded. "I remember findin' out that my Da was just a man. I was devastated. He was supposed to be all-powerful; nothin' could defeat him. It was quite a shock."

Greame chuckled. "I remember yer Da."

"Ye do?"

"Oh aye. He was all powerful, but in a way that was kind when it was called for, and ragin' wi' fury when he saw an injustice."

Cat's dimples deepened. "He was like that. Fair. That's why people listened to him, even the Prince, to some extent."

"Prince Charles? The Bonnie Prince?"

Cat nodded. "He nearly had the Prince convinced that the moor at Culloden was no' a good place to fight wi' Highlanders. It was the Prince's advisors who angered him so wi' their bickerin' that he didna make the right decision."

"How ... wait, do I *want* to ken how ye hae this information?"

"No. It would confirm too many o' yer theories about me. I'd much prefer to remain a mystery," she said with a smile.

"When ye put it like that, I *ken* I dinna want to hear it," he agreed.

A bark at the door prompted Greame to let the dogs in. Both of them were covered with snow and shook themselves off, sending showers of droplets across the kitchen. Greame stood in the open doorway with his arms folded across his chest, studying the weather. Dawn had arrived with little fanfare; the snow made it seem like a dream, all gray and soft. It was getting colder now and the wind was still howling, making the trees dance so wildly, he wondered how they remained standing. A sudden blast of wind-driven snow hit him in the face and he shut the door on it.

"I'm glad there are no trees close by. There will be many that dinna survive this storm."

A wind gust hit the cabin, making it creak and snap. It was going to be a long day.

ॐ

Around noon the first of the men began arriving. As each of them came in, they gave a weather report. Geoffrey said the snow was nearly a foot deep already. He brought with him some blankets and an armload of wood. Kenny and Robbie were next, about a half hour later, also bringing blankets, wood and some jerky. Kelvin and Gregor entered just before dusk, rounding out the small community, which was now gathered in Cat's large cabin. She hardly minded, though. They were keeping her mind and her hands occupied.

"Snow's over my knees," Kelvin said, limping from the pain in the left one. "Dinna look like it's goin' to let up anytime either."

For the rest of the night the clan talked and ate until they were too tired to continue. One by one, blankets were laid out on the floor. Cat suggested that someone should take Jim's bed, since it was unoccupied for the time being. Kelvin jumped at the chance and was snoring before the rest of the men had even made their sleeping arrangements. Gregor found the settee to his liking. Geoffrey made fast friends with Gent and Bogle and the threesome took up the floor in front of the stove. Cat and Greame closed the door to their bedroom and soon the only thing heard was snoring and the whistling wind, with an occasional fart to break up the monotony.

Sometime during the night, loud crashes woke some of the group. They knew it was the sound of trees coming down, unable to withstand the relentless wind and heavy snow. When it was light enough to see, they tried to look out the windows to assess the damage. The snow was so deep it covered the bottom mullions. Windblown snow plastered the rest of the window panes, making it impossible to see outside. Greame opened the door for a better look, and to his and the rest of the household's amazement, the snow was chest high.

"Christ," he said quietly.

"It must be a drift. There canna really be that much snow out there … can there?" Cat said.

"Ne'er seen nothin' like it," Kelvin stated, scratching his bristly chin.

"And it's still snowin'!" Robbie declared.

Gent whined from behind them, indicating his need to go out. But one look at what he'd have to wade through to relieve himself, he went back to the stove and laid down next to Bogle.

"Well, that wilna last for long," Greame said, knowing full well all of their bladders will have to be emptied soon. "We'll need to dig ourselves out sooner or later, and it may as well be sooner, aye?"

Cat went into her bedroom and appeared with two shovels she'd brought in before the storm and handed them to Greame. Greame accepted one and donned his cloak and gloves. Gregor took the other after he dressed for the occasion. Together, they cleared the doorway and began the long process of digging out a path to the privy.

About an hour later, red-nosed and breathing heavily, they returned. Cat poured them each a cup of hot chicory after they got out of their wet clothes.

"Is it as deep as it was in the doorway all the way to the privy?" She asked.

Greame and Gregor just nodded as they sat with their hands wrapped around their warm mugs.

"Well, I'll be back shortly. C'mon dogs, we're goin' for a walk."

After a little persuading by Geoffrey, Gent and Bogle went out with Cat. The wind was fierce, biting into her skin. She pulled her cloak tighter around her to keep it from flying free. She walked as fast as she could and finally made it to the privy, where she slammed the door on the wind.

The fierce gale shook the tiny wooden structure to the point where she wondered if it was safe to be using it. She could hear the brutal snowflakes smashing into the wood with such savagery it seemed as though they could have made indentations. When she emerged, Gent and Bogle were sitting beside the door with their eyes squinting against the wind and snow. Cat did a quick survey of the woods and noticed it looked a bit sparse behind the house. Several of the tall spruce had snapped off, leaving just jagged stumps of varying heights.

Then a heavy snow squall hit and she could barely make out the cabin a hundred feet away. It was an eerie nightmare. The wind howled around her and tree branches snapped, making thuds when they hit the snow-covered ground. She thought how easy it would be to get lost and die a rather cruel death if there wasn't a path to follow. Then she thought of Smiles at Everything, Gray Eagle and Little Hawk. How did they make it through this kind of storm?

Her fingers were getting numb, so she began the walk back to the house quickly and slipped, landing on her side. Gent nosed her, apparently trying to make sure she wasn't hurt.

"It's just my pride that's been bruised, Gent, but thank ye for yer concern."

She took more care and made it to the house, where Kenny and Robbie had just stepped out.

"Looks like it could use another pass wi' the shovel, eh?" Kenny shouted over the wind to be heard.

"Probably best if we each make a pass every hour or so. It'll be easier than havin' to do feet of it again," she agreed from the doorway.

"Did ye fall?" Greame asked when Cat got inside.

"Aye. No damage, save my pride," she assured him, as he took her cloak and hung it near the stove.

Gregor poured her a cup of tea, which she placed on the counter in the kitchen, and began breakfast.

"Did ye see the trees?" She asked anyone who was listening.

"Aye," Greame answered. "Did ye hear the sea?"

"No. Not o'er the wind. Did it sound rough?"

"Worse than rough. I'm fearin' for the *Revenge*."

"She'll be fine, laddie," Kelvin said confidently. "She's anchored well in the lee o' the island."

"I hope so."

ॐ

For three long days, the storm raged. On the morning of the fourth day, the dawn brightened with a clear sunrise. The wind had subsided some, but was still gusting, sending white clouds of snow that obscured the landscape momentarily.

Greame donned his snowshoes, grabbed a shovel and beat a path to each of the cabins, retrieving Kelvin's and Gregor's snowshoes. Geoffrey, Kenny and Robbie fetched theirs as well and they all made the trek to the other side of the Cape to retrieve the *Revenge*.

The woods were littered with trees that the hurricane force had winds wreaked havoc upon, making the normal pathway impossible to follow. Buried branches caught the open weave of the snowshoes making for a snail's pace, at best. What normally took about an hour to traverse took three hours of hard work.

When they reached the shore where the long boat was tied, they found that a tree had come down on top of it, crushing it under its weight. All that was visible was the ropes that secured it to the trees on either side. The boat itself was a splintered pile of wood. Now there was no way of retrieving the ship once they'd found her.

They followed the shoreline in search of the *Revenge*. She should have been visible by now, but so far there was only an empty harbour.

Greame was becoming frantic. To lose his ship would be devastating, not only for him, but for the entire village. They would in essence, be trapped here. No way to get supplies or trade. No way to escape the English. He felt the world close in on him.

Kenny had walked up ahead and was the first to see her. "Captain! Over here!"

The *Revenge* was on her side on the rocky shore of a small cove on the island. It was Greame's worst fear come true, and his heart sank. From this vantage point, he couldn't tell how badly damaged she was, but there was no way she was unscathed.

Gregor put his hand on Greame's shoulder and said, "At least she's all in one piece."

It was true. She could have been dashed upon the rocks and had her entire hull ripped out, but from here, at least, she looked repairable.

"Damn it!" Greame swore. "How are we goin' to get to her?"

"What about wi' this?" Kenny said, uncovering a canoe that somehow managed to escape being crushed.

Geoffrey and Robbie helped him dig it out of the deep snow and drag it to the water's edge. Greame's face lit up with a grin.

"Nice find!"

The oars were salvaged from the longboat and Greame, Kelvin and Geoffrey got into the birch bark canoe. It wasn't far to the island and they were there in moments. Greame jumped from the canoe and ran to his ship. The tide was low so they'd have to wait to get her back into the water, but at least he could see what kind of damage she had sustained. He climbed up the hull and onto the deck, then shimmied his way below deck. She had been tossed about wildly from the looks of everything below, but at least it was still dark down here. He couldn't see any light coming from outside.

Walking on the ship's curved walls was an odd experience. Greame moved the strewn desks, chairs, and chests out of the way to get to the center of the ship. That's when he saw daylight. Right where she rested, a sharp boulder protruded through the hull below the water line. It looked as though the jagged rock caught her there and the sea's relentless wave action hammered away until she was ruptured. The open wound and splintered oak could indeed be repaired, but it would have to be done here.

Greame checked the rest of the hull to be sure that was the only damage. There were a few more soft areas that would need attention, but for the most part, that was it. He crawled out to receive Kelvin's report on the two masts.

"They seem structurally sound, Greame, but I wilna be sure 'til we get her upright," Kelvin said. "These booms, though, dinna look so good. I'd feel safer if they were replaced. The sails should be fine. They'd been lashed down verra well and nothing splintered to tear them. All in all, she fared all right."

Greame had his hands on his hips and his head bowed, taking in what Kelvin was telling him. They could certainly do the repairs themselves, but would have to wait for fairer weather.

"She'll be all right here 'til spring, barring any more storms like that one," Greame said. "Once the weather breaks we'll begin repairs. Until then, let's keep a sharp eye out for two replacement masts and booms. Now, let's go before we freeze to death out here."

❧

It was nearly dusk when the group returned home. Cat had a big venison stew and a couple of loaves of bread ready when they came in. She had already seen what Greame saw, but waited for him to elaborate on the details and his feelings. The men were quiet as they ate. Cat suspected they were exhausted and all a little let down that the *Revenge* was damaged.

"So, is anyone goin' to enlighten me on the condition o' the ship?" Cat asked.

"She didna fare too badly, considerin'." Kelvin commented. "We can repair her back to her seaworthy self."

"She's got a hole below water line and her booms are weak, but it could hae been worse," Greame detailed.

"She'll be good as new when we get done wi' her," Kenny said between chews.

Cat smiled at the positive reactions, but felt an underlying tension from Greame. She would ask him later in private what was really going on.

All the men spent the night in her cabin again. The next morning, after breakfast, each of them left with their blankets, indicating they would return to their own cabins for the night. It seemed abnormally quiet when they left, but Cat enjoyed the peace for a change.

As she began tidying up, she had the strange sensation that someone was watching her. She looked around the house. It was empty. Since the day was clear and calm, Greame and the men were out shoveling and clearing out woodpiles. Cat looked out the windows, but knew in her heart the intruder wasn't in the physical form. She closed her eyes and concentrated on Black Devil, knowing full well it was him. This time, there was no need for the red eyes disguise he usually presented to her. He appeared as himself, smothered in animal skins in the glow of a fire.

"What do ye want, Black Devil?" Cat demanded.

Why are you so hostile? I only want to talk, he said in a wounded voice.

Even telepathically, she could tell he was up to something.

"I hae nothin' to say to ye. Now leave me be."

But I enjoyed our engagement before. You cannot tell me you didn't feel the same.

"I *can* tell ye that, and I *dinna* feel the same. What do ye want?"

I only want to have an equal. You are that equal. Think of what we could do together. What we could have, he said in a pleading voice.

"Dinna be daft. I may be yer equal, but we are on different sides, and I hae no intention of havin' anythin' to do wi' ye. Now leave me be!"

Come now, Garnet. You must admit you are curious about me. About my powers. We can change the outcome of this war. All this can be ours, instead of the white man's.

It took Cat a minute to process what he had just predicted, and she didn't like what she heard.

"What war?"

He laughed maliciously. *I knew that would get your attention, you having such a history with war.*

"What war? And what white men are ye speakin' of?" she shouted.

Come with me, Garnet. We can change everything!

"Get out o' my heid!" she screamed.

Suddenly, he was gone. The door burst open and Greame and Gregor stood there looking around for the person she was yelling at. Greame walked over to her and held her.

"Black Devil?" He said.

Cat nodded on his shoulder. "Did ye see him, too?"

He released her and looked into her eyes. "I felt him."

"Did ye hear what he said?"

Greame shook his head.

"He said there was goin' to be a war and the white men would take control o' this place."

"Was he warnin' ye about it?"

"No. He wanted me to join him and change the outcome," she said, walking in the kitchen to sit down.

Greame followed and sat next to her. Gregor listened while standing beside her.

"How? Did he tell ye?" Greame asked, peeling his gloves off and rubbing his hands together.

"No. That's when ye came in and he disappeared."

"I see no good comin' from this, do ye?"

"Dinna be daft. He's a madman. Gregor, ye ken more about who will be involved in this damned mess. Where do the Mohawks' loyalties lie?"

A sad expression came over Gregor's face, as though he didn't want to drag her into what was inevitably going to happen.

"Tell me. Apparently, I hae no choice in the matter now."

"With the English," he said.

"Perhaps ye should hae a seat. I think we need to talk."

It's Deja Vu
All Over Again

The sun disappeared behind an ominous dark cloud for the entire duration of Gregor's exposé, as though in a premonition of the event. The more details he revealed, the more *déjà vu* Cat experienced. For a brief moment she wondered how all of this had been going on without her knowledge. Then she remembered; it was because she didn't *want* to know about it. When she was in Boston, she was in the thick of things, privy to all that was happening, but that was not what she wanted. She had a different path to take, one that led her to the Province of Maine, but for what purpose? Was she really destined to be a part of this new war? Was Black Devil correct in seeing the entire country owned by the white man, meaning the English or the French? What would happen to the Indians? Would they become slaves like the blacks?

Suddenly, she could take no more. Gregor was still talking, but Cat had stopped listening. Her face got hot with fury and she pounded her fist on the table, effectively startling both Greame and Gregor, then bolted to her room.

Greame threw an angry glance at Gregor before going to check on Cat, and said, "Ye couldna see that she wasna listenin' to ye anymore? That she'd had enough?"

Gregor sat at the table all by himself, wondering what had happened to his audience.

❧

Cat was leaning on the edge of the window twirling her hair when Greame silently walked in. She didn't need to see him to know he was there, but she made no motion to acknowledge him. She was still sorting things out in her mind, and nothing he could say would make her feel any better right now. He must have sensed this because he left the room, closing the door behind him.

How she would have preferred to stay ignorant of the whole affair. To not know that two years ago, after the English fought the French for Louisbourg, they gave the fort to France in return for Madras in southern India. What kind of politics was that? Now the French and English were vying for territory west of here, in some place called the Ohio Valley. New York and Pennsylvania, she thought Gregor said, were also on the firing lines, being raided by Indians because settlers were literally stealing their lands, pushing the natives further and further out of their own territories. Six tribes formed a nation calling themselves the Iroquois Confederacy, and they were siding with whoever could supply them with the goods and trade they came to rely on.

Gregor also said the French were building more and more forts to keep the English settlers from entering their land, although the Indians were the rightful owners of it. She remembered Far Eyes telling her that man could not own the land, that man was merely here to tend to the land and, in harmony, use its bounty. Hell, it worked for them for thousands of years! Now, all of a sudden, Europeans come in and wipe out an entire way of life for their own greed. Cat wondered if she even wanted to continue being here. Not just being in Maine or America, but living, period. It all seemed so hopeless, so futile. There was so much land and space here. Why couldn't everyone enjoy its resources and live together? Apparently, that was too easy. This group couldn't get along with that group, and both groups wanted it all for themselves. Stupid.

"And here I am rantin' about," she said out loud, throwing a shoe across the room.

The younger Cat would have asked what she could do to change it. This Cat wanted nothing to do with it. Didn't care about it. Wanted only to live in peace, but where? One thing she was sure of, and that was the conviction not to be part of this next confrontation.

ॐ

The sun began staying up a little longer each day. It was still very cold, but it hadn't snowed for nearly three weeks. 'Course, there was so much snow covering the ground, no one missed it falling from the sky.

Greame was out splitting wood with the men. There was no shortage of spruce, with the decimation from the big storm, and it took so much wood to keep the cabins warm. In Scotland, it was the digging of peat with much the same regularity, then drying it and hauling it to the crofts. Wood still seemed more labour intensive.

Cat was making bread when she was assailed with a feeling of utter sorrow. Tears sprang to her amethyst eyes for no apparent reason. By the time she wiped her hands off, she was sobbing. She sat at the kitchen table wiping her eyes, but unable to control the flow. She tried to analyze the cause, but could find no reason for this sense of depression.

As suddenly as the feeling washed over her, it was gone. Greame walked in to see her wiping her eyes, and sat down beside her.

"What's wrong, *a ghaoil?*"

Cat looked at him for a long moment before trying to explain what had just happened. At the end, she just shrugged.

"Ye'er feelin' alone, is that it?" He asked, rubbing her arm.

Another shrug.

"How would ye like it if Kelvin brought the pipes o'er tonight?"

Cat regained some of her composure, and said, "Aye, that'd be fine."

"Ye canna tell me why ye were so sad?"

Cat shook her head. "It just came o'er me. Just a feelin' o' sorrow so deep, it hurt."

Greame nodded, as though understanding perfectly. "My oldest sister was prone to such things in winter. It was dark for so long, ye remember. Much longer than here. She would tell me that the walls were closin' in on her. She always felt better when she went outside for a while, just gettin' some fresh air and sunshine. Perhaps ye should try that. Want to come out wi' me now?"

Cat thought about it for a moment. Fresh air sounded nice. She glanced at the mound of dough on the counter, then said, "I'll be out as soon as I finish kneadin' the bread, then I'll help ye stack the wood."

"Well, ye dinna hae to do that, we can take a stroll along the beach. There's no wind today."

Cat smiled and blew her nose, making a tooting sound. "All right."

She got up and resumed the kneading. Then the smooth dough was patted into two rounds, placed in bowls and covered with linens to rise. Within minutes, she had her boots and cloak on, and Greame guided her out the door.

"How would ye like to hae another woman here to help ye wi' yer chores?" Greame asked.

Cat looked at him with curiosity, wondering what brought that up. "Am I no' doin' my job well enough?"

He sent her a scowl. "That's no' what I meant. I just thought it would pass the time faster if there was someone ye could talk to when I wasna here."

"Hae ye someone in mind?"

He smiled, knowing full well she knew who he had in mind.

"Sings Like Bird? Are ye trying to tell me somethin'? Does Gregor want to take her for his bride? Will ye answer me and wipe that smile off yer face?"

Greame laughed, in turn making Cat smile.

"Aye, I mean Sings Like Bird, and aye, he's been talkin' about her a lot, so I'm just tryin' to get yer opinion about the situation."

"I think it's a fine idea, as long as that's what she wants."

"We'll ken in the spring," he told her, wrapping his arm around her waist.

What sounded like a stampede behind them turned out to be Gent and Bogle running wildly on the pebbles, then stopping suddenly with their rear ends in the air, then dashing off again.

"Bogle will be comin' into heat soon," Greame said. "We'll hae a whole family o' very strange lookin' wolf-dogs come April."

Cat laughed at the picture of them in her mind. "What will we do wi' them?"

"Perhaps we can get them to haul wood."

"Speakin' o' that, are ye sure ye dinna want me to help wi' the stackin'? I'd much rather be out here than inside today."

"I think ye should do whate'er ye want to do, and if that includes stackin' wood, then by all means," he said, with a formal sweep of his arm.

"Let's go then. There's too much to do to be dallyin' on the beach."

Kelvin filled the cabin with music that night, and everyone went home in a happy mood. When all was quiet again, Cat tried to figure out what had brought on the sudden bout of sadness that morning. She came away without a cause. The fresh air and sunshine did make her feel better. Was that really all it was? She wondered if Far Eyes had heard of such things, and decided to try and contact him on a telepathic level.

Cat sat in the chair in her bedroom, and picked out a lock of auburn hair to twirl. As she rocked back and forth she closed her eyes and pictured Far Eyes. It had been quite some time since she'd practiced this ability, and felt a bit rusty. All at once, she saw Far Eyes sitting under furs in his wigwam. The fire lit his features, making them dance in the warm glow; one minute soft, the next, harsh. She knew she'd made contact when he looked up and smiled. In her head, she heard him say, *Garnet, is it you?*

"Aye, Far Eyes, it's me."

Good to see you.

"Good to see ye, too. I hae a question."

Yes. The sun is powerful healer.

Cat laughed. "Thank ye."

Tell me of Black Devil.

Suddenly, it felt imperative that she say nothing. It was as if Black Devil was monitoring her thoughts, and with his name spoken, he was now listening.

"I'll see ye in the spring, Far Eyes."

She abruptly broke off communication and got up from her chair, shaking off the feeling that Black Devil was still watching. She walked into the keeping room where Greame was writing in his journal. He'd been doing that with more frequency, and it made Cat curious.

"What do ye write in yer wee book?"

He looked up with a smile, "What goes on around here."

"Is it so yer cousins in Boston can read it and ken what went on up here in the wilds o' Maine?"

"Aye. They canna possibly hae near the entertainment we do. As soon as the weather breaks, we'll start repairs on the *Revenge*, then take a trip down to check on them, and the teashop."

"That would be nice," she said, a little distractedly.

"What were ye doin' in there?" He gestured toward the bedroom.

"Ye dinna miss a thing, do ye?" Cat wondered if she should say anything.

He patiently waited for an explanation, watching her every move. After a few minutes, she knew he wasn't going to let it go.

"I was speakin' wi' Far Eyes."

Greame's eyebrow raised, as if to say … *and?*

"Black Devil was listening in on our conversation."

"What?" He put the quill down. "He can do that?"

"Well, I wasna as cautious as I probably should hae been. I didna put up defenses for intruders; ne'er thought I would hae to."

"Do ye think Far Eyes kent Black Devil was listenin'?"

Cat turned a ghostly white. What had she done? Would Black Devil realize her alliance with the Penobscot and set against them in retaliation? She had to warn Far Eyes.

"Talk to me," he said anxiously.

Cat saw the fear in his eyes. He was thinking the same thing she was.

"How can I help ye?" He moved closer to her on the settee.

Cat's mind was racing. She knew that alone, she wasn't powerful enough to keep Black Devil from spying, but didn't know if together with Greame, they were strong enough either. She grabbed his hands, looked him in the eyes, and said, "We're goin' to need more help."

Cat wanted to do this right. Her thoughts were consumed by strategies of strengthening her protection. She deduced that during the daylight hours would be stronger for her. Black Devil liked the dark. It's what fed him. Cat would have to be the light in this confrontation, his opposite. Anna would have to be called upon to watch her back. She also felt a strong attraction to a protective stone. She wished she had the *clach na braitach,* but would have to make do with something else. But what? Her ring wasn't enough. Even the garnet-encrusted dirk wasn't enough.

"Garnet, isna there somethin' I can do to help ye?" Greame asked as he watched Cat pace back and forth in front of him.

Cat stopped for a second, and said, "Oh aye, ye can fetch me a wee crystal from the beach." She was being sarcastic, but Greame took it to heart.

"Wait here. I may hae somethin' of use, if all ye need is a crystal."

Cat watched in disbelief as he disappeared into Jim's room. She heard him pull out a chest and rummage through it. One of these days, she thought to herself, she would have to see what was in those chests. She walked over and stood in the doorway, arms crossed under her breasts, watching to see what he came up with. It seemed like a veritable treasure trove he was sifting through. Cat picked up a small wooden box he had just discarded, and opened it. It had a set of tiny silver spoons in it. Something wrapped in royal blue velvet caught her eye and she unwrapped it on Jim's bed. There were two sticks in it. Only these weren't ordinary sticks. They were made of rose wood, about six inches long. Attached to the tops were ornately carved gold dragons with small emeralds for their eyes. Cat was amazed at the extraordinary detail of the dragons, but couldn't figure out what they were used for.

She held them up, and said, "Greame, what are these?"

He glanced up quickly, distracted from his task, then stopped and smiled. "Oh, I forgot about those." He stood and took them from her hand. "Twist yer hair up," he requested.

Cat's curiosity was piqued and she did as she was asked. When the waist-long mass was reined in and collected at the back of her head, Greame inserted the two sticks so they held her locks in place. Cat went to the looking glass and smiled, marveling at the sheer simplicity of the items.

"Where did ye get them?" She eyed them critically, adjusting them so she could see the miniature dragons.

"From the same chest as the Chinese coins that landed on my shore in Scotland. They look beautiful on ye. Why dinna ye keep them out? They may as well be gettin' some use, aye?"

"Thank ye, Greame. What else do ye hae in those chests o' yers?"

He had already resumed the hunt, pulling out bolts of silk, more wooden boxes that only he knew the contents of, and finally, with an *ahh haa!* came an oval box made of pink stone. He handed it to her, gesturing her to open it, while he put everything back into the chest.

Cat held the eight-inch-long box and gently touched its smoothness with her fingers, amazed at the craftsmanship. It was carved so thin it was nearly translucent. Carefully she took the cover off and to her amazement, inside, lying on a bed of light rose velvet, was the most incredible purple amethyst crystal she had ever seen. It was about seven inches long, over two inches around with smaller crystals at the base, and went to a sharp point. She picked it out of its stone sarcophagus and held it up to the light. It was perfect.

"Will it do?" Greame asked.

Cat stared at him with her mouth open for a few seconds before she nodded her approval. After a moment she controlled herself and asked, "Why didna ye tell me ye had this when Bogle and I went in search of the watcher?"

"Ye didna ask," he said, in all innocence. "Ye said ye wished for the ensign stone. I didna think anythin' else would do."

"I'll ask ye again, what else do ye hae in those chests o' yers?"

He laughed. "Another time we'll go through them together, all right?"

"Ye can count on it. Now, I need to cleanse this crystal and direct its protective properties to the matter at hand."

"How is that done?" He followed her back into the kitchen where she placed the pink stone box on the table, then put her cloak on. He followed suit, curious to see the procedure.

"I need to wash the crystal in the sea and let it dry in the sunlight. That places the elements into it. Then I'll direct my intentions to it and by tomorrow it will be ready to work."

The dawn bloomed in a lemon sky. It was already warm, and icicles dripped in a torrent of wet prisms when the sunlight hit them. The bay stood still in the windless morning, making the water seem more solid. The first signs of a January thaw.

Inside, on the kitchen table, Cat laid out the emerald, indigo and raspberry silk square, three candles, the garnet-encrusted dirk (one couldn't be too careful), and the amethyst. Her mission was to contact and warn Far Eyes without Black Devil perceiving it.

"Do ye mind if I watch ye?" Greame asked.

"No. I want ye here ... just in case," she said, a bit cryptically.

"What about Bogle? Should she be wi' ye?"

Cat thought for a moment. Perhaps it wouldn't hurt to have her keen senses along. "Aye. Would ye call her in?"

When Greame opened the door, Bogle was sitting on the other side, as if already knowing she was wanted for a task. "Sometimes this is a wee bit spooky, Garnet," he said, closing the door after Bogle walked in.

Cat giggled. "And ye've such a rare fine nature about all of it, Greame. Thank ye."

After the candles were lit, Cat and Greame began their protective prayers. Hearing Anna's voice in their heads confirmed her presence.

Cat looked at Greame and held his hand and put the other on Bogle's head. Greame placed his hand on Bogle's nape and the circle was complete.

"Are ye ready?" Cat asked.

Greame nodded and closed his eyes.

"We only want to speak wi' Far Eyes," Cat commanded. "There's to be no interference or interlopin' from anyone no' connected wi' our circle."

Instantly, Cat, Greame and Anna were in a cave. Bogle was guarding an unseen entrance. From out of the darkness, Far Eyes appeared, and they all sat around a central fire.

"I see Black Devil when we talk last," Far Eyes said in a low voice.

"I was so afraid o' what he would do to ye to get back at me," Cat said, looking around to make sure they were still alone.

"Dinna worry, lass, we're safe here," Anna said.

"I dream of Black Devil. He will come. We will be ready."

"Can we truly be ready for the unseen?" Cat asked.

"Ye just answered yer own question, Garnet," Anna stated.

"We'll make sure he's seen," Greame said.

"Aye. And to do that—" Anna began.

"Must mark his energy," Far Eyes interrupted.

"When I am Bogle, he wears a red light wi' purple, silver, yellow and white."

"That's how we see on my side," Anna said. "That's how each person is identified."

"So how can we make him show his colors to everyone, no' just us?" Cat queried.

That seemed to be a stumbling point.

"Remember when ye hit him wi' yer wee stick, Anna?" Greame asked. "He went down just like any other man would hae. How was that possible?"

Anna cackled. "Ye've a rare smart man here, Garnet. That's the secret!" When everyone sat there with blank looks on their faces, she elaborated. "His third eye, his vision center," she pointed to the center of her forehead. The dawning light on everyone's faces indicated their grasp of the concept.

"That still leaves us wi' a problem," Cat said. "It's no' like we can sneak up on him and bash him between the eyes."

"Not in real world, but from this side, we do," said Far Eyes, smiling.

"Ohhh. Block his sight like he did to me," Cat said.

A growl from Bogle indicated they must solidify a plan immediately or risk being overheard.

"But how do we do that permanently?" Greame whispered, his unease growing when Bogle growled again.

"Make likeness," Far Eyes said.

Bogle was growling more now. Black Devil must be too close. Suddenly, the fire went out, jolting Cat and Greame back to the kitchen table.

"What happened?" Greame asked, checking to make sure Cat and Bogle were safe.

"Black Devil was near. Our collective fear brought us out."

"So what now? We make a likeness of him and blindfold him?"

Cat grinned, "Och, ye *are* a rare smart man."

The foot-long muslin doll didn't look a thing like Black Devil, but then it didn't need to. It only needed to represent him. Cat used her herbs to dye it red with purple and yellow. Around its neck she tied one of Greame's silver spoons and the doll's head was left white. Cat tied a black ribbon around the doll's eyes, in essence, blindfolding it.

Greame studied the figure for a minute, then disappeared into the bedroom. When he came out, Cat noticed he carried the ceremonial dirk. She watched in fascination as Greame placed the point of the dirk in the center of the doll's forehead and skewered it to the table.

"That should keep him where he belongs," he said.

It's All in the Eyes

For the remainder of the winter, life was normal and quiet. There had been a few more snowstorms in February and March, but nothing resembling the wicked blow. It was now nearing the middle of May. Most of the snow was gone, except in the darkest of the woods. Small red flowers budded out on the maples, and caterpillar-like catkins fell from the birch to litter the ground with greenish-yellow fuzz. And while the sun was warm, the air, especially by the water, was still immersed in late winter cold. The trees were decorated with songbirds that were returning from wherever they went during the deepest winter. Gulls of all types were crying day and night as they paired up and nested on the small sheltered islands out to sea.

Cat, dressed warmly in her woolen dress and cloak, took her cup of tea out on the rocks by the shore. It was mid-morning, her bread was rising in the kitchen, Greame and the men had begun repairs on the *Revenge,* and life was being reborn all around her. She wanted to witness it firsthand. A raven, which didn't frequent the area all that often, landed on a thick, dead branch at the top of a spruce. It instantly brought Cat back to her childhood when she would have the curious and intelligent black birds send messages to her brother Lachlan. She smiled, remembering the way Lachlan's face lit up when he received his first message. She couldn't remember what the message was, but from then on, she and Lachlan strengthened their telepathic bond, eventually rendering the raven's assistance unnecessary. All they had to do was think about each other and send an image in their minds. God, she missed him. Even though she still spoke to him and could see his face from the other side, it wasn't the same as having him beside her in flesh and blood.

Cat stood and drained the dregs of her tea onto the ground. She had started back to the cabin when the hair rose on her arms and her neck tingled. Someone was watching her. She seemed to be having a hard time distinguishing friend from foe anymore. They all evoked the same emotion—wariness. She stood perfectly still, except for her eyes. They searched the clearing around the cabin and as far into the woods as she could see. No one was there. Her eyes went to the trees and the raven cawed its raspy call as though taunting her. The black bird took flight and the feeling left.

"So, ye still want to play that game, Black Devil?"

There was no reply, but she derived pleasure in knowing he could see only through the eyes of a messenger now and apparently couldn't speak.

❧

When suppertime rolled around the men came in announcing the Penobscots' return, and Cat simply forgot to tell Greame of her own news.

"Far Eyes said he'll be by to talk wi' ye soon," Greame said. "Oh, and Jim's wi' them," he added casually.

Cat's face beamed. "How is Jim? Has he changed much? How is Jumpin' Turtle? Are they still gettin' along well?"

Greame chuckled at the barrage. "He said he'll stop by tomorrow, says he has some news."

"What news?"

"He didna say." He looked up from his plate of food when Cat remained quiet, and clucked his tongue. "Aw, now dinna do that," he chided in an exasperated tone. "Let him tell ye. Let someone surprise ye for once."

Her eyes had gone far away, indicating she was finding out in advance. Deep dimples gave away her discovery. Cat waited a few minutes before asking him why he wasn't curious in finding out what the news was.

He looked her square in the eyes and said, "Because I happen to like surprises."

❧

Cat had just enough dried apples for one more pie, and she figured now would be as good a time as any to use them. She was certain Jim hadn't had a pie in a while. As promised, Jim and Jumping Turtle stopped in for a visit around mid-afternoon.

It didn't take a formal announcement to anyone with or without the Sight to figure out what the surprise was. Jumping Turtle was about six months along. Her ball-like belly strained against the deerskin dress in a taut giveaway.

Cat squealed with delight and accosted both of them with enormous hugs. Jim blushed, but the smile never left his face. Jumping Turtle was a bit overwhelmed, and held Jim's hand for quite some time.

"So tell me, Jim," Cat said, passing out slices of apple pie and pouring cups of tea for each of them. "How did ye fare durin' the winter? And especially, that blow in January."

A look of awe came over Jim's face at the mention of the storm. "I couldn't believe how much it snowed. It was chest high! And the wind … well, I didn't think our wigwam could take it, but the snow seemed ta actually hold it down so we didn't blow away!" He laughed a little, because now he could. "It was a frightenin' storm, though. Smiles at Everything, Gray Eagle and Little Hawk stayed with us. They arrived in the middle of the night, just as a thunderstorm, of all things, hit! Said they ran most of the way ta beat it."

Cat sensed it was the first time he'd spoken of it. She felt his terror, though he did well to hide it. "Aye. All the men stayed here during the storm. It was just easier to all be in one place. We ate, told stories and Kelvin played the pipes."

"Never cared for the pipes," he said, shaking his head. "They bring out an anger in me."

Cat thought about that for a moment. The pipes were what Scotsmen used to terrify the enemy; usually the English. Jim was English, so she guessed that somewhere down the line, he—in a former life—may have bore the brunt of a Scottish battle cry.

"What pipes?" Jumping Turtle asked, now feeling a bit more relaxed.

"Can ye stay for supper?" Cat asked the both of them, clapping her hands together.

Jim said something to Jumping Turtle in Wabinaki, got a nod from her, and simply said, "Yes."

ॐ

Jumping Turtle had both hands over her ears and an enormous grin on her face as Kelvin played several reels and jigs. Jim entertained himself with Gent and Bogle far away from the skirl. And the few times the wind carried the distant sound to him were not unpleasant.

Greame caught up to Jim when Kelvin was finished with his concert. He wanted to make sure Jim was aware of the turmoil that was beginning among the French, English and Indians. He would probably be involved in one way or another; whether he remained with the Penobscot or came back to make a home in the settlement.

Jim told Greame that Smiles at Everything had enlightened him on several occasions from his return trips with Gregor.

"Yeah, the Mohawk seem ta have most of the nations stirred up," Jim stated. "The English have the most supplies and weapons, so they're sidin' with them. They say there's a white man named William Johnson who lives in upper New York. The Iroquois made him a colonel. He deals with the whites on both sides ta make sure the confederacy and the crown maintain good relations. But, there's also talk of the French building forts in Pennsylvania and New York ta keep the English and Indians out. It won't make for good relations for anyone if that happens."

Greame took this new information in. So far, at least, the brunt of the activities were far to the west of Maine. Perhaps their little settlement could remain out of the conflict altogether.

"I'm glad ye're stayin' on top o' these things, Jim. Garnet wouldna be happy wi' me if ye were in danger and I didna say anythin' to ye about it."

Jim chuckled. "Garnet's quite a woman." He spoke like suddenly he knew what "quite a woman" meant. Perhaps he did now. He had learned a lot over the winter living with Jumping Turtle and the rest of the Penobscot women. Skin color, he found out, made no difference to human attitudes. Native women argued and bickered the same as white women. Native men could be cocky and greedy the same as white men. There was no distinction he could see. But Garnet stood out among women. He couldn't put a finger on why, but she was definitely different.

Greame clapped Jim's back and grinned. "I'll no' argue wi' ye there, Jim."

è&

Jim and Jumping Turtle stayed in Jim's old room for the night. The peepers were loud outside. The tiny frogs, which were nearly impossible to see, filled the small ponds. Their miniature splashes were the only indication that they existed. If one got too close to them, the entire collective would go silent, not starting up again for a long time. Each one had a distinctive call, but when hundreds all called at the same time, it was nature's music serenading the village.

Cat lay next to Greame unable to sleep. He wasn't having any trouble, as he let out a snort then rolled over. Her mind was filled with agendas that, as unimportant as they were, didn't seem to want to wait 'til morning to sort out. One such agenda was the trip to Boston they were planning when the *Revenge* was back in working order. She was oddly looking forward to it. Maybe Greame was right back in the winter when her moods were black and nothing but sunlight and fresh air could dispel them. Maybe she did long for the company of women, if for nothing else but to chat about normal things, not impending wars, or guns, or angry shamans. Cat smiled at the thought of trying to get Greame to "chat." She had to silence a giggle into her pillow at the idea. Then she thought about having a woman sharing the same house all the time, like Sings Like Bird. It didn't sit well. She still wanted her privacy, her aloneness, her freedom. "Huh," she said out loud, just coming to the realization of her wants and needs.

She slipped out of bed and tiptoed into the keeping room. She added a couple more logs to the fire to take the chill off and sat down on the settee. Gent and Bogle never stirred from their sprawled out postures on the floor. It seemed everyone was sleeping soundly, except her.

The fire grew slowly in the fireplace. Its mesmerizing flames cast its spell and Cat was hooked. In the orange and yellow glow were images. She saw *Slios Mín,* the long field that overlooked Blair Castle, and the ship she sailed on to get to America. They were memories. In her short life she had done many things her mother had never done, seen things her mother had never seen. A tear gently coursed down her cheek. How would things have changed if her entire family hadn't died? Where would she be? She just wanted to grow old the same way everyone else did.

The path no' taken could lead ye to better or worse places, Garnet. Anna's voice was as clear as though she were sitting right beside her.

Cat sniffed and said, "I guess I took the wrong path, 'cause I dinna think it could hae gotten worse."

Trust me, ye could hae done much worse. What are ye feelin' sorry for yerself for?

"I dinna ken," she sighed. "It seems like all I do is the same things over and over again, day after day. Nothin' happens. It's just the same routine every day."

A soft cackle from Anna made Cat wonder what could possibly be so amusing.

"What?" Cat asked.

Ye just said ye wanted to grow old like everyone else does.

"And yer point is?" Cat replied testily.

Ye are, and ye dinna ken it. Ye're dyin' inside, no' usin' yer powers.

Cat thought about that for a minute. If that were true … "Christ," she said in acknowledgement.

Another cackle let Cat know she was back on the right path. Cat would never be happy without conflict in her life. It wasn't in her nature. She lived to solve problems, to challenge herself. How could she possibly do that in the routine she was in, never venturing outside to see what could be changed?

"So why Maine? The war between the English, French and the Indians wilna be here," she thought out loud. "Wait!" She sat up on the edge of the settee. "I'm no' goin' to chase down the war in Ohio! I wilna do it! There has to be another reason why I feel so strongly about bein' here."

When Cat finished ranting, she looked to see Gent and Bogle sitting side-by-side, staring at her as though she'd gone mad. They seemed pretty confident that this speech wasn't for them, but they were giving her their undivided attention, just in case.

ले

Cat was awakened by the sounds of the kitchen. She opened her eyes, wondering who was making all the noise, to find Jim searching for the chicory in the cupboards.

"Second one from the left," Cat said groggily.

Jim's sleep-tousled hair made Cat smile when he poked his head around the door jamb to apologize for waking her. Cat waved it off and went into her bedroom to get dressed. When she emerged, Jumping Turtle was sitting at the table with Jim drinking a cup of chicory. Cat noticed a mug was set out for her, and took the seat it was closest to.

"Sleep well?" Cat asked the two of them.

Jumping Turtle just nodded. She mustn't be a morning person.

Jim said, "Yup. I take it you didn't."

"Och, ye ken me," Cat said, warming her hands on the mug.

"So what's this I hear about Black Devil?" Jim said.

Cat looked at him for a moment with her head cocked and her brow knitted. For some reason, she didn't want to answer him. That was odd. He had every right to know, especially living with the Penobscot. He stared at her, waiting for an answer. She had to say something.

"I think we've heard the last of him," she said.

Cat caught Jumping Turtle's eyes and didn't like what she saw in them.

"Would ye excuse me? I've got to get Greame up."

Cat walked into the bedroom to find Greame sitting on the edge of the bed. Cat closed the door and sat beside him.

"Why is everyone up so early?" He said after an enormous yawn.

"I hae something to say, but I'm no' sure I believe it myself, so hear me out before ye say anythin'." Cat whispered.

Greame nodded with a frown furrowing his forehead.

"The other day when ye and the men were making repairs on the *Revenge,* I had a visit from a raven. He was a messenger from Black Devil, but couldna speak, he just watched me for a moment, then flew away. I forgot to tell ye, wi' Jim and Jumpin' Turtle showin' up, and all. Anyway, just a moment ago, Jim asked me about Black Devil."

Greame opened his mouth to say something, but remembered Cat's request and remained quiet.

To answer his unasked question, Cat said, "Aye, that's what I thought. How does Jim ken about Black Devil? And, when I caught Jumpin' Turtle's eyes, they were … well, the best way I can explain it is that they werna hers. Would Far Eyes talk about Black Devil or is this some kind o' trick?"

Greame raised an eyebrow, silently asking if he could speak.

"Oh, ye can talk now."

"Thank ye," he said, in the same soft voice to not be overheard. "Do ye think Black Devil can be *inside* someone?"

"I dinna ken. He has powers I would ne'er hae thought of."

"I dinna like this, Garnet. We canna go around thinkin' everyone to be a spy for him. Who could we trust if that were so?" He took her hand and pressed a kiss on it. "What did ye tell Jim?"

"I hated to, but I lied and told him we'd heard the last of Black Devil."

"Well, under the circumstances, that was probably the right thing to say. I'll get dressed and walk them back to their summer village. Perhaps I can get some information out o' them. I'm a better liar then ye," he grinned.

Cat decided to begin her meditations again. She had to find out what was going on with Black Devil and the only way to do that was to strengthen her powers. Taking advantage of having the cabin to herself for a while, Cat went into her bedroom and sat in her rocking chair beside the window. Just as she had for as long as she could remember, she grabbed a thick lock of auburn hair and began to twirl it around her thumb and forefinger. She rocked back and forth in a slow momentum, keeping pace with her heart rate. The world slowly faded away. The shadows of her mind became clearer as visions started flowing from her subconscious. At first, they were soft gray nonsense; just leftover thoughts and feelings. She discarded them until all that was left was a blank canvas. Now she was ready.

Her intentions were to travel around the settlement and the Penobscot village to see what the summer would bring. Would they be safe? Would hunting and fishing be abundant? Were the English and French in the area? The Mohawk? Black Devil?

As she gazed through time, all seemed pretty normal on the outside, but there was a feeling, an ever present doom lurking behind the scenes. Cat checked in with Jim and Jumping Turtle. Jim was

thrilled to be the father of a healthy baby boy. Jumping Turtle, however, was not herself. She didn't want to have anything to do with the
bairn. Cat strained to hear her telling her mother how she felt, and
knew she was right all along.

In her native tongue, Jumping Turtle told Raven that the baby
wasn't hers. Raven argued that it wasn't possible to give birth and not
have it be her baby. "Look at its eyes!" Jumping Turtle screamed.
When Raven looked, she saw only that the bairn's eyes were blue,
like his father's. She could not see what Cat and Jumping Turtle saw
in those blue eyes.

Relinquishing Possession

Cat ran most of the way to the Penobscot village, making the normal hour-long journey in half the time. The first person she saw was Far Eyes. He'd been waiting for her. While she caught her breath, they walked down to the shore. It was windy and the tide was going out. The noise of the water would assure their privacy.

"I feel you come. What wrong?" Far Eyes asked as they sat on the rocks at the water's edge.

"I had a vision," Cat said. "It was Jumpin' Turtle's bairn. I wanted ye to see if ye can tell if the lad will be … well, normal."

Far Eyes looked at her in a curious way. "You mean all toes and fingers?"

Cat shook her head. "No, I mean wi' the right spirit."

His eyebrows rose high, then he frowned and squinted, sure he hadn't heard her correctly. "You tell me what you see."

Cat explained what her vision entailed to the best of her ability. Far Eyes remained stone-faced throughout the account. When she was finished, his only reaction was a look of awe he let slip onto his face for a moment, before quickly erasing it.

Cat waited to hear what he thought, but Far Eyes just kept shaking his head, going over all the possibilities in his mind, then disregarding them as useless. After a few minutes he opened his mouth to say something, then closed it without uttering a word.

"I not know how to tell this. If this true, very bad medicine."

"Bad medicine, indeed. If Black Devil can take over a person's spirit, then there's no way to stop him, besides the obvious."

"Kill him."

"Aye, but will he die?"

Far Eyes stood and walked back to the village, still shaking his head. Cat remained on the rock letting him go on alone. They both had some thinking to do.

Cat looked to the sky and said, "Mistress, I may be needin' yer help soon."

I'll always be here for ye, was Anna's reply from the other world.

Greame came home to an empty cabin. The stove was cold and supper wasn't made. He was just about to search for Cat, when the door opened and she appeared.

"What's wrong?" he asked while stoking the stove. "Where were ye?"

"I had a terrible vision and I went to Far Eyes for some advice," she said, banging pots around in preparation for supper.

As she worked, she told him what she saw and her conclusions. Greame stood open-mouthed, unable to fathom the story's reality.

"Cat, if this is all true, then … how … how?"

"I think he's shape-shiftin'. When he's in that state of bein' in two places at the same time, the physical man is at a disadvantage."

"Ye'd better explain," Greame said, taking a seat to grasp the details.

"Remember when ye, me and Bogle went to find the watcher?" She waited for Greame to nod his head. "Our bodies were still here sittin' at the table rather helpless 'cause we were doin' battle in another place. What do ye remember of yerself at the table? Nothin', right?" Another nod of comprehension from Greame. "The physical body is in a vulnerable state when the mind is creatin' in another realm. If we can locate Black Devil, I think we can sever the link to Jumpin' Turtle and her bairn."

"Ye mean kill him, dinna ye?" he said angrily, the gravity of the situation hitting him.

Cat's eyebrow rose and she shrugged. "Aye. I think it's the only way to end this. If ye can see a better way, by all means tell me."

Greame stood abruptly and walked around the kitchen, rubbing his chin. Periodically, he'd stop and almost say something, but, much like Far Eyes, seemed to discount each theory and remain silent. Cat watched him attempt to sort out his thoughts without interruption. She was willing to listen to any other solutions, but was pretty sure it was the only answer.

After a few minutes of silence, Greame sat back down at the table. He ran his hands through his long, chocolate hair, then dropped his head into his palms. "I dinna care for this," his said, his voice muffled in his shirt.

"Then tell me another way."

Greame lifted his head and stared deep into Cat's violet eyes. He remained silent for a few moments. Cat let him consider his options.

"When?"

"Now's a good a time as any. He canna be allowed to take over Jumpin' Turtle's bairn. I feel that if he does, his physical body can die and he'll live on through the bairn. She's due in just three months. We must act quickly."

Greame was mentally calculating who would go, what they should take, and how long it would take to get there. He looked sadly at her and shook his head slowly, "Sometimes I wish ye had remained sightless."

Cat stretched across the table and kissed his cheek. "No, ye dinna."

Three days later, a small party consisting of Greame, Cat, Geoffrey, Far Eyes and Smiles at Everything—who had just returned from New France with Gregor—was ready to set off for New York, where Cat thought Black Devil was residing. Gregor was still at the Penobscot village "trading," Smiles at Everything said with a look of mischief in his eyes. Cat assumed he wouldn't want to make the long trek anyway, especially after he'd just returned from one.

Earlier, Cat asked Far Eyes and Smiles at Everything not to disclose to Jim or Jumping Turtle where they were going or what they were doing. This venture could only work if the element of surprise was on their side. They agreed not to speak of it to anyone.

As the group gathered as much as they could carry for the trip, they were interrupted by what sounded like a stampede. All eyes were trained on the woods when suddenly, into the clearing came eight horses with Gregor leading the herd. His hair was wild around him and the grin he wore was a sight to see. If ever there was a clearer picture of a Highlander in action, Gregor epitomized it.

"These rare fine beasts should make the trip easier on us all, dinna ye agree, lass?" He shouted to Cat, reining the herd in and dismounting as agilely as though he were twenty years younger.

Cat ran to him and hugged him fiercely. "Once again, I am amazed by ye, *mo charaid.*"

Gregor patted her back and said, "Oh, aye. So when are we leavin'?"

"I'm no' goin' to ask if ye're up for the trip," Cat giggled. "We leave as soon as we pack these *rare fine beasts.*"

The six of them left within an hour. Because of the horses, they were able to take more supplies and would make it there much quicker.

As the days passed, they traveled through open blueberry barrens that reminded them of the heather moors of Scotland, thick forests that smelled sweetly of balsam, cedar and pine, and high, rolling hills. They crossed rivers using ancient Indian trails, and borrowed canoes in a ferry system to get their supplies across.

The mountains were the most difficult. Once again, the Indian trails proved invaluable, but no less hazardous. As they continued on, the hills they thought were mountains were dwarfed by the snow-covered peaks they were seeing to the south.

"We have to cross those?" Geoffrey asked in a panicky voice.

Smiles at Everything told them that they were using trails that went to the north of them. They were all relieved.

They noticed that the further inland they went, the warmer it became. Grasses were tall and the leaves on the trees were out full, not miniature versions of themselves like when they left. Deep in the valleys, rivers ran with clear, cold, sweet water; sometimes in raging torrents, sometimes in wide, lazy flows.

The landscape had flattened out in front of them and a clearing near a wide, shallow river became their campsite for the night. After another very warm day, Cat could take it no more. She needed a bath. Her hair felt like straw and her skin was gritty from sweat and dust. After supper was cooked, she informed Greame she was going to the river to bathe.

"I'll go wi' ye. I could do wi' gettin' some dust off, too," he told her, searching the packs for a fresh pair of breeks and sark. He met her down by the water with a clean shift for her, as well. He threw her a bar of soap, which she captured after it hit her shoulder and bounced into the water. "Dinna lose it! It's the last bar until we can get back to Boston."

She was still in her shift, figuring to wash it while she wore it. It permitted her a small sense of modesty, even though the looks Greame was giving her made her think that was not the case.

"Christ, Garnet, ye're a fine lookin' woman," Greame said in a husky voice.

She was not prone to blushing anymore, but the tone of his voice produced a pink glow, turning Greame's nearness and his nakedness, into an ache she would have liked quenched. It was not to be, though, as Gregor and Smiles at Everything burst through the brush at the water's edge with the horses.

Gregor saw them first and chuckled innocently. "I didna interrupt anythin', did I?"

The glare he got from both of them only made him laugh harder. Smiles at Everything became aware of what was broken up and true to his name, grinned widely.

"C'mon horses, drink quickly. We're no' welcome here," Gregor said, taking the opportunity to dunk his head into the clear water and freshen up. When he came up for air, he shook the water from his thick hair like a dog and said, "By the way, dinna stay here too long. We're in Mohawk territory and they dinna take kindly to whites trespassin'. I'm goin' to take a look around."

Cat and Greame finished bathing and dressed quickly, never meeting each other's eyes to see the unfulfilled desire in them. They dried their hair by the fire and remained quiet until it was dusk. A full yellow moon rose in the lavender sky. Gregor had just returned from the scouting mission and sat beside the fire.

"What did ye see?" Greame asked, breaking the silence.

"I rode a fair piece and didna run into anythin'. I dinna think we hae more than a day or two before we reach the Mohawks' central village."

"Did ye see open farmland?" Cat asked.

"No."

She nodded and asked to have everyone gather around. When they all got comfortable, Cat began with her instructions.

"This may sound odd to ye, but I need ye to no' think about what we're doin' here. Dinna think about *him,* dinna even say his name. We're close to his village, a day or two away. He's a verra powerful man and, well, let's just say he could be listenin'." She held up her hand to halt the doubting grumbles. "I ken it sounds farfetched, but it's entirely possible."

Cat had only disclosed her vision to Greame and Far Eyes. The rest were told that Black Devil was planning on destroying the Penobscot village, and he must be stopped before he could strike. It was hardly a lie.

"Will ye trust me on this?" she asked, and got nods all around.

"What do ye suggest we think about to keep him from findin' us out?" Geoffrey asked.

"Well, it should be something believable—" she started.

"That we're fetchin' yer woman, Geoffrey," Greame said to the chuckles and snorts of the rest of the men. "And that her French Commander father doesna want her to go wi' ye to Maine, so ye may need to take her by force."

"I take it ye've had such adventures, Greame?" Cat asked with a straight face, bringing Gregor nearly to tears with laughter.

"Wi' a face like his, it would have been the only way!" Gregor said, wiping his eyes.

Cat elbowed him in the ribs good-naturedly. If nothing else, this was relieving some of the tension that hung over the camp.

"Oh, aye. This French Commander is standin' in the way of me happiness," Geoffrey played along.

The fabrication grew as each person added more and more details, until the story wove into an elaborate saga of love found, then lost. When they had all agreed on the plan, most headed for their blankets to get some sleep, each wearing a smile on their faces.

Gregor pulled Cat aside before she made it to her blanket, and asked if he could have a word. He waited for everyone to be out of earshot before he began.

"Ye may look like yer Mam, but ye've yer Da's way about ye, lass," Gregor said with a smile in his voice. "I'm right proud o' what ye've done wi' yer life. Ye dinna scare easy and ye ken how to lead men. No easy task." He put his big hands on her shoulders and moved close to her face. "Now, do ye want to tell me what's really goin' on?"

"Ye wouldna believe me if I did, Gregor."

"Try me."

Cat wavered for a minute, but remained steadfast. "It's enough for ye to ken that this man must die. Quickly and cleanly, wi' no witnesses. He stays alone, so that shouldna be a problem, but he can do things that may appear real, but aren't. He can play wi' yer mind. That's all I can tell ye."

Gregor kept his eyes locked with hers in a kind of willing of information, but Cat was too strong for that. He finally gave in and walked into the darkness. Cat could sense his disappointment, but it couldn't be helped. She had given him enough facts to complete the task. As long as they all followed her instructions, she was sure they would prevail. They had to.

As the sun rose the next morning, the small group edged closer to the confrontation Cat was dreading, but knew had to be done. By late afternoon, Cat began recognizing the terrain from when she ran as Bogle. She asked Gregor to scout ahead to see if there was any open farmland like she had seen before. She told him that if this were the correct place, there would be a river coming from steep ravines.

"Far Eyes, do ye feel him nearby?"

"No. You?"

Cat shook her head.

"Not worry. We protect with ceremony."

"No! It canna be anythin' he'll see or sense. We must remain like shadows. Protect yerself inside only," Cat said.

Far Eyes agreed. "Very wise."

They ate some jerky while waiting for Gregor's return, watching the sun advance ever-so-slowly in the sky. They talked among themselves quietly, then Smiles at Everything pointed to a small dust cloud towards the west. As the cloud loomed closer, they realized it wasn't Gregor making it, and they scurried for cover in the woods.

It was a small detachment of English soldiers patrolling the area. The Redcoats obviously weren't expecting to see anyone because they stayed in the open, trudging past the group without even looking into the forest. When the dust settled, Gregor emerged from the woods behind them, startling the group enough for curses.

Once Cat's heart began beating again, and the prickly feeling dissipated, she said, "What did ye find?"

Gregor dismounted and scuffed a clear spot on the ground. He proceeded to draw a map of the village and the river leading from the ravines. "Is this what ye saw?"

Cat nodded. "How far? Did ye see anyone?"

"About five miles due west. The Mohawk were in their village and there were some in the fields," he pointed with a stick, "but no' the one ye're lookin' for."

"He wouldna be in the village anyway," Cat stated confidently. "He'll be somewhere verra private so he can conduct his business wi'out fear of bein' disturbed. He'll be where I saw him before. Up in the cliffs." She used her finger to locate him in the area where Gregor drew the ravines.

"So now what?" Greame asked. "Wait until dusk to move closer, then surprise him at dawn?"

Cat looked at Gregor, who shrugged and nodded. "Seems like a fine plan, Greame."

No fires were lit in the camp they made in the shrubbery a little ways below the ravines. Just before the moon came up, shining so brightly it threw shadows, Smiles at Everything noticed the faint glow of a fire up in the cliffs.

"We're still too far away to make a surprise attack. Those cliffs will take some time to climb," Greame whispered, pinpointing the fire with his telescope. "We'll hae to start climbin' well before dawn."

"Moon bright. No trouble," Far eyes said.

"How many of us are goin'?" Geoffrey inquired.

"Good question," Gregor said. "Someone needs to stay wi' Cat—"

Before he could say anything else, he was staring into a face of fury. Cat's. "If ye think for one minute I'm waitin' in camp like a bairn, ye've another thing comin', Gregor Macgregor!"

Greame let out a chuckle, as did Far Eyes and Smiles at Everything.

"Did ye actually think ye were goin' to get away wi' that comment, man?" Greame clamped his hand on Gregor's shoulder.

"It was worth a try."

"We're all goin'." Cat said, daring anyone else to challenge her statement. "It will take all of us to complete this task. He kens the terrain and the area, and he's tricky."

"Let's get a couple hours o' sleep," Greame said. "We'll be leavin' soon enough."

Cat was sure no one slept. She spent the quiet time protecting and preparing her mind to distract Black Devil. Anna Macpherson was already waiting to aid on the other side, to make sure that, once Black Devil was dead, he remained in the other world. Cat's plan was to get within sight of Black Devil and lure him into her mind, while the men, except Greame and Far Eyes, went after his physical body. Greame and Far Eyes would be her backup on that other plain. She figured she would need all the help she could get.

In the light of the moon, Cat opened the satchel that sat at her feet and dug around until she found the pink stone box with the amethyst crystal in it. Setting it close to her, she continued rummaging until she found the ceremonial dirk. She laid it next to the crystal and went in for one more item, the candles, which she wrapped in the silk square. All the items she needed to perform her ceremony were cleansed and instructed on their purpose. The remaining contents in her satchel were herbs, bandages and poultices, just in case anyone was injured in the fray.

She was ready.

Far Eyes had been secretly watching Cat perform her ritual in the bright moonlight. She had some fascinating items he would ask to see when Black Devil was dead. He tried to hear her thoughts as she prepared herself, but he was unable to locate her in the gray of the ethereal. He marveled at her powerful mind and wondered if he had the strength to do what she was attempting.

But he wanted to stand beside her when she went to the other side to separate Black Devil from Jumping Turtle and her baby. He felt it was his right to care for his people and to learn more about these unusual powers shamans could attain.

Garnet had a warrior's heart. He respected her greatly for that, but she also had a shaman's spirit, one that was used to being alone. This part was the stubbornness she possessed. It also made her strong, but he knew all too well how all needed to have help at times. He had learned that the hard way. Maybe if he had asked for help when the Mohawk raided his village many years ago, he could have prevented his wife and sons from being killed.

ʔ⚓

It was as though everyone's internal clocks were set for the same time, for within seconds of each other, Greame, Gregor, Smiles at Everything and Geoffrey sat up and began rolling up their blankets.

"Did ye sleep at all?" Greame asked Cat.

"Too much to do," she replied. "Would ye stay wi' me and Far Eyes when I go in and … how did ye put it, Far Eyes? *Separate* 'him' from Jumpin' Turtle?"

Far Eyes smiled, his white teeth shining in the moonlight. "You hear me?"

"I didna mean to eavesdrop, but …"

"Glad you did. Make easy to ask to help you."

"I need all the help I can get, Far Eyes. I canna do this wi'out ye and Greame. Anna will be joinin' us from the other side."

"Must work. Will work."

"He's right, Garnet. It *will* work," Greame said. "So I take it ye'll want me and Far Eyes to stay wi' ye."

"Aye. We'll get as close as we can and *entertain* his mind, while the rest o' the men find and dispatch him quickly and quietly."

"We're ready," Gregor told her.

"Quietly, and remember, we're gettin' Geoffrey's woman from the French Commander, just as we discussed yesterday, aye?" Greame said to everyone.

They walked quietly in their moccasins upon the newly greening grass beside the river. The moonlight made them look like shadows, gray and unreal. The sounds of the water masked their footsteps as they slowly trekked further and further into the ravine.

Once they reached the cliffs, Cat, Greame and Far Eyes remained at the bottom. Gregor silently directed Smiles at Everything and Geoffrey—armed with only silent weapons, a bow and a dirk—where he wanted them to go.

Gregor looked up once again, following each man's advance, then whispered to Cat, "Be sure to give us enough time to reach the top before ye start."

Cat nodded, then found a flat rock to lay out her silk square and candles, though they would remain unlit it was still part of the ritual. The dirk and crystal were set on the silk, and the three of them sat on the ground around the rock.

Cat began her protective prayers, indicating Far Eyes and Greame to do the same. After waiting for what she thought was enough time for Gregor and his men to get up the cliffs, she asked if Greame and Far Eyes were ready. They nodded and took each other's hands, forming a circle. Cat closed her eyes and, within moments, was on the other side.

ೀ

Gregor took the trail up the center, while Smiles at Everything flanked to the left, and Geoffrey flanked to the right. It was steep, and they each had to watch their footing, making sure they didn't loosen stones and send them crashing onto the rocks below.

Geoffrey and Smiles at Everything made it up their sides faster than Gregor. He was much older than they were, though still in excellent shape, but it winded him a little. He wanted to have enough energy to kill Black Devil, so he had to conserve a bit.

The fire in the shallow cave Black Devil occupied was glowing brighter, but Gregor had a few more yards to go before he was close enough to throw his dirk. He could see the silhouette of Geoffrey above him to the right. Smiles at Everything hid himself too well to be found.

Gregor pulled himself up one last escarpment and as his head peeked over it, he noticed that there was a deep, wide ravine between himself and the cave. Black Devil knew how to choose his lair. Gregor was sure he couldn't cross it and would have to go around. Valuable time lost.

ೀ

The space that occupies the mind is much larger than given credit for. It encompasses the entire universe, and that's why it's so difficult to protect. One can communicate with another across the earth, or beyond it into the next realm. Somewhere far in the distance, there's another realm that's rarely explored. It's where titans rule and only the strongest get to exhibit their talents. This was where Black Devil and Cat would do battle.

Cat entered the semi-familiar territory and called Black Devil's name, finally giving rise to her purpose. At first, she felt confusion in Black Devil's energy. Cat had done her undercover work well apparently, because he wasn't expecting her. She stood alone in the void; Far Eyes and Greame lagging behind, giving Black Devil the illusion of a one-on-one with a much less powerful energy.

In a show of ego, he appeared naked in a ball of red light hovering a little above her. His black hair floated around his shoulders as though he were underwater. He held something in his hand but she couldn't make out what it was.

How nice of you to come, Garnet. To what do I owe the pleasure? Have you reconsidered my offer?

She could feel his power growing, drawing away from Jumping Turtle. It was almost painful, but she remained steadfast.

"I want to ken more of the war. Tell me how I can help the Indians keep their land."

She was correct in assuming his ego would want her to hear how he could help her. Her ears were ringing now. She wasn't sure how much more she could take without calling in another's energy to take some of the brunt away from her.

He laughed as though he knew all along she would go to him.

Surrender yourself to me. You have the power, just let me inside of you. Together we can beat armies of men and rule this land forever!

Cat's hands flew to her ears. His voice was nearly deafening. She was just about to call for help when Far Eyes and Greame appeared on either side of her. The look on Black Devil's face was pure rage; a hatred so deep, Cat wondered if they would live through this fool's errand. Did she actually think she could beat the man on his own ground? No, she couldn't waver. That's just the advantage he would look for. Weakness, and she wasn't about to give up that easily.

Just then, far in the distance, a familiar cackle. Anna! Cat's confidence soared and the power of four with the same pure intention became stronger than Black Devil. Suddenly, a blinding white light engulfed all four of them. Cat didn't know if Gregor could hear her in his mind, but she screamed at him, *do it now!*

Gregor felt an overwhelming urgency to get to the cave. He moved stealthily around the ravine, but still could not get there; another wide crevasse barred him from his mission. He had to climb down into it, then back up out of it if there was any chance of putting his dirk into the man.

As Gregor started down, he caught sight of the menace. Black Devil was sitting cross-legged with his back against the wall of the cave. His head was lying on his chest as though he were asleep. Gregor knew better. He was an ordinary-looking man, clad in just a breech clout. His body shimmered in sweat and was littered with scars. Gregor wondered idly if he'd been tortured to garner so many wounds.

He continued deeper down the crevasse then lost his footing and slid roughly down a few feet. He thought for sure he'd been heard as the slide of stones rained down, bouncing off the rocks below. He looked up and waited a moment to see if Black Devil would appear above him, but the top remained clear.

A little further down, then he'd be at the bottom. He had to hurry now. He'd lost valuable time with this sidetrack. His head was pounding with urgency as his foot touched the bottom and he began his ascent.

Black Devil grinned widely. He was enjoying this match of strength. Cat felt his ego growing, as though he imagined himself a teacher and this was her first lesson. Still encapsulated in his red light, he stood and held out his hand, opening it so Cat could see what he was holding. It was a baby boy. He was going to take possession of Jumping Turtle's bairn! If that happened, he'd have control and live on. They had to stop him now!

As the realization hit the four of them simultaneously, the white light exploded, sending Black Devil reeling backwards. His own red bubble of light disintegrated, leaving him exposed. As if they had poked him with a stick, Black Devil showed his true self and began hurling red fire balls at them. Anna stepped up with her staff and easily warded each one away.

Do it now! Cat screamed the mental command again to Gregor.

Gregor's head was splitting. Cat was screaming in his mind, but he was powerless to do anything about it. He had to reach a suitable place to throw his dirk. He couldn't risk firing his pistol for fear of the entire Mohawk nation coming down on them. He climbed up further; a few more feet, then finally, his hand landed on earth instead of stone. He'd reached the top.

Gregor pulled himself up, but the earth he felt wasn't the top, just a ledge that crumbled beneath his weight. He slid down several yards, his breeks ripping on the jagged rocks. He'd never make it up in time now.

Once again, he climbed the rock face, this time using a different route. It took a little longer, but when he pulled himself up, his head peered onto flat ground looking right into the cave at Black Devil. Gregor was halfway over the top when soft footsteps came up behind him. He turned just in time to see Smiles at Everything pulling back the bow and letting an arrow fly. It whizzed passed Gregor's ear so close, he heard it *whoosh!*

The brawl continued as Black Devil scrambled to his feet, and held the baby up over his head. This was their only chance. If they waited any longer, Black Devil would enter the bairn. Far Eyes leapt onto Black Devil knocking him to the ground, and tried to wrestle the baby away from him. Greame jumped into battle with the silver dirk, grabbing Black Devil's arm and holding it down. Far Eyes grabbed the bairn and held it close, while Greame took the dirk and in a high arc, plunged the silver blade through Black Devil's heart. Black Devil roared in a deafening scream of pain, then went limp.

Gregor watched Black Devil's body convulse and shake. Suddenly, his arm lifted into the air, holding something unseen. Gregor watched as though it were a dream in slow motion, as the arrow found its mark in Black Devil's chest. It was a perfect shot. The Indian opened his mouth in a silent scream, then went limp.

Cat, whose power was keeping them all in that realm, let one more burst of energy out to make sure Black Devil was truly dead. Right before their eyes, he seemed to fade a little, then a little more. His light was going out. With a blink, it was extinguished altogether. Suddenly, the three of them were back at the rock. The sun was up and a light breeze blew. It was over.

The trio released hands and stood up, shaking circulation back into their extremities. They were exhausted from the effort it took to be in that other realm, yet exhilarated at the same time.

"Are ye both all right?" Cat asked, struggling to hold back tears of released tension.

Greame hugged her tightly and Far Eyes nodded. It seemed to be just as hard on them as it was for her.

Greame released her, then in her mind, Cat heard Anna say, *Thank ye for a wee bit o' amusement for this old woman.*

Greame and Far Eyes must have heard Anna as well, because they each wore smiles on their faces, as though it were all for her entertainment.

"That woman has a strange sense o' humor," Greame said.

"I like her," Far Eyes remarked.

Cat looked up into the cliffs and found Gregor, Geoffrey and Smiles at Everything winding their way down the jagged rocky outcroppings. Gregor carried the lifeless body of Black Devil over his shoulder. They had to dispose of the body so his tribesmen would never find it.

Once Gregor reached the bottom, he let Black Devil's body slide off his shoulder. It landed with a thud on the ground. "Ye all look a bit wore out," he said with a grin. He was truly in his element as a mercenary, though no one was paying him. He did it because he enjoyed it, and it served all of them well to have him as an ally.

"Somehow, after what we just witnessed," Greame stated, looking down at Black Devil, "I pictured him to be a much younger and bigger man."

"Obviously, size doesna matter," Cat replied.

Gregor opened his mouth to comment, but thought better of it and clamped it shut.

No Rest for the Weary

By the time Black Devil's body was buried, some much-needed rest was in order. The small band went back to where they had made camp the night before, though that seemed like a lifetime ago. The forest afforded them the shelter they needed from the English and the Mohawk, but they still slept in shifts, always someone remaining awake to stand guard.

It was the end of June. The weather was hot and humid. By late afternoon, thunderclouds loomed on the western horizon. Unused to this kind of heat, Cat slept in fitful naps. Her mind was still acting out the entire scene with Black Devil, reliving each tortuous moment. At one point, Greame shook her awake so she could have some peace. She went right back to sleep, only to wake herself up a little later drenched in sweat.

She sat up and let the breeze cool her a bit, but it wasn't enough. She glanced around camp to see that Greame, Smiles at Everything and Far Eyes were sleeping. She walked a ways and found Gregor down by the river soaking his feet.

"Do ye mind if I join ye, Gregor?"

"Och, no. Looks like ye could use some o' this cool water. Ye're as red as a rose."

Cat stepped into the water up to her knees. It didn't matter that she soaked her breeks, she just had to cool down. She splashed the cool liquid on her face, letting it drip down the front of her blouse. She lifted the mass of heavy hair and patted water on the back of her neck, breathing in sharply at the extreme temperature change to her body.

"Better, aye?" chuckled Gregor.

"Christ, that feels good!" She let the cooling breeze blow on her wet skin.

"Tell me what it was like."

Cat looked at him for a moment, assessing to see if he meant what she thought he meant. "I dinna think ye really want to ken. Ye remember how ye were when I showed ye the Picts in the faerie dùn. Ye got a bit panicky, if I recall."

"That was a long time ago, and besides, I've gotten used to the fact that ye're a bit odd," he asserted.

"And ye say that wi' such love."

Gregor laughed. "Ye ken what I mean. But really, I want to ken what ye did."

Cat saw that he was truly curious. She shrugged, what the hell, she thought, and began with the images she got of Black Devil in the red light. Then how loud his voice was, and Greame and Far Eyes battling him, while Anna used her staff to ward off fire balls.

Gregor shook his head through most of the story. When Cat finished, he said, "When I saw him, he was sitting in his wee cave, head hung low. I could hear ye in me heid screamin' to do it now, but I couldna reach him. Black Devil was twitchin' around somethin' fierce and holdin' up somethin' I couldna see. Then Smiles at Everything pierced his chest wi' an arrow from behind me. In a way, it was fittin' that he got the chance to kill him, what with Black Devil bent on destroyin' the Penobscot village and all."

Cat knew he wanted the real reason down to the last detail. He didn't seem too shocked by what she had already said, so with another shrug, she elaborated on the partial truth she had told him before.

"Hopefully, ye can fathom this, Gregor, 'cause it's the honest truth. Black Devil was tryin' to possess Jumpin' Turtle's baby. This way his physical body could die, but his spirit would live on to wreak havoc through another body. Black Devil would spread his evil through the lad, tearin' the Penobscot apart from the inside. We couldna let that happen. We nearly couldna stop it either." She pondered for a moment, then said, "I wonder if Smiles at Everything heard me in his heid and that's why he took the shot?"

"I hear you clear," Smiles at Everything said, startling them from behind. "I feel you and others in battle with Black Devil." He could see Cat and Gregor's expressions of curiosity. "I am Shaman. It what Shaman do. We hear other side good."

"Did ye ken what Black Devil was goin' to do?" Cat asked, sitting down on a large rock keeping her feet in the water.

He shook his head, wading into the river next to her. "Not know until you fight him. Then I hear plan. Like you say, almost too late. Gregor too far away for long knife. I shoot with bow. Good shot, too," he said with a wide grin.

Gregor splashed a handful of water at the lad, showering him and Cat, making her squeal and prodding Smiles at Everything into a water fight. By the time they were finished, all three of them were soaked to the skin, but feeling better. They walked back to camp to find everyone up and tending to the horses.

"I'm goin' to start supper before it rains on us," Cat said to anyone listening, eying the darkening sky.

"Good," Greame said. "I want the camp dark like last night, so perhaps ye can keep it simple and we can put the fire out before it gets dark."

Cat nodded as the reality of where they were hit her again. Enemy territory. As she prepared the food, she did a mental search of the area for English or Mohawk. For the time being, they were alone. She wondered for how long.

It never rained, just thundered in the distance. As darkness fell, each person took to their blankets and slept. Cat let her mind free itself of its turmoil and slept soundly through the night. Greame woke her to a red dawn. The air was still and humid, brimming with static.

"I dinna care for this weather," Greame said. "I ken we were to leave this mornin', but I'd feel safer if we waited this storm out. I'm sure it wilna be long before it hits."

Life on the sea had taught him about the weather. Events like this could be deadly. As calm as it was right now, the wind could kick up at any minute with hurricane force. Lightning bolts jabbing from the sky could strike anywhere. They'd be safer in the woods than they would out on the open flats.

Within the hour, as predicted, torrents of rain fell from the sky and bolts of lightning struck all around, sending thunder rolling across the landscape. When it was over, the air was freshened and had cooled considerably.

By mid-afternoon, the group was on their way home, following much the same trail. Two days into the journey, Smiles at Everything, who always seemed to be the first one to spot anything, noticed movement in the valley below. Everyone came to a halt as Greame took out his telescope.

It was the same small detachment of red-coated English soldiers they had seen several days ago. Odd how his scar tingled. He got the same feeling when he saw the detachment before, too. It made sense since it was an English sword that had sliced him at Falkirk. He'd use this forewarning to his advantage one day, he was sure of it. Right now, he was sure all they had to do is give the detachment a wide berth and they'd be home free.

Commander George Wilson was being punished. At least that's what he thought when he was given this post in the middle of nowhere. It bordered the lands of New France and New York. His orders were to search for insurgents and report their numbers. Who or what was he expected to find out here? The French, obviously, but there weren't many of them. A few savages, possibly, but even they were hard to track down, disappearing into the forest like ghosts when spotted. For the last two months he and his detachment of twenty men patrolled just for something to do. He loathed America, and New France. His posting was supposed to be in Boston, but that was altered when the previous commander of this desolate hellhole disappeared. His subordinates—the men he had traipsing all over the countryside—said the man never returned from the privy one morning. If he were smart, he'd still be running, George Wilson thought.

He was a young, good-looking man who prided himself on the women he conquered. Royalty usually, for George Wilson had high expectations for himself. He'd marry wealth and power to rise to the rank of general before he was thirty. But his plans were being destroyed out here. Royalty! Hell, there wasn't even a white woman within a hundred miles. Indian women were used when his need became overwhelming and he used them mercilessly, but, afterwards, he had no further use for them. Many, he knew, would never be found.

The more George Wilson stewed about his predicament, the harder he'd push his troops. He needed an incident. That's it! Something he could start, then quell and be noticed for outstanding service to the Crown. But, hell, there was no one around to pick a fight with, for Christ's sake.

Just as Greame suspected, the English detachment pressed on through the valley without noticing a thing. Gregor scouted on ahead and reported back with no sign of anyone in their general path.

Cat was getting a prickly feeling on the back of her neck, but couldn't figure out what was causing it. She wondered idly if it was from the English soldiers, then recalled she had the same feeling when she saw them the last time. Culloden. Would it ever go away? The brutality beyond words she saw on that battlefield would forever be a scar on her memory. Time would never erase the loss of her brothers, fallen nearly side-by-side.

She shook off the vision in her head. No need to relive that again. Concentrate on today. And today, she didn't care to have Redcoats so close to her. A vicious cycle it was turning out to be.

The group moved ahead. Day by day, the terrain changed, and even though they traveled the same trail, it looked different.

That night, as they made camp near a quiet stream, Cat once again got that prickly feeling on the back of her neck. She mentioned it to Greame as they lay side-by-side on their blankets under the stars.

"That's strange," he said, his voice raspy from the day in the dust. "I noticed my scar tingled when the Redcoats went by us. I said to myself that the warnin' would come in handy someday."

Cat touched the thicker line of skin near his ear. "Is it tingling now?"

"Well, it wasna 'til ye touched it."

"Seriously."

"I am."

"Greame! This is serious."

"All right. Take yer fingers away and give me a moment."

Cat smirked. Now he sounded like she did.

"Nope. I dinna feel anythin'."

"Good ... I guess."

"Ye'd probably feel them before me anyway, dinna yet think?"

"I'm hopin' to no' feel them at all."

They fell asleep in each other's arms and woke hearing Gregor and Smiles at Everything in a heated discussion.

"What's wrong?" Greame asked, sitting up on his blanket.

Cat got herself up on one elbow and listened for the explanation.

"Smiles at Everything thinks he sees movement coming up behind us," Gregor said.

Greame's eyebrow rose. "How close?" he directed his question to the Indian.

"Few hours."

"And why are the two o' ye arguin' about it?"

"He fell asleep!" Gregor said, getting angry again. "He should hae seen them well before now."

"Dinna ye think ye're bein' a bit harsh, Gregor?" Cat asked, sitting up now.

Before Gregor could answer, Smiles at Everything said, "No. He right. Should see before."

"Who are they?" Cat asked, curious as to whether or not she should be concerned about it.

"The Redcoats we passed a few days ago," Gregor answered.

"Christ!" Cat and Greame said in unison.

"And ye think they're after us?" Greame asked Smiles at Everything.

"Yes. English follow our tracks."

"What would they want wi' us?" Cat asked, rubbing the back of her neck.

"I dinna ken, but we're no' goin' to let them catch us to find out. Let's disappear," Gregor said.

By then, Geoffrey and Far Eyes were up and had heard the gist of the conversation enough to know breakfast would be deer jerky on the back of a horse.

Commander George Wilson's men crossed the tracks nearly three days ago. Eight horses. Indians, he imagined, because the horses were unshod and the footprints were moccasined. God was listening when he asked for an incident. If nothing else, he could take out some frustration on the savages, but if he played his cards right he could make it look like the French did it. Mohawk didn't like the French. An unprovoked attack would be more than enough instigation for the savages to retaliate against the French, and with any luck, spark a large enough skirmish to be recognized and get him out of here.

He knew his men were bone tired from the extra long patrols. He had only let them sleep for two hours, and they'd get no real rest until their prey was caught. Incentive enough, he thought.

"I'd say they're not far off now, sir," a skinny red-haired young man said to George Wilson.

"How far is not far off, Corporal? I want more precise timing than that."

"We should be on top of them by mid-day, sir."

"See, now how hard was that, Corporal? Let's pick up the pace then, shall we?"

Far Eyes knew the territory well enough to find Indian allies and enlist their help. Gregor and Geoffrey went with him. Smiles at Everything took Greame and Cat on a different route. It was unlikely the English would split up their forces to hunt both groups down. More than likely, they would see that they were following a small hunting party. Nothing to be worried about, therefore they would halt the pursuit. That was the consensus anyway.

Cat couldn't shake the feeling that this was more than just a patrol doing its duty. She had a suspicion that the English officer was after something more. She wondered if he knew he was tracking whites, not Indians. Every step her group made was Indian. Though they could not take even a moment to stop so she could do a meditation, the conclusion to her intuition was that this officer could not be trusted.

Smiles at Everything's effort to hide their trail bordered on over-cautious. They traveled in streams to hide their tracks. They rode on solid rock where they could, and when riding in the forest, if a branch caught their clothes, they had to make sure nothing was torn off to leave a trail. It made for a longer trek.

Smiles at Everything knew of an overlook nearby. He informed Greame that he was going to take a look and see if the detachment was still following. He rode off, disappearing into the thick woods.

"I want to stop for a moment to do a meditation. Perhaps I can see if they're still after us," Cat said, reining in her horse and dismounting.

Greame dismounted and took advantage of the bushes to relieve himself. He returned to find Cat sitting cross-legged on the ground under her horse, twirling her hair. He watched her quietly as she rocked back and forth with her eyes closed. Her breeks fit tight to her figure, enhancing her curves. Her blouse, though certainly modest, only left him wanting to explore what was under it. He shook his head to clear the scandalous thoughts flooding into it. His timing left a bit to be desired.

In Cat's mind, she watched the English Commander push his men's tolerance to the extreme. He was driven by greed and power, stopping at nothing to get what he thought he deserved. Truth was, he had only reached his rank because his father—another cut of the same cloth—bought his position. The commander never earned it and used it only to further himself in the eyes of women.

On the subject of women the man was lecherous. His depravity was rivaled only by his greed. The commander's reason for pursuing Cat's small group was to promote himself out of this territory by fabricating an incident where he came out smelling like a rose. He thought he deserved a much better posting like Boston, where he could rub elbows with people of culture, not savages and lowly cavalry soldiers.

The more Cat saw, the more she despised this man. A twig snapped beside her and she opened her eyes to find Greame standing there.

"We need to go. Smiles at Everything is coming back."

Cat stood and brushed the spruce needles from her butt. As soon as she was atop her horse, Smiles at Everything reined in beside her.

"Did ye see them?" she asked.

"Yes. They stop where we camp."

"So we're a half a day ahead of them now," Greame said. "Do ye think they will follow us?"

Before Smiles at Everything could answer, Cat said, "He'll be comin'. He thinks we're Indians—no reason for him no' to, given our trail. But he wants to create an incident to get himself noticed and promoted out o' this no man's land."

"What kind of incident?"

"The kind where no one's left to dispute it."

35

Strained Truce

The camp was deserted when the detachment arrived. Commander George Wilson was not happy at this turn of events. He thought about shooting his corporal, thought hard about it, but in the end, what good would it do? The corporal's saving grace was that he was an excellent tracker. Besides, these stupid savages couldn't outwit an officer of the Crown for long. He'd hunt them down if it took all summer.

George Wilson let his men rest there, only because he was tired. It was a lovely spot to set up camp. Rations were opened and the men ate, then crawled onto the softest piece of ground they could find and slept, some before they finished chewing. It was the kind of sleep where the world could come to an end and they'd be blissfully unaware of its demise.

It was dusk by the time most of the men stirred. Even George Wilson slept like the dead. They remained in camp until dawn the next morning, then true to his word the commander marched his troops further east until the trail split.

"What do you mean you've lost their tracks?" Commander George Wilson bellowed angrily to the corporal. "Find them you idiot! They didn't just disappear!"

"Permission to take a few men and scout ahead, Commander?"

"Yes, yes," George Wilson waved his delicate hand in dismissal. "We'll stay on this trail. Find us when you've found them."

Cat, Greame and Smiles at Everything stopped very little over the next few days. Smiles at Everything pushed them, feeling the urgency to get back to familiar territory. He had a bad feeling about this Redcoat who followed them. Smiles at Everything knew Cat felt it as well.

When they stopped for the night, Smiles at Everything asked Cat if she still saw the Redcoats behind them.

"Oh, aye, he's still comin'. He wilna stop 'til he finds us. How long do ye think before we cross the Panawanskek River?"

Smiles at Everything thought for a minute, gazing towards the east, as though seeing the water in the distance. "One week, more if weather bad."

"Are ye all right to keep up this pace, Garnet?" Greame asked.

"Well, my legs are feelin' a bit tired and my butt's bruised, but we dinna ken how close they are, so I guess we must."

"Not far ahead, place to see far away. Stop tomorrow, find Redcoats."

Cat and Greame nodded their approval.

Far Eyes, Gregor and Geoffrey rode hard. Gregor told Far Eyes that their mission was to get help from whatever tribe was friendly and hated the English. That meant getting out of Mohawk territory, then they could enlist the Mohican, or Pennacook, or any other Abinaki tribe. Tomorrow they would be in Mohican land.

Commander George Wilson couldn't have been more pleased when he himself found a trail of four horses. When his corporal finally caught up to him the following day, George Wilson couldn't stop pointing out that fact to his increasingly red-faced subordinate. He never stopped to wonder how that made the corporal feel. It was the corporal's duty to follow orders, and by god, he would do as he was told.

George Wilson said, "Corporal, do you think you might be able to follow this trail and find the Indians, or would you prefer that I do it for you?"

"I'll do it … sir," the Corporal said through gritted teeth, spurring his horse savagely in the ribs.

"Thank you, Corporal," George Wilson said in a mocking tone. He was feeling quite good about himself.

≥•

"I not see Redcoats," Smiles at Everything said, scanning the area behind them with Greame's telescope.

"Might I hae a look?" Greame asked, holding out his hand for the eyepiece.

Smiles at Everything passed the telescope over and Greame made a long, sweeping scan of the area behind and ahead. Far to the northeast, he could see smoke, indicating a village of Indians.

"How much farther 'til we're out o' Mohawk land?"

Smiles at Everything pointed to the ridge in the distance. "There Mohican land. Friend to Wabinaki."

"Will they help us cover our trail?"

Smiles at Everything grinned and nodded.

≥•

In the small Mohican village there were at least a dozen braves, along with women and elders. Far Eyes asked to have a meeting with the elders. Gregor wondered why such formality was shown, but Far Eyes said, "If I ask you to fight and you not know why, would you fight?"

"Ye've a point, man."

As with most things that could change the course of a lifetime, heated discussions filled the wigwam. Gregor and Geoffrey weren't allowed to participate, so they had to rely on how convincing Far Eyes could be.

"We do not have quarrel with the whites," said the Chief.

"This white is not ordinary. He is vengeful and angry at Indians. He only wants to kill them, not live among them in peace. Will you wait until he comes to this village and kills your family and rapes your women?" Far Eyes silenced them with that scenario, and was asked to leave so they may discuss it amongst themselves.

Gregor watched Far Eyes emerge from the wigwam alone. He wasn't sure if it was a good sign or a bad one.

"We wait," Far Eyes said, and found a comfortable place to sit.

Corporal Thaddeus Bakeman was used to taking orders, but had more than he could take from this ass of a commander. He knew all too well how his commanding officer's position was bought, not having a lick of common sense to his name. Thaddeus wondered how far the Commander would take this. If George Wilson did what Thaddeus suspected he was going to do, the ramifications went beyond incompetence; they went to madness. The fragile peace the Crown held with the French, never mind the Indians, would be toppled. He wasn't ready for a war.

When Cat saw how far it was to safe land, she was deflated. She just wanted to go home, but in a leisurely pace, one where she could enjoy the scenery. So far, it all seemed like a dream; too hurried to remember the details.

She slept fitfully, sure she was keeping Greame awake. He denied it, but she could tell by the darkness under his eyes he was tired.

Smiles at Everything was a man possessed by his task. He always found something positive to tell her, though she found little to be enthused about. Maybe she would feel better after today. Smiles at Everything said they would be in Mohican territory by nightfall. Hopefully, then they'd be able to rest.

George Wilson picked up the pace. He thought he knew where the savages were heading. They would be out of Mohawk territory in another couple of days. That left some other tribe, one he wasn't familiar with, but probably just as easy to trick into letting his troops into camp. He needed some release, then he could proceed with his plan.

He smiled to himself, then prodded the corporal by saying something lewd. He enjoyed watching the corporal's face turn an unnatural shade of crimson.

As day turned to night the elders bickered on about what they should do. Gregor was frothy by this point and ready to find another ally, one that wasn't afraid of getting a task done. He sat in front of the fire tossing pinecones into the flames. At least they were fed a hot meal. The stew left a bit to be desired, but after what they'd been living on, it was rib sticking.

Gregor stood to take a walk and stretch his muscles, when the flap opened on the wigwam and one of the elders motioned for Far Eyes to join them.

"Finally," Gregor grumbled under his breath.

Not long after Far Eyes went in, he returned to the fire with Gregor and Geoffrey. "We go in morning. With help," he smiled.

Greame told Smiles at Everything they weren't moving until Cat woke herself up. They had made camp just inside Mohican land last night. To Greame it was a small measure of comfort, and he knew Cat was exhausted. He was wavering within his own endurance and noticed Smiles at Everything's slower pace as well. Peace was not to be, though. Greame's scar was tingling. He looked at Cat and she was fidgeting. She could feel them, too. He woke her by pressing a kiss on her forehead. She opened her eyes and smiled, melting him a little, then she realized where she was.

"Let's ride," she said, rubbing the back of her neck.

Corporal Bakeman edged out onto the rocky overlook with his telescope. He saw smoke a few hours away. He wondered if the commander would really go through with his plan.

"How far, Corporal?" George Wilson asked, standing right beside him.

"Just a few hours, sir."

"Good," he said, and turned to go. "Well, what are you waiting for, Corporal? Let's go. We're wasting daylight."

Far Eyes led Gregor, Geoffrey and the twelve Mohican braves back to the planned rendezvous he hoped Smiles at Everything had reached. The braves didn't have horses, so they took turns holding the pommels of Far Eyes', Gregor's and Geoffrey's saddles to conserve energy when they ran. Gregor was amazed how they all kept up. At this pace, they'd reach Cat in a few hours.

಻

It was just before noon. The sun was bright and warm. On any other day it would have been perfect, but today wasn't any other day. The woods were quiet; even the birds knew something wasn't right.

The back of Cat's neck was tingling strongly. She felt the English closing in behind them. When she glanced at Greame, he was rubbing the scar on his neck. They had to get to the Mohican village. There they would have safety in numbers.

Smiles at Everything stopped them with a raised hand and twisted his head, hearing something. Cat strained her ears, but didn't have to hear to feel who was coming.

"It's Gregor," she said with a smile on her face.

Before Gregor reached them, horses were heard from behind. The Redcoats burst through the trees at nearly the same instant as Gregor and his band of Mohicans, all stopping within feet of Cat. It was a stand off with all sides eyeing the other with a potent mixture of curiosity, hatred and fear.

"What have we here?" Commander George Wilson asked, eyeing Cat's form-fitting attire with leering intent.

"What is it ye want, Commander?" Cat asked, sitting tall in her saddle.

"What I want I would rather keep private until I can whisper it in your lovely ear."

Cat was thunderstruck at the comment. He'd said it as though he were the only man standing there. As if Greame and Gregor and over a dozen Indian braves wouldn't kill him on the spot if he even *thought* of saying what he just uttered out loud.

Cat wasn't sure who was first to draw weapons, but the sound of unleashed steel reverberated through the woods. The Redcoats had their rifles pointed at the Indians, and the Mohicans had their arrows trained on the English.

She edged her horse close to George Wilson's, then bent close to enough to see the fair, soft hair attempting to make a beard on his face. "I've killed men for less, *Commander.*"

She said it with such disgust, a few of the Redcoats chuckled. This enraged George Wilson. No one spoke to him in such a manner, especially an Indian-loving Scotswoman. With startling quickness, George Wilson's sword was under Cat's chin. He was breathing heavily and his provoking expression dared her to challenge him.

Cat lifted her head an inch—just to get more comfortable—never taking her eyes off of him.

"So what will ye do, *Commander?* Cut me heid off in front of all yer men? How far do ye think ye can go wi' so many witnesses? But, I suppose ye could kill all o' them, too, aye?" She taunted him, and he pressed the sharp blade into her skin, indenting it under the pressure. One slight move and she would be sliced.

No one dared to breathe. Each side stood frozen, waiting to see what action the Commander would take.

"You, my sweet little thing, need to be taught a lesson."

As George Wilson brazenly looked her up and down, she saw him notice the pistol in her right hand aimed at his chest.

Cat smiled when the realization registered on his face. In a tone dripping with sarcasm, she said, "Would ye like to wager which would be quicker, Commander? Yer arm or my finger on this trigger that's twitchin' right now, 'cause I'm verra frightened at the moment."

Gregor laughed from behind her; an evil laugh that spoke volumes. She could hear Greame chuckle as well. Cat was glad they thought she had the ability to weasel herself out of this predicament on a positive note. Right now, she thought it could go either way.

Further incensed by the laughter, George Wilson's face contorted with rage. Cat could see his arm tense under the wool jacket. He wouldn't—no—couldn't stop now for fear of what damage it would do to his reputation to have a *woman* get the best of him. She watched his eyes open wide then squint, and knew she had to act now or have her throat slit. The trigger tightened under her finger and the muzzle blasted out a cloud of blue-black smoke before the blade could do its worst.

George Wilson screamed as the lead ball hit his cheek then took off the top of his ear, while the burning powder singed into his fair skin. In slow motion he fell off his horse and landed hard on the ground. He lay writhing and screaming with his hands covering what used to be a handsome face, then passed out.

Chaos ensued as some of the soldiers' horses reacted to the shot by rearing up and dislodging a couple of riders, while the other soldiers struggled to remain seated. Guns went off recklessly into the air and instantly, the Redcoats lost their advantage over the Indians' arrows, still at the ready.

The Corporal was shouting, "Hold your fire! Hold your fire!"

When the soldiers collected themselves, Gregor said in a firm voice with his pistol aimed at the Corporal, "Hae yer men drop their guns."

Immediately, the Corporal told the group in a quietly commanding voice, "This was not our intent." He looked at his men and said, "Lower your weapons, it's over. Tend to the wounded."

The Redcoats did as they were ordered, then the Corporal said to Gregor, "I'd like to tend to my Commander, sir."

Gregor nodded, and Corporal Bakeman dismounted and searched his satchel for bandages.

As Thaddeus Bakeman began wrapping the unconscious George Wilson's head, he looked sadly up at Cat and said, "Please accept my apologies, miss. He'll not bother you again. I promise."

The Mohicans lowered their bows and disappeared into the forest. Cat and her group of men followed, wanting to get as much distance as possible between the Redcoats and themselves.

Once out of sight of the English, Greame stopped, stepped off his horse and walked over to take Cat down from hers.

"I dinna think that's wise, at the moment, Greame," Cat told him, not moving from her position.

Greame looked up at her and frowned. "Is there something wrong?"

"I dinna think my legs will hold me up."

Gregor laughed. "Hell, I dinna even think mine would hold me up after an act of foolishness such as that."

"Can we just go home?" Cat said.

"Oh, aye," Greame said, mounting his horse. "I'm lookin' forward to a life o' boredom."

"And a bed," she said, feeling the enormity of her actions weighing on her like stones.

ଏ୰

After three days, George Wilson regained consciousness. The Corporal, who had tended to him as though he were a child, told him it was time to change the bandages.

Under the confines of the linen dressings, George Wilson's hearing wasn't very good. His ear kept ringing, but he attributed it to the inadequate medical care from his corporal.

"Hand me my shaving kit, Corporal," George Wilson demanded. He wanted to see for himself what damage was done to his face. It felt large and heavy under the dressings. He took the looking glass from the kit and watched, unaware that he was whimpering as the Corporal unwound the bloody bandages. A grinding pit formed in his stomach as each layer came off and his face didn't resume its normal shape.

"Are you sure you want to see this just yet, Commander? It's still very swollen."

"Just get it over with, Corporal!"

The last layer peeled away to George Wilson's horror. The powder blast had left black pellets imbedded in his previously flawless skin. An angry red gash split his cheek where the lead ball had hit, and his ear was misshapen beyond recognition. He looked like an ogre. Rage filled his heart. He would never fulfill his plans now. No woman would ever look at him, never mind a wealthy one that would further his career. In a wounded roar, he shouted, "That bitch! That bloody bitch! She will pay dearly for this!"

To be continued ...

Gàidhlig Glossary

A Ghaoil = a GHOoil = my love

Bean-sìdhe = BAN she = faerie woman

Bòdhran = BO-rahn = drum

Bràithrean = BRAY-hren = brothers

Brighid = bree-GEET = Bridget the saint

Catrìona = ka-TREE-na = Catherine

Ceilidh = KAY-lee = party or visit

Ciamar a tha thu? = KIMmar ah HA oo = how are you? (familiar)

Clach na Brataich = clack na BRA-teck = ensign stone

Clan Donnachaidh = clan DON-a-key = children of Duncan

Dà Shealladh = da SHAYlahk = two sights = second sight

Gàidhlig = GAAH-lik = the Scottish language

Glè mhath = glay VAH = very good

Iain = EE-ine = John

Iolair-uisge = ee-YOlar OOSH-kah = osprey

Lachlan = LAHK-lan

Mo Nighean = mo NEE-an = my daughter

Mòrag = MORE-ek = Marion

Pìob Mhor = Peep Vohr = large pipe (bagpipes)

Prig = preek = prick

Sassenaich = SAH-sen-ache = English

Seumas = SHAY-mus = James

An Sgeulaiche = ahn SKEUL-lah-kay = the storyteller

Slàinte mhath = SLAN-cha VAH! = good health

Slìo Mìn aig Aulich = slees meen ek AW-lick = smooth slope at Aulich

Tapadh Leat = TAH-pah laht = thank you (familiar)

Here are a few words in broad Scots:

Ken = know

Kent = knew

Dinna = don't

Dinna Fash = don't fret

Penobscot Glossary

Kolóskape = Gloos-KAH-bay = the creator

Igrismannak = ee-GREES-mahn-ack = English

Weliwoni = well-e-WONI = thank you

ABOUT THE AUTHOR

Mary Duncan is an artist and graphic designer when not writing. She's designed each of her book covers. Her love of genealogy and history were the sparks that ignited writing about 18th century Scotland. Though not of Scottish descent (in this lifetime, anyway), she has a deep passion for anything Scottish (with the exception of haggis). Mary lives with her husband on the Downcoast of Maine.

Visit her website at
www.eyesofgarnet.com

☙

Printed in the United States
206974BV00003B/43-87/P